"AN OCCASIO... a fast-paced... mystery so ve... literary distinction to the genre. It is also something else. Mr. Silvis has created original, fully developed characters—again a rarity in the genre—and his protagonist is one of the most appealing and poignant figures in the recent history of crime fiction. The novel is a stunning performance by a young writer of exceptional talent and promise."

—JOHN W. ALDRIDGE
Author of *Talents and Technicians*

"Vibrant prose . . . Silvis settles into the action, lacing his narrative with astute observations and hard truths. . . . This work succeeds in leaving dark images to linger in the reader's mind."

—*Publishers Weekly*

"AN OCCASIONAL HELL is, quite simply, one of the best-written modern crime novels I've ever read. One has to go to Graham Greene or Thomas Berger for a worthy comparison. With this one effort, Randall Silvis shows what a skilled writer of literary merit can do within an already distinguished popular genre. The standards of crime writing have been on the rise for some years now, and they've just been raised by several more notches. Silvis's secret is in his flawless, sensual style and in the irresistible detective/writer Ernest DeWalt. I am dazzled by this book."

—WILLIAM ALLEN
Author of
Starkweather: Portrait of a Mass Murderer

By Randall Silvis:

AN OCCASIONAL HELL*
EXCELSIOR
DRIVEN TO ACTS OF KINDNESS
THE LUCKIEST MAN IN THE WORLD

*Published by Ballantine Books

AN
OCCASIONAL
HELL

Randall Silvis

BALLANTINE BOOKS • NEW YORK

Copyright © 1993 by Randall Silvis

All rights reserved under International and Pan-American Copyright Conventions, including the right to reproduce this book, or parts thereof, in any form, except for the inclusion of brief quotations in a review. Published in the United States by Ballantine Books, a division of Random House, Inc., New York, and distributed in Canada by Random House of Canada Limited, Toronto.

Library of Congress Catalog Card Number: 92-31129

ISBN 0-345-38727-9

This edition published by arrangement with The Permanent Press

Manufactured in the United States of America

First Ballantine Books Edition: July 1995

10 9 8 7 6 5 4 3 2 1

The author gratefully acknowledges the Thurber House in Columbus, Ohio, Mercyhurst College in Erie, Pennsylvania, and the National Endowment for the Arts for their generous support during the writing of this work. Individuals who contributed their expertise are too numerous to mention, but include Brenda Fulton, Charles Walton, and Dennis McNair.

This book is for Rita,
and for Bret,
and for Nathan

Prologue

To Ernest DeWalt, the investigation of a crime seemed not at all dissimilar to the writing of a crime story. As an investigator, he began always with a few known facts, as many as, like the sweet cream of invention, might float readily to the surface. Thus equipped, the investigator, the storyteller, in any case an outsider miles and hours from the radiant heart of the genesis of these truths, would then mix a mortar of *possible* truths—that is, an honest fiction—and with this putty piece the larger chunks together, hard truth with pliable truth, adding and subtracting bit by bit, ascribing muscle and bone until a working model was formed, an acceptable truth, an agreement of imaginations; something all concerned could live with.

Such truth, he told himself, is, after all, how history is formed. It is what our lives, looking back, become.

Such truth, when it turned virulent, was never a pleasant thing for DeWalt to handle, no matter whether the handling was meant to edify or entertain. He had handled and reconstructed and fabricated truths for both purposes. Notwithstanding the wounds inflicted, success in both professions had come easily to him.

Neither talent was what he would have called a gift.

And now he had been handed a mere portion of truth once more. Like a forensic anthropologist given a shard of skull, a splintered tibia and a few broken teeth, he warmed the fragments in his hand. Gradually and painstakingly he filled their silent gaps with the soft clay of imagination. He attempted, with little success, not to let his presence contaminate or discolor the facts. And he tried, again and again, to conceive of the whole unruly beast. . . .

Chapter
One

This much DeWalt knows or can imagine:

Alex Catanzaro and Jeri Gillen have been coming to this place, this tiny inlet beside the Monongahela River, this lover's venue only a few hundred yards off the highway but completely isolated, unobservable, coming to this place in Alex's car, a silver Honda Accord, every Saturday morning for over a year and a half. Jeri is a waitress at the Colony Restaurant in the college town of Menona, a town whose name is thought to derive from the Indian word *menaungehilla*, which means "river with the high banks that break off and slide down."

The Colony Restaurant, on Main Street, is a five-minute walk from the Shenango College campus. It serves only breakfast and lunch, seven days a week, closing at five PM each day, its customers the students, faculty and other employees of the college plus those few townspeople who don't mind the academic chitchat, discussions about tenure, exams, who's doing what to whom.

Jeri Gillen is twenty-five, a tall slender unnatural blonde with large almond-shaped eyes. She has the high cheekbones of a fashion model, the sharp points of those cheeks invariably highlighted with too much lavender blush. Except for a nose that is a bit too broad and a wide mouth with full lips set permanently in a pout, she might in fact have become a fashion model, except too that she has had no such aspirations for herself, no expectations of success whatsoever until she met Alex Catanzaro.

She is married to Rodney Gillen, a musician and vocalist with the rock band the Kinetics, a group that plugs itself as a "Classic Rock" band, which means they will include in their repertoire any four-chord thumping melody at least six weeks old. The Kinetics play every Friday and Saturday night at fraternity mixers, in local bars, at weddings and private parties.

Jeri and Rodney Gillen were married the year they graduated, both by the skin of their teeth, from high school. They have lived ever since in their one-bedroom second-floor Thurman Street apartment. They have no children.

On most Saturday mornings Rodney does not return home until five or six AM. He then drinks a beer and swallows a couple of Seconals and falls into bed beside his wife. When he awakes ten or twelve hours later, he will find Jeri in the living room leafing through a magazine or watching television. On those few mornings when he awakes early to find her not in the apartment, she later explains that she had walked to the post office or to the grocery store. In most cases, however, he does not question her absence.

Jeri Gillen first met Alex Catanzaro several years ago. He is forty-four years old, an associate professor of American History, married, the father of two children: Christopher, age 11, and Nicole, 8. His name for Elizabeth, his wife, is Betts or Betsy; her friends call her Beth.

Alex is an attractive man, five feet nine inches tall, with a full head of prematurely silver hair, a broad Mediterranean face, strong chin, steady green eyes, Anthony Quinnish. Sartorially he is of the starched and natty school, buttondown collars, colorful silk ties.

4

He has been a regular customer at the Colony Restaurant since before Jeri Gillen began to work there, but approximately three years ago his patronage of the restaurant becomes more frequent; he will sometimes pop in twice a day for a take-out coffee, even though there is always a fresh pot in the faculty lounge, two doors from his office.

Later he begins to show up every weekday at 2:00, after the lunchtime rush and during Jeri's regular fifteen-minute break, which she often spends sitting across from him in a booth. They laugh and flirt openly and do not appear to be hiding anything. Alex is popular with the other waitresses too, as he is with his students; he consistently receives some of his department's highest marks during the student evaluation sessions each semester.

Approximately a year and a half ago, Alex Catanzaro stops coming to the restaurant with any regularity. Once or twice a week he will appear in the morning for a coffee and pecan roll to take with him to his office. He remains friendly with Jeri, but not overly so. He flirts just as warmly, it seems, with Della or Elaine or Sunny, whichever waitress happens to serve him.

Saturday mornings, he explains to Beth Catanzaro, are the quietest times at the college library, where he goes to research a novel about the War of 1812, a war that began the day after both sides had agreed not to fight, a war that continued after both sides had agreed to stop, a war that resolved none of the issues over which it was fought, a comic-opera war, a bloody irony.

Alex soon establishes a routine of visiting the library early every Saturday morning. He reads and writes for a couple of hours—he tells his wife—then cools down with a workout on a stationary bicycle in the field house. Then a swim and a sauna. He leaves his home at 7:45 each Saturday morning and returns by one in the

5

afternoon. This routine begins at approximately the same time as his regular patronage of the Colony Restaurant ceases.

It is on a Saturday morning, sometime between ten and ten-thirty, when Beth Catanzaro receives a telephone call from an old friend living near Williamsburg, Virginia.

"She was calling from an estate auction to tell me about some Civil War diaries that were going to be sold. Diaries written by a soldier who had fought at Gettysburg under Longstreet. Anyway, she knew Alex would want them—he's a collector of Civil War memorabilia. That's his true passion, the War between the States."

"Not the War of 1812?"

"No. The only reason he was writing his novel about that war was because there are already so many Civil War novels. And . . . I don't know, but I don't think he had enough confidence in his abilities to put his work up against that of Cantor and Shaara and all the others."

"So you told your friend. . . ."

"She said the diaries could go on the auction block at any minute, so I told her I'd get in touch with Alex and call her right back. Because I personally had no idea how much they might be worth. I guess, in the end, I had no idea about a lot of things."

She telephones the college library but her husband can not be located in any of the carrels or common areas, nor do the library employees recall having seen him there that morning. She telephones his office but there is no answer. The equipment manager at the fieldhouse assures her that her husband is not yet in the building.

"He usually doesn't get here until well after twelve. And then only for a quick shower. You want me to tell him you called?"

6

"No, please don't," she says, and tries to keep her voice from trembling. "It's nothing important."

She telephones her friend at the estate auction and tells her to forget about the diaries. She then drives into town and searches each of the campus's five parking lots for Alex's car.

When Alex returns home in the afternoon, his hair still damp from the shower, Beth asks, "How was your workout?"

"Great," he says.

"How's the book coming?"

"Slowly but surely." Then, as is his routine, he goes to his study above the garage, to, as he explains, "organize my research notes," and she does not see him again until late in the afternoon. She makes no mention of the telephone call from her friend.

The following Saturday, Beth watches as her husband's car leaves the garage. She waits until the car is out of sight down their long hemlock-lined drive. She then climbs into her own car and follows her husband into town.

"What about the children?"

"I left them watching cartoons. And I know what you're thinking—"

"I'm not thinking anything."

"Well, you'd have the right to. It was stupid of me to leave them alone like that. What if something had happened to them while I was gone?"

"Nothing did though."

"No, but it could have. I hate myself for doing that."

"You were upset. Confused."

"I was *enraged*."

She follows Alex at a distance but close enough to see when he, at just a minute or two before eight, drives up close to the rear entrance of the county courthouse. The building is locked and the parking lot deserted. The sky is as blue as a gas flame, clear, scalding bright. It is late Spring, new leaves, new growth, the season of youth and hope.

Alex drives within four feet of the rear entrance, and stops. He leans across the seat and pops open the passenger door. From the shadow of the recessed doorway steps a young woman, smiling. She slides in beside Alex, pulls shut the door, leans across the seat and kisses Beth Catanzaro's husband.

"Why didn't you follow when he drove away from the courthouse?"

"I don't know, I was. . . ."

"You said you were enraged."

"I was, until I actually saw the woman with him. The girl. Then it was like ... I don't know. I couldn't lift my foot off the brake."

"How long did you sit there like that?"

"Long enough to watch thirteen years of marriage fall apart. Long enough to think all kinds of things."

"Did you think about killing him?"

"In a dozen different ways."

"You didn't tell the police that, did you?"

"Do I strike you as an inordinately stupid woman?"

The next Saturday she follows him again, having all week kept silent, having stilled the efflorescence of dread with the impossible allowance of an alternative explanation for her husband's action, some dissembling innocence to that furtive kiss. Again she parks in an alleyway unseen and again watches the same young woman step from the courthouse shadows to climb into her husband's car; again watches and this time follows the car down the steep highway to the river, across the bridge's quivering gridwork, six miles along the river road to the entrance of a narrow and deeply-rutted dirt lane.

A sign at the mouth of this lane reads PRIVATE: NO

TRESPASSING. She sits staring at this warning even as the veil of dust raised by the other car's trespass settles on the weeds. It is not the sign that keeps her from going further, but the fulmination of hope. She will not drive through her husband's dust, will not darken her lungs with it, will not breathe the suffocating wake of his deceit. No more evidence is needed; no alternatives possible. She knows too much already.

For what must seem a very long time to Elizabeth Catanzaro she keeps her knowledge to herself. She keeps the unavailing rage and ineffable grief to herself. She keeps that coil of slippery fear lashed tightly around her, that constricting braid of terror. She lives alone with these elements and does her best to display to her family no sign of infection, even though it taints her every perception and rumination and in her mind it explains those times when Alex was irritable or distracted, when unduly solicitous, when angry for no apparent reason, when amorous and when too tender after love—as tender, she now understands, as only a guilt-ridden man can be.

What she knows quickly numbs her because numbness is the only practical response to such killing pain. But at the same time, her knowledge renders her keenly aware in a way she has never been, aware of her past and the ever-fleeting present. The future is a blank, a darkness. But in the past she can now detect nuances, corners and facets and adumbrations she had previously strolled past without noticing.

She lives inside this world of heightened and terrible perception through another seventeen Saturdays, always waiting for that one Saturday morning when Alex will linger over his coffee and instead of hurrying out the door look at her nostalgically and utter something perfectly banal and revivifying, "Let's spend the morning together, Betts. I don't feel like working today; let's take the kids on a picnic."

But this hope too becomes untenable when she realizes that the part of her gone numb is more important than the surviving part, that she is dead to everything except knowledge and the selfish bitterness of it, and that it has to end.

And on that Saturday morning she watches her husband's car speed away and she goes into her bedroom and closes the door and she sits calmly at the telephone and punches in the seven numbers that have been pulsing in her brain for too long now, the number of a telephone in a second-floor apartment on Thurman Street, a number obtained by spending a Saturday noon parked in view of the courthouse, finally seeing the young woman being deposited there just as she had been picked up some four hours earlier, then following Jeri Gillen as she walks home alone, Alex on his way to what he believes will be a purifying shower at the fieldhouse.

Elizabeth Catanzaro follows her husband's lover and sees where she lives and inquires of the waitress's name from an older woman who emerges from a neighboring apartment twenty minutes later, and Elizabeth Catanzaro thereby adds to the store of bitter knowledge she keeps to herself, has kept to herself until she hears and feels the telephone ringing in her hand. Twenty jangling rings and then Rodney Gillen finally stumbles out of bed and into the living room and picks up the phone. And Elizabeth Catanzaro's silence comes to an end. And she finally tells somebody everything she has never wanted to know.

Things change so quickly, and not at all.

This is what Ernest DeWalt told himself on his way to meet Elizabeth Catanzaro. He had seen her picture in

10

the newspaper and her face on the evening news, and now, little more than an hour ago, he had heard her voice on the telephone. Her husband was dead—with a musketball through his forehead—and Elizabeth Catanzaro needed someone to help her prove that she had not had a hand in the murder.

But DeWalt did not want to have to prove anything. He had bailed out of that business five years ago, had gotten out by pulling a Wambaugh, as he called it—that is, by writing a novel about his former profession, which in his case had been a profession less noble than Wambaugh's, DeWalt's a profession of snoopery, of eavesdropping and Peeping Tomism and of softporn shot through telephoto lenses. But his novel *Suffer No Fools* had been too successful and he had had to get out of that profession too—because in truth he had not wanted success, he had wanted catharsis, an exorcism, and so had endowed his book with three hundred pages of hate and anger, every page soaked in blood; and after writing it had become embarrassed by it, ashamed; ashamed too because he had not made any of it up except for the chronology of events, twenty years compressed into less than one, the creativity of a minor artist, a juggler; and ashamed most because the book's success made him little more than a panderer, pimp to a bloodthirsty world.

And so, two and a half years ago, at the overripe age of forty-six, he found himself, quite by accident, awarded a sinecure thanks to his embarrassing success as a novelist, a comfortable position in the only sanctuary that exists for a man too skeptical for the monastery, the only refuge from real life left to the civilized but cowardly, that tweed and ivy enclave of self-reassuring insularity: academia.

And that's the truth, isn't it, DeWalt? That you've

been running from life, looking for a place to hide, ever since you were shot.

Not running very fast, DeWalt.

But fast enough to stay ahead of yourself, am I right?

Apparently man was meant to run. We have legs and feet, don't we? Not roots.

Do feet of clay count?

Shut up, DeWalt.

Get off your butt, DeWalt. You're getting fat and lazy.

I'm not going to do this thing. I'm not equipped anymore for investigative work. I'm not equipped physically or temperamentally. Investigation is a job for somebody who cares.

Keep talking; sooner or later you'll find an excuse you believe.

I don't need an excuse. I'm not obligated to anybody.

For over twenty years he had been a private investigator, working first in Chicago for an agency that specialized in the recovery of lost individuals and objects. It was satisfying work but seldom exciting or dangerous enough for a young man, so he and a friend drove to Los Angeles and went into business for themselves. But then the friend had an abortion and stopped being a good friend, and a year later she swallowed too much phenobarbital and stopped being a good partner.

Glib, DeWalt. You're so fucking glib.

Eventually he overcame his friend's absence and the absence of his own passion and with time he gained a reputation for solid yeomanlike work. He steered away from any case too ambitious for a one-man operation, and, as Los Angeles changed, he changed too in the opposite direction, creeping backward toward the fifties as the city galloped through the seventies.

As street gangs proliferated, their members enrolling in night school to sharpen their business acumen, learning the rules of supply and demand, memorizing the Periodic Table, schmoozing with South American entrepreneurs, Ernest DeWalt snooped on unfaithful wives and husbands. He saw more tits and ass each week than in a month of HBO. While other investigators sank small fortunes in hi-tech listening devices and state of the art surveillance gadgetry, DeWalt maintained fidelity to his telephoto lens. He worked the uppercrust neighborhoods and made a conscious attempt to stay well within their borders. He knew that the rest of the world was out there, the dirty needles and dirty fucks, the methadone grocery lines and the bag sniffers and the punks and pukes and paltry lives, but he had no use for them, no truck, as his uncle used to say.

Then one of the uppercrusters hired DeWalt to locate a prodigal son, and DeWalt in his typical workmanlike way located him, spotted him finally on a street in Indio and followed him to a four-star hotel and went inside the hotel and found the boy's door standing open and walked across the threshold and caught three slugs from a .380 automatic fired by the coke-brave prodigal son, who had mistaken DeWalt for the lover his lover was doing on the side.

Don't be bitter, DeWalt. The boy apologized, didn't he? It was a natural mistake.

Sometimes even now DeWalt could hear the dialysis machine clicking in his ear. He could hear his blood churning through the wash and wear cycle. It was a maddening sound, that barely audible whoosh, that sudless agitation of his soul. He had come out of it all right, though. He wore a fourth hole in his gut now, this one for the catheter just below his naval. Four times a day he needed to find a clean and quiet place so that he could unroll from around his waist that long tube attached to the catheter, and unroll the empty plastic bag attached to the tube, and lay the bag on the floor and watch it fill with fluid from his peritoneal cavity. Then he would clamp off the tube and dispose of the full two-liter bag, then attach a new bag, this one filled with the dialyzing solution called Dialysate. He would drain this solution into his peritoneal cavity, then wrap the tube and emptied bag around his waist again, tuck in his shirt, buckle his pants, and be perfectly all right.

It was called continuous ambulatory peritoneal dialysis and it kept him off the big machine. Maybe someday he would have a kidney transplant but AB positive blood was difficult to match. Lots of things were difficult to match. But maybe someday it would happen.

Sure, DeWalt. And maybe someday the world will be filled with peace and love, and we'll all sit around singing harmony and crocheting doilies.

Ironically, it had been DeWalt's liver, not his kidneys, shot by the jealous coke-head. DeWalt lost so much blood as he lay there on the Turkish rug that his unscathed kidneys turned themselves off—which is how the body protects itself, DeWalt learned later; the body shuts down all nonessential functions so as to keep itself alive. He eventually recovered five percent renal activity, which meant that he sometimes was still required to visit the men's room, although a large thimble would serve just as well as a urinal.

He had to restrict his fluid intake these days but he was okay. He couldn't drink alcohol anymore but he was just fine. He had to maintain a low potassium, sodium-restricted diet, and he had to take medication to keep his blood pressure down, and he had to guard against catheter infections, which might lead to peritonitis, but otherwise he was doing swell.

There was an additional side effect too but he didn't have a girlfriend anyway so it really did not matter, he was A-number one.

Top of the heap, DeWalt. King of the hill.

It was during his convalescence that he, having already resigned as an investigator—a decision made facedown on the Turkish carpet—became a writer. In the beginning he did not know whether he could write or not but this did not worry him because he had read hundreds of books and many of their authors could not write either. He had enough characters and plots in his memory bank to keep him busy for the next twenty years if necessary, if his uncooperative organs allowed him to hang around that long, and they probably would not.

To his delight and later dismay he found that he had a knack for writing, a facility that surprised himself and everyone who knew him and what surprised him even more was the extent to which he enjoyed those hours with pen in hand and a yellow legal pad balanced on his knees. He liked how on good days he would evaporate but for the hand holding the pen and the knees bracing the tablet, that his teeth would not ache from too much clenching, nor his head pound, nor his neck be as stiff as a post.

He liked disappearing between bags and he even came to enjoy the second bag exchange of the day, it was the most trancelike of the daily treatments, the most meditative and salubrious. He finished it, after a morning of writing, feeling truly cleansed; although he knew it was the writing that had cleansed him, the writing that expurgated more of his poisonous fluids than did the dialysis.

So he could write, he decided, but he was no writer. The type of book he could write was popular enough, in fact too popular, and that was what bothered him. Its easy success made him feel like a woman who sits behind a glass wall and talks dirty and fondles herself while her paying customer, on the other side of the wall, masturbates. DeWalt did not have the spleen for another

15

book, just as he did not have the kidneys or the liver to be an investigator again. What choices were left to a hollowed-out has-been such as himself?

There were two choices but he did not like the taste of the first one, it tasted of cold metal and smoke and there was no telling what the aftertaste would be. The other choice was to slink away to the has-beens' sanctum sanctorum, where there are always vacancies and the benefit package is good.

DeWalt moved back east then, through the Mississippi and Ohio Valleys and into that quiet heartland where by all appearances the carcinomas of drugs and despair had not spread. They had spread there too of course and were easily detectable if you wanted to look closely, but they were also easy to ignore and that was what DeWalt decided to do. It was a small college and the perfect place for a two-time washout with a couple of body parts missing. He felt comfortable in his old suits again and with money from the novel he was able to buy a small house on a quiet street. He had a twenty-five-year-old bachelor's degree in political science but he was hired by the English Department to conduct two courses each semester, a workshop in *The Writing of Popular Fiction*, and the other, because his book had been made into a movie and because he had actually lived in Los Angeles, a course called by the college catalogue *The Visual Metaphor* and called by DeWalt *An Excuse to Watch Movies for Academic Credit*.

There were seldom more than twenty students in each of his classes, and maybe one or two of them had actually read his book. They either lionized him or ignored him and for the most part they talked of harmless things and none of them ever tried to shoot him.

He never finished the second novel, which he had begun while waiting for the first one to appear, and he had no intention now of ever finishing it, and when a colleague or student asked how it was coming along he always answered, "Just fine, thank you. It's coming along just fine."

He was a wholly useless and expendable adjunct to the college and he was comfortable as such. All too soon he would be a fifty-year-old man with no romantic attachments and he had made himself more or less comfortable with that too. Not so long ago he had lain in a hospitable bed for two months and he had thought about life and his in particular, and he had decided finally that none of it amounted to anything in the end, it was here and then gone and if you left any tracks at all they would not last long either, and he was trying to get comfortable with that as well.

Then Alex Catanzaro, a colleague from the History Department, had gotten his brain parted with a musketball. DeWalt watched Catanzaro's widow grieving on TV, he had seen her lash out at the reporters, and he had tried not to feel curious about any of it. Then Elizabeth Catanzaro telephoned him. Her response to his refusal of help—that awful silence of hers coming through the receiver, that quivering breath and nothing else, no words at all for the next thirty seconds until he finally hung up—that tremulous silence of hers so unsettled him that he now felt compelled to tell her no in person, and now, on his way to do so, he once again felt too big for his favorite old summer suit, he felt pinched by it, choked, as if it were shrinking at that very moment.

Chapter Two

In the beginning, the more one learns, the more there is to learn. The thing you have been constructing seems to change of its own volition. You place it in the center of the table and you try to view it from another side, another angle. If you are lucky and attentive, it will tell you something new. . . .

"Good morning, beauty," Alex said.

Jeri slid in smiling and kissed him quickly. Then she sat back against the door as he drove away from the courthouse and toward the river. He was in a hurry but careful not to drive that way. She was with him now so there was no need to drive too fast, there was no need to draw attention to his car, which many people might recognize.

It was a gray August morning and Jeri had brought the smell of it into the car with her, the scent of summer dew and sweet damp shadows, and unbelievably she smelled too of the heavy clouds and the low rumbling thunder, every nuance of the morning filtered through her warmth and scent so that it all became an extension of her, properties of the day otherwise inconsequential until her nearness gave them meaning.

And you can smell her yourself, can't you, DeWalt? Not Jeri exactly but the scent of a couple of young women just like her, that nosegay freshness and the cloud-wet fragrance of desire. That's *one* ability you haven't lost, the art of unsolicited memory, and one you would be better off without.

Between them on the seat lay Alex's briefcase, a soft-sided black leather attache case with one snap that did not work, a birthday present from his wife ten, maybe eleven years earlier. The briefcase was stuffed with tablets and bulging manila folders filled with newspaper clippings and magazine tearsheets, the research for his book. He carried it with him every Saturday morning but he would not open it until mid-afternoon when alone in his study, alone with the dulcet exhaustion of another secret morning, of this one just begun.

He kept the briefcase in the middle of the seat to prevent Jeri from sliding too close. He did not want to have to remind her not to. He was as hungry for closeness as she was but he could wait until they were safer. He could wait but knew that she would not without that barrier between them. She was young and heedless and wanted everything right away. This was one of the qualities he loved her for but it was also what he feared the most. Her marriage was not important to her, nor was her job or his nor what people might say about them. He enjoyed being the only important aspect of her life but at the same time he worried about it. It was flattering to a man his age but it was also very dangerous.

"God, it's been such a long week," she whispered, as if even inside the moving car somebody might be listening.

To see her eyes watching him that way excited him, those doe eyes so bright with impatience. She was wearing straw sandals and a pale rose-colored dress he would undo by untying the tiny straps behind her neck. He knew she wore nothing underneath the dress and this excited him too. He wanted to take a hand off the steering wheel but he would not let himself do it just yet. When they had crossed the bridge and there were no more houses he would do it. He would lay a hand just above her knee and then suddenly she would be against him, her mouth against his ear and her hand slipping inside his shirt.

"Once a week just isn't enough anymore," she said, and still with her back to the door she stretched out a leg and rubbed the back of his calf with her toes.

"I know, baby," he answered, smiling, enjoying the self-denial, and stared straight ahead.

"I want it every night."

He almost reached for her then but stopped himself. It was always better when he waited.

"And every morning," she said, her toes pushing under his thigh now, one foot raised to the seat so that if he wanted to he could confirm with a glance what she was wearing beneath the summer dress.

"And twice every afternoon," she said.

He looked at the mist on the river now, and as the car came onto the bridge he rolled his window down so that he could smell the mist, its sadness and its longing.

"Four times a day?" he asked. "What do you think I am—a machine?"

"You could do it," she told him. "I know you could."

And now because she knew he would not stop her she picked up his briefcase and laid it on the back seat and with the next motion she seemed to be half-atop him, kneeling beside him with one hand on the back of his neck and the other at his belt.

"Wait," he said, but was glad when she ignored him. And now that she was lying on the seat and had her head in his lap he could not keep himself from driving faster.

This is slipping toward burlesque, DeWalt. Better stick with what you know.

Later they would discuss how they had spent their

20

week and any interesting things that had happened. Discussion was impossible now however and like everything else it could wait. Before Alex met Jeri he had lived a long time without the madness of sex—not without sex itself but the wonderful terrible insane burn of desire—and having enjoyed it again for the past eighteen months he did not want to ever be without it. He found that he could work happily and energetically until at least midweek knowing what awaited him on Saturday. By Thursday he would be incapable of not thinking ahead to it and it would distract him from his work, but the early part of the week was always wonderful. He felt young and strong again, a confident and unassailable man. He flirted with other students and with one of his colleagues in particular and he sometimes toyed with the idea of having an affair with her too because he was sure he could pull it off.

Then Thursday would come and he would catch a faint whiff of Jeri's perfume. That vague musky odor might rise up off his briefcase, or be waiting when he climbed into his car. Then it was Saturday as it was Saturday now with her scent going through him with every breath, and his hands wet on the steering wheel and his mouth dry, his lungs aching and his chest feeling crushed. He knew how she looked underneath that dress and as he drove he pictured his hand letting the straps fall free, and then even with four miles to go it was not enough to just picture this happening so he slipped a hand behind her neck and freed the small bow.

"Oh god," she said, as if gasping for air, the nipple suddenly hard between his fingers. He drove with his left hand and he kept watching the speedometer, glancing into the rearview mirror and then down at her blonde head moving and her mouth so hungry and warm and it had never been like this before no not with anyone else and he put a hand beneath her dress and the

21

slickness of her thighs and she gasped again but then shoved herself hard against his hand. "Oh god Alex I want you to fuck me. I want to suck you too but I want you to fuck me, I wish you had two cocks I want you all through me, this is the way I want to die."

Too much, DeWalt. Whatever happened to understatement and subtlety? Say what you mean but don't say too much.

Silence is the only voice that truly says anything, DeWalt.

But sometimes even silence lies. Think of this as compensation for the silence.

Usually she did not become so excited until after they had been parked for several minutes. But it was getting bad for her lately and she seemed more eager each Saturday morning. In fact he sometimes envisioned having to fuck her right there in the courthouse parking lot before she would let him drive away. Right there in the dooryard of justice. He would stand her up against the wooden door. Her body banging against it. Loud knocks echoing down the tiled halls. The janitor in the boiler room sipping his coffee, cocking an ear. . . .

DeWalt, please. This is getting ridiculous.

Sometimes her eagerness worried him but for now it warmed and fueled his own. The river and its mist were running along beside them now and very soon he would be turning onto the narrow dirt lane and he could turn his full attention to what she was so expertly doing to him. Her thighs were clamped around his hand and her ass moving slow and rhythmically and she was using her tongue even though this was not the most practical position for it. She wanted everything right away and for the moment he had to agree that immediately was the best way to have it.

Three hours later he was dead with a significant portion of his brain dislodged, his body naked but for his wristwatch and wedding band. The car keys were still in the ignition, the radio tuned to an easy listening station but the battery weak by the time the police arrived. One of Jeri's sandals, the left one, was found inside the car, in the back seat with Alex's briefcase and her neatly folded summer dress, the second shoe some twenty yards down the lane. Not far from the shoe lay her handbag, spilled open, shoulder strap broken. Other than that, Jeri Gillen had disappeared.

"Hello, I'm calling for Mr. Ernest DeWalt?"

"This is he."

"I'm sorry for disturbing you so early in the morning, Mr. DeWalt, but . . . my name is Beth Catanzaro. My husband Alex taught at the college with you. I mean not actually with you but—"

"Yes, of course. I'm very sorry, Mrs. Catanzaro. It's a . . . a terrible, terrible thing that's happened. I'm truly sorry."

"Yes, well. . . ."

She gathers herself with a long slow breath, a tremulous breath he hears quivering going in and also when released just as slowly. He is standing on the threshold of his kitchen, standing at the end of the telephone cord's reach, watching as at the other end of the kitchen his omelet fries in a skillet. It is a three-egg omelet fat with Monterey Jack cheese, slices of red bell pepper, tomato and onion and capicola ham, and as it is filling the kitchen with its wonderful aroma it is burning because a woman somewhere unknown miles away is struggling to keep the tears from her voice. He will not hurry her but those are his last three eggs.

"I was wondering if I could talk with you a few minutes today," she says. "I need somebody . . . experienced, I guess."

23

"I honestly don't think I could be of much help," he says.

"The thing is, the police have this idea in their heads. . . ."

"Have you been charged with anything?"

"They're convinced I did it," she says. "Or that I planned it or something ridiculous like that."

The cheese is oozing out of the folded eggs now, filling the skillet bottom. Curling up. Turning brown. "But you haven't been charged," he says.

"It just isn't true," she tells him. "I can understand how, to them, it might look like the truth. But it isn't!"

It seldom is, he thinks. The ham is burning now too, the scent of charred flesh. Everything is burning. "I can put you in touch with a good agency," he says. "Or maybe your lawyer can recommend somebody."

"My lawyer was my husband's lawyer. He was Alex's friend so. . . . Anyway, I don't have a lawyer."

At what temperature will butter combust? But there is probably no butter left in the skillet by now, an unpalatable brown crust, brown stink. He says, "This is out of my league, Mrs. Catanzaro. Even when I was investigating, and that's a good while back, I never got involved with anything like this. I was strictly third-rate. I'm sorry."

He should not be eating eggs and butter and cheese anyway, at least not all at once, not in the overdose quantity there in that skillet. He shouldn't but the hell with shouldn't, he wants an omelet this morning, damn it.

"I just thought that since you and my husband were colleagues, that you might take a more personal interest in it. Because you knew each other. That you were friends or . . . whatever."

"I'm afraid I've never even spoken with your husband," he says.

24

There is a long pause. "I got your number off his desk blotter. It's on his calendar in no fewer than six places."

"I've never once spoken to him," he says.

"Then I don't. . . . But apparently he must have intended to call you. I mean, why else would he have written down your name and number so many times?"

Those are his last three eggs and there is nothing left to eat but cold cereal. The kitchen stinks of burned, still burning peppers and cheese and ham, and he is going to have to start the day with toast and corn flakes.

"I'm sorry, but I really don't see how I could be of any help. I honestly didn't know your husband at all, I wish I did. And as for the investigative work, I've been out of that for too long. I'm in no shape for it anymore, believe me. Not for something as important as this."

Elizabeth Catanzaro says nothing. Her silence is anything but silent, he can hear the fear inside each breath, the terror of helplessness in each inhalation. He had once made a career out of listening to silences and in learning to differentiate them, to discern their weight and depth, and hers is the kind he always liked least to overhear. There is no anger in it nor expectation nor any emotion that might eventually lead her somewhere. It is a dead-end silence because there is nowhere left to go, it is the silence at the end of the road, the silence at the bottom of the well. It is a dead-end silence here in his sunny kitchen stinking of the smoke of incinerated food.

"I'm sorry, Mrs. Catanzaro. I wish I could help. But it's just impossible. I'm sorry."

She says nothing and he knows that that is the end of it. She will stand there in silence holding the phone to her ear until he gives her a reason to stop.

"If you decide you want the name of that agency," he tells her, "or the name of a lawyer you can trust, call me back. I should be here most of the morning."

25

Again he tells her he is sorry and that he is going to hang up now, but he holds onto the receiver another thirty seconds, he knows she is doing the same. He doesn't want to let her go too brusquely, doesn't want her to think he doesn't sympathize, he does. He has been gutshot himself and he knows some of the effects. But he slips the receiver into its cradle finally. He feels embarrassed; he has an urge to wash his hands.

Instead he goes to the stove and shuts off the flame. There is not a salvageable bit of food left in the skillet. He stares at the charred scab of egg, a blackened clod. Cowflop. With a metal spatula he tries to scrape the omelet into the trash but the omelet and the Teflon are one now, indivisible. It is an old skillet anyway, already scratched and dented, the handle loose. He has a habit of holding onto things too long.

He cools the skillet with cold water in the sink, the metal hisses at him, spits hot black spit. When the skillet is silent he drops it in the trash.

Now if he wants any breakfast he will have to eat cold cereal. But he does not want any breakfast now. The smoke or stench or silence of the bright summer morning has turned his stomach.

"Hang up the goddamn phone," he says, and he stands there a long time waiting for it to happen. He stands there a long time listening, as if he will somehow hear that other phone unknown miles away being replaced. As if he will hear in the distant click of finality something to change the way he feels.

Chapter Three

Alex says, "Are you hungry yet, baby?"

And Jeri says, "A little, I guess. Are you?"

"I'm starved. Slip your dress on and we'll go."

"Why can't I just go like this?"

"You go like that and the produce manager is going to jump you in the melons."

"Maybe that's what I'm counting on."

At the Shop & Save in Pawtawney, fifteen miles up-river, Alex Catanzaro purchases a quart of orange juice, a halfpint container of artichoke salad, a half-pint of Tahitian fruit salad, one rye bagel, one jelly doughnut, two peaches and two large cups of coffee. The receipt, containers, and uneaten portions of food will be found in the grocery bag in the back seat of the car. The cashier who rang up the purchase at approximately 10:45 AM can not state emphatically that Catanzaro shopped there every Saturday morning, but she and other store personnel have definitely seem him on more than one occasion. No one can recall having seen the girl.

"Did you get my jelly doughnut?" Jeri asks when he returns to the car.

"They were all out of blueberry. You'll have to settle for raspberry this time."

"And what else?" she asks.

He hands her the bag. "One of these days you're going to have to start eating right, you know."

She holds up the container of artichoke salad. "I suppose this oily mess is your idea of eating right."

"The only reason I buy that stuff is because it makes my tongue slippery."

"Hurry up, take a real big bite."

Later, driving back toward the river, he tells her, "Open up one of those coffees for me, okay?"

She punches down the V-shaped flap on the lid, then hands the cup to him. Coffee splashes out of the cup and onto his trousers. "Ouch, damn it," he says.

"Oooh, it didn't burn him, did it? You want me to blow on him and cool him off?"

"Keep it up and I'll spill the rest."

They return to the spot where they had earlier parked, at the end of the narrow private lane a quarter-mile from the highway, the lane dead-ending where the river forms a shallow inlet. On the landward side of this lane are thickly clustered oaks, maples, chokecherry and sassafras trees, here and there a black walnut, long-reaching slender-armed scarlet sumac, an occasional fir tree or pine.

These woods continue for another half-mile behind where the car sits, the woods ascending in a rise of two hundred feet over that half-mile, bordering finally but not subjugated by—in fact threatening to reclaim—the grassless dooryard of the Jewett family. It was Clifford Jewett who posted the NO TRESPASSING sign at the mouth of the lane, Clifford Jewett who owns all the property from the inlet upward to his sunless clapboard house.

Except for the encroachment of the inlet itself, flanked on both sides by a curtain of cattails—the center of the cattail wall cut away as an entry to the inlet, a place to sit on a maple stump and fish for bottom feeders, bass and catfish; an entryway wide enough for the launching of a rowboat—this lover's rendezvous is

28

concealed too from the pleasure boats which traverse the wide brown river May through September. Along the river grows a collonade of slender birches and other young trees, their trunks all but hidden in the tangle of choking weeds that spring from the flattened matting of previous years' growth, of decayed foliage regularly added to by the floods of April and October.

Close all around the inlet and lane, between the car and the woods behind, between the car and the river birches, grow thin blonde straws of scrubgrass, clumps of weed, Indian tobacco, elderberry bushes and Queen Anne's lace.

Remember smoking Indian tobacco when you were a boy, DeWalt? How old were you then—ten? eleven?

Older. Everytime you'd smoke you would get an erection. The smoking made you want to throw up but there was something very sexy about it.

Maybe you should smoke some Indian tobacco now.

Maybe you should concentrate on the job at hand.

What's the matter, DeWalt—afraid of your memories?

Memories are the hemorrhoids of the mind, DeWalt. What good are they except to annoy, intrude, interrupt? They keep a man from being who he has to be. From doing what most needs done. If a man could live without memories, DeWalt. . . .

Ten feet in front of the car, close enough so that Alex Catanzaro must be careful not to drive over it, is a fire pit built of seven rounded stones. The pit is full of ashes and charred wood, fish scales and bones, the ringtabs of beer cans.

On sunny warm days a buzz of insects resonates from the grasses around the inlet. Water skippers and tadpoles and sometimes a sluggish gray bass hug the shadows beneath the cattails. Redwing blackbirds flit from one cattail to the next. Dragonflies skim the water.

On this morning, the 16th of August, the sky is not sunny. Even when Alex picks Jeri up behind the courthouse, nearly three hours earlier, already the sky is gray, low with cumulus clouds. Now, with their early lunch from the Shop & Save finished, the car parked again in its weed-trampled space, facing the fire pit, the river, with Jeri Gillen's dress again neatly folded and laid atop the rear seat, Alex's clothes beside hers, even more meticulously folded, there is a wind in the sky now, a wind as blue as serge, scratchy and hot. The clouds look like Brillo pads thumbsqueezed flat, oozing dirty suds. From these clouds come growls of thunder; muffled detonations. The air is as thick as silt, so muddied with heat that all the car windows are rolled down despite the gnats and other biting insects harried by the scent of rain.

Alex thinks to himself that it is probably raining already in Menona, the storm is coming from that direction. During these latter sessions of lovemaking, after the early madness and then lunch and then a slower, more measured consideration of pleasure, at these times he often finds his mind wandering, distracted from the damp and sticky gleam of her skin, his thoughts turned to other concerns, to needs not so easily gratified.

She is a wonderful girl but inexperienced in everything but this, and their conversations are not what he would term meaningful, they are of trivial matters, of movies and television shows she has seen, of gossip about other professors and students who frequent the restaurant where she works.

The only thing she is especially good at talking about is sex. She is as good talking as she is doing. She can make a double entendre from any phrase he utters, whether she understands the phrase or not, and even though she has no idea what *double entendre* means. She could turn that term into a double entendre too, just by the arch of her eyebrows, the suggestive curl of her smile.

He supposes he loves her in a way but he can never separate the thought of her from the idea of sex and he can not imagine being with her and not fucking her. He likes the way she says *fuck* and the way she asks for it and the ways she tells him what she is going to do to him. She is easy with all the words that he, even after three martinis and in the company of his colleagues, can not say without a consciousness that they are novelties for him, words at most times foreign to his mouth.

She is for him the embodiment of sex. He loves her for this and even loves the need she invokes in him, loves being addicted to her despite and maybe because of the danger of the addiction.

In fact during the latter half of these mornings he can be aroused more easily by the abstractions of sex than by the physical proximity or the palpable textures of it. When she wants to make love again but he is not yet ready, he will ready himself not by touching or being touched but by playing with the knife of possibilities.

"When we finally get the chance to spend a whole night together," he says, "maybe even go away somewhere for a weekend, what are we going to do with all that time?"

"Guess," Jeri says.

"Tell me. What do you like to do best?"

"I don't want to do anything except fuck."

"That might get boring after a while."

"Not the way I do it."

"And how's that?"

"You'll see when the time comes."

"I want to hear about it now."

And so she relates to him in exquisite detail all the joys of her tongue and mouth and ass and cunt, of how hard she will fuck him and how deep and fast and slow and of the times he will come in her mouth and the things she will wear and touch him with and the improbable positions and acrobatics of love. He will see these things in his head while smelling her very real perfume and the perfume of their earlier union, and he will feel her body moving again, excited by her own promises, and he will be ready for her once more.

And now he does not see the rain as it begins to fall in fat heavy drops, pocking craters in the loose dirt of the lane, splashing crowns of moisture from the river's surface. He does not heed the thunder nor the sudden bursts of light and noise as startling as discovery. Perhaps he feels the coolness of rain as it blows in through the open windows, he feels the spray across his naked legs and back, but he does not heed this breath of wind, he does not rise in time to look, to flee from whomever it is now standing there outside his door. He has no time to defend himself, to run. He sees and heeds none but the last of the signs, the final lightburst, the gunshot itself, that culminating explosion of censure he has always expected and feared but never in a form so conclusive.

Whether imagination, delusion, or actual memory, DeWalt could not name it; he knew only that when this intrusion came upon him, it ruined him for the rest of the day. It always came without announcement, as unexpected as a cluster headache, as damaging, a kind of internal movie from which he could not look away. Usually it came at night, a brief nightmare preceding sleep. But occasionally it came in full daylight, which somehow made it all the worse. If he were to describe it to someone, and he never would, he would compare it to a petit mal seizure. An observer would probably not even notice it, but DeWalt would notice, and it would leave him shaken and weak for the remainder of the day.

This time when it happened he was halfway to Elizabeth Catanzaro's house, the afternoon sun glaring off the windshield. His left forearm rested on the windowsill, warm air streaming past his face. Miles Davis was on the tape player, the elegiac "Sanctuary" cut. There was nothing happening that should have set DeWalt off again and yet suddenly there it was, that imagined or remembered thing.

He is in the ambulance and the ambulance is cold and he can feel through his back the speed and vibration of the vehicle's rush to the hospital. He can feel his heart trying to push itself out beat after beat through the holes in his belly. He is aware of all this, even aware of being aware of it, as if he is experiencing everything now from two perspectives, in first and third person. Then there is a click in the back of his head and the first person awareness disappears. His nostrils are no longer clogged with the paste-thick scent of blood on a Turkish carpet in a room that smells of sandalwood incense. Now he smells nothing at all.

Moving in silence, the pain still there but different somehow, more like a heaviness than a piercing throbbing ache, a weighty kind of numbness, he stands up in the back of the ambulance. The two attendants, both male, do not seem to be looking at him. He turns to the rear door and pushes it open. The doors swing out wide and he jumps clear, landing hard, rolling on the pavement, and he wonders how he knew to tuck and roll like this, how does the body know to do such a thing?

When he rights himself and on his hands and knees looks up, there is not a sign of the ambulance anywhere, no wink of red taillights, no fading whine of siren, no stink of exhaust. He looks around and does not know this place, this stretch of road bare of buildings and people and empty of all traffic. "Where were those bastards taking me?" he wonders aloud.

He is somewhere outside the city, somewhere so far from the city that he has never seen this place before. The ambulance must have been moving very fast, he must have passed out a while, because it is early in the morning now, the light is gray and the fog just beginning to lift from the road, a macadam road, black-topped, smooth, newly surfaced.

Before and behind him the road continues without turn between two broad fields of wild mustard, fields stretching uninterrupted to each far horizon. He is resting on his knees on the left edge of this road, his feet in the soft clean dirt of the shoulder. The fog is thinning quickly. He can distinguish through this haze the ripe golden clusters of mustard seed. There are no trees in any direction, only the wide yellow field with the black road cutting through it. There is a song in his ear like the plucking of a guitar string, a high metal whine, short, stiff, a single note repeating.

Approximately two hundred yards behind and then the same distance in front of him the road gently lifts onto a ridge, blue-gray morning all around. He is lying in the lowest part of a shallow basin, its field of yellow flowers appearing at its farthest points as uniformly colored as a pool of golden water, a sunset lake.

When he looks again at the sky it is surprisingly clear, so purely blue. Wondrously so. Not a cloud. Not a bird. Unusual. Too clear, that sky. He has never before seen such a sky. So wondrously pure. It makes him sad to look at it. You will never see a sky like this again, DeWalt. The inevitable loss of it seems terrible, he can not bear it. His chest is thick with grief, his throat constricts.

He becomes aware then of a vague ticking noise far to his right, a clicking faster than the tick of any clock.

34

It is coming from over the ridge behind him, in the direction from which he believes he himself has come. Then something crests the hill, a slowmotion shadow in the center of the road, a blurred silhouette against the lightening sky.

The ticking grows louder and the figure closer. It begins to assume definite shape and then color and then feature. It is a boy on a bicycle. The boy appears to be around nine or ten years old and he is pedaling very hard to reach DeWalt. Attached by a clothespin to the rear fork of his bike, so that it will click in the spinning spokes, is a baseball card. The boy wears a red baseball cap but DeWalt can not make out the insignia on it, the team's name. The bicycle shines like new but it is a type DeWalt has not seen for a very long time, a red 24″ Schwinn with fat tires and wide fenders, red and yellow plastic streamers whipping back from the handlegrips.

The boy stands on his coaster brakes and slides to a halt beside DeWalt. "Climb onto the crossbar," the boy says. His forehead is shiny with perspiration. There are beads of moisture above his lip.

DeWalt flattens his hands against the cool black road and tries to push himself up.

"We're just going to the other side of the hill," the boy tells him. He is short of breath but smiling, breathing hard.

"I can't get up," DeWalt says.

"I'm not supposed to get off my bike."

DeWalt reaches out and grabs hold of the chain guard and drags himself closer. Reaching progressively higher on the frame he manages to get to his feet.

"Sit on the crossbar," says the boy. "It's not far now."

DeWalt drops his weight onto the crossbar. The metal is cold across his buttocks. There is no strength in his stomach or back to hold himself up so he has to lean

35

forward over the handlebars, laying into their U, his body twisted at the waist.

The boy turns the wheel against DeWalt's weight and aims the bike up the center of the road. He stands on the pedal to set them moving again but they do not go anywhere.

"You'll have to lift your feet up," the boy says. "Hold them off the ground. Quit dragging them."

"I can't," DeWalt says.

"You're too heavy, I can't get started. You should be lighter than this."

"I'm sorry, I can't lift my legs. I'm cold, I can't stop shivering."

"You're not supposed to be like that."

"Tell me what to do if you know. I don't know what to do."

"You'd better get off," the boy says.

"You can't just leave me here. Can you send somebody else?"

The boy jerks his handlebars hard to the right and DeWalt falls off, he lands on his knees and then falls forward with his hands sliding into the soft dirt. He turns and reaches for the bicycle but the boy pushes away, he glides around in a full circle so that he ends up facing the same direction as before but out of DeWalt's reach.

"Does anybody know I'm here?" DeWalt asks.

The boy lifts his cap and with the flat of his hand wipes the sweat from his forehead. He resets the brim to hang low over his eyes.

"Tell me what you smell," the boy says.

DeWalt does not understand.

"What can you smell?" says the boy. "Tell me if you smell anything."

Until now DeWalt has not realized how congested his

sinuses are, how prohibitive of scent. He shakes his head no.

"You can't smell the mustard seed?"

DeWalt tries again. "I'm sorry. There's so much of it. It's beautiful but ... I wish I could."

The boy looks away. He seems annoyed now; somehow disgusted; as if he has been tricked. DeWalt feels inclined to apologize again, but before he can speak the boy shoves away, pedaling hard, standing, elbows pointed out like wings as he hunches over the handlebars. The boy grows small in the distance, the steady *ticktickticki*ng fades. Then his silhouette crests the hill and then sinks out of view and the clicking of the wheel dies away so softly that it is impossible to tell when it actually stopped.

By now the sun is bright on the fields and road. DeWalt feels the sunlight on the side of his face, warm and skin-tightening, but the warmth does not go deep enough and he can not stop shivering. The wild mustard is a brilliant yellow in the sun, a blinding beautiful yellow glare that stings his eyes finally so that he has to look away from it. He lays his cheek to the road and tries to smell the mustard seeds. The macadam is cool and a dull even black. It is all he can see for a very long time. It seems to him that he sleeps for awhile. When the coldness wakes him and he reaches for the pain in his belly, everything is white except for the woman wearing a dark blue dress and wide-brimmed blue hat who is holding his hand.

"I couldn't smell anything," he tells her. She smiles and squeezes his hand, and after that he sleeps again and while he sleeps the woman goes away.

And then that was the end of it and where it always ended. He awoke expecting to find himself in the hospital but this time he was in his car. It took him a few moments to remember what he was doing there. He glanced down at his odometer and saw that he had gone too far, he had missed the turnoff to the Catanzaro house. The postmaster in Menona had told him to drive six miles out of town and then look for a gravel drive-way on his right; there would be a white mailbox with a Confederate flag on it. He turned the car around, drove a mile and a half and saw the mailbox.

The driveway was long and gently winding and bordered on both sides by hemlocks, so tall and dense that only broken strings of sunlight reached through to the needle-matted floor. With the car window down he could smell the hemlocks and the wonderful coolness beneath their branches and he could hear crows somewhere but he could not see them. It was not until the car rounded a corner, turning at a right angle past the final hemlock, that he found the crows, four of them heading for the trees at the back end of the cornfield a couple hundred yards behind the Catanzaro house.

DeWalt turned off his tape player. Still fifty yards from the house, he brought the car to a halt. A pleasant sense of déjà vu had come over him. Emerging so suddenly from that shadowy tunnel of hemlocks, breaking into this wide sunny clearing of yard and house and cornfield, it put him forty years into his past. One of his uncles had owned a place like this, secluded and peaceful, a place that seemed to pop up out of nowhere, a parcel of order and cleanliness and reassuring routine.

The lawn surrounding the Catanzaro home took up well over two acres, was flat and neatly mown and the two-story white frame house sat in the center of it. The near side and the rear of the grounds were flanked by fieldland, tall dusty-tassled spears of corn for as far as DeWalt could see to his right, but giving away behind the house to a stand of mixed timber, aging massive oaks, the white-barked aspens and paper birches.

These same woods encroached closer on the far side

of the house, continuing forward to the highway. The house and property were shielded then on all sides, shielded, at least, from the noise and view of the highway, if not from the more insidious contagions.

DeWalt had spent many weekends at a place like this when he was a boy, weekends and summers with his aunt and uncle. But they had divorced when he was fifteen and a coal company bought their farm and stripmined it. The pond where he had caught frogs became a catch basin for sulphurous runoff. He had seen the place eviscerated and he had not returned to it since. The land had been reclaimed of course but that was not enough reason to return to it.

But this place could easily have been a reincarnation of his uncle's. Scattered behind and to the sides of the house were peach trees, Seckel pear trees, Granny Smith and Golden Delicious apple trees, a plum tree, a grape arbor, raspberry vines, a garden as big as a basketball court, a three-tiered strawberry patch, two bluebird boxes, a hummingbird feeder, patches of peonies, lilac, marigolds and chrysanthemums.

"This woman has her hands full," DeWalt said.

It was beautiful but of a hard-won beauty and it was the kind of place where DeWalt would live if things had been different for him. He had made a lot of money from his novel but he had lived off that money too long, doing nothing. Now he lived in a small house on a quiet street filled with small houses, and he had no practical need for a place this large.

But certain needs are anything but practical, DeWalt.

That's true, DeWalt. But you're not here to enjoy the sights, are you?

He could have let it end with the telephone conversation that morning, but all day long he had thought of her standing in an empty house holding a dead telephone receiver to her ear. It was absurd but he could not shake the feeling that she was still in that position, still waiting. So he had written down the names and addresses of some reliable people he knew and he had that paper in his shirt pocket now.

So get to it, DeWalt. Do something different this week: do somebody some good.

The front door was not locked but there was no answer when he knocked on it. There was a side entrance that opened onto a pantry, and here through the unlocked screen door he could see into the pantry and a portion of the kitchen. He knocked again but the house was silent. He tried not to think of her upstairs sitting on the edge of the bed with an endlessly beeping receiver in her hand. He took the slip of paper from his pocket and was about to wedge it between the door and metal frame when a couple of dogs began to bark somewhere behind the house.

Toward the far corner of the wide backyard there was a small kennel, a doghouse the size of a child's playhouse, with attached to it a chainlink dog-run. Elizabeth Catanzaro was inside this enclosure, had apparently just then entered it, a large bowl of dog food in each hand. Two Golden Retrievers were barking happily and leaping up and down beside her, their front paws reaching well above her head with each jump. The dogs appeared ecstatic but not once did they touch her. She set the bowls on the ground, stepped back and watched the dogs as they ate, long snouts deep inside the bowls, bowls wobbling and skidding across the packed earth, tails whipping back and forth. In little more than a minute the dogs had emptied the bowls. They looked up at her then, grinning and licking their black gums, tails snapping like whips.

Elizabeth Catanzaro picked up the bowls and squeezed out past the gate, pushing the dogs back with her foot. She was halfway back to the house before she looked up and saw Ernest DeWalt standing there. She gasped out loud, startled, and stopped moving.

"I'm Ernie DeWalt," he said quickly. "Sorry, I should have cleared my throat or something," and he smiled, hoping to elicit a smile, but did not.

She came forward again, again looking at the ground as she walked. She knelt at a water tap attached to the rear of the house and rinsed the dogs' bowls clean. She filled one bowl with water and set it on the ground, then filled the other bowl.

"I just dropped by to give you this," said DeWalt, the slip of paper between his finger and thumb. "The name and address of that agency I mentioned on the phone."

She cocked her head and looked at him. Cold water splashed into the metal bowl. When the bowl was full she shut off the tap and picked up both bowls and started toward the kennel again. Without looking at him, she said, "I'll be right back."

She was an attractive woman but this did not surprise him. Even if he had not already seen her face on TV he would have expected her to be attractive. As a young investigator he had often wondered why men married to comely women are so frequently unfaithful, and not rarely with a far less attractive woman. But over the years he had learned that this was the rule and not the exception. The same held true for unfaithful women, of course, who often chose extraordinarily unlikely partners. It was a matter of ambition, he supposed. The attention and flattery and ego-gratification attractive people feel entitled to. There were other explanations too but it was all a matter of ego. Ego was a simplistic explanation but satisfactory because he did not require much in the way of explanation anymore. People lied to and cheated the people they loved while being inordinately kind to strangers, it was an observable fact. He

41

did not have to understand gravity either to feel the effect of it.

Elizabeth Catanzaro was a small woman but she walked into the kennel without fear of the two large and noisy dogs. She appeared to be maybe five feet four inches tall, maybe one hundred and fifteen pounds. The dogs yelped and leapt for the bowls but still they did not touch her, they maintained a respect she had apparently instilled in them long before today.

She's not the kind of woman, DeWalt hypothesized, to blame herself for her husband's infidelity. She wouldn't blame herself for driving him away. She would feel betrayed by him; angered. But was she capable of rage? Of a methodical exorcism of her rage?

She scratched the heads of both Golden Retrievers as they lapped sloppily at the water. Then she stepped outside the kennel and locked the gates and came striding toward him, her step long and purposeful, legs and hips thin but certainly not shapeless in pale faded jeans, the long-tailed yellow cotton shirt not tucked into the jeans, sleeves rolled above the elbows. She wore tennis shoes and had the kind of small strong body that would look very good in tennis whites on the country club courts. It also looked very good returning from feeding the dogs—all of which made DeWalt too aware of his own body, the chronic fatigue and weakness, his paunch of half-living, half-plastic flesh.

She had a strong chin and dark intelligent eyes, short brown hair stylishly cut although not at that moment stylishly combed, lovely small breasts and strong square shoulders. She wore no make-up and there was a natural paleness to her lips, her mouth thin and unsmiling, tired, the curve of a crow's wings in the distant sky. She had spent too many hours in the sun as a teenager and those hours and her young laughter had etched deep lines at the corners of her eyes. Still, he admired the confidence with which she moved and the unselfconscious sureness of her body.

She came toward him with her hands in her hip pockets, walking without hesitation but with eyes lowered until she stopped an arm's length away, then looked up, squinting a little, squinting, he now saw, because the whites of her eyes were streaked with red.

"Those are beautiful dogs," he said.

"You want them?"

He tried another smile. "I live in town. In a house not much bigger than that kennel out there."

"Then maybe you should buy this place," she said. "Make me an offer."

Again he held the slip of paper toward her. "This is a good agency, Mrs. Catanzaro. If they say they're too busy to take you on, which they probably are, you mention my name. Tell them I promised you that they would take the case. They'll call me up and give me hell for that, but I don't mind."

She took the paper and even looked at it, but without unfolding it to read what he had written. She held it by a corner between finger and thumb, delicately, as if it were a butterfly perhaps, a curiosity, a captured thing.

Still looking at its blank face, she said, "Whatever you were involved in with my husband, I think I have the right to know." Now she looked up at him.

"I told you on the phone. I've never even spoken to him. In any case, not more than a passing hello."

"Then why is your name and phone number on his desk calendar and in his other papers? *Call DeWalt,* it says, with sometimes your home number, sometimes your number at school."

"He never called me. Or if he did, he never reached me."

She studied him hard for ten seconds more. Then with a small nod she brought her eyes to the folded pa-

43

per again, staring as if to read through it, to read something not written there. Almost imperceptibly, she shook her head.

He thought of touching her, a hand on the shoulder. He wanted to do it. But he was afraid that his hand might feel cold against her, and then how would she react? His fingertips often felt numb with cold, knuckles stiff, muscles as taut as frozen rubber bands. There was frost in his nostrils, he could smell it with every breath. Even in summer there was snow in his lungs.

"Well," she said, and looked up. "You came all this way out here . . . can I get you something to drink? Coffee? or a beer? a glass of iced tea?"

"Thank you, no." He looked at the field of corn behind the kennel. He could see no barn or equipment shed large enough for a tractor. Behind him and to his right was a two-story garage, but no other buildings.

"Who does the farming?" he asked.

"We own the property, but we lease it out to a neighbor. He lives down that way. You can't see it when the corn's so high."

"How many acres do you have?"

"A hundred and eighty. Don't ask me why."

"You don't care for rural living?"

She started to say something, but stopped. Finally she said, "It wears thin after a while."

Owning so much acreage had been her husband's idea, that was what DeWalt read into her remark. It had been her husband's idea but he had always been too busy to do so much as mow the lawn. The dogs were his dogs because he had thought how wonderful it would be to take them pheasant hunting on his hundred and eighty acres but the dogs had probably never even seen a pheasant unless one happened to fly past the kennel, and it was Elizabeth Catanzaro who cared for them and loved them. She had probably been a good

44

tennis player once but DeWalt doubted that she had visited the club recently. She could have been a faculty wife getting bloated and stupid on ten AM martinis except that her gentleman farmer husband had never had time to feed the dogs.

DeWalt figured that he had met more than his share of faculty and corporate wives and he was pleased that Elizabeth Catanzaro did not fit the mold. There was no reason to be pleased because he was not going to have anything to do with this case, but the pleasure was there anyway. There was no evidence in her of that typical hostess mentality he had grown to abhor, that shallow self-centeredness of women whose days are comprised of lunch, tennis, and cocktails, of wives utterly dependent upon their ambitious if neglectful husbands, women who because they take frequent shopping trips far from home see themselves as liberated and independent, women independent of nothing but self-honesty, arrested in development somewhere between Sak's and L.L. Bean's. All such women struck DeWalt as particularly asexual. He much preferred the company of working women, that category to which Elizabeth Catanzaro most certainly belonged. His preference was a useless one, of course, but it existed nonetheless.

She walked away from DeWalt now, she went to the metal basement door beside the water tap, the door canted at a forty-five degree angle between the ground and the house. She sat down on this door with her elbows on her knees and her hands clasped between them.

"It's just that I've been away from this kind of work too long now," DeWalt said, even though she had asked for no explanation. "I'm in no shape for it anymore. I couldn't do you any good."

She looked at the dogs, who were standing with their noses to the fencing.

"The police don't have any evidence against you, do they?" he asked. "If they did, you would have been charged by now."

"Just the phone call," she said.

"What call is that?"

"The one I made to Rodney Gillen."

"Rodney Gillen being Jeri Gillen's husband?"

She nodded.

"When did you call him? And why?"

"The same morning Alex was murdered. And I called him to tell him exactly where he could find his wife and my husband."

DeWalt blew out a slow, heavy breath. Yes, she certainly was a woman who would be angered by betrayal. "Why did you want Rodney Gillen to have that information? What exactly was it you wanted him to do?"

She looked to the side, looked at the ground, head cocked, jaw held crookedly.

The phone had rung at least twenty times on the morning of August 16th, twenty times before Rodney Gillen, groggy with barbituates, stopped shouting for his wife to answer the phone, crawled out of bed, stumbled into the living room, and snatched up the receiver in the middle of a maddening ring.

"Yeah? What?" he had answered.

"Is this Rodney Gillen?"

"Who's calling?"

"Are you married to Jeri Gillen? The waitress at the Colony Restaurant?"

"What about her?" Gillen had asked, coming awake now, awake with suspicion, a flowering of fear. "Who is this?"

"My name is Elizabeth Catanzaro. And I thought you might like to know that your wife and my husband are together at this very minute. As far as I can determine, they've been together every Saturday morning for the past year and a half."

Gillen said nothing, neither encouragement nor denial.

She continued, angered by his silence, another form of collusion. "Just in case there's any doubt in your mind as to what they're doing together, you can go see for yourself. They're parked in my husband's silver Accord on a private road beside the river. You head out of town on Third Street, turn left off the Abrams Hill bridge, then follow route 38 north for five and six-tenths miles. On your right there'll be a dirt road with a NO TRESPASSING sign at the entrance. That's where they are."

Again she waited. She expected her information to be challenged, her veracity questioned. She had more to say if he wanted to hear it. But Gillen said nothing. In silence he held the phone for half a minute, and then he hung up.

"And what did you do after that?" DeWalt asked.

She laughed. A small laugh, soft, self-deprecating. It was the first she had laughed since DeWalt met her.

She said, "I went upstairs and got all of Alex's clothes and carried them downstairs. I was going to burn them out on the front lawn. I wanted him to see the smoke on his way back home."

"But you didn't go through with it?"

"I never even noticed it was raining until I stepped out onto the porch with a bundle of clothes in my arms. And it was raining hard. Thunder, lightning; the water was already an inch deep on the driveway."

"So you changed your mind."

"It was like. . . ." She smiled to herself and shook her head. "I put his clothes back in the closet, and then I got in my car and drove to a little Presbyterian church a few miles from here. I didn't try to go inside or anything." She looked up at DeWalt now. "This is getting pretty melodramatic, isn't it?"

He smiled in return. "I can take it."

"Anyway, I just sat there in my car. And I prayed, I guess. I just wanted everything to be made right again."

"How long were you there?"

"Close to an hour. Long enough to start thinking maybe it was a mistake to have called Rodney Gillen. That maybe I'd given him the wrong idea or, I don't know, that I'd *had* the wrong idea about what should be done."

"You were afraid Rodney would go down there and kill them?"

"I don't know, I just had a feeling. I felt strange all of a sudden. Sick to my stomach but . . . not physically sick. Do you understand?"

"Of course."

"So I went to the nearest phone and called Rodney Gillen again. There's a phone booth outside a bar maybe a mile or so from the church. Anyway, there was no answer this time."

"Which made you even more worried."

"Terrified." She plucked a tuft of grass, then let it fall. "So I called the police. And they sent a car down to the inlet. And it was too late."

"And now you blame yourself."

"I am responsible, aren't I?"

"Not in a criminal sense. Not unless you suggested the course of action, or offered payment for it, or supplied the weapon."

"Are you asking me if I did? Go ahead, ask. You wouldn't be the first one to ask that question."

DeWalt chose to say nothing. He did not need to know. He was not involved.

"I know how it looks," she said. "Because the murder weapon was a musket, and because Alex was a collector, and because I called Rodney Gillen and told him where to find them ... don't you think I *know* how it looks?"

"Has Rodney implicated you in any way?"

"Rodney Gillen, like his wife, is still 'whereabouts unknown.' Same as the musket is. All of which leaves me with no way to defend myself. With nobody on my side."

For some reason, DeWalt's heart was racing. The air was muggy, thick, it sat in his chest like mud. It pooled on his forehead, oozed down his spine. And yet he felt frozen in that hollow space beneath his heart, he felt the coldness of the plastic bag folded against his belly, the chilly pinch of the catheter.

He thought it peculiar too how words could come so easily when directed through a pen, and so clumsily when he tried to speak aloud. Maybe if he pursed his lips to pensize, tightened the flow ... nope; now he would not only sound like an idiot but look the part too. Fortunately she was staring at the ground.

If he could count on her to not look at him again, maybe he could get away from here unscathed. Slink back to his little house that was easy to keep clean and quiet and back to his tiny backyard with its cedar block-ade fence that kept him from seeing beyond it. But out here in the open he was having a difficult time contain-ing his thoughts, they went out and on forever, they were crows in the distant trees, calling for him to find them.

He asked, "So how do you think Rodney Gillen got hold of a musket from your husband's collection?" A single crow took to the air; a black frown against the gunmetal sky.

"It wasn't from Alex's collection," she said. And now she looked up at him. "Nothing of his is missing.

You can check with the insurance company; Alex had everything insured."

If she was lying she was very good at it. But he did not think she was lying. But whether he believed her or not did not matter. His heart had slowed down now and was beating heavily again, dully, a hammer pounding clay. As for its brief freneticism—why do hearts do that? he wondered. Do they possess a secret knowledge, a way of knowing, or fearing, what the mind does not?

Anyway he would not be taking this or any other case. He looked to see if she was still holding the slip of paper he had given her. She was. It hung between her thumb and middle finger, brushing the grass, a yellow leaf about to fall.

"You call those people," he said, and nodded toward her hand. "They'll straighten things out."

"I thought that's why I was telling *you* all this," she said.

"Sorry," he said. "I'm sorry I gave you that impression." He could have left then but didn't. He stared at the treeline. "You should probably change your phone number too, get an unlisted number. Or at least an answering machine. You'll be receiving some crank calls before long."

"I've gotten several already."

He nodded. "The DA isn't going to charge you unless he can come up with something solid, so you can relax about that. Their first job is to find the Gillens and the murder weapon."

"I don't care about being charged, Mr. DeWalt. No, that's not true, I do care. Most of all, though, I want the truth."

"You know the truth."

"I think I do. But that's not enough."

"Sometimes it's all we get."

"It's what we get if it's what we're willing to settle for."

"I'm sorry," he said. "It's just impossible for me right now."

"Aren't you curious as to why my husband would have written down your name and number so often?"

He smiled. "I'm trying not to be."

"I don't understand how you can do that."

He kept smiling, even though the smile felt crooked somehow, ersatz. "Good luck," he told her, and turned away.

Conscious of every step, he walked back to his car. By the time he reached the car he was out of breath and his heart was racing again. His legs felt rubbery, feet like sweaty slabs of ham. Damn it, he told himself, I'm not that far out of shape that I can't walk fifty yards without collapsing. Get ahold of yourself, DeWalt.

Inside the car he started the engine, turned on the air-conditioner and closed the windows. Cool air flooded over him finally but it had an unpleasant odor, it left a sour taste of metal on his tongue. When he had his breath back he slipped the car into reverse, backed up to the garage and faced the highway again.

It was then he noticed the treehouse twenty feet up in a tall black oak, the boards of the small cabin as dark as bark, a ladder of short and variously tilted boards nailed to the thick trunk. It made him catch his breath again, his breath snagged on something sharp inside his chest.

Children, he thought. He had heard about them on the news. How could you forget about the children, DeWalt?

He shut off the car, got out and walked to the rear of the house. She was still there, still sitting on the basement door.

"How many children do you have?" he asked.

"Two," she said. "Nikki and Chris."

"And they are how old?"

"Nikki is eight, Chris is eleven. Why do you want to know?"

"And where were they the morning you called Rodney Gillen?"

"I had sent them the night before to stay with their grandmother, about thirty miles from here. So that they'd be out of the house when I made the call. And also when Alex came home afterward and we'd have it out. Or so I thought."

"And those mornings when you went to check on your husband and the girl?"

"I left them here watching television. Saturday morning cartoons. And I know what you're thinking—"

"I'm not thinking anything."

"Well, you'd have the right to. It was stupid of me to leave them alone like that. What if something had happened to them while I was gone?"

"Nothing did though."

"No, but it could have. I hate myself for doing that."

A few moments later he asked, "Where are the kids now?"

"They're staying with my mother. I want them to stay there until this thing is cleared up. Before school starts, I hope. Which is eighteen days from now."

"You should have told me you have children," he said.

"Why should that make a difference?"

He remembered the scene from the six o'clock news. She had been standing on her front porch, top step, late afternoon of the murder, looking down, arms hugging herself. A spa-slender mustachioed reporter in a powder blue suit pushing a microphone in her face. "How do your kids feel about what's happened?" he asked. And she, looking almost sleepy with grief, insentient with her surfeit of loss, she had lifted her head then and with blazing eyes asked in a low even voice, "You asshole, how do you think they feel? How would *you* feel? Or do you feel anything? Maybe you can't feel anything, maybe the only thing you're capable of doing is sounding like a goddamn idiot!" And she turned and stormed inside, the screen door banging shut. Her expletives had been cut but there was no mistaking what she had said. The reporter faced the camera then, nodding mournfully, looking appropriately sympathetic as he made his closing inanities. It was good theatre, it was real. They ran the same clip again at eleven.

"How long were you married?" DeWalt asked.

"Thirteen years. I was one of his students when he was a graduate assistant at Penn State. I guess he had a weakness for younger women even way back then."

DeWalt could not look at her now, did not think she would want him to. And when he did not look at her and they did not speak, it was as quiet there as had been his uncle's place. His aunt had raised chickens and there were no chickens here but the crows in the far trees were a suitable substitute. It was just as clean here and as quiet and it made him wish there were a way to be young again.

He glanced at her now and saw that she was staring at the grass between her feet. He could hear a woodpecker in one of the trees left of the house, hammering its brains out. He could hear his own breath rasping in the hollow of his chest and he could hear her finger and thumb rubbing up and down across the slip of paper he had given her.

"Is there anything else I should know about?" he

53

asked then, not as a reprimand but gently, an apology for ignorance.

"Lots," she said, and looked into the sky.

He stepped closer and extended his hand.

Chapter
Four

In structure the Jewett home was much like the Catanzaro home, a two-story frame house covered with three-inch clapboards, a long covered porch stretching from one front corner to the other, a side entrance, overhanging gables and a steeply-pitched roof. But there the similarity ended.

An original coat of white paint on the Jewett house was all but erased now, the boards blistered and warped, the house the color of chalk dust, a variegated gray. Beside the front door, beneath the porch roof, someone had once begun to repaint, this time with an ochre colored pigment, but even this area—no larger than that which a man could reach to both sides and above his head without stretching—was old enough to have lost all trace of sheen.

At the side entrance, the lower half of the screen door's frame was scorched black, most of the screen itself melted into clots of metal held suspended by a few threads of wire, like empty insect shells trapped in an abandoned web. The wooden door stood intact, however, the glass of its small triangular window replaced with cardboard covered with aluminum foil, the outer skin of the door charred in an inverted chevron pattern whose point reached nearly to the window, the varnish having been boiled into bubbles long since hardened into tiny black agates. There remained only enough of the three incinerated steps that had once led to this door to suggest their original purpose.

The roof of the house was splotched black with tar in six places visible from the front, six wide black shadows flattened against the curled and brittle leaves of the shingles. Growing thirty feet to the side of the porch but extending branches over the porch roof was a hundred-year-old oak, all but leafless now, dying from the inside out, its heart full of sawdust and beetle shells. One gnarled limb grew with several crooked fingers thrust against an upstairs window; the glass was cracked but not yet broken through. Last year's leaves, acorn husks, twigs and windfall branches littered the roof and ground.

The property surrounding this house seemed to be returning to its primal state. Maple and oak seedlings sprouted at random in the dark earth virtually bare of grass. The light was dim, a few broken shafts, weak straws of timid yellow. The air smelled vaguely musty. Depending on the breeze there were other odors as well, the least pleasant the scent from a hole being sunk ten yards off the left side of the house, where Clifford Jewett and his brother Draper were excavating the septic tank.

Ernest DeWalt parked his car, a professor's car, a maroon-colored Acura, beneath the oak whose branches were about to poke through the upstairs window. Ten minutes earlier he had been at the inlet where Alex Catanzaro had been murdered, a place now four miles away by car but less than a half-mile downhill by foot. He shut off the engine and, moving slowly, wanting to appear in no hurry, climbed out. Clifford and Draper Jewett leaned on their shovels to watch him approach.

They were pale; their skin, where it showed on the arms and face and neck, as white as their dingy tee-shirts. Draper had not been doing much of the work: the hilt of his shovelblade remained fairly clean, not caked with orange clay mud, as was his brother's. Draper's boots too, and the cuffs of his jeans, were not soiled to the extent of Clifford's, who wore the ochre stain of muck as high as the crotch of his trousers. A tear of sweat swung from the tip of Clifford Jewett's nose.

Draper Jewett looked like a sickly twin to his older brother—Clifford being fifty-four years old, Draper fifty-two—both men bald but for their horseshoe fringes of stiff black hair, both men squinting at DeWalt through the sweat-filmed lenses of black-framed glasses.

Draper's pot gut was not appreciatively smaller than his brother's but in fact appeared more distended, grotesque, because of his scrawny limbs; he weighed forty pounds less than his brother's 195. And Draper's chest heaved even as he watched DeWalt walking toward them; he seemed to be struggling to pull another breath from the dank air. Yellow threads of perspiration shone on his forehead, another clustered above his upper lip, another in the hollow of his long lupine chin. His skin was several shades darker than Clifford's but it was not a healthy coloration, a saffron shade of jaundice. He had the face of a yellow stone, the mouth a mere scratch, empty gouges for eyes. Clifford, on the other hand, despite his more robust physique, his round bulb of head with features too small, features undeveloped like those of a fetus, his coloring was more than merely pallid, it was achromatic.

DeWalt smiled at both men. He was about to call out a greeting when a loud pop sounded behind him; he felt his stomach turn, felt for just an instant all the strength flee from his legs. Then the sound registered and he knew it had not been a gunshot and he turned to look at his car; a dead chunk of branch had dropped onto the roof, scratching the finish. He looked at the Jewetts and saw them grinning, Draper's sneer broad and wolfish, showing yellow teeth; Clifford's thin-lipped smile as tight as a scratch.

DeWalt laughed uneasily. Jesus, he thought, your nerves are shot. You don't belong out here anymore.

"Howdy," he called then, and immediately regretted it, knowing they might think his rhubarb greeting a mockery, patronizing.

Because it is patronizing, he told himself. You better watch your step, buster.

No sooner had DeWalt walked past the front porch than a tiny brown blur came streaking through a tear in the screen door, a short-legged low-slung streak of teeth and noise, yelping shrilly, charging for DeWalt's leg. As near as DeWalt could determine it was a cross between a Dachshund and a Chihauhau, a frenetic hairless thing that seemed all belly and teeth, a short stub of tail and pointed bat ears. It seized the cuff of DeWalt's trouser, and, drooling spittle, whipped its rodent head back and forth, growling, nearly standing on its chin as its hind legs scrabbled air.

"Unless you give him a good kick," said Draper Jewett grinning, "he's not about to let go of you."

DeWalt watched the dog a moment longer; the animal appeared to be generating energy rather than expending it. Or perhaps DeWalt was feeling weaker by the minute, unprepared for falling branches and laughable attack dogs, unprepared for the incessant absurdity of life beyond his small house, his classroom.

He slipped the toe of his right foot under the dog's belly finally and exerted a gentle pressure upward, lifting until all four stubby legs were pumping air. The dog unbuckled its teeth from DeWalt's cuff, flipped off his foot and onto the ground, righted himself and attacked DeWalt's other leg.

"Tippy!" Clifford Jewett growled. "Goddamn you

mutt, get away from there." He picked up a clump of dirt and threw it. The clod struck the ground just short of DeWalt, exploding in a spray of small wet chunks. Tippy turned and looked at him.

"Go on, get out from there!" Clifford said. Tippy retreated to the top porch step, where he turned, faced DeWalt, and launched into a chorus of highpitched barks.

"Leta!" Clifford called toward the house. "Come and get your goddamn dog out of here before I bash him with a shovel!"

Aleta Jewett came to the door then. She held open the screen and said, not loud, without a glance in DeWalt's direction, "Come on here. Inside now." Then both she and the dog disappeared from view.

DeWalt had had but a glimpse of her but enough to be surprised by her age, which, to his eye, was close to seventy years; surprising because, according to the Menona policeman he had spoken to an hour earlier, the only woman who lived with the brothers was neither mother nor sister, but Clifford's wife.

Now, with the dog gone, DeWalt felt engulfed by the silence. He was perspiring heavily and his clothes felt heavy on him, trousers dragging on his waist, thin shirt pulling on his shoulders. This damn humidity plays hell with a man's dignity, he thought as he hitched up his trousers. Then, having tugged them too high, he had to free them from his sticky crotch.

He forced a smile. "Good watchdog you got there."

"Beats the shit out of a German Sheperd," Draper said. "Strikes quicker and eats less."

Nodding agreeably, DeWalt approached the ragged edge of the wide hole in which both Jewetts stood, their heads perhaps two feet below his own. He tried to keep his expression free from any reaction to the rich warm scent rising up from the hole.

59

"Full up, is it?" he asked.

Neither Jewett replied. Clifford had ceased smiling.

Now DeWalt hunkered down on the edge of the hole. "My name is Ernie DeWalt," he said, and held his smile. "I'm doing a little work for Elizabeth Catanzaro."

"Who's she supposed to be?" Clifford asked.

DeWalt kept smiling. "The name Catanzaro doesn't sound familiar to you?"

Again the men said nothing. The lenses of their glasses seemed smoked, fogged with the film of dried sweat.

DeWalt said, "Alex Catanzaro was the fella who got himself shot a few days ago on that piece of land of yours down by the river. Elizabeth is his wife. Or widow, I guess, to be exact."

"Who says it's my land?" Clifford asked.

"Court records."

Clifford stared at him a moment longer. Then, leaning the shovel handle against his chest, he removed his glasses. With the soiled tail of his tee-shirt he cleaned the lenses, all the while studying DeWalt. Clifford's eyes surprised DeWalt. They were as green as a lizard's and just as protrusive: bulging, naked eyes, unshaded by eyelashes or even transparent filaments of hair. And when he blinked, as he did but once during the next full minute, the action was unnaturally slow, a lugubrious rolling of naked skin over the bulging green balls, so slow that DeWalt could actually see the eyeballs roll upward in their sockets. DeWalt looked away then, he looked at the yellow ground, until he saw peripherally that Jewett had replaced his glasses.

"What I was wondering," DeWalt said, "is if any of you folks up here might have heard anything unusual that day."

"I heard a rabbit fart," said Draper. "Now that's something you don't get to hear too often."

DeWalt smiled and picked up a small clump of sticky earth. He squeezed it between his finger and thumb until it broke apart. "But you didn't hear a gunshot? Or maybe a woman screaming? It would have been around eleven AM or so."

Clifford said, "The state police already took down everything we know about that."

"I just thought you might have remembered something new since then."

"That'd be pretty hard to do if there's nothing new to remember."

DeWalt nodded, then broke another clod of dirt.

Clifford said, "I haven't been bustin' my ass here just so that you can knock dirt back into this hole, you know."

DeWalt looked up. Clifford's lenses were still opaque. "Catanzaro and his girlfriend spent every Saturday morning for the past year and a half parked down there on your property. How is it that none of you were aware of that?"

How is it that you let yourself get talked into this, DeWalt?

"Seems to me," DeWalt said, "that in all that time, it being your property and all, one of you would have wandered down there at least once and maybe caught them going at it."

"Seems that way, don't it," Clifford said.

"What do you folks usually do on a Saturday morning? Not last Saturday in particular. Any Saturday morning."

"We mind our own business," Clifford said. "What do you do?"

DeWalt looked at Draper now. "That's a nice little inlet down there. What's the biggest bass you ever pulled out of those cattails?"

Clifford said, "She's still claiming she didn't do it, is that it?"

The stink from the septic tank stung DeWalt's eyes. "You folks were home last Saturday morning, weren't you?"

"What'd we tell the police?" Clifford asked.

They had told the police that at or about eleven AM on August 16th, Clifford Jewett was underneath his pickup truck in the front yard, repacking the ball bearings in the rear axle. Draper and Aleta Jewett had spent the entire morning inside, making piccalilli relish and putting it up in canning jars.

"It just seems to me," DeWalt said, "that if somebody was down there in that hollow, probably screaming her head off, you would have heard it up here."

"What makes you so sure she was screaming?" asked Clifford. "Maybe she never made a peep. Maybe she's the one shot him, you ever think of that?"

"I have thought of that, yes. But then I have to ask myself, if she did shoot him, why would she go running off naked, leaving even her shoes behind. Where could she go like that?"

"There'd probably be lots of places happy to take her in looking that way. How about it, Drape?"

"Wouldn't even charge her admission," Draper said.

"That path that leads from the inlet?" DeWalt said. "Up through these woods of yours? I guess the police found a couple strands of her hair snagged on one of those tree limbs."

Clifford laughed and said, "And I guess you're full of shit."

"So how do you know she *didn't* come up that path? Wouldn't you, if somebody were chasing you?"

"Not barefoot and naked, I wouldn't. If you saw that path you saw all the vines and stickers too."

"I doubt she'd be overly concerned about a few scratches, seeing as how she'd just watched her lover's head get blown off. And probably figured that the same thing or worse was going to happen to her too."

Draper chuckled. "What'd be worse than taking a steel ball through the forehead?"

"For a woman, lots of things."

"Like what?"

DeWalt only smiled.

"Well," Clifford said, "if she's still around, somebody'll spot her sooner or later. In the meantime, this shithole isn't digging itself out."

DeWalt smacked the dirt from his hands. "And I've taken up too much of your time already." He put his hands to his knees as if to push himself up, but stopped.

To Draper Jewett, whose skin seemed the color of congealed chicken fat, DeWalt said, "How long have those kidneys of yours been on the fritz?"

Draper said nothing, surprised.

"Mine went bum on me about five years ago," DeWalt told him. "They work a little bit, but not enough to earn their keep."

"I was born with just the one," Draper said.

"And what happened to it? Infection?"

Draper shrugged. "It started acting up on me awhile back, so I took a bunch of pills Aleta had laying around. But that just seemed to make things worse."

Antibiotics, thought DeWalt. You poor dumb sonofabitch, you overmedicated yourself. "You on dialysis?"

"Fuck no. Nobody's plugging me into some damn machine."

"It's not like it used to be," DeWalt said.

"I don't give a shit what it's like."

63

"You've got to keep your blood cleaned out though. Otherwise you can be poisoned to death by your own blood."

"Fuck if I care."

"You might, one of these days."

"I don't see why."

"Because you could die."

"You think you can't?"

DeWalt smiled. "How about I come and take you into the dialysis center some day? Let you see for yourself there's nothing to it."

"The day I decide to do that, I'll put a gun in my mouth."

"That's what I used to think too."

"Yeah, well you ain't me, are you?"

DeWalt chewed the inside of his cheek. He tasted blood. Finally he pushed himself erect, knees stiff, leg muscles quivering and sore. As he stood, the charnal reek assaulted him again, and this time it showed on his face.

Clifford Jewett grinned. "I got another shovel if you feel like pitching in."

"Thanks," said DeWalt. "But I don't think I want to be within sniffing distance when you take the lid off."

"Stick around. The honeydipper'll be showing up any time now."

DeWalt felt sick to his stomach, he felt light-headed, body-heavy. He smiled a last insincere smile and said, "Thanks, it sounds like fun. Maybe next time."

As he turned away he heard the thrust of Clifford's shovel, the blade stabbing into the earth, and he felt the impact in his stomach, his mouth tasted dark and wet. Inside his car he sat motionless for a moment, closed off, not looking in their direction. His neck and back ached but it felt good to let the sunwarmed leather seat support them.

You went soft fast, he told himself, seeing those eyes in the rearview mirror, fast because now it did not seem like another man's life to him, that past, did not seem like somebody else's memories inadvertently telegraphed into his head. It was his life and it had not been so long ago after all.

But you went downhill fast, he thought as he drove toward the highway. You went soft, DeWalt, and you got rusty, and your reflexes are shot to hell. And worst of all, he thought as he opened all the windows and turned the air-conditioner fan to high, man oh man, DeWalt, you stink.

Sometimes you get hold of a truth you would rather not lay hands on. You do not know what to do with it and it is probably not good for anything. Finding it suddenly in your hands is like being at a dinner party and surrounded by the hostess and her influential guests. You are recounting a wonderful anecdote and they are hanging on your every word. But your nose is itchy, so you reach up to scratch your nose and something from inside your nose comes off on your finger, not a little something either but as long and elastic as a worm pulled from wet ground. Now it is there on your finger, and right in the middle of your very witty story. You are stuck with it and you have to do something. None of your choices is droll.

Such was the kind of impractical truth DeWalt was handed in Alex Catanzaro's office on the second floor of the garage. Here Catanzaro had his desk and word processor, a short box sofa and a telephone. Here he kept his notes and research for the book he was writing, plus a small cassette tape recorder and several tapes containing information he had dictated or read, a stack of students' papers to be corrected, numerous magazines and books, maps of Lake Erie and the fortifications and the sites of naval battles.

Along one full wall was a glasstop display case containing Alex's collection of Civil War artifacts: cartridge belts and powder horns, knives, bayonets, a blue serge jacket, a confederate cap, buttons and other insignia, a 135-year-old train schedule, photos of weaponry plus two handguns (both reproductions), and a broadside proclaiming Brown's victory over evil at Harper's Ferry. The display case was locked and its contents neatly arranged, with no indication that any item, especially one as large as a musket, had been removed.

Once an item was placed in the display case, Elizabeth Catanzaro had told him, her husband seldom moved it. He had looked at his collection often and enthusiastically showed it to visitors, but he rarely allowed the items to be touched or handled. He certainly would not have had a loaded musket in his possession, nor would he have allowed even the handgun reproductions to be fired. He prized his collection for its historical relevance. That the individual items had no practical application in today's world was precisely why he valued them.

On floppy disks he had stored the first seventy-two pages of his historical novel. DeWalt scrolled through it, reading paragraphs at random. It was competent writing but dry, filled with the minutae academics adore. Maybe it could have been published by a university press if Alex had promised to make it required reading for all his classes. There were a lot of facts in it but the piece had no lungs, it did not breathe. It was all head and no heart. Just the opposite, DeWalt thought, of Alex Catanzaro's other abiding passion.

And such was the irony of Alex Catanzaro's life: that the passion he lived by and with, his passion for history, for an era he must surely have considered nobler and more civilized than his own, an era reflected in the sobriety of his dress (pinstripe suits on class days, nothing more casual than a tweed jacket on any other), reflected too in his southern civility and charm (although he had been born in New Jersey), and reflected even in his home, this gentleman farmer's estate, that this first passion had conspired with a second one, a passion by all appearances the shadow reflection of the first—that is, prurient and vulgar and anything but noble—that these two passions, embodied in the heat of a young woman and in the cold lead of a musketball, had acted in concert to bring about Catanzaro's death—DeWalt considered this an irony of the highest form. But was it irony contrived by man or God?

"Ready for the rest?" Elizabeth asked after DeWalt had leaned away from the word processor.

He looked up at her. Nothing he had read or seen so far had been particularly illuminating, except as it applied to Henry James's theory of character illumination. But the quality of Elizabeth's voice now—she sounded like a child who, wanting to appear brave as the doctor raises the innoculation needle to her skinny arm, says, "Sure, let me have it."—this tone of forced insouciance signaled to him its opposite.

He wished she would turn on the air-conditioner before revealing anything new. The temperature was at least ninety degrees in the small closed room; his breath did not come easily.

"Show me what you've got," he said.

She went to the corner of the display case then, sank to her knees and ducked beneath the case. Her fingers slid along the wall to its intersection with the case's bottom. Here there was perhaps a half inch of space between the display case and the garage wall. Looking down from the top of the case, no space was discernible. But it was large enough to conceal what Elizabeth soon brought forth: three cassette tapes and a packet of photos.

She crossed the room and handed them to DeWalt. He asked, "How in the world did you find these?"

"I came up here one time," she said, "I don't remember the reason. But anyway I guess he didn't hear me coming. It was, I don't know, five or six months ago. And I saw him kneeling there with his head under the display case."

DeWalt looked at the photo envelope but he did not yet remove the photographs. The cassette tapes were untitled, marked only as number *I*, *II* and *III*.

"When I asked him what he was doing, he said the display case felt wobbly and he was checking the bolts. At the time, I believed him. Then later, when I found out about the girl. . . ."

DeWalt knew even before he looked at the photos what they would show. Elizabeth Catanzaro stood with her eyes averted, mouth unsmiling.

The photographs had been taken with a 35mm camera and developed at a one-hour processing shop in a mall nearly forty miles away, a place that provided double prints for the price of one. There were twenty-four photographs in all, a full roll. They were dated December of the previous year.

When DeWalt turned the first photo over to check the date printed on its back, Elizabeth said, "He seems to have had a very Merry Christmas that year, didn't he?"

All but four of them were shots of Jeri Gillen, taken inside Alex's car. In some, Alex had apparently been standing outside the car, shooting in through an open window or door. In others she lay across the back seat as he shot from the front. The four taken outside the car included Alex as a subject. In two of these, the girl was fellating him; in another, their positions were reversed; and in the final one—all of these four with the woods as background, and therefore accomplished, DeWalt guessed, by positioning the camera on the car's trunk lid and setting the automatic timer—the photo showed Alex standing sideways to the camera, the girl clinging to his neck, her legs circling his thighs, head thrown back, mouth agape.

DeWalt slipped the photos into their envelope and handed the packet to Elizabeth. "I assume that the police don't know about these," he said.

"I can't think of any good reason why they need to."

"Then why show them to me?"

"I don't know," she said.

And he thought, Because it hurts too much to keep them to yourself.

"And these?" he asked, picking up the cassette tapes.

"The movie soundtrack," she told him.

She started to turn away, then stopped for a moment. She dropped the packet of photographs onto Alex's desk. She seemed ready either to cry or to explode in rage; the same emotion, different responses.

You might at least take her hand now, DeWalt told himself. Show a little compassion.

He said, "There's no reason why you need to hang around and listen to these again."

She nodded. "I'll go put some fresh coffee on."

"How about something cool instead?"

"Iced tea okay?"

"Perfect."

As soon as she was gone, he turned on the air conditioner.

Chapter
Five

"How about another one?" Della asked. She picked up the saucer that had held DeWalt's Colony Roll, a softball-sized pastry of cinnamon, raisins, pecans and sticky caramel sauce, the saucer empty now but for a smear of caramel.

"You want to see how I'll look with *three* chins, is that it?"

"You don't have a double chin, Ernie. That's just baby fat. I think it's cute."

"If you think I'm so cute, then sit down here a minute and talk to me. I need some information about Jeri Gillen."

Della flashed a look toward the kitchen. Then she slid in across from him in the booth. He had timed his visit for the restaurant's final half-hour of business, hoping that just such a conversation would be possible. Of course he could have met Della outside after work, could have sat with her in one of their cars, but he preferred these days to meet with women in public places, especially if the woman was as flirtatious as Della.

There was only one other customer here now, a student more interested in his *Wall Street Journal* than in the resident novelist schmoozing with a waitress fifteen years his junior.

She was one of the first people he had met when he moved to Menona five years ago. She had served him his first cup of coffee there. On his second visit to the restaurant she surprised him by bringing out a copy of *Suffer No Fools* and asking him to autograph it. She had said, "Write something like, 'I'll never forget all the crazy times we've had together.' It'll drive my husband nuts."

Della was a plain-looking girl, a woman actually, already into her thirties, the mother of three. Her oldest, a boy, was in high school, tenth grade, the same approximate age as his mother when she gave birth to him. She was one of those women who appeared to have been put together in haste, by a god inattentive to his work. She had thin shoulders, small breasts and a narrow waist, but from the waist down she became another woman, broad-hipped and thick-ankled, splay-footed. She moved heavily, almost waddling, as if the upper body had a hard time keeping the lower half in motion. But DeWalt had never known her to greet a customer with less than a smile and an ebullient, "Hey! It's about time you came by to see me!"

DeWalt liked her and often asked about her children. They were all fine, she would tell him, except for Travis, the oldest, a bright boy destined either for the penitentiary or the governor's mansion. When DeWalt asked about her husband, she would answer, "My what? You mean that skinny baldheaded guy who uses my bathroom? Geez, and I thought it was the TV set he was married to. He sure plays with it a lot more'n he plays with me, I'll tell you that!"

"Tell me about Jeri," he asked her now, his coffee cup resting in both hands, the cup still nearly full, coffee cold. He had to restrict his fluid intake and so allowed himself only an occasional sip, but the cup was a comfortable prop, a legitimization of his fondness for coffeeshop ambiance. The Colony Restaurant in partic-

71

ular was always clean and seldom noisy and the people who worked here never hurried him to leave.

"I still can't believe what happened to her," Della said.

"What happened to her?" he asked.

"You don't believe she's still alive, do you? I don't."

DeWalt shrugged. "Did any of you know that she was dating Dr. Catanzaro?"

"Hey, Jeri used to flirt with every second guy to come through that door. She made more in tips than the rest of us put together."

"Did she ever mention Alex Catanzaro in particular? Ever hint that she was involved with him?"

"Not that I remember, no. She did seem to have a thing for older men, though. I mean a guy your age would come in and she'd say something like, 'I bet that one's got a lot of notches on his pistol,' or maybe, 'Old guys are better because they take their time, they always think their next one might be their last.' But I don't know, we all say things like that. What else is there for us to talk about in here?"

"She ever talk about her husband?"

"Only to say what a loony bird he is."

"In what way?"

"Take your pick."

"Give me an example. I'm an old guy, remember?"

"Well, you know, he did a lot of drugs and stuff. According to Jeri, you could never tell how he was going to act."

"What kinds of drugs?"

"What kinds are there? Anything he could get his hands on."

"Jeri too?"

Della shrugged. "We got high together a couple times after work, so I know she smoked. She said she had stopped using coke, but I'm not so sure."

72

"Why do you say that?"

"I just don't think she did is all. I never saw her doing it or anything, but she could be moody, you know? Plus, she was always complaining about how she and Rodney never had any money—so where'd all their money go? They never bought anything, that's for sure. You ever see the furniture in that apartment of theirs?"

"You've been in the apartment?"

"A couple of times, yeah."

"Was Rodney there?"

"Yeah, but he never came out of the bedroom. She'd be all bitchy and complaining when we'd get there, and then she'd go into the bedroom and close the door, and a couple minutes later she'd come back all smiles and ready to take on the world."

"But Rodney always stayed in the bedroom?"

"According to her, that's where he practically lived. He'd be in there half the day with his headphones on and plugged into one of those electric keyboards of his."

"So you think she'd go in there and do some coke with him."

"Well what's it sound like to you? I don't know, though; I guess it's none of my business. She was a good waitress, no matter what she did at home."

DeWalt nodded. "Other than staying in the bedroom all day, what other things about Rodney made him a loony bird?"

"He had certain ... quirks, I guess."

"Such as?"

"I guess weeknights were kind of weird for him," she said. "When his band wasn't playing somewhere, I mean. And he had to spend all night at home."

"Weird how?"

"This is just what she'd tell us, you understand? I have no idea whether she was making it up or what."

"I understand."

"Well, the thing he liked to do best, I guess, after it got good and dark outside, was, he'd go out on their balcony, you know? And she was supposed to stay inside and pretend that she lived there alone."

"I don't think I follow."

"She was supposed to act like he was dead, like he had died and she lived there all by herself. Rodney got a real charge out of that. Pretending he was dead and then peeking in through the curtains to see what her life was like without him."

"And what would Jeri do while he was outside?"

"Watch TV, read a magazine, paint her toenails, I don't know. Probably the same things she did when he was holed up in the bedroom. The difference was all inside his head, you know what I mean?"

"Did this have anything to do with their sex life?"

Della grinned. "The way Jeri told it, it was their sex life."

"Tell me how Jeri told it."

"You want me to go into detail about this?"

"Not if it makes you uncomfortable, Della. I know how shy you can be when it comes to talking about sex."

"Okay, smart guy. Rodney didn't seem to have much interest in sex. Not in the usual way, that is. Once in awhile he'd ask her to go down on him, but that was about as typical as they ever got."

"He had a preference for oral sex," said DeWalt.

"I wouldn't call it his preference, no. It was one of the few things they did together though. Until, that is, Jeri kind of discovered one night how to *really* turn him on."

"And how was that?"

"Well, this one night, see, there he was out on the balcony, pretending to be dead and all. And Jeri, I don't know, just to see what he'd do, I guess, she started touching herself. She said it was kind of exciting to know that he was out there watching her. So anyway, she's there on the couch, having a good time with herself, and pretty soon the balcony doors slide open. She stops, because she thinks he's going to bitch her out. But instead he goes and stands over in the corner and takes his own pants down and tells her to keep going! And to talk about it out loud, you know? Like there's somebody actually doing it to her? And the dirtier she talks, the more excited both of them get."

"And?" said DeWalt.

"Now *you're* excited, aren't you?"

"Della, please."

She laughed and patted his hand. "So, anyway, that was the only way she could get him worked up enough to do it. The only problem was, he wouldn't put it in until he was almost done. So it was like, what good was he doing her?"

"Do you think Rodney was capable of killing her?"

She considered it a moment. "I think he could kill Dr. Catanzaro. But I don't know, now that I think about it, I'm not so sure he could kill Jeri."

"Why do you say that?"

"She tried to break up with him once. It was, lemme think, early last fall sometime."

"She was going to divorce him?"

Della nodded. "And Rodney just fell apart. He started crying and crawling after her all the time, begging her not to leave him. He'd call or come by here five or six times a day. She said it was even worse at home. He started getting up before she did every morning, ironing her uniform, polishing her shoes, making breakfast, waiting on her hand and foot. He even shaved her legs

75

and washed her hair for her! And I guess she loved it at first—she said she made him screw her three or four times a day for awhile. Jeri did love to screw, there's no question about that. But anyway, eventually she got sick of him threatening to kill himself if she left, so finally she just told him okay, no divorce."

"You think maybe they had some kind of agreement after that? That she could do what she wanted with other men?"

"All I know is, she stopped talking about getting a divorce. She said it was easier just to let him stay. Plus, I think she was a little bit afraid of him too. Because he was so unpredictable and weird, you know?"

"But you still don't believe he could actually kill her, is that right?"

"I don't know, I guess it's hard to say. I guess, in the end, a man might do just about anything. Don't you think?"

Yes, DeWalt, you do.

Now that he was wholly and inextricably involved in the case, it was time to let the police know. In the past he might have delayed this longer, knowing how private investigations can be handcuffed by the enmity of certain police officers. But rural police, he had learned, are not so immediately affrontable, not so tense. In the rural areas are places where an angry heart can go to be alone; space and solitude to spew out one's bile without embarrassment; the privacy to throw off for a moment the mask of manhood, to get oneself clean, and emptied; to expunge the surplus hate or grief and get back to that level of emotion one can live with. But in the city if you find an empty space you can never be sure there is not someone lurking in the darkness, someone even angrier than you; and such suspicion exacerbates instead of heals.

And so, crimes in the country tend to be simpler crimes, unpremeditated and therefore lacking the convolutions of claustrophobic planning. Rural cops, therefore, are easier to get along with. They are less suspicious of the con. More willing to accept a man at face value. Plus, they share an attitude of their constituency that it is unbecoming to ask for help but churlish to turn away a proffered hand. Which means that the adversarial element need not be so intrinsic to an investigator's relationship with a country cop, but depends to a large measure on how smoothly the investigator intrudes himself.

In this case DeWalt would be working with the State Police, for which he was grateful. He might be inclined to wonder about the motivations of a small town cop who will put in long hours for $14,000 a year, but it could be assumed that a state trooper earning twice that amount is not necessarily a bully, an incompetent, or a physical reject from the academy.

A state policeman might ignore a traffic violation in exchange for a half-hour of afternoon delight but he would not risk his career for a handful of food stamps. Most of the state boys DeWalt knew were motivated to keep people out of jail rather than to put them in. They placated rather than antagonized. Held in at least moderate esteem by the people they served, they remained salt of the earth, reasonably paid, moderately feared and respected; somewhat Godlike in their aloofness and deadpan compassion.

DeWalt knew one such individual here. Trooper Larry Abbott had introduced himself to DeWalt at the autograph party the English Department organized to welcome DeWalt to Shenango College. The reception had been held in the Student Union, a dim windowless basement room that housed a half-dozen tables and chairs, four vending machines, and a jukebox. Abbott had seemed an anomaly in the small crowd gathered to hear DeWalt's reading, an audience of nine females and three other males, three pale men whom DeWalt would come to know as fellow English professors, men who spent a great deal of time reassuring one another that they wrote far too well to ever get published.

Abbott's posture as he sat attentively in a metal chair was tall and straight without appearing forced; a goodlooking young man in his late thirties, suntanned and blue-eyed, his short blonde hair parted neatly on the side. He was dressed that night in blue jeans, moccasins with no socks, a short sleeve pale blue cotton shirt. DeWalt pegged him as either the baseball coach or a campus cop.

After DeWalt's brief talk, when everyone else had left except for Dr. Andrea Banks, the English professor who had organized the reading, Abbott purchased a copy of *Suffer No Fools* and collected DeWalt's signature on the flyleaf.

"I read your book a couple of months ago," Abbott told him. "I'm a State Trooper, and it seemed to me that you told things pretty much the way they are."

It was the kind of compliment DeWalt most appreciated—no fawning, no sychophanous slavering. "Thanks," DeWalt said.

"Do you mind if I ask you a question, though? It says on your bio that you worked in Los Angeles. Is that where you're from? I mean, were you born there?"

"I was born and raised in Ohio. A little town just this side of Columbus."

"I thought so," said Abbott. "I couldn't imagine, after reading your book, that you grew up in California. From my observations, and I spent over two years in San Diego, if you lived your childhood in Southern California, you're fucked for life."

DeWalt laughed. He felt as if, here in this foreign

land, he had finally found someone who spoke his language. "How about a cup of coffee somewhere?" he asked.

"Sounds great."

DeWalt was relieved not to be left alone with Professor Banks. He knew what she was up to with her meticulous wrapping and packing of hors d'oeuvres. Her attention to detail bordered on psychosis, especially when she began to return walnut crumbs to their original places on the cratered cheese ball. But she was not a psychotic, she was stalling for time. As some people are aroused by pornographic films, Professor Banks was aroused by poetry and fiction readings. Her passion for words was literal as well as figurative. If books came with penises, she would have been a librarian.

DeWalt would have been happy to accommodate her passion had circumstances permitted. But there were circumstances beyond his control now. Circumstances he did not care to explain. Women were too damn understanding and it would only make her want him more. Look at Lady Brett for example. She had been mad for what she could not obtain. But DeWalt did not wish to be the Jake Barnes of the Shenango English Department, not even in this day and age, this era of high technology. Even modern science could not turn Jake Barnes into Don Juan. It could give Jake a permanent erection, which was something no other literary figure had had, except perhaps for Cyrano, who had worn his on his face. But in this particular case, DeWalt decided, it would be better to let Professor Banks think he was a Truman Capote.

Hearing DeWalt's and Abbott's plan, Professor Banks was crestfallen. She took a quick look at the handsome young trooper. Then another look at DeWalt. "Have fun," she told him. She recognized her loss as an occupational hazard. She would have to see to it that DeWalt got acquainted with the Theatre Department.

After that, DeWalt and Abbott met from time to time for lunch or for a couple of drinks at the end of a day's shift. When DeWalt ordered a soft drink the first time they met at a local bar, then barely touched it through the course of the evening, he explained, even though the trooper had had the tact not to inquire, "I took a slug in the kidneys awhile back. Have to be careful about my fluid intake." It was a partial truth but sufficient. DeWalt might have told him more, might have told him everything, in fact, had Abbott asked.

Spending an hour or so with Abbott was for DeWalt akin to lifting his head from the trough of pedagogical bullshit for a gasp of fresh air. Whenever the academic atmosphere grew too thick for DeWalt, when it began to reek of departmental gladhanding, handjobbing, back-stabbing and buttlicking, he would call Abbott and in-vite him to lunch.

Now DeWalt called him again. They shared a corner booth at the Colony Restaurant. DeWalt waited until the trooper had finished his half-pound cheeseburger before he said, "That girl who disappeared last week was our waitress last time we were here, remember?"

Abbott nodded. "Crazy, isn't it?"

"I've been picking up a little information about her here and there."

"Writing another novel?"

DeWalt merely smiled. Half a minute later he said, "Elizabeth Catanzaro hired me to do some digging for her."

"No shit? I thought you gave up that kind of stuff."

"I thought I did too."

"You told me you weren't going to be looking up anything from now on except young girls' dresses."

"That was my plan. Thing is, none of them wear dresses anymore. Ain't it a bitch?"

"So ... what really changed your mind? She make you an offer you couldn't refuse?"

"Don't be crass, Larry. She's a grieving widow and the mother of two kids."

"Yeah, but how's she look in a bikini?"

DeWalt said, "Is this the kind of cooperation I can expect from you?"

Abbott chuckled. Then, "Sgt. Tom Shulles," he said. "He's the man in charge. I'll put you two together and maybe something will turn up. Right now they've got diddly."

"You're not a part of the team?"

"I could maybe get myself assigned."

DeWalt signalled to the waitress to bring the check. To Abbott he said, "Who's doing forensics?"

Abbott grunted. "There are four hundred forensic pathologists in the whole country, Ernie. How many of them you think live around here? The coroner did the forensic autopsy."

"The coroner. Also the local funeral director."

"We've got what we've got. This isn't Chicago, you know. Investigating murders isn't a fulltime career around here."

"I don't suppose the murder weapon's been found yet."

"Not unless you happened to bring it with you. In my opinion, though, we find Gillen, we find the weapon."

"No sign of him yet either?"

Abbott shook his head as he dragged a french fry through a smear of ketchup.

"Any predictions as to where he might turn up?"

"I have no opinion on that," Abbott said. "Except to say that, if anybody knows Gillen's whereabouts, it would be your client."

"She's never laid eyes on the guy."

Abbott nodded, unsmiling, but DeWalt could tell that the trooper did not concur.

"What we're doing now," Abbott said, "is we're checking with a couple of muzzle-loader and black powder clubs hereabouts. Seeing if they've had any weapons stolen or misplaced recently. Seeing if we can connect any of the members with Gillen."

"How's it looking so far?"

"Like a serious waste of time."

"How about this, Lar. How about if one of those muzzle-loader afficionados was doing some target practice down near the inlet. And Alex Catanzaro was unlucky enough to catch a stray ball?"

"That ball was no stray. It went exactly where it was aimed. Point blank."

"How about the ball itself? Learn anything from it?"

"Nothing revelatory. It was made from the same kind of lead as used in fishermen's sinkers. Nearly all the local muzzle-loader nuts mold their own."

"What about matching the ball to a specific mold?"

"There's a man working on that. Thing is, it could take months. My guess is, we'll locate Gillen first, and he's going to tell us exactly where the weapon came from, and the answer will be the obvious one."

"Despite Elizabeth Catanzaro's disavowal that it belonged to her husband?"

"Would you really expect her to admit that it *was* his?"

"I don't know. But I'll tell you this. If the weapon did belong to her husband, she knew nothing about it. Trust me on this."

"I don't have to trust you, I'm not even on the team yet. And neither are you."

DeWalt conceded with a smile. "Are you and Laraine still trying to make a baby?"

82

"Yeah, but we've cut down to five times a day now. I told her I'd better pace myself, just in case this takes awhile."

It seemed to DeWalt that he and Abbott always began and ended their conversations this way, with sophomoric jabs or rotomontade. But there was comfort in this familiarity, there was solace. Larry Abbott was, DeWalt realized, his only friend.

"You want a last refill on that coffee?" DeWalt asked.

"Naw, I'd better not. I gotta watch my sperm count."

"Right there's your problem," DeWalt said.

"What do you mean?"

"You're not supposed to *watch* your sperm, Larry. That's not how babies are made. I have to admit, though, that it's damn interesting that yours can count."

"Hey, you ought to hear them singing 'The Star Spangled Banner'."

Chapter
Six

It would be wrong to think of Ernest DeWalt as an exemplary human being, a man of consummate morality, a man who never entertained a duplicitous or savage thought. He did not love all mankind; in fact he loathed a fair proportion of it. He did not believe that all men are inherently good. He did not wish well of everyone he met.

The anger in him was never fully suppressed. It kept him company at night, warming his narrow space, his share of darkness. It was one of the few things that *could* warm him, for he was always chilled, even on a sultry August night, chilled in that hollowed-out center of his being.

On particularly frigid nights he would welcome the warmth of anger and huddle close to it, a campfire to keep the beasts away. In the living room the television would be left on, volume low, the brightness of the screen dimmed to gray, whispers and flickerings of light sufficient for the ordinary hours of loneliness. But on particularly frigid nights he needed more. He would think of causing some damage, an unprovoked act, a violation in kind.

A man could take a fair-sized rock—an intelligent man; a man smart enough to have no motive, no greed or jealousy or passion fueling the act—he could take his rock and, wearing gloves of course, walk down to Sec-

84

ond Avenue at four AM—it was now 3:47 AM; close enough—and standing across the street from, say, Kingman's Jewelry Store, sail his rock through the plate glass window, and, having never emerged from the shadows himself, seen by no one, unidentifiable, walk away, stroll briskly home to the music of the store's whining alarm, never be caught or suspected, sit at his breakfast table the next morning as if nothing unusual had ever happened to him, nothing the least bit adventuresome, and be an overall happier man for his secret, a more productive man, his attenuation slowed.

But a middle-aged man is hope betrayed. Time subverts his plans. Dawn arrives too quickly, before strategy can become execution. And yet, another chill night has been outrun. The day lies ahead, another search for one's soul.

He sits on the edge of the bed and stares out the window. He is silent and motionless but something is happening. He is coming to grips with another day dawning in the chill of the shadow of the past.

There is no question that every effort of the coming day must fail. An understanding of this is the only possible success.

Yes, to live another day is a Cadmean victory. We are all sprung from dragon's teeth. And on a fog-enshrouded battlefield, on this day or the next, we will each of us be slain.

Every Tuesday and Thursday evening the Kinetics practiced in a two-stall garage behind the home of the drummer's parents. The carport doors were kept locked and the windows had been blacked with paint. DeWalt drove slowly down this street, window open; he could hear the Kinetics from a block away.

To DeWalt's ears the music was all volume and no heat. Bessie Smith had heat, as did Billie and Dede

Pierce, Bix Bierdecke, Coleman Hawkins, Aretha Franklin, Miles Davis, Gene Krupa, Benny Goodman. But when DeWalt pulled open the garage's side door, the sudden blast of noise made him shiver. The reverberating chords seemed as hard as the concrete floor.

The drummer and the electric bassist looked up at DeWalt as he stood there in the doorway, but they kept playing, kept pummeling the notes. DeWalt smiled and nodded; he slapped his hand to his thigh, hoping to find a beat, looking as if it was all he could do to keep from breaking into the funky alligator, the convulsing monkey, or whatever gyrations kids were doing these days. The lead guitarist, bent almost double over his instrument, grimacing as his fingers stabbed the frets, the guitar extruding from his crotch like an odd red phallus being madly massaged, had not yet noticed DeWalt. Rodney Gillen's electric keyboard stood empty.

They were in their early twenties, DeWalt guessed, these jean and tee-shirt clad musicians. Town boys, he could tell at a glance. They did not attend college and if asked would profess revulsion of the very notion of college, would complain that their hometown had been ruined by college assholes, but they were secretly flattered when asked to play their music at a frat house every weekend, secretly enamored of some classy cold and impossible college bitch, then openly disdainful of any coed who eventually revealed her rural roots by actually sharing her pussy with him.

DeWalt kept smiling, nodding and slapping enthusiastically, even though the catheter in his gut was vibrating from the noise, tickling his skin. Except for the boys and their instruments, the room was virtually empty: a cardboard barrel brimming with beer and soft drink cans; a ratty brown sofa partially covered with a green army blanket, the blanket abundantly stained by a variety of fluids DeWalt made no attempt to distinguish.

The room smelled vaguely of marijuana, although DeWalt could spot no evidence of a joint, no roach in the ashtray at the feet of the bassist. The preeminent odor, however, was of old woodsmoke, the smoke of a fire that had blackened the rafters and left a sizable scorch stain on the concrete floor. One of the carport windows, now patched with plywood, had been smashed out, and the fire stain on the floor lay in a direct path approximately six feet inside this window, half a step from where the lead guitarist squeezed and thrummed his instrument. His left forearm from wrist to elbow was pink and thin, discolored by a wide scar that had the look of melted plastic.

He did not unbend from his strings until the last note quivered away. Even in this silence, DeWalt's abdomen tingled. The guitarist finally unwound and noticed him.

"You guys have quite a sound," DeWalt said. Not unlike that of a mastodon polishing his tusks on a blackboard.

"You want to hire us?" the guitarist asked. It was more of a challenge than an inquiry.

"My name's Ernie DeWalt, guys. I'm investigating Jeri Gillen's disappearance."

"You mean murder," the drummer said.

The bassist told him, "You don't know that, man. Shut the fuck up."

DeWalt smiled. "Nobody knows a thing at this moment. That's why I'm here. I was hoping maybe you fellas could clue me in on a couple of things."

DeWalt grinned broadly now, to show that he knew his question was a ridiculous one. "Anybody know where I might find Rodney Gillen?"

"Try Jamaica," said the drummer.

The bassist said, "Fuck, and get blown away in a hurricane? He'd never go there."

"That's where I'd go if I was him."

"Not me, I'd stay right here in town. Right under the cops' noses. That's the last place they'd think to look."

DeWalt asked, "Is that where you think Rodney is?"

Nobody answered.

"He couldn't stay around here without help," said DeWalt. "He'd need somebody to keep him supplied with food, do his laundry, that kind of thing."

Again, no response.

Finally, the lead guitarist asked, "So what do *you* think? You think he wasted that guy?"

DeWalt shrugged. "Like I said, I don't know enough yet to form an opinion. Tell me something, though. Was Rodney into guns?"

"What do you mean, into?"

"Whoever blew Catanzaro's head off was fairly knowledgeable about firearms. Especially old ones. Muskets, muzzle-loaders, that type of thing."

"Shit," said the bassist. "Rodney barely knew how to shoot that little twenty-two of his. I think he was scared of it. Couldn't hit a fucking beer can from ten feet away."

"Shut up, asshole."

"Rodney had a twenty-two?" DeWalt asked. "Rifle? Automatic? Revolver? What?"

"Revolver," the bassist told him. "But so what? I got one too. We all got guns. Sometimes we go out to the dump to shoot rats and tin cans, shit like that. There's nothing illegal about it."

DeWalt smiled. "I'm not a cop, fellas, so don't worry about me. I don't even like cops very much."

The lead guitarist dug his fingers into the scarred skin of his forearm, scratching, clawing at a deep itch. "I can guarantee that Rodney didn't know shit about guns," he said. "Hell, the guy's practically spastic."

"So what's he hiding from?" DeWalt asked.

"Think about it."

88

"Let's just suppose then," DeWalt said, "hypothetically. I mean, not did he do it, but could he have? Is he psychologically capable of that kind of thing?"

Said the drummer, "Anybody's capable."

"Yeah, right," the bassist scoffed.

"They are, man! In the right situation, you push anybody too far, they're going to push back. It's human nature."

The guitarist told him, "He wouldn't have wasted Jeri, I know that for sure."

"How heavy was his drug use?" DeWalt asked.

"Drugs?" said the drummer. "You mean, what? Like penicillin?"

DeWalt laughed. Good joke, asshole, ha ha.

Anyway he had seen enough. The garage was little more than a shell, exposed rafters and concrete floor—nowhere to squirrel Gillen away. Nor did the Kinetics appear to be concealing information. Liars would be more sincere than these young men; sincerely helpful or sincerely hostile.

"When was the fire?" DeWalt asked.

"Which fire was that?"

DeWalt nodded toward the dark stain on the floor.

The drummer told him, "That's where we have our weinie roasts."

To the guitarist DeWalt said, "Is that how you burned your arm?"

Again the drummer answered. "Yeah, reaching for somebody's weinie!"

They were a riot, these boys. A fun bunch of guys. "Well, anyway," DeWalt said. He half-turned toward the door. "Where will you be playing this weekend?"

"Theta Chi house," the drummer said.

Said the bassist, "The I-ate-a-thigh house."

"Even without Rodney?"

89

"Our sound's got a hole in it as big as a truck," the guitarist answered, "but yeah, we're still playing."

Your sound's got a hole in it as big as the Grand Canyon, fellas. "You never know, maybe Rodney will show up by then."

"Yeah, right," said the bassist.

At the Theta Chi house, fifteen minutes later, DeWalt found a half-dozen clean-cut young leaders of tomorrow engrossed in a *Star Trek* rerun. Four of the students knew him. He said he was working with the state police on the investigation of Professor Catanzaro's homicide case, and when they asked if he was going to write a book about it he said only, "We'll see how it goes."

They were polite and conservative young men, even anxious to tell him what little they knew. Except for their boom boxes and wide screen TV they might have been boys from his own college days, leftovers from the Eisenhower era, atavistic Dobie Gillises with their short hair and short-sleeve starched shirts, their creased chinos and Bass loafers and their winning Crest smiles. They were all very likable and unmemorable but they could not tell him anything useful about the professor and his town girl. About Rodney Gillen they knew a bit more. His group played at the Chi house regularly, at least every other weekend. The students suspected that the Kinetics used drugs—"You could just sorta tell, you know, by looking at them. They're all a bunch of deadheads."—but drugs were never permitted in the house, not even marijuana, no sir. But maybe Craig Fox would know something more about Gillen. Fox, a senior, Theta Chi VP; in charge of booking the bands, organizing smokers and other functions.

"His room's on the second floor, sir. Go on up and talk to him if you want. His door's the one with the picture of Donald Trump on it."

DeWalt went upstairs and knocked on Trump's forehead.

"Nobody home!" came the reply.

DeWalt opened the door and peeked inside. "I'm not disturbing you, am I, Craig?"

He had not recognized the name but he recognized the student the moment he saw him, a familiar face in the hallways, a confident and smiling young man always with an arm around a pretty girl. A starter on the tennis team, Michelangelo's David with a double major in Marketing and Economics. He was at his desk, a textbook open in front of him. Startled, he swiveled around to face the door.

"Professor DeWalt, hello. What, uh ... ?"

DeWalt smiled amiably but said nothing for a moment, letting the boy worry, letting him sort through the dozen unhappy possibilities for a faculty member making a personal call on a student he had never taught. Besides, he needed to get his breath back. He had taken the stairs too quickly, wanting to get to Fox before a warning could reach him from downstairs.

There was no place to sit except on the waterbed's padded frame, and DeWalt needed to sit. But as he moved toward the bed, Fox quickly stood and offered his desk chair.

"Here, sir, sit here. I'll sit on the bed."

DeWalt then explained the reason for his visit, at the same time appraising the room. The kingsize waterbed enclosed in a padded velveteen frame, a velveteen coverlet the color of port wine. On the walls were framed prints of Peter Max and Leroy Neiman paintings. A carpet of three-inch white shag on the floor. A windowbox air-conditioner, a stereo, a nineteen-inch color television with video cassette recorder, and, within easy reach of the desk chair, a squat little refrigerator. There was also an anomalous scent to the room, vaguely musty, dry, almost chemical; a familiar yet elusive and unpleasant odor DeWalt could not name.

"You wouldn't have anything cold to drink in there, would you?" DeWalt asked, and nodded toward the refrigerator.

"Yeah, sure, let me just—"

But DeWalt leaned forward and pulled open the door before the student could cross the room. Inside were ten or twelve soft drinks, a bag of cookies, a quart of milk, half a loaf of bread, a package of deli ham, a jar of brown mustard. Nothing interesting.

DeWalt chose a bottle of New York seltzer. "Anything for you, Craig?"

"No, I had a soda not long ago. Thanks."

DeWalt swiveled the chair so that he faced the bed. He unscrewed the bottle cap. "The guys downstairs told me that if anybody here knew Rodney Gillen, it would be you." He looked up at Fox and smiled.

"Well, yes, I guess that's true. Except that I don't know him all that well myself. I'm the guy that hands him their check, and tells him when we need them, and all that, but otherwise. . . ."

"Strictly business."

"Exactly," Fox said.

"They play here fairly often, don't they?"

"Well, you know, they're local, and they're reliable, and. . . . they'll never make it on MTV though, that's for sure."

"How much do you pay them?"

"Three hundred a night."

"That seems like a lot of money to be laying out for a band every week."

"We've never lost money on them."

"No?"

"We get two or three hundred people in and out of here over the course of the evening. Three bucks admis-

92

sion for the guys, two for the girls. So we still turn a profit, even after refreshments."

"And where do all these profits go? You're a nonprofit organization, am I right?"

"They pay our expenses here, part of the rent and insurance, things like that. Plus, we have two major social functions every year. And each Christmas, we make a contribution to a charity. Last year we gave a thousand dollars to Children's Hospital."

"That's something to be proud of," said DeWalt. He took his first sip of seltzer. "About Rodney Gillen though. Is there anything you might know about him? Anything at all that could help us track him down?"

"I wish I could think of something. But I'm sorry, I can't."

"Did you ever see him with any particular girl when he was here? Other than his wife, I mean."

"As far as I know, his wife was never here. I can't remember meeting her if she was. And as for him being with other women . . . I don't think I ever saw him with anybody, no."

"When his band finished playing at the end of a night, did they pack up and leave, or would they hang out for awhile?"

"A little of both, I guess. What I mean is, while they packed up their equipment, they'd drink a few beers, help themselves to some munchies, things like that."

"Do a few lines maybe?"

"Sir?"

"I hear that Rodney used cocaine regularly."

"Rodney Gillen? Seriously?"

"So I was told."

"By whom? Not by one of the guys downstairs."

"Let me think. . . . I guess it might have been a student, I've talked to so many people today."

93

"Well, he didn't do drugs here, that's all I know. Not in this house."

"You sound fairly adamant about that."

"Well for one thing, we could lose our charter. And I mean permanently. As an officer, I could never allow us to take that risk."

DeWalt nodded, a warm paternal gleam in his eyes. "You knew Dr. Catanzaro, I'm sure."

"I had him for a couple of classes. My freshman and sophomore years. He was a great guy."

"Did you ever hear anything, gossip, rumors, whatever, about him and Gillen's wife?"

"Nada," said Fox.

DeWalt watched the pale bubbles ascend from the bottom of his bottle. Finally he looked up and smiled. "I've run out of questions, Craig."

Fox held out both hands, palms up. "I've run out of answers, sir."

DeWalt screwed the cap onto his bottle, then placed the bottle in the oak-finished trash basket beside the desk. He saw nothing in the trash to tell him the source of the thick earthy scent sticking in his nostrils.

He pushed himself to his feet. "I hear the Kinetics will keep playing, even without Rodney."

"One more weekend anyway," Fox said. "But I'll tell you what. That keyboard really filled out their sound. You know the Door's tune, *Light My Fire*? Try to imagine that without a keyboard."

"I don't think I can," said DeWalt.

"My prediction is, the Kinetics will die fast and hard without Rodney Gillen."

"A sad day in musical history," DeWalt said. He took a step toward the door, then paused. "Did Rodney or any of the other band members ever mention having a fire at their garage?"

"What kind of a fire?"

"Any kind."

Fox thought for a moment. "Like I said, I really didn't know any of them on a personal basis. I'm sorry."

Ten minutes later, in his own bedroom again, DeWalt sat on a straight-back chair and watched the clear dialysis fluid trickling through the long tubing attached to his waist. The bag on the floor was beginning to swell, its liquid contents reflecting the overhead light, a polluted moon. He knew that he should consider himself a lucky man, just as a paraplegic must learn to love his wheelchair. He knew this and he accepted it as truth. But there were times when the plastic bag seemed a cannonball; times when the slender tubing dragged like chain; times when he remembered the buoyancy of youth, those years of levitation. And then, looking ahead, seeing all his tomorrows draining into a swollen bag, this bag or the next, a thousand hopes to be quietly flushed away, he could only curse his rare good fortune.

Chapter
Seven

I am getting nowhere and it angers me. It shouldn't, because that is the nature of the business. You spend a lot of time getting nowhere, marking time, treading water, and then suddenly you are there.

What am I trying to prove to myself? You are not the light of the world, DeWalt, so stop expecting to shine. You are a thirty-watt bulb with damn few kilowatt hours left.

I've got too many metaphors for truth, that's my problem. Truth is a sculpture crafted from the clay of experience. Truth is a light to illuminate dark corners. Truth is a laboratory hybrid of fact and imagination.

These are all good metaphors but they imply that truth can be constructed bit by bit, or sneaked up upon, unearthed, systemically revealed. It isn't so, damn it. Truth is an epiphany, a sudden unexpected and often undeserved blessing. Most often, it comes only after all hope of discovery has died.

Maybe truth is a koan: If you wish to achieve the fulfillment of your dreams, you must first wake up and rid yourself of desire.

Only on the calmest of nights may you hear your soul rustling in the wind.

Only in the absence of love may you know love's fullness.

Christ, why did I waste my time as an investigator, a

writer, a teacher? I could have been a famous pop philosopher, Baba Ram Ernie. Could have counseled the Beatles, hung out with Leary. Could have kept my organs intact, my piano in tune. Could have dispensed truth like jelly beans; been as reflective as aluminum foil. . . .

Hey Ernie, listen to yourself. You're thinking in the first person again. No wonder you're confused. Better get yourself out of the picture, professor. You're blocking the view.

DeWalt nudged his car in beside Trooper Abbott's empty blue and white, taking the last space in the apartment building's lot. DeWalt had telephoned the trooper earlier, requesting an opportunity to examine the Gillens' apartment, and Abbott agreed to meet him there at three in the afternoon. By DeWalt's watch, it was now 2:57.

The air in DeWalt's lungs as he climbed the outside stairway felt as heavy as oatmeal. He wished he could get some energy back, some motivation. He went through the motions as thoroughly as he knew how and he would continue to do so but he felt as drab as the sky. The sky today was a chalky white but if he looked at it directly there was a glare that stung his eyes.

He found Abbott standing in the middle of the Gillens' small living room, standing motionless as he stared at the blank wall, squinting hard at the beige surface as if angered by what he saw there, a pale oval of reflected light from the ceiling fixture, an innocuous golden stain illuminating nothing.

"If you're meditating," DeWalt said softly from the threshold, "I can wait. Let me know when you hit nirvana."

Abbott turned. Deadpan, he said, "I have been to nirvana, but I came back. The food was terrible there."

"I should have known you'd be thinking about some-thing to eat."

DeWalt knew in fact that food was, right now, probably the last thing on Abbott's mind. Larry Abbott was one of the most intelligent cops DeWalt had ever met, one of the few with an active sense of humor, a wide-ranging mind and a catholic appreciation of knowledge.

Ducking under the police's yellow plastic strip that stretched across the doorway, DeWalt stepped inside. "Might as well close that door," Abbott told him, and DeWalt did so.

For a few moments then DeWalt walked slowly about the room, looking closely at each banal object, hoping to see in one of them what he knew he would not.

Abbott said, "I convinced Sergeant Shulles that you and I have a good working relationship."

"In other words, you told him you could keep me in line."

"I told him I'd try. Plus, I promised him an acknowl-edgement in your next book."

"That was generous of you, Lar."

"I'm a generous guy," the trooper said. "So Ernie, listen. What exactly is it you're looking for here?"

"I wish to God I knew."

"You read the report already. You saw the photos of the crime scene. You know as much as we know, and we know there's nothing here."

"Sometimes it helps just to get the feel of a place."

"This place feels weird, if you ask me. You notice how clean everything is? It's all garage sale stuff, but it's like ... it's just not talking, is it?"

"You notice a peculiar smell, Larry? Kind of stale? Dry?"

"The place needs airing out, that's for sure."

But it was something else. It was the same odor DeWalt had detected in the frat rat's room, although less strong here, older. The scent that comes off the earthen walls of an unlighted basement ... but not quite. The scent of a pile of dead leaves overturned. No, more like the dusty, cloying scent of pollen spores.

Or maybe it's yourself you smell, DeWalt. Old mold and rot. Cobwebs and insect shells.

"All of the girl's belongings still here?" DeWalt asked.

"As far as we can tell. Anyway, the closet and dresser drawers are crammed full. Plus the entire range of feminine toiletries."

"Rodney's stuff?"

"Some empty hangers, and a couple of drawers only half full. It looks like some things might be missing. There's no shaving kit, and only one toothbrush in the holder. And no sign of that portable keyboard he practices on here."

"How about magazines? Anything pertaining to muzzle-loading weapons in particular?"

"Last month's *Cosmo* and *Self*, plus last week's *TV Guide*. And a copy of *Hollywood Wives* in on the nightstand. But don't worry, Ernie, I'm sure they both read your book. Probably lent it out to a friend."

DeWalt said, "Fifty-eight percent of graduating high school seniors can't read a newspaper. Seventy percent of America has never been in a bookstore."

"Those figures sound a little low to me."

DeWalt stepped into the bedroom. Abbott followed a moment later.

"Any suggestion of unusual sexual practices?" DeWalt asked.

"I haven't suggested anything yet, no. What do you have in mind?"

The bed was neatly made. "Okay if I look at the sheets, Larry?"

"Just don't sniff them in front of me, all right? That's a side of you I'd rather not know about."

"Killjoy." DeWalt peeled back the worn chenille coverlet. The sheets and pillowcases were clean, unwrinkled by the weight of a body. Interesting, he thought. He smoothed the cover back into place.

"What's this about unusual sexual practices?" Abbott asked.

"According to a waitress at the Colony, and this is what Jeri told her, Rodney couldn't get it up unless they made a game out of it. He liked going outside and peeking in at her, looking at nude pictures of her, things like that."

"Weird guy."

"You didn't find any pictures though?"

"No nude shots of Jeri, if that's what you mean. Do you know for certain that such pictures exist?"

DeWalt did not answer for a moment. Then he said, "I'm extrapolating is all."

"I stopped doing that when I got married."

DeWalt smiled. He returned to the living room and took another slow turn around it, then into the kitchen, careful not to touch anything. The place was too clean; cleaned before the police got to it. Dishes washed and put away. Furniture dusted, carpets vacuumed. Bedsheets changed and bed neatly made. But by whom? Had Rodney done all this, calmly preparing for his departure prior to the murder? He would scarcely have had the time, not if Elizabeth Catanzaro telephoned him at 10:30 AM, and her husband had died sometime during the next hour. Had, then, Rodney murdered Alex, returned here with the body of his wife in tow, either alive or dead, and proceeded to clean the apartment? And what was the cleanliness meant to conceal that Rodney's disappearance had not already revealed?

DeWalt stared into the empty sink. "Exactly what do we know at this point?"

"We know what we don't have," said Abbott from the living room.

"Which is?"

"We don't have a single piece of incriminating evidence here in the apartment. At the murder scene we've got no prints other than those expected. No fibers, no hair or blood—except for the victims', of course. We've got no eyewitness reports, no tips, no clues, no lead. We've got a primary suspect, complete with motive and opportunity, except that we don't know where he is. The only thing we *do* have, Ernie, is your client. Who, by the way, also comes equipped with motive and opportunity."

"You've got a whole lot of nothing, my friend."

"I've got the sun in the morning and the moon at night."

"So your guys are playing it as a straight double homicide?"

"Until Jeri Gillen turns up as queen of the Autumn Fair, yep."

"Maybe it was contrived to appear like a double homicide."

"Contrived by whom?" said Abbott.

"You're short one victim, right? Who didn't leave any of *her* blood at the scene, am I right?"

"You're suggesting that she and Rodney offed the professor."

"She wasn't the naif she appeared to be."

"I never had her pegged as a naif, Ernie. I talked with some of the boys who knew her in high school, and she was, how shall I say, extraordinarily popular."

"Borderline slut," said DeWalt.

"From the other side of the border."

101

"It's unlikely that Dr. Catanzaro knew that about her, though. Or about her cocaine habit."

"Where did you get *that* information?"

"She and her husband both. Regular users. And another thing. It appears that Rodney Gillen knew about Jeri's affair long before Elizabeth Catanzaro clued him in to it."

"What's the source of this information, Ernie?"

The source was a combination of what Della had told him in confidence, what she had implied, and what his instincts whispered to him—a difficult source to identify. "It's solid, okay? There's nothing to be gained by having your guys reinterrogating my informants and having them clam up on me. So just take what I'm giving you, all right?"

"Just make sure you don't hold back on us."

There it was, that first hint of suspicion, first glimmer of distrust. Fucking business, DeWalt thought. He said, "So anyway. Considering Rodney's proclivities, maybe he didn't mind his wife getting banged by another guy. Maybe it turned him on. Nothing you haven't come across before, right?"

"There's nothing I haven't come across before."

"Or maybe Alex Catanzaro was, I don't know, I'm just thinking out loud here. But maybe he gave her money, bought her presents, and, for whatever reason, financial or otherwise, Rodney went along with it. Or maybe Jeri told Rodney she'd leave him if he didn't let her fuck around on the side."

"So what you're saying is, either Jeri helped to set the whole thing up, or else, after she saw her sugar daddy get blown away, she willingly ran off with her husband."

"What I'm saying is, where's Jeri Gillen's body?" And why, DeWalt asked himself for the hundredth time, why in the world did Alex jot down my phone number so many times?

"Her husband shows up, puts a lead ball in Catanzaro's brainpan, and she goes off hand-in-hand with Rodney, even though she's naked as a baby?"

"Maybe Rodney brought extra clothes for her, precisely so they could leave the old ones behind and make it look as if she'd been abducted."

They looked at one another for a long time. Finally Abbott shook his head. "Ninety-nine percent of the time, the simplest explanation is the correct one."

"That figure sounds a little high to me."

"Your scenario just doesn't fit, Ernie. I mean what did they get out of it? They didn't even take his wallet, for chrissakes."

"Maybe they did it for kicks."

"Whew," said Abbott, and blew out a breath. "I'd hate to think that was the truth."

"The youth of today are the leaders of tomorrow."

"The thing I still don't understand, though ... why make it look as if Rodney killed Jeri too? I mean the heat's already on him for blasting Catanzaro. Why, if they're going to stage something, why implicate Rodney in not one but two murders? Why not fabricate an alibi for Rodney, in which case he might eventually be able to collect on an insurance policy for Jeri. If, that is, there had been one."

"There wasn't?"

"Not a dime."

"Jesus," said DeWalt. "None of this fits together."

Abbott said, cautiously, "There was a nice-sized policy on the professor, though. Two policies, in fact."

"Forget it, Larry."

"Even if she had to split it with somebody—"

"Forget it, all right? It's a dead-end."

"At least you want it to be a dead-end."

103

"What I do or do not want doesn't figure into it."

Trooper Abbott nodded, a concession, an apologetic smile. "Want to know what I really think, Ernie? I think it's going to take a crystal ball to call this one. You know as well as I do, if a case isn't solved while the trail's still hot. . . ."

"Trouble is, the trail on this one was never hot."

"It hasn't even gotten warm yet."

Now Abbott was being wonderfully agreeable. This session was over. DeWalt smiled warmly. "It's a ballbuster. On that we can agree."

"It's a fucking A-number one bitch and a half. A bowlegged bitch with a high-pitched squeal. And you're the guy to blame for fixing me up with this date."

DeWalt chuckled. "You're waxing poetic, you must be tired."

"I'm past tired, I'm dead. I haven't slept in two days for thinking about this thing. I can't even make love to my wife, Ernie! We've missed two nights in a row now."

"Geez," said DeWalt, and thought, I've got you beat by about five years, pal.

Abbott said, "Funny how failure goes straight to a guy's penis, isn't it?"

"It's a deflating experience, all right."

"You have that problem too?"

"Always," said DeWalt.

104

Chapter Eight

Beyond the inlet the river was as brown as mud and just as slow, the steep bank on the far side lush with waxy green rhododendrons and white-trunked birch and, higher up, young red-skinned chokecherry trees intermingled with oaks. The foliage glistened with the dew of morning but the air smelled of night, of wet wriggling things that push up blindly through the damp soil or are cast ashore to strangle on too much air.

DeWalt had been sitting at the inlet for nearly two hours now, since dawn, sitting on a stump rolled close to the fire pit, his feet perched on a round chilly stone. He had come to watch the river fog, to attend its slow ascension. Maybe it would lift and reveal something he had failed to see before. This was always his hope, inarticulate, unreasoned; that he might glimpse what he had never seen; recover a tremor of understanding; be made privy to a knowledge few living men deserve.

Upon his arrival here the fog had been a solid wall of white against the charcoal trees and ashen sky; a well-defined battlement of hoary silence; a bulkhead. Gradually the curtain rose, lifting whole, exposing the river's far edge and the groping rhododendron, clearing finally the trees and hanging grapevines and the sky itself, an August sapphire sky that soon surrendered all beauty to the sun.

At DeWalt's foot set a thermos of coffee and a brown paper bag. He removed the thermos's plastic cup and filled it, smelling the warm steam, warming his hands around it. He could allow himself only a sip or two but he had made enough to fill the thermos; the coffee would stay warmer that way. He raised the cup to his lips and tasted the coffee; a sip so small, so prized and delicious, that his tongue seemed to absorb it all, leaving nothing to swallow. There had been no particular reason for him to come here at dawn, or why he now chose to wait, no purpose other than the hope that a purpose might introduce itself, might ... might what, DeWalt? Might chirp at you from the cattails, *Here I am! Here I am!*

When he held the cup of coffee between his knees he lost its scent and smelled instead those cold chunks of charred wood at his feet; or, if a timid breeze blew, he smelled the river. But the scent of ash did not tell him anything he needed to know. Nor did the water tell him anything, nor the fog, nor the ancient stones.

He balanced his cup of coffee on one of those stones and took from the paper bag the two-inch heel of a baguette, fresh at five AM, and removed the bread from its plastic wrapping. Over the wound, the white flesh of the bread, he had spread honey-butter. He bit into it now and tasted the sweetness first on the roof of his mouth, and then his mouth filled with sweetness, and he held it there, a yeasty pastille, until it had all but dissolved.

As he ate the bread, tiny flakes of crust flew from his hand to the ground. A sprinkling of crumbs, DeWalt, from a moment of your life. Evidence after you are gone that you were here.

Except that a bird will soon be along, a chickadee or sparrow, to feed on those crumbs.

And then the bird will fly away and the bird will be

the evidence. Because the evidence of one's life is always in transit, DeWalt, always elusive. It lasts as long as it lasts, and then it changes, and it is what we have as truth.

He finished the bread and had another sip of coffee. He placed the sticky plastic wrap inside the paper bag, folded the bag flat and slipped it into his pocket. Now that the fog was gone the air would warm quickly. There was no reason to be here and nothing to learn.

But as long as we have anything more to do, Melville had said to Hawthorne, we have done nothing.

Silence is the only valid response, said Samuel Beckett.

I'm disgustipated, said Popeye the Sailor Man.

He laughed softly at himself, a capitulation. Then he turned on the stump and once again looked at that narrow space where Catanzaro's car had been parked. He had seen the police photos, so he superimposed those images on the flattened weedgrass and he saw the pale blank headlights of the square-faced silver Honda pointing at him. He saw the door on the driver's side sprung open. He saw Jeri Gillen's rose-colored dress folded neatly on the back seat. He saw one straw sandal just outside the car. Jeri's purse with the shoulder strap broken and the contents spilled twenty yards down the lane.

Both front seats are reclined at a forty-degree angle. Catanzaro is atop the girl. Her right foot is hooked over the steering wheel. The radio plays softly: 99.6 FM, station WZYZ, bedroom music, instrumental and innocuous. Jeri supplies the lyrics.

"God, how I love to fuck you," she is saying. "You feel so big inside me, I love your big cock. Fuck me hard, baby. Fuck me hard."

DeWalt has heard her voice and he has seen pictures

107

the police have not seen but he still knows not enough. Until he knows it all he knows nothing.

There is a sound outside the car then, a sound of . . . what? A twig snapping? The hammer of a musket clicking into place? A small involuntary grunt, a whimper of jealousy, unsuppressable groan of rage? Whatever the sound, Alex hears it. He raises himself up on his hands, his gaze finds the window. For just an instant he freezes, incredulous. Does he realize in that instant the impossibility of escape? Does he taste the futility of life, the bitterness of hope and ambition? Is there time enough in that moment for a silent admission of regret?

Is there time enough to understand?

His body, instantly dead, is thrown back by the percussion. His spine strikes the steering wheel and he recoils forward again, he falls atop Jeri, still inside her (still erect?), a good portion of his forehead gone.

Is she still rocking her hips? Still murmuring her vulgar endearments?

Does she scream?

Or does she lie mute, wanting to scream but shocked beyond words, beyond comprehension? Does she pass out?

Does she push Alex's body aside, shove it away, struggle to crawl from beneath it? Does she squirm and scratch her way out of the car and onto the rainslick ground, clawing insensibly, scrabbling helplessly for purchase until she is lifted up, or struck unconscious, or strangled, or somehow irrevocably silenced and spirited away?

Or does she, after Alex crumples atop her, does she enjoy for a moment the still-warm weight of death? Does she smile, unafraid, unsurprised? Then calmly slides from beneath him. Then steps outside the car, bloodied, perhaps even excited by the blood. Gratified.

Rearranges her props. And walks calmly away with her companion.

For DeWalt, this last possibility was scarcely tolerable. It chilled him inside and out. A taste of charred wood filled his mouth; he smelled the dew-wet ash. Did such behavior actually exist in the repertoire of human response?

He knew the answer even before he finished forming the question.

And that, he decided, was all he was destined to learn this morning. There was only so much knowledge to be gained by sitting on a stump and staring into the fog. The fog was gone now and the morning light too palpable, intrusive. He couldn't concentrate now. Insects buzzed in the weeds. Ten yards away a starling sat on a limb and screeched at him, wanting his crumbs, his perch.

He dashed the cold coffee into the ashes, emptied the thermos, and screwed on the lid. Just as he was about to stand he heard a gearbox grinding, somebody downshifting out on the highway, slowing to make the turn into the lane. DeWalt stood and went to his car where it blocked the lane. He glimpsed the blue pickup truck just an instant before its driver noticed DeWalt's Acura. Again the gearbox whined, this time as Clifford Jewett braked, then immediately shifted into reverse. Draper Jewett, sitting on the passenger side with his head lain back, eyes closed, abruptly sat up and looked straight ahead as the truck sped backward. A moment later the vehicle swung onto the highway, and DeWalt lost sight of them.

There was no sign of the pickup truck at the Jewetts' house, but the front door stood open. DeWalt walked onto the porch, listened for a moment, heard nothing, and knocked on the screen door.

Instantly DeWalt's knock was answered by a shrill barking. Tippy flew at the screen, bounced off, landed on all fours facing the opposite direction, claws scribbling at the bare floorboards until he managed to turn himself and attack the screen again, the tiny hairless dog as nimble as an acrobat turning flips off a trampoline—a canine Donald O'Connor somersaulting off a wall—and all the while yelping.

Aleta Jewett appeared out of the far grayness of the house. "Shush!" she said to the dog, and pushed it aside with a foot. Tippy scurried away in a wide half-circle but quickly returned to stand at her heels, eyes bright, rat-head quivering.

She did not say anything to DeWalt nor did she reach for the door to push it open. Her face showed no expression at all, neither recognition nor surprise nor annoyance.

"Good morning," he said, and smiled. Her eyes were the color of smoke. No, not smoke; river ice. The milky blue of river ice two feet thick, dirtied shoreline ice cracked and piled high, a whole winter's accumulation.

"I'm Ernie DeWalt, I stopped by a couple of days ago? To ask about what happened down at the inlet?"

She said nothing. Not even a nod. DeWalt could see past her into the living room, a portion of it anyway, braided rug on the hardwood floor, plaid sofa, cushions permanently indented. He could see part of a cherrywood sideboard that was probably an antique. Cream-colored wallpaper with a design of tiny green flowers, the colors faded, probably decades old. He could see two large water stains on the plaster ceiling, amoeba-shaped adumbrations the hue of old blood. He could see into the kitchen too: linoleum floor, a corner of the white-enameled sink.

The woman herself was as tall as DeWalt, her face and figure broad but not heavy. Hair the color of pewter, a simple but not severe cut; she probably gave herself a permanent every few months, as his mother had—he could still picture his mother on a kitchen chair, winding locks of hair around the pink barbed curlers, bobby pins in her mouth, the pink foam squares he had loved to touch, to fill with water and squeeze dry, the smell of solution, ammoniac, eye-stinging, it would linger in the house for days.

The hem of Aleta's blue calico dress fell to midcalf, its pattern of miniature roses so faded as to have all but disappeared. Her feet were bare. In her left hand she held a raw sweet potato.

"I just thought I'd stop by for a minute and talk to Clifford again," DeWalt said.

"He's not home," she answered. Her voice was smoky too; leavesmoke; damp leaves that smoked but would not catch flame.

"How about Draper then? Is he around anywhere?"

"They're off together," she said.

"Son of a gun. I guess this was a wasted trip." He pursed his lips and stared past her, as if thinking, struggling for an idea. Then, a smile. "Any chance I could use your phone? It's a local call."

"Clifford don't allow people inside when he's not home," she said. Was there a note of embarrassment in her voice? Any hint of apology, challenge, fear? DeWalt tried to distinguish as much, but could not.

He nodded. "Any idea when the boys will be back?"

"When they get here. Not before."

"You wouldn't happen to know where I might find them, would you? I want to double-check a couple of things."

"I wouldn't know," she said.

"Maybe they went down to the inlet to do a little fishing this morning, you think?"

"They didn't go fishing."

"They do go down there occasionally though, don't they? Whether to fish or whatever."

She had not yet turned her head or otherwise glanced away from him but neither did she look directly into his eyes; she seemed to be staring at the side of his head, at the top of his ear perhaps. He suppressed an urge to scratch it.

But those eyes of hers, they appeared almost frozen. Or rather, the irises were frozen, thick circles of ice. But the pupils, those jagged black dots, these were the holes that had been punched through the ice, holes deep with a dark liquid chill. You could not go into them for long, you would not survive the shock.

"You might look for them in town," she said.

DeWalt grinned. "They didn't go off to the movies now without taking you, did they?"

Aleta Jewett did not smile. "They went in to see about a submersible pump."

"You folks out of water?"

"Pressure won't stay up is all."

"Boy, I bet those new submersibles must cost an arm and a leg."

"I wouldn't know."

Despite its flatness of expression her face retained an angularity barely softened by the weight of years, a sharpness of features which, punctuated by those forbidding eyes, must have lent her, in younger times, a striking countenance, that ascetic and perhaps cautionary appearance that certain men are drawn to. DeWalt suspected, however, that she had long ago ceased thinking of herself in that regard, she had moved beyond sexuality and its derisiveness and into a further stage of being, a place he could not name, having never been there himself. But there was to Aleta Jewett an inwardness, a tranquility born of detachment. He sensed that she would stand there forever if need be, succinctly re-

112

sponding to his questions, made neither nervous nor impatient by them, neither amused nor angered. She was beyond guile because guile depends on fear and she was fearless now. Maybe she had always been fearless; he had no way of knowing. He had glimpsed this quality in others on a few occasions but it had always been in faces more obviously pummeled by circumstance, beaten past caring, beyond fear or wonder. Faces so empty that we read into them a most profound and irreducible peace.

He knew he could not startle or frighten her. And so he asked, "Don't you agree that it seems highly unlikely, Mrs. Jewett, that none of you people up here would have heard that gunshot?"

"Apparently that's what you think."

"Yes, I do. It seems a whole lot more reasonable to me that you did hear it. But by the same token, just hearing a gunshot doesn't make you in any way responsible for it, does it?"

He waited. Just when it seemed he would receive no reply, she said, "I don't know what it was I heard."

"But you did hear something."

"I don't even know that."

"I understand," he said. "A sound like that, it happens out of nowhere and it's over in an instant. You don't know whether you really heard it or not. It might have been an acorn falling on the roof. Or a car backfiring."

"It might not have been anything."

"But it seems to you that you might have heard something like a gunshot, am I right? Except that it could have been something else entirely. But the girl, though. A girl's screams would be hard to mistake, wouldn't they?"

"I didn't hear anything like that."

"Okay," said DeWalt. "That's something anyway. I

113

don't know what, but it's something." He tried a smile; no luck.

"About what time do you think it was when you heard the gunshot? What *might* have been a gunshot, that is."

She inhaled deeply, her eyes never straying far from their focus. "A couple of hours before dinner," she said.

Dinner meaning lunch, he thought. "So that would be what—about the same time of morning as right now?"

"Later," she said. "Sometime after ten."

"And Draper was with you at the time. In the house, canning vegetables."

"He come and went all morning. He's not the kind to stick to one thing for long."

"I would imagine he gets tired out fairly quickly. Because of his kidneys, I mean."

She said, "He does."

"But it seems to you that he was with you when you heard the sound that might have been a gunshot."

"As far as I remember."

"Did you say anything to him about it?"

"A gunshot's nothing unusual hereabouts," she said. "It's not something to stop work over."

DeWalt nodded. "And let's see. Clifford was out here in the yard, underneath his pickup. So if you could hear a gunshot while inside the house. . . ."

"He says he didn't. He probably had the radio going in the truck."

"He never mentioned that he was listening to the radio."

"He says he didn't hear a gunshot," she told him. "And Draper says he didn't. And I don't know if I did or not."

Now, for the first time, she looked away, she looked down at the dog. She slipped her bare foot beneath the animal's belly and scratched it with her toes. Tippy rubbed against her.

And DeWalt asked himself, What difference does it make anyway? What does it matter if anybody heard the shot or not? It doesn't matter. But why lie about hearing it, that was the question that troubled him. And why had Clifford backed away from the inlet, his own property, when he spotted DeWalt's car there?

"How's Draper doing?" DeWalt asked.

"About how you'd expect."

"He'd better not put off that dialysis too long."

She said nothing. She stared at the dog.

"Maybe if you talked to him about it," he said.

"What he does is up to him, not me."

"Well," said DeWalt, but then dropped it. She would stand there and listen if he wished to talk to the air but it would have no impact on her.

"Thanks for your time," he said. "I hope I didn't interrupt anything." To the quivering dog he said, "So long, killer."

Tippy yelped and flew at the screen. The dog was still yapping, alone at the door, as DeWalt drove away.

Chapter Nine

The telephone was ringing as he walked up the sidewalk to his front door. With luck it would stop ringing before he could reach it. He needed to do a bag exchange and then he was going to make some lunch, a couple of vegetable taco rolls—shredded cabbage, carrots, celery, onion, red bell pepper and tomato steamed and rolled in a warm flour tortilla, and drizzled with picante sauce—and then he was going to go back to bed. He had begun to feel sluggish at the Jewett place, sluggish almost to the point of indifference, heavy in limb and movement and head. He doubted that he could sleep this feeling away but it was better than staying awake with it.

There were times when he thought life's ruin inexorable, beyond repair or reclamation, a wrecked car abandoned by the side of the road to be consumed by weeds and time, not worth salvage or notice. There were times when he thought life's ruinous ways malicious, calculated; other times, ruefully hilarious. At any of these times he might think too of his handgun, the .44 in a manuscript box in a corner of the closet. But he knew the weapon's taste and the memory of this sickened him, it froze his throat and stomach with the same icy smoke of fear that had earlier frozen his hand.

There were other times, however, when he thought of life as a beautiful but failed experiment. He could not

116

say as much of his own life in particular but of all of life, a lovely sweet idea too quickly gone awry, by accident or design or perhaps by poor execution, a matter of reach exceeding grasp. With this type of thought he was moved quite differently, empowered, it seemed, with a peculiar kind of energy, the second wind of the recalcitrant pipsqueak determined to remain on his feet while the bully bashes his brains out.

This was not the way he felt just now, however, as he took his time closing the door and then moving toward the jangling phone. He waited to see if the phone would ring one more time. It did. He picked it up and said hello.

"Oh god, finally, where have you been? I've been calling since seven o'clock!" It was Elizabeth Catanzaro, breathless and shrill.

"What's wrong?" he asked.

"Could you come out here please? I need you to come here right away."

"Tell me what's wrong."

"I just need you to come out here and see something, all right? I don't want to talk about it on the phone."

"Why can't you talk about it? Is somebody there?"

"No. I don't know, I don't think so. Just come out, all right? God, I've been calling since first thing this morning. I didn't think you were ever going to answer."

"If you think there might be somebody in your house, I want you out of there right now."

"No," she said, and seemed to be calming now, "no, there's nobody here now, I'm sure of it. But will you come out, Ernie, please? I need you to explain why somebody would do such a thing to me."

"*What* thing, Elizabeth? Tell me what happened."

In her silence as she calmed herself further he realized that they had called each other by their first names, that her fear and his response to it had erased a distance

117

between them. His reaction to this was a kind of anger, a tension which, for the moment, supplanted fatigue.

"Are you all right?" he asked. "Just tell me that."

"I'm fine, Ernie, really. I'm sorry if I sounded hysterical, it's just that ... I really would like you to come out here if you can. It doesn't have to be immediately but ... the sooner the better."

"A half-hour?" he said. He had already begun to unbutton his shirt, to expose the plastic bag and rubber tube flattened against his skin.

"A half-hour's okay," she said. "I can wait another half-hour."

"Goddamn it," he said after he had hung up the phone. He unbuckled his trousers, unwound the tube, tossed the empty bag onto the floor. He wanted to kick the thing away from him, tear out the catheter, undo the past.

"Goddamn fucking shit."

She was sitting on the front porch, on the top porch step, smiling wanly as he approached. She had pulled a thin satiny robe on over her summer nightgown but her feet were bare and she had not brushed her hair yet nor washed her face. She held her hands clasped between her knees, knees and fingers squeezing hard.

"It's in the kitchen," she said.

Inside, DeWalt paused on the threshold. The overhead light in the kitchen was on. At first he could see nothing unusual, walls of yellow-painted wainscoting below white wallpaper adorned with butter-yellow stripes and miniscule red and blue hummingbirds. A floor of shiny brown ceramic tiles. The kitchen table and counter empty. The glass pot from the coffee maker, however, was lying on its side on the sink counter, the glass cracked. Something had made her drop the pot as she was about to fill it with water.

118

He went to the sink. The left basin was empty. But in the other one, stuck in the drain that emptied into the garbage disposal, pushed down so that its face was flush with the bottom of the metal basin, its eyes open, staring up, was a cat. A calico cat, small, probably a kitten. Mouth parted as if trying to mew.

DeWalt did not touch the cat. He touched nothing in the room except for the wallphone. Abbott was not at the barracks but the dispatcher took the number and radioed the message to Abbott's car.

Elizabeth turned to look up at DeWalt as he came out onto the porch. "What did you do with it?" she asked.

"Nothing for the moment. The state police should be here in ten or fifteen minutes. Are you all right?"

"Who could do such a thing?" she asked. "And why?"

He sat beside her and took her hand. "You found it, when? First thing this morning?"

"Yes. God, I was barely awake. I think I even turned on the water and. . . ." She shuddered, she shook her head, she blew out a noisy breath.

"Did you hear anything through the night?" he asked.

"I took a Valium before going to bed."

"How long have you been doing that?"

"Five, six months now."

"Maybe it's time to stop."

"Obviously you don't know what it's like to lie awake every night with a horror movie running through your head."

He stared out across the lawn. "What time did you go to bed?"

"Eleven, eleven-thirty maybe. I don't look at the clock much these days."

"And you got up around seven? You said on the phone that you had been trying to call me since seven."

She nodded.

"You keep all your doors and windows locked at night?"

"The doors, yes. But it gets so hot upstairs that we have to keep most of the windows open. But there are screens on all of them."

Her eyes were wide and bright and there was a kind of smile on her face, but the smile was involuntary, the tension of incredulity, and the glint in her eyes came from the dark light of fear.

She said, "Maybe I should ... change my clothes or something. Get dressed."

He squeezed her hand. "Let's just sit here for awhile."

She sat motionless, her breath audible. Her pulse throbbed inside his hand. "Why would somebody do this, Ernie?"

"There are a couple of possibilities, I guess."

She looked at him and waited.

"It could be the work of some crank," said DeWalt. "Some self-appointed judge who wants to punish you for what he thinks you did. Some friend of your husband, for example. Or it might have been somebody who saw you on TV and, for whatever reason, decided he or she didn't like you. It might be somehow ritualistic, it's hard to say."

"Satanic?" she asked, and he saw the terror flare in her eyes.

"Naw, I doubt it. It's highly unlikely."

"Or it might have been done by the same person who killed Alex," she said.

DeWalt thought, Cat. Kitten. Kitty. Pussy. Dead pussy. You're dead, pussy. Garbage disposal. Garbage. Disposable.

"Can you think of anybody who might have had something against both of you?" he asked. "Somebody who might have had reason to resent not just Alex, but you too?"

She squinted, thinking, trying to think, then shook her head. "I'm sorry, my mind's a blank. I'm lucky I can remember my own name right now."

"Of course," he said. He looked down at her hand in his, the small fingers, the warmth. He had not held a woman's hand for a long time. He turned her hand over, exposing the back of it, and he touched the fingertips of his free hand against it, stroked gently the lovely small knuckles and the warm valleys between them.

A moment later he caught himself, and stopped. He loosened his grip.

She withdrew her hand from his then. With both index fingers she picked the sleep from the corners of her eyes. "I'm a mess," she said.

"You look fine."

"I look like hell."

He smiled. Then he thought of something. "Was it the kids'?"

She did not understand.

"The kitten. Did it belong to your kids?"

"No, we've never owned a cat. The kids have a Sheltie, it's with them at my mother's. But no, I don't know whose it is, I never saw it before.

"How long before the police come?" she asked a moment later. "God, Ernie. I want that thing out of here."

When Troopers Abbott and Brown arrived nearly twenty minutes later, Brown carrying a black plastic tackle box, DeWalt escorted them into the kitchen. Elizabeth remained outside. DeWalt filled them in on the little he knew. Trooper Brown, a man younger than Abbott, thinner, his neck scarred from acne, then donned a latex glove. He grasped the kitten by the fur between its ears, having to work his fingers into the

121

drain, and gingerly extracted the animal from the sink. There was no body, only the severed head.

"Jesus Christ," said Trooper Brown. Water dripped off the exposed muscles and tendons. Abbott held open a paper bag, into which Brown deposited the head.

This done, the bag sealed, Abbott leaned over the sink and peered into the drain. "She didn't hear the garbage disposal running?" he asked.

"She took a Valium," DeWalt said. "Besides, I don't think the disposal was used. The cat's head is small enough, it would have gotten sucked down into the blades."

"What if somebody was holding onto the head?"

"There'd be more body left. To the front legs at least."

"I don't think a garbage disposal can chew up bones, can it?" Brown asked.

DeWalt shrugged. "Even if it can, it wouldn't do such a clean job of it. The neck would be more chewed up. It looks to me like maybe the head was whacked off with a hatchet."

Abbott laughed, not at all amused. "It's like a fucking B-movie," he said. "Where do people get these ideas?"

Brown laid the paper bag atop the kitchen table, then opened his plastic tackle box. "The sink and what else?" he asked Abbott.

"Yeah, dust the sink, and the back doorknobs, and . . . shit, whatever you want, you're not going to find anything anyway. Anybody sick enough to pull this stunt is smart enough to wear gloves. We'll just end up wasting a week and a half matching prints to the people who live here. So forget the sink. Do the back door. We'll need something to prove to Shulles we weren't in here just jacking each other off."

To DeWalt Abbott said, "You check around for forced entry?"

"Let's do it now."

Ten minutes later they returned to the kitchen. DeWalt said, "So somebody had a key."

"Or knows how to spring a deadbolt."

"Alex might have given Jeri a key, though I can't imagine why. Except that he was thinking with his dick. More likely, she stole it from him."

"And somehow Rodney got hold of it. Which suggests to me that our primary suspect is still in the neighborhood."

"Possibly," said DeWalt. "I mean I can understand him wanting to blow away his wife's lover. Maybe even his wife. But considering Rodney's knowledge of her affair, even his encouragement of it—"

"You don't know that for certain."

"I don't have an affidavit to that effect, no. But let's assume, okay, Rodney murdered Alex and murdered or abducted Jeri. Why come after Elizabeth? What's to be gained by killing her?"

"Not a thing. Which is exactly why we pulled a cat's head out of the sink and not her head. Rodney's trying to make a point is all."

"And what point would that be?"

"Don't bristle on me, Ernie, okay?"

"You think she made a deal with him to kill her husband."

"Her old man's fucking around on her," Abbott said, his voice low, conspiratorial. "She wouldn't be the first woman to get pissed off in a situation like that."

"But now she won't pay up. Or else Rodney is trying to squeeze a little extra out of the deal. And so, this gentle reminder in the sink."

"You've got to admit, Ernie. It makes sense."

123

"Based on two criteria only. Her telephone call to Rodney, and the nature of the murder weapon."

"You think those criteria should be ignored?"

DeWalt shook his head, not in answer but in disgust. He felt sick to his stomach. "So why would she hire me to look for the truth if the truth is precisely what could convict her?"

Abbott did not respond to this question. He was looking at the sink again, absentmindedly scratching his Adam's apple. "There's another possibility too," he said.

Trooper Brown nodded. "Kitty's a red herring," he said.

DeWalt laughed softly then, a tired laugh, and sour. "I'm having a hard time picturing Elizabeth Catanzaro whacking off a cat's head and shoving it down her garbage disposal. I'm sorry, but I am."

"That's because you're a romantic, Ernie." There was a broad smile on Abbott's face as he said this, but the statement had more layers than the smile implied. The resentment was building, DeWalt could feel it. Abbott was starting to regard him not as an ally but an obstacle. "Let's go chat with the missus now, shall we?" Abbott said.

Dewalt nodded toward the paper bag as Trooper Brown picked it off the table. "Keep that thing out of sight. She hasn't had her breakfast yet."

They walked single-file through the living room and out onto the front porch, where Elizabeth Catanzaro was sitting now on the porch glider to the right of the door. Brown shifted the paper bag to his left hand, holding it close to his leg as he carried it to the car. DeWalt stood a few inches behind Abbott, just off his right shoulder, so that Elizabeth could see his face clearly while speaking with the trooper.

DeWalt said, "Trooper Abbott would like to ask you

a few questions, Elizabeth. You're under no obligation to talk if you don't feel up to it."

"I'm okay," she said.

Abbott proceeded to ask the same questions DeWalt had asked just a half hour earlier. She gave the same answers.

"What about the dogs?" Abbott asked. "Did you hear them barking last night?"

"Not that I remember," she said.

"They would bark though, wouldn't they? If somebody came sneaking around the house at night?"

"I imagine they would, yes. They bark at deer, and rabbits. Sometimes I think they bark at each other. But whether they did or didn't last night, I didn't hear anything."

"You must have been unconscious," Abbott said. "I understand you took a Valium."

DeWalt said, "The dogs didn't bark when you arrived, officer. So maybe there wasn't any barking to be heard last night either."

From where he stood he could see Abbott's neck stiffen, and he had a fair idea of what Abbott was about to say to him. But Elizabeth Catanzaro spoke first.

"I probably was unconscious," she said. Both men looked at her. "I also had, I don't know, maybe half a bottle of wine."

DeWalt felt a flush of anger then, not because she had withheld this information from him earlier but because of the stupidity of mixing drugs and alcohol, guilt turned to self-destructiveness. It angered him because she was too smart for that, too responsible.

But so what, DeWalt; what's it to you? Since when did you become a crusader? Don't pretend you wouldn't like to engage in a little of the same.

"Anyway," Elizabeth said, "not that I see why all this

matters so much, but they're bird dogs, they're trained not to bark."

Abbott smiled. "Not at birds, in any case." He held his smile a few moments longer, until she looked away. DeWalt had never seen the trooper in action before and he wished he didn't have to now. That condescending smile was too familiar, he knew the effect of it too well. Sometimes the things you like least about a person are the ways they remind you of yourself.

Abbott said, "Trooper Brown and I will take another stroll around the outside here before we go. Maybe we can spot a footprint or something." He held out his hand to DeWalt. "Thanks for your help, Ernie. I'll be in contact."

As they shook hands it occurred to DeWalt that this was the first time he and his friend had touched. It felt like a gesture of some kind.

Soon Brown and Abbott disappeared around the corner of the house. Elizabeth said, "I guess I can't sit here in shock all day. I'd better go disinfect that sink."

"You get dressed," DeWalt told her. "I'll take care of it."

"You don't have to do that."

"I like doing housework. I was a maid in a former life."

She stood then and came close to him and took both his hands, holding them against her body just below her breasts. His knuckles could feel the plastic bag through his shirt.

"I'm glad you're around," she told him, and squeezed his fingers. He felt his breath catch in his chest, felt it snag on something sharp. In response he merely nodded. He wondered if his smile looked like Abbott's.

After she had gone upstairs he went into the kitchen. He found a bottle of bleach under the sink and poured half the contents over the stainless steel basin. The fumes stung his eyes and burned his lungs. He stepped to the back door, stuck his head outside and cleared his lungs. Then, holding his breath, he returned and rinsed the sink clean.

He filled the sink with hot soapy water, opened the drain and turned on the garbage disposal. He repeated this a second time. As he was washing his hands with dishwashing detergent he glanced out the window and saw Abbott standing there in the yard, looking in at him. Abbott motioned for DeWalt to come outside; he waited in precisely the same spot until DeWalt joined him.

"Where is she?" Abbott asked, his voice low.

"Upstairs, getting dressed."

Abbott lifted his gaze to the upstairs windows.

"What's up?" DeWalt asked.

Abbott turned his back to the house. For chrissakes, DeWalt thought, do you think she's going to read your lips?

"I had a thought," Abbott said.

"Didn't hurt yourself, did you?" DeWalt regretted it the moment he said it.

"You want to hear this or not?"

Their relationship was changing, and DeWalt could think of no remedy for it. He hoped it was nothing more than a situational change: the change a rubber band undergoes when subjected to stress. If it is not pulled too far it will snap back into place. So DeWalt moved a step closer to the trooper, he faced the woods, he let up on the tension.

"Sorry," he said. "What's your idea?"

Abbott nodded to himself a couple of times, thinking it out. "No sign of forced entry," he said. "No footprints in the flowerbed. Whoever was here last night went straight to the backdoor. No pussyfooting around."

He smiled, proud of himself.

127

"Ha ha," DeWalt said.

"So let's say that Jeri Gillen did have a key. How she got it, we don't know. But she had one."

"Okay."

"And say too, she's not dead. She saw whoever it was shot Catanzaro, but she herself managed to get away. For the sake of argument, all right?"

"I'm still with you," DeWalt said.

"So where would she go? She's naked, right? Doesn't even have any shoes. Scared shitless probably."

"I imagine so."

"Somehow, some way, she gets in touch with her husband. Breaks into a house maybe, and uses the telephone. Or flags down a car, hitches a ride, and—"

"Buck naked?"

"Would you stop to pick up a naked girl? A naked girl built like Jeri Gillen?"

"Is my mother in the car with me?"

"So Jeri's out along the highway somewhere. She stays out of sight until she spots a car with a lone male occupant. That's you. It's Saturday morning and you're on your way to the bakery to buy your fat wife a bag of doughnuts. She's sitting at home watching cartoons and picking her toenails. This is what you have to go home too. Suddenly there's a naked girl standing in the middle of the road and waving her arms for you to stop. Are you going to stop or not?"

"I'm going to stop and have a heart attack."

Abbott chuckled, then shook his head. "This is getting too elaborate. I'm not writing a novel here, this is just a scenario. And the scenario is this. Somehow she gets away from the murderer. Somehow she gets in touch with Rodney, who comes to her rescue."

"Rodney Gillen is not the murderer?"

"This is an entirely different scenario, okay? Scenario B, let's call it. And in this scenario, right, Rodney didn't kill him. But Jeri knows who did. In fact, she has, in a drawer back home, a key to the murderer's house."

DeWalt, smiling at the ground, slowly shook his head.

"Now wait," said Abbott. "Just consider it, okay?"

"You shouldn't even be talking like this to me, Larry. You're talking about my client here."

"I'm not talking to *you*, I'm talking to myself. And here's what I'm saying. Jeri knows that the murderer is not going to let an eye witness go walking around town as if nothing happened. So she and Rodney go back to their apartment, grab the key and a few other things, and go into hiding. After a couple of days they decide to send a message to the murderer. The message is, Forget what you're thinking, lady, or next time it will be *your* ass in the disposal."

"Why leave a message at all? Why not just walk upstairs and plug her?"

"For one thing, maybe they don't have a weapon."

"Rodney has a .22 pistol."

"Who told you that?"

"The boys in the band. They've all got them."

"Okay, so he's got a popgun. But this woman they're dealing with is something else. Jeri saw her put a musket to her old man's forehead. I doubt that they want to get too close to her."

"It's appropriate that you're calling this scenario B," DeWalt said. "B for Bullshit."

"Even someone in your position, Ernie, has to try to maintain objectivity. You've got to consider all the possibilities."

DeWalt almost said, Don't lecture me, squirt. But that would have been going too far. And he was not the contentious type anymore. He was too tired to slug it out.

129

Jesus, why did an argument always make him want to lie down and go to sleep?

"So you're saying that Elizabeth telephoned Rodney, but not to enlighten him, as she claims, but to what? For what reason?"

"To implicate him," Abbott said. "To get him to go to the scene of the crime, maybe leave some evidence. Also, the telephone call shifts the blame off her."

DeWalt asked, "Did she kill her husband before or after she called Rodney?"

"That's hard to pinpoint, but the coroner's report suggests that it was after."

"So she calls Rodney—not even knowing, by the way, what, if anything, he might do—then she hurries down to the inlet, blows her husband away, lets Jeri run bare-assed out to the highway to flag down a car, then comes home again, waits an appropriate amount of time, and calls the police to say she's worried that Rodney might have done something drastic. Sure," DeWalt said, "that sounds logical. It probably happens everyday."

"Well, I can see there's no use discussing these things with you, Ernie."

"What's to discuss? The way you see it, Elizabeth either hired Rodney to do it, or else she did it herself and tried to make it look as if Rodney did it."

"The murderer's choice of weapon is more than coincidence. Fuck, man, open your eyes."

"There is absolutely no evidence that the weapon in question belonged to the deceased."

Abbott stared at the horizon and chewed on the inside of his cheek. "The only reason I got myself assigned to this thing was as a favor to you, Ernie."

"I know that," DeWalt said, eyes fixed on the field of

130

corn. "And maybe you're right. Maybe I'm not keeping an open mind about this."

"On the other hand, you *are* getting paid to look out for your client's interests."

"That only goes so far," DeWalt said. Then, fifteen seconds later, "Fuck."

Abbott turned slowly to look at him. He was smiling now. "That better not have been a proposition."

He held his smile a moment longer, then glanced once at the upstairs window. As he walked away he lightly jabbed his fist against DeWalt's chest. "You watch yourself, my friend."

DeWalt waited a few minutes after the police car had pulled away; he then returned to the house. Elizabeth was busy in the kitchen now, chopping celery for a bowl of tuna fish. She wore jeans and a yellow knit shirt, blue cotton socks but no shoes. She had washed her face but had not put on any make-up, and her face looked pale, her smile thin and uncertain. Her hair was wet close to the scalp and he could see other streaks of dampness too where she had drawn a wet comb through her hair. She seemed to him so vulnerable and so small, a homeless animal, unloved and underfed, a cat in the rain.

"Sit down," she said as he stood at the threshold. "I'll have some sandwiches ready in a couple of minutes."

"I can't stay," he said.

"Just for lunch?"

"I have an appointment. I'm sorry."

She looked at the shredded fish. "I was hoping you wouldn't leave right away."

Her hand, holding the chopping knife, rested on the edge of the table. A splash of sunlight lay upon her hand, quivering. A finch of sunlight, small golden bird, breathless, too long in the air. A moment later she

131

looked up at him and her hand flicked, a nervous twitch, and the startled lightbird flew.

"How about if I come back for dinner," he said. "Around six."

"That would be good."

"Nobody's going to bother you in broad daylight, I promise."

"I know. I know that, and yet. . . ."

The way she looked at him, he had one of two choices, one of two directions to go.

He broke eye contact and looked at the back door. "I'm going to stop at the hardware store and pick up a couple of safety locks," he told her.

"I'd feel safer with a whole new set of deadbolts. I'll call into town and have somebody come out."

"Good idea. A security system wouldn't hurt either, as long as you can afford it. It might take a week or so to get something like that installed, though."

She smiled now. "This isn't the city, Ernie. I know who to call. I can have him here within the hour."

Probably an old boyfriend, thought DeWalt. Or at least a man enamored of her. A hardworking dirt-under-the-fingernails kind of guy. A guy who adores his wife and kids but who can always find an excuse to dawdle in the presence of a woman like Elizabeth Catanzaro, feeling a certain ineffable grace in her company, a gentility, a delicacy he can never achieve in his own life.

But at least there would be somebody with her until DeWalt could return. DeWalt nodded, then asked, "Did Alex ever complain about having lost a house key?"

"Not that I remember. Why?"

He did not answer.

"You think it was Rodney here last night, don't you? That he has a key he got from Jeri?"

132

"The thing is, I can't imagine Alex ever giving her a key."

"He wouldn't," she said. "He would never have let her come here."

"So she must have stolen it from him. Maybe when they drove into town one day for lunch, while he was in the supermarket, she took the car keys and went into another store to have a copy made. Assuming that he kept his house key on the same keyring."

"House, office, garage, everything."

"It wouldn't have been all that difficult for her to get a duplicate made without his knowledge."

"But why would she want a key to our house?"

"I'm just speculating here, okay? But from what I understand, she used drugs fairly regularly. Grass, cocaine, et cetera, et cetera."

"My god."

"There's no chance that, you know, Alex—"

"Never!" she said. "He wouldn't even take an aspirin when he had a headache. No, it's impossible. He wouldn't even let anybody smoke a cigarette in the house."

"All of which would seem to suggest that Alex didn't know about Jeri's habit."

"He couldn't have. I mean," she shook her head. Her eyes were shimmering. "He wouldn't have had anything to do with her."

"Then ... let's say this. Let's say Jeri knows how Alex feels about drugs, which puts her in a rather tenuous position. Or maybe he's been showing signs of getting bored with her. Obviously he has no intention of leaving you and the kids. As you said, he was not a stupid man."

"Thank you," she said.

"If Jeri has any brains at all, she knows that the relationship is doomed. She's thinking of ways to benefit from him even after he dumps her. She surely knows that he's a collector. Being curious, she's probably come by to look at the house a couple of times, just to see the kind of place where he lives. By her standards, he's a wealthy man."

"She stole his key so she could rob us," Elizabeth said.

"Cocaine's an expensive habit."

"So . . . she couldn't have really loved him."

DeWalt did not think it wise to volunteer a confirmation.

"Was she just using him, Ernie? Taking an infatuated older man for all she could get?"

He waited too long to answer. "Alex would surely have sensed it if she was."

"But that's not what you believe, is it?"

It was one thing for a woman to discover that her husband had been unfaithful, had sought to de-annuate himself between the legs of a beautiful younger woman. A wife could then blame not herself but the years, the erosion of passion, the slow dissolution of desire. But to be told that her husband, an intelligent man, a man she respects, has been played for a fool—it would take a certain kind of woman to glean pleasure from such knowledge. Elizabeth Catanzaro was not that kind of woman.

DeWalt told her, "I think a girl like Jeri Gillen couldn't help but to be very nearly in awe of a man like Alex."

She looked at him with eyes narrowed and mouth frowning. He could almost see the seed of suspicion taking root in her mind. She would mull it over for a while, would worry it from every angle, but eventually she would uproot the suspicion and be done with it. She would not allow her husband to be further reduced in

134

her memory. She would not allow their history to be re-written.

"Is she still alive, Ernie?"

"Trooper Abbott thinks she might be. I have my doubts."

"But if it wasn't her last night . . . if it was, who? Her husband? What was the point? In fact whoever it was, what was the point?"

"That's what we're trying to figure out."

He drove home trying to figure it out and trying to understand his need to do so. He had gotten involved and was involved now for untenable reasons. He was more emotionally involved than intellectually, and the emotions washed over him like hot and cold running water, fever and chill, tenderness and rage.

A man does not go into this line of work, he told himself, unless he has a taste for violence. He might see himself as a humanitarian out to do the world some good but he is not above achieving that good by violent means.

But exactly what kind of work do you mean, DeWalt, by *this line of work*? Investigative work? Writing? Teaching? Self-flagellation?

The work of living in a violent world, yes.

He wished he liked weapons more. He wished he had retained his old fondness for guns. But the last gun he held had left a bad taste in his mouth. Sometimes he would remember it in his dreams and wake up gagging, wanting to vomit. He wished there were something just as loud and quick but more tasteful. The noise was important. There had to be enough noise to deaden all hearing. A concussion grenade maybe. Except that a grenade was not as certain as a .44 fired through the roof of your mouth. Unless maybe you put the grenade in your mouth. That should cut down on the margin of error. But the time delay, those seven seconds or what-

135

ever it was after pulling the pin, those few seconds could be disastrous. No, a grenade had noise and relative certainty but it wasn't quick. Not quick enough. Nothing was. And nothing that had not already happened ever would be.

Chapter
Ten

There is a song in your ear like the plucking of a guitar string, a high metal whine, short, stiff, a single note repeating. Is it outside or inside your head? It is inside, somewhere behind the eyes. It reverberates in the throat, choking, a tight string, too tight, about to break.

It is an insistent song, trying to tell you something, but you do not understand and you would like it to stop. Maybe the ritual will help. It is time for the ritual again and even the house seems to know it, the house is quiet, dim and hushed. The bedroom is your altar. Here you unwind the plastic tubing, carefully, in no hurry. You feel it with your thumb, press out the crimps. You unroll the empty plastic bag, sticky with your perspiration. Make sure the clamp is secure. Lay the bag out at your feet. Double-check everything. Free the clamp near the catheter. And watch the gravity flow begin.

The plastic tubing is transparent and so is the bag, and the dialysis solution that drains from you as you sit on the bed is clear too, innocuous looking, pure, and yet it is full of impurities. During the next twenty minutes you do not resent your plastic appendages. They are part of your viscera exposed and you understand their workings better than you understand the spleen and appendix, the stomach and lungs and the heart. For a while now you are a man turned inside-out and the design of the convolutions becomes a tiny bit clearer.

You know that the dialysate is filled with toxins and that if you hold onto these poisons they will affect the way you feel and the way you think. So now as you watch them draining away, as pure as filtered water, you imagine your body growing lighter, stronger, your head clearing. You feel as if you have been enveloped in a fog but now the fog is draining away. It speaks to you in a clear strong whisper only you can hear. This fog is truth or the illusion of it and if you pay very close attention it might tell you something you did not know you knew.

Rodney Gillen was aware of and perhaps even condoned his wife's affair, says the fog. It aroused him to think of his wife with another man. Also, he would benefit from any generosity bestowed upon his wife, especially if it came in the form of cash or gifts redeemable for cash. His is an unpredictable personality, however; he might encourage adultery, yet in the next instant fly into a jealous rage.

Up to this point, says the fog, the explanation fits or can be made to fit. But this is an early point and you must look farther.

Where would Rodney get his hands on a musket? Not difficult, says the fog. Working reproductions are available at department stores, hardware stores, by mail order catalogue. So then, not how but why? His motive for such acquisition? Two possibilities: A. having evidenced no intrinsic interest in the weaponry himself, he acquired it so as to sell to a collector; or B. he acquired it so as to perpetrate an act of high irony, i.e. the murder of an individual enthralled with the very instrument that would destroy him.

If the answer is A, why would Rodney have delivered the weapon primed and loaded? Would he command the expertise to accomplish these tasks? And why would Catanzaro be inclined to buy a reproduction he could more easily have obtained firsthand? Could the weapon possibly be authentic? How would someone like Rodney Gillen come into possession of such a valuable firearm? And would it, if authentic, still be fireable? Why jeopardize its monetary value, why risk personal injury, by firing a weapon that might blow up in your hands?

All of which, says the fog, makes possibility A unlikely.

By default then, we are left with possibility B. Premeditated murder. After which Rodney abducts or escapes with Jeri Gillen. Why then send a cat's head to the victim's wife? More bizarre kicks? Risk capture, arrest, imprisonment and possible electrocution for the thrill of terrorizing an already devastated woman?

Possible, says the fog. But not likely. In the end, unacceptable.

Explanation, says the fog: Rodney Gillen did not murder Alex Catanzaro. Or, Rodney Gillen did murder Catanzaro but is not responsible for the cat's head.

And if Rodney Gillen is not the murderer, who? Elizabeth Catanzaro? Jeri Gillen? An unknown third party?

If Elizabeth, why hire an investigator to look for the truth? Because you feel certain he won't find the truth, due to incompetence or infatuation or whatever other shortcomings sent him running for cover in the ivy tower? Possible, says the fog.

But unacceptable, says the man.

If the murderer is Jeri Gillen, why would she have brought the affair to an end? Because the thrill was gone. Joyride over. Because Alex himself was planning to end it. Okay, says the fog. Any of the above is acceptable.

But why would Jeri flee the scene leaving her clothes, purse, even her shoes behind, making it look as if she too were a victim, her husband the most logical suspect? Obviously, if she can masquerade as victim, she won't be pursued as suspect. As for casting suspicion on her husband: accidental, a last-minute screw-up. She would have had no foreknowledge of Elizabeth's incriminating call to Rodney. Only after the murder, or too late to stop it, would Rodney realize that he had suddenly been cast as primary suspect, and would therefore disappear along with his wife.

Plausible, says the fog, but weak. Jeri's motivation for the crime is insufficient. She murders her lover because she has grown bored with him?

Her opportunity is doubtful as well. Somehow she acquires a musket, keeps it secreted or at least conceals its intended purpose until such time as she can prime and load it and aim it at Catanzaro's head? When there is nothing material to be gained by such action?

Let's suppose this, says the fog. Alex Catanzaro already has the weapon in the car. The latest addition to his collection. Forget for a moment the fatuity of actually firing such a collectible; for some not yet conceivable reason Alex prepares the weapon and hands it to Jeri as she stands outside the car. She has been naked outside the car on other occasions, so her modesty or lack of it is not a consideration here, not a problem. She is standing on the passenger side of the car, holding the loaded weapon. She starts playing around. Teasing. Alex cautions her to be careful, a gun is not a toy. He lies prostrate on the seat (why?), then lifts his head to look at her. The gun goes off. Accident. Jeri, in a state of shock, still clutching the weapon, wanders away. No; in that condition, dazed, somebody would have encountered her. No, when she fled she did so purposefully; she had enough sense to keep out of sight.

But if she had enough sense for that, why not sense enough to get dressed? Or to conceal Alex's body? Get in the car and drive away? Why take neither her money nor his, why leave her purse spilled in the dirt as if it had been ripped from her hand?

The tube is empty now, the bag full. The fog waits, breathless, pulse throbbing in the catheter. Clamp off the bag, put aside. Attach a new bag, this one full of dialysate, sugar-sweetened blood cleanser. Elevate; free the clamp; fill the abdominal cavity with this new fog now, purer, wanting pollution.

Why does Ernest DeWalt's phone number appear a half dozen times in Catanzaro's papers?

Why do the Jewetts' claim to have heard no gunshot on the morning of the murder? And, more significantly, how could they have not been aware that for a year and a half their inlet was being used as a low rent rendez-vous?

And why, just eights hours ago, did Clifford Jewett attempt to avoid being seen on his own property?

The new bag is empty now, the peritoneal cavity full. The fog is silent. The fog is truth but sometimes even the truth does not know. You clamp the cathe-ter and then bind yourself with tube and bag and your movements seem dreamlike. Physically you feel okay and a certain clarity of purpose has returned to you, but you are slow to finish up and somewhat reluctant to quit the room. You know what awaits outside. You have a bag of poison to flush and even this simple act holds you longer than it should. But the delay is all part of the process of reassembly, the putting-together of a man ap-propriate for the day. You have been in the fog and it is never an easy place to leave.

DeWalt arrived at the Catanzaro home at four-thirty in the afternoon. He had come early, he told himself, because there was work to do in Alex's study. The sun, lingering just above the treetops, was as orange as the heart of a gas flame, the sky a scalding blue. In the trees behind the field, crows had gathered, were calling noisily.

DeWalt, as he stepped from the car, found their cries in the distance and felt somehow reassured. As a boy when he had stayed at his uncle's farm he would awaken at first light to a similar chorus of caws and shrieks. Years later, after sitting up all night in a car, trying with camera and binoculars to catch people in the act of temporarily warding off their own emptiness, the sunset would be his morning, first light of a new clandestine day.

And now, with those two elements combined here, the sunset and the crows, he felt as if something new was starting for him. It was a vague kind of premonition; and probably, he told himself, illusory. Deceptive fragment of memory. Juxtaposition of old hope on a new landscape, a self-enticement, self-delusion: this notion that any moment for a middle-aged man could be the beginning of something rather than its end.

Even so, DeWalt, what harm does it do to admire the sun hanging bright and swollen above the trees?

Even a sunset is an illusion, DeWalt. Feeling safe is an illusion. Feeling somehow joined to another person's life. Feeling that a virtuous life will make a difference. That someday the pain will stop.

Yes, of course, even a sunset. Sunset, sunrise, floating fragments of memory, all of it. But if you know this and do not accede to the fraud, don't be taken in by it, there is still the possibility of beauty or pleasure. You can enjoy the many illusions of life but you must never place any value in them.

Yes, even a good deadbolt lock can be a thing of beauty, he thought. There was a new one on the back door. And yet this door stood open, open to him and the air and whatever else came along. Through the gray mesh of the screen door he could see into the kitchen.

Elizabeth was at the sink, water running from the faucet as she rinsed a handful of broad red-tinged lettuce leaves from the garden. She was humming softly, sipping occasionally from a glass of white wine. He thought she looked as good from that angle as she did from the front, her profiled face pleasantly angular, jawline neither too fleshy nor taut, firm but with a softness, a womanness that made him not want to go inside just yet.

She was dressed in baggy green chinos and moccasins and a silky white blouse; half practicality and comfort, half femininity. He imagined that if he were close enough he would smell apricots in her hair. Music played softly in another room, something airy, almost ephemeral, a single flute, the tinkling of a glass celesta, a delicate breeze of violin.

Finally he tapped on the metal doorframe. Softly, yet still he startled her. When she turned he was surprised to see the glisten of her eyes, lashes jeweled with tears.

But why should that surprise you, DeWalt?

She brushed the tears aside with the knuckle of a finger. "Come on in, I've just started the salad."

Before he stepped inside he tapped the wooden door. "This is a good lock," he said.

"There's one on the front door too."

"You should use them."

She, tending to the lettuce again, now rewashing the leaves one at a time, said, "The security system will be installed tomorrow."

"You get things done fast."

"I've got connections," she said, and smiled. Then, half-turning, "I'm having a glass of wine. Can I get you one?"

"No thanks."

"How about a beer? Whiskey? Vodka?"

"I don't drink," he said. It sounded too abrupt; sanc-

143

timonious. "I used to drink. Too much, in fact. So now I don't drink at all."

She picked up her glass of wine and looked at it.

"Don't stop on my account," he told her.

"Are you sure? Because I don't mind. I mean if it makes it easier for you. This is my second glass anyway."

"It doesn't bother me a bit. Enjoy your wine."

Before being shot he had relied heavily on alcohol and he had learned how to sustain over several hours that harmonious and bouyant numbness that precedes drunkenness, how to pace consumption so that the buzz of optimism did not drop away into despair until he was ready for sleep. It had been necessary in his line of work to find an acceptable narcotic. Alcohol softened the focus so that what he viewed nightly through his telephoto lens was not so startling nor ugly and in the cumulative not as dismaying as it might have been to a perfectly sober and reasonable man. The only other panacea to come close to it was sex with somebody he truly liked. He had made frequent use of that remedy too but the problem with sex was that the cure lasted only until your feet hit the floor. Sex was not a portable cure. You could not always engage in it spontaneously or without fear, suspicion, guilt, or remorse. A hangover was its own penitence but there was no penance for inappropriate sex. Still, he had relied upon both alcohol and sex and now both medicines were denied him and he had not yet found a reliable substitute.

All he had found were various ways to lie about his need for the medicines. It sometimes surprised him that a man who valued truth so highly could lie so often and efficiently. He tried to limit himself to lies of omission, but this too was not always practical.

Elizabeth Catanzaro took another small sip of wine and then set the glass on the sink. She rinsed the last of the lettuce leaves, shook the water off and then laid them on a paper towel. "I'm afraid dinner won't be ready for awhile yet," she told him. "I didn't know exactly what time you'd be coming. I planned for around six."

"That's fine," he said. "I have a little work to do first anyway."

She nodded. "It's stuffed roasted chicken with garlic and thyme. Plus just about everything I could get from the garden. Do you like sliced tomatoes with mozzarella and basil?"

"You grow mozzarella too?"

"You don't grow mozzarella, city boy; you make it."

"And you make your own?"

"As a matter of fact," she said, "no."

He smiled, watching as she dried her hands on a dish towel, enjoying just this, the sight of her, the sunwarm kitchen and its odors, fruity wine and greenery and the sweet distant melody of an unfamiliar song. He watched too long probably, watched in a way that did not see until finally he realized that she was no longer holding the dish towel, it lay folded on the counter, and Elizabeth was standing there not quite looking at him but waiting for him to get on with it, to move or speak, do something to erase the moronic glaze from his eyes.

"What kind of work do you need to do?" she asked.

And he came quickly back, out of that region of unthought which you can never get to if you try. He said, "I'd like to take another look at Alex's papers. If that's okay with you."

She turned to the cupboard, opened the door and, after reaching behind the spice rack, produced a key. "Do you think the police might have overlooked something?"

He stepped forward to take the key from her hand.

"They're working under a different set of assumptions than I am."

She nodded, said nothing more, told him with this silence that she understood the implication. She went back to her glass of wine and sipped from it as she faced the sink. He bounced the key in his hand.

"They're small this year," she said.

He did not understand, but waited.

From the bottom of the sink she lifted a handful of fingersize carrots. She turned on the cold water and held the carrots under the stream.

"It's been so dry this summer. If we don't get another good rain soon, the melons and pumpkins won't be any good. The kids will have to buy their jack-o-lantern pumpkins at a store."

He remembered one thorough rain of the summer, only one. And not a good one, but a drenching, a washing away of tracks, of clues, a submersion of bodies.

He said, "You put a lot of time into that garden, don't you?"

"It's something to do," she said.

"It's more than that."

She smiled faintly, turning the carrots back and forth in her hands under the splashing water, the carrots no bigger than a child's thumb. "The first summer we lived here," she said, "I didn't do a garden. I went to lunch everyday with all my new friends from the university. Played tennis, drank martinis, gossiped, giggled a lot. A very meaningful life." She laughed softly. With her thumbnail she scraped a dark spot from one of the carrots.

DeWalt asked, "So what happened to change you?"

"Wax," she said.

"As in . . . ?"

"As on cucumbers and peppers and apples and nearly everything else I bought at the store. You can't wash it

146

off, you know. I tried, but all I had was the shiniest produce in the county." She laid the carrots in the sink again and shut off the tap. With a paring knife she began to nip off the carrots' roots and stems.

"Even around here," she said, "where we're surrounded by so much farmland, even here all the food in the stores has been trucked in from hundreds of miles away. It's artificially grown, artificially ripened, artificially attractive. I began to think about what stuff like that might do to my kids. A lifetime of junk like that. It gave me the shivers."

"So you abandoned your life of leisure."

"Yep," she said. "Not that the kids appreciate it, though. They'd live on candy and chips and cookies if I'd let them. But what responsible mother would?"

"I never even tasted a store-bought cookie until I went away to college," he told her. "My mother made everything from scratch. And the way she made them, with oatmeal, raisins, honey and brown flour—cookies like that cost a dollar each in the mall these days."

"That's the way I make cookies too." She looked at him and smiled. "I'll make you a batch sometime."

So now it was time to leave. Without realizing it he had closed half the distance between them. That was a bad sign. Reminiscing about cookies was a bad sign. Dinner was going to be dangerous. "I'd better get to work," he said.

As he opened the screen door, she asked, "What exactly are you hoping to find out there?"

Yes, DeWalt, what are you hoping to find? It's a simple enquiry, give us a simple answer. Tell the lady what you're after here. Tell her what you will not admit even to yourself.

"Connections," he said.

"That's one thing the police overlooked, you know.

The connection between you and Alex. Your phone number appearing so often, I mean."

"That's one of the things I want to explore."

"Do you think it's related?"

"At this point, knowing nothing, I've got to assume that everything is related."

"Good luck," she told him.

He had no choice but to believe that she meant it. "Give me a holler when dinner's ready."

The study above the garage was as stuffy as an attic, but DeWalt did not turn on the air conditioner. Instead he opened all the windows. He wanted to smell the field-scented air and to hear the crows. The sterile white noise of an air-conditioner would make him too comfortable, almost drowsy, but what he needed now was a fidgety kind of alertness, the tickle of sweat on his skin, the fragrance of memory, sadness, a jabbing caw of alarm. Without external stimulations, even annoyances, there was always the danger of getting too close to your material, blurring the small print. And he did not want to miss anything this time around. That metal one-note song was still pinging in his head, a reminder that there was something he should know but didn't, something he should remember but couldn't. There was something he had looked at but had not seen, and this time he meant to discover it.

The first thing he did was to make a calendar of the dates Alex had intended or had reminded himself to phone DeWalt. DeWalt's office extension was noted five times on the desk calendar, starting in January and ending in March, always on a Monday, Wednesday, or Friday. Apparently Alex had gone to the trouble of looking up DeWalt's teaching schedule. Also, there was a pencil dot beside DeWalt's home number in the faculty directory, but DeWalt could ascribe no date to this.

When satisfied that Alex had made no further reminders to himself to call DeWalt after the last one in March, DeWalt put the calendar aside.

Okay, DeWalt. Now what? Now what do you look for?

He picked up the large manila envelope in which Alex had kept his business receipts for the current year, and he dumped these receipts onto the desk. Most were typical deductions: receipts for floppy disks and printer ribbons, postage stamps, books and magazines and photocopying services. There were hotel and restaurant receipts from Niagara Falls, plus the stub of an admission ticket to Fort Erie. All legitimate business expenses related to Alex's research for his book, no doubt. Except that the hotel bill was for a double room for four people, the restaurant stub for four also. Alex, Elizabeth, and the kids, thought DeWalt. A combination business trip and family vacation. Easily verifiable.

Then DeWalt found something to pique his interest. Two withdrawal slips from Alex's account with the State Teacher's Retirement System. In early April he had withdrawn $2500. In July, another $4500. DeWalt laid these receipts aside. He sorted through the remaining pieces of paper, found nothing else of particular interest, and finally returned the manila envelope to the desk drawer.

From another drawer he lifted a bulging accordion-type folder. This folder contained magazine tearsheets, photocopied pages from texts and other books, newspaper clippings, plus Alex's typed or handwritten notes to himself; all, upon first look, seeming to pertain to the War of 1812: disparate pieces of research, descriptions of uniforms and weaponry, chronicles of naval engagements and ground battles and the comic political maneuvers that precipitated and perpetuated that meaningless war.

Upon his second examination of this material, how-

149

ever, DeWalt discovered three newspaper clippings that seemed somehow anomalous; in a sense, anachronistic.

The first was a *New York Times* announcement that an archeological dig at Old Fort Erie had unearthed the remains of several soldiers killed during the northern campaign of 1814. In addition to human remains, a small cache of "medical and military artifacts" had also been recovered.

The second clipping, this one from the *Toronto News* and dated over three months later, told of a burglary of the Fort Erie Museum, the theft of several unspecified items on display with artifacts "unearthed during a recent archeological study."

DeWalt added the dates of the dig and the museum robbery to the calendar of events he was compiling. He then searched through Alex's desk until he found a map detailing the geographical arena of the War of 1812. This map confirmed that Niagara Falls, where Alex had taken his family on vacation months after the archeological discovery, was located just across the Niagara River from Fort Erie.

The third newspaper clipping, its news unrelated in even the most tenuous way to Alex's research, made DeWalt's breath sit heavy in his chest. The clipping, from the local newspaper, had been printed last May. In it was a brief account of the fire-bombing of a privately owned two-stall garage on Arlington Avenue. A garage used as rehearsal hall for a rock band called The Kinetics, who, said the report, had been in the garage at the time of the fire-bombing. A Molotov cocktail made from a Pepsi bottle had been thrown through one of the glass panels on the garage door. It exploded on the concrete floor, causing serious injury to the lead guitarist, Robin Janicki. He suffered third degree burns about the right arm, chest and abdomen. Motive for the attack was unknown. Police were investigating.

"I hollered three times so far," said Elizabeth Catanzaro from the threshold. She was smiling, holding a wine glass in one hand, holding to the doorframe with the other, swaying just slightly, her body framed in fading light. "Are you ignoring me, or do you *prefer* your dinner ice cold?"

"Sorry," he said. "I guess I was involved in this stuff."

"Find something interesting?" She walked over to him and, standing close, placed a hand on his shoulder. Her weight and her warmth went inside him. The kitchen scents, the scent of her hand. Her hip touched his shoulder, leaned into him. He wondered how many more glasses of wine she had drunk. Her hand slipped around to the back of his neck. There was something hard and heavy in his lungs.

"First things first," he said as he swept the newspaper clippings into a drawer. He picked up the sheet of paper on which he had made his calendar of important dates, folded it three times and shoved it into his shirt pocket.

He slipped out from under her hand, stood beside her, caught her as she swayed, held her gently by the arm. "Let's eat," he said.

Chapter
Eleven

A soft summer evening. One of those quiet August dusks which, quite unexpectedly, resonates October. DeWalt hoped to do nothing to disturb it. As he and Elizabeth walked back to the house from Alex's office he felt it, the hint of October, a gathering readiness for change.

She held lightly to his arm as they walked, a deliberate lightness, a lightness to belie the lethargy of her other movements. Her eyes looked heavy, eschewing of distant glances. Her mouth was formed in that vague kind of smile impossible to assess, a reflection of hope; fear; ineffable sadness. What it probably indicated was an excessive consumption of wine. But how much is too much, DeWalt, for a woman in her situation? In this case maybe there is no such thing as too much. In this case maybe any amount that does not induce unconsciousness is not enough.

The crows were silent now. Somewhere off to DeWalt's left, a mourning dove purled from a telephone line.

All through dinner the October feeling stayed with DeWalt. He understood it to be—assumed, in any case; never trusting wholly the intellectual explication of emotion—a kind of sickroom melancholy; a moribundity evoked from the information newly gleaned from Alex's papers, the half-information that had not yet jelled but surely suggested a diversion of accepted truths.

For tonight anyway, DeWalt resolved not to worry it. He would allow the information to settle; by tomorrow, perhaps, some of the murkiness might have cleared.

But still he could not shake the feeling that something was about to be lost, something else gained. He sat across from Elizabeth at the rectangular dining room table—she had used the china, a pair of silver candlesticks with white candles, a slender crystal vase holding three tiger lilies—and looked past her through the wide bay window to the backyard and the woods beyond. Every indication was of a summer in full ripeness, the grass a verdant green, the fields lush, the multigreened thick-leafed branches of the trees. But in this house and all around it a new Fall had begun.

As if to confirm this, a chill rippled through DeWalt. He looked at Elizabeth as she too-delicately cut a bite of chicken breast; her face was flushed, a thin glistening line of perspiration on her forehead, another in the hollow of her chin.

Behind her, the sun settled deep inside the woods, was resting on the forest floor. Its soft fire burned through the irregular collonade of trunks. But there was no smoke and the fire dimmed instead of grew. It was a cold fire that would eventually put itself out.

She had asked if he had found anything important in Alex's papers and he had said it was too early to tell. She let it go at that because she did not wish to talk about it anyway, did not want to think about the violence or betrayal or any of the other virulent ways people hurt one another. He complimented the dinner and so as not to offend her ate more heartily than was his habit. She ate delicately, with an appetite diminished by more than wine alone. She kept her movements deliberate and slow, but they were unsteady nonetheless.

He hoped he was wrong about what he thought he sensed from her tonight, and yet all the while guarded against the possibility of being right. If what he expected to happen actually happened, he would have no appropriate defense for it. He felt more than a little unsteady himself; shaky with desire, weak with the heaviness of resistance.

"Tell me what it's like to live alone," she said.

Yes, it was coming. He would have to be very careful with her tonight.

"You needn't worry about that," he told her. "School starts in a couple of weeks, right? So the children will be coming back soon."

"I was asking what it's like for you, though."

"Boring," he said, and smiled.

She smiled too but his answer did not satisfy her. She picked at her food a moment longer, then pushed the plate aside. She reached for her glass of wine.

"Do you believe there's a God?" she asked.

The abruptness of her question startled him, that tone of challenge, the invitation to controvert her own suspicions. He looked at the vase filled with tiger lilies, the leaves softly curled, three fluted orange chalices that would soon be closing for the night.

"Somebody you care about dies," she said, "especially the way Alex died. . . ."

"Of course," he said.

"What makes it so hard is that I don't even know what I *want* to believe. If I accept that God exists, I have to also accept that he allows things like this to happen. But I can't. I won't."

"Nor do you want to accept that there is no God. No truth or purpose whatsoever."

"You know what I see every time I close my eyes?" she said. "Alex's coffin. With him inside it. I just can't stand the . . . finality of that."

154

"If it is final," he said.

"You have your doubts?"

"Doubts or hopes, whatever you want to call it."

"Then . . . you believe there's a heaven?"

"I'm afraid I have my doubts about that too."

"What do you think, then, becomes of the dead?"

"I think they live in the grief of the living."

"And who grieves for the living, Ernie?"

"Maybe God, I don't know. Or maybe we're supposed to grieve for each other."

She shook her head. "If there is a God," she said, "he's not what we think. Not what I used to think."

Judging by the grip she had on her wine glass, the grim set of her mouth, he guessed that she was about to heave the glass at a wall. He understood such a response and would not have tried to restrain her. A certain amount of breakage was inevitable.

But she did not. Her grip relaxed. "Tell me what you really believe, Ernie. You're a smart man, and I respect you. So tell me what you really believe so that I can believe it too. I need something to believe right now."

He waited a moment; tasted the bitterness of his words. "My belief won't do you any good."

"I want it anyway."

He held her gaze as long as he could. "I guess I believe that, if God does exist, we can't count on him for much."

She smiled. He wished he had had something else to give her. Confidence; even arrogance. A revivifying lie.

"We're supposed to accept it all on faith," she said.

"So I've heard."

"Faith." It was a word she felt no fondness for. "Just have faith, people, and everything will turn out fine. But oh oh, look out, everything isn't fine. Well, have faith anyway, have faith and it will all work out. But you know what? It can't work out, not unless people can come back from the dead. Well, gee, have faith, it's all part of God's plan and it's not for us to question. Because if we don't have faith, things will *really* turn out bad. Maybe not in this life, though, because in this life the faithless prosper. Am I right, Ernie?"

"It's a pretty mean set-up, I agree."

"It stinks." She drank off the rest of her wine. She looked at her glass a moment. She pushed back her chair and stood. "Time to open another bottle."

"Do you really think you should?"

"Absolutely." She dragged her hand across the back of his neck as she walked past him into the kitchen. "It's what we have instead of God."

It's what *you* have, he thought. You and Hemingway, who said it first. DeWalt liked that she had read Hemingway and could quote him unobtrusively. Not that DeWalt was looking for a reason to feel affectionate toward her. Not that he needed one.

From the kitchen she said, "I almost forgot, I made a coconut flan for dessert. I don't think it's set yet though. You might have to eat it with a straw."

There was a tremulous quality to her voice and it told him not to leave her alone for even a few moments now. When you have given up on God even an unjelled flan can move you to despair. Once you have given up on God, God becomes an enemy, no repository of hope, and all such resentment only further distances you from reconciliation. It is an unproductive place to be; a difficult place to find your way out of. DeWalt had been to all those places already. He did not want any company there.

He went into the kitchen and took her by the arm. "Let's go sit on the porch awhile."

The rhythm of the porch glider brushing slowly back and forth on metal tracks had a salutory effect on him. He eased down into himself; the darkness softened his thoughts. Elizabeth sat close, their hips touching. He could smell her wine and the cooking scents on her clothing. He thought them wonderfully natural scents and he was glad she had not tried to suffocate them in an unnatural fog of perfume. After a few minutes of gentle rocking she leaned into him and drew her feet up, turned sideways at the waist so that her feet rested on the glider and her head on DeWalt's shoulder. He slipped his arm around her. He smelled the clean fruity smell of her hair, not an apricot-scent as he had imagined but the nostalgic fragrance of watermelon. They watched across the dusk-filled yard at fireflies twinkling in the trees beyond the driveway.

The dark shell of the children's treehouse stood out high in the darkness. He could not see the board ladder or even the trunk to which the boards were nailed, but the outline of the small empty house was clear to him, a shadow upon a shadow.

When Elizabeth spoke he knew that she had been looking at it too. "I miss the kids so much," she said.

He could not respond to this in any honest way, and so he said nothing. If he was aware of an emptiness in his own life it was not the same kind of emptiness Elizabeth Catanzaro must have felt. In fact every emptiness is different, he told himself, no matter what similarities they might share. And he had never found anything to be gained by the public display or comparison of private emptinesses.

"Did you use to catch fireflies when you were a kid?" she asked.

"Sure," he said.

"I guess all kids do. Christopher likes to fill up a jar with them, and then when he goes to bed he sets it on the nightstand so that he can fall asleep watching them."

"I used to do that too." He would lie atop the cool

157

sheets, wearing only his undershorts, and he would watch the green winking lights and he would listen to his father across the hall, his father taking off shoes and trousers and shirt, kneeling beside the bed and the bed creaking as he leaned into it, *The Lord is my shepherd I shall not want . . . he maketh me to lie down in green pastures.* Sometimes Ernie and his mother would say the *Lord's Prayer* together or she would look in and remind him to say it, and he did without fail because he was afraid not to say it, until, that is, after his father had died and then Ernie found the courage necessary to stop.

But his father's prayer had been the *Twenty-Third Psalm.* Even as a child DeWalt had liked his father's prayer better than the *Lord's Prayer.* It seemed at once more poetic and more realistic; more adult. *Yea, though I walk through the valley of the shadow of death. . . .* Not the valley of death but the valley of the shadow of death. Even now he did not understand why the writer had made that distinction, except for poetic reasons. It gave a beauty to fear. A luminosity to human ignorance.

DeWalt had always intended to learn the Psalm but too many other things had affected his ability to memorize it. Still, he found its rhythm soothing. Maybe, DeWalt, that is the value of prayer. Maybe people are soothed by their own voices and they do not realize it. They are comforted by the poetry of their fears.

"It's good your kids have a place like this to grow up in," he told her. "You weren't serious about selling it, were you?"

"I was angry when I said that. I guess I'm still angry, though. . . ."

He did not say anything. There was warmth and comfort to the feel of her body against his. He had not held a woman for a long time now. If he let himself think about this it could destroy him for tonight and for a

158

long time after but he had gotten past thinking about such things. Just as he had gotten past thinking he should respond to Elizabeth's uncertainty with some reassuring platitude or abstract axiom of promise.

"What do you remember best from your childhood?" she asked. "What's the one moment that stands out clearest in your mind?"

He was not convinced there was any value in this either but the memory was already there. "The winter I was eight years old," he said.

"The whole winter?"

He smiled, and shook his head. "It was during Christmas vacation. After Christmas but before school had started again. I was downstairs in the basement, supposedly practicing with my new roller skates. But what I was really doing was fooling around with the coal furnace. Something I'd been warned a thousand times not to do. But there I was with the furnace door wide open, burning pieces of wood, broomstraws, anything I could find. And I ended up setting a whole pile of cardboard boxes on fire. With me wedged into the corner behind them. I knew I'd done something terrible, so I didn't start yelling for help until it was almost too late. The flames were as high as the ceiling. Then I heard my Dad's footsteps pounding down the wooden stairs. Then his bare arms coming reaching through that wall of fire. He just stepped right into it, grabbed me and yanked me out."

"My god," she said. "Were you badly burned?"

"I remember Dad's shirt being scorched. And how all the hair on his arms was singed off. He never complained that he was hurt but I'm sure he must have been. His arms were red for several days. But I was fine. Untouched, in fact."

"You were lucky," she said.

"He beat my butt until it glowed," said DeWalt. "But

later that night, when he thought I was asleep, he came into my room and sat on the edge of the bed. I figured he was still angry, so I didn't move a muscle. He laid his hand on my back, and then he just sat there. After a while I heard him crying. At first I didn't know what the sound was, because as far as I knew, my old man had never shed a tear in his life. He cried pretty hard that night, though. And I didn't know what to make of it."

DeWalt stared across the yard to the treeline. The playhouse was lost now in the darkness. Everything lost. " 'Don't you ever play with fire again,' Dad whispered. 'Don't you ever do that. Please honey, don't. And don't ever drive a car.' he said. 'Don't fight in a war. Don't climb trees, or swim in the ocean, or play football. Don't ever do anything dangerous where you might get hurt. Don't take chances, son, please. Just stay home, stay right here in this house with your mother and me. Just stay here forever, it's safe here, you won't ever have to leave. Please, son,' he said. 'Please, God. Please, don't ever let my boy get hurt.' "

Elizabeth said nothing for a while, for too long. And then, finally, "Children change everything." Her voice was as soft as his father's hand lifting away had been. DeWalt had never before let anyone into this room with his father and him but now he had brought Elizabeth Catanzaro in and it seemed to be all right. He could feel the dampness of her cheek against his shoulder.

"We stop hurting for ourselves and start hurting for them," she said. "I think that's the hardest thing a parent has to overcome. That desire to protect your kids from everything that can possibly go wrong."

For some men it is not so hard to overcome though, is it, DeWalt? Some men die young enough to overcome everything. Some men disappear just when their sons are beginning to look at them closely.

160

That's enough, DeWalt. You can't fill up the emptiness with memories. You're getting heavy with it. Cold
rain-soaked wet to the skin soul-drenched heavy with
remembrance. You've got to cut this shit out, DeWalt.
You're not a green stick anymore. You're not a spring
twig, you don't bend, you don't float. You are water-
logged and soft, old man. Get out now or sink.

She raised his hand to her lips then. He barely felt the
kiss.

"You know what I think?" she said. "I think the only
mercy God ever bestows is the mercy we give each
other while waiting for God to get started."

He tightened his arm around her shoulder and mo-
mentarily drew her closer. There were new locks on all
the doors but he and Elizabeth were outside the locks
and all the doors were open. It had been a long time
since DeWalt had been in a place like this. He was here
now, unexpectedly, unintentionally, and although it was
a surprise he did not allow the darkness to fool him into
believing that Elizabeth Catanzaro had come here for
the same reasons.

"Put me to bed, Ernie," she said a minute later.

"You only say that because you've been drinking."

"I've been drinking so I would have an excuse to say
it."

He did not move or consider a reply too quickly.
"There are reasons why you think you want to do this,"
he told her.

"I know all the reasons, Ernie. I've thought about
them all. But what difference does it make what the reason is? I need to have you close to me tonight. I need
you to want me."

She stood, holding his hand, waiting for him to decide.

Sometimes, DeWalt, we sharpen the blades of our
memories. But sometimes we have to blunt them.

161

He stood and followed her upstairs.

There were no lights on in her bedroom and very little moonlight filtered through the window. He watched her undress as a shadow and come to him. He felt the cool shadow of her breasts against his chest and her hands in the small of his back. He tasted her mouth and the warm sweet wine of her hunger for him.

Now in the darkness he realized that she was drunker than he had first thought. There was no steadiness to her now, there was only need and no attempt to conceal or control it. Her hands were on his belt and clumsily working to free it, but he stopped her hands and held them together in his and kissed them once. "First this," he told her, and leading her to the bed helped her to lie down. He lifted her ankles and kissed them and placed them on the mattress. He leaned over then and put his mouth to her breast, he took the nipple into his mouth and felt it firm against his tongue, his hand on the warm flesh of her thigh. He kissed one breast and then the other, her skin so sweet and warm he could have lain his head against her and slept, so healing and tender her submissiveness, her trust in him an affirmation he had told himself he would never again experience.

His mouth worked its way down over her belly and he felt her stomach muscles quiver, her hands on the back of his head. He moved down the length of her until he was between her legs. With his hands beneath her buttocks now he lifted her toward him as he knelt at the foot of the bed, her legs falling over his shoulders and crossed at the ankles, heels against his spine. With his first taste of her and the gasp as she pushed against him he imagined that everything might change, that the scented pull of her thighs and the salty heat might finally put an end to the uncertainty of his own body, might end that debate once and for all.

Her pelvis established a rhythm which he with the

languorous slippage of his tongue reaffirmed, a slow eager beat he wanted to prolong forever, forever consuming the taste and scent and heat that encompassed everything now. Her pace quickened but then slowed again, deliberately stalling, holding back, extending the pleasure until it would not be held back, this racing of the heart, this warming, filling, aching empty almost dissolution of the self, this slow falling away into nowhere, into everywhere at once, until her hands pulled at his head pulling him into her and her legs pulling him in and the wings of her shadow opening wide to enfold and pull him in and down with her into the long fast moaning slide into nowhere.

Her legs held him for a few moments as her body quivered. He felt the spasms in her thigh, the twitching muscle. Finally she unwrapped her ankles. He slid up beside her and held her in his arms. She was still breathless and she clung to him as if she might again fall away somewhere. After a while her breath softened and he could tell that she was drifting away. He kissed her lightly on the cheek.

"You get undressed now," she murmured, but her voice was weak with sleep, drowsy with too much wine.

"Soon," he told her, and he kissed her a final time.

He lay beside her for nearly an hour, even after she in her sleep turned her back to him and curled up on her side. He lay there thinking things out in every direction. He felt that he had walked fleshless past the unfinished framework of her need and that he had snagged his heart on a nail. To move in any direction would only rip the muscle further. Finally he admitted that there was no way of thinking of it that was not destructive. He moved away from her. He stood and covered her with a blanket.

In the hallway he paused for a moment outside the

163

boy's room. The bed was small but he thought he could be comfortable there. It would be good to sleep as a child again and surrounded by the baseballs and heroes and plastic toys of a child's world. It would be good but that would be impossible too. He had a routine to carry out and it was time for it again. He was supposed to create a sterile field for himself and his hardware but that wasn't always practical. Anyway it does not matter because I am a sterile field myself, he thought.

He went downstairs and outside to his car, and from the trunk he took a bag of dialysate. In the house again, he watched the empty plastic bag fill, and then he emptied the new bag into himself and he rebuttoned his shirt and was finished.

In the kitchen he sampled the flan; it was the color and consistency of milk and it was not going to gel, she had done something wrong. He locked the new deadbolts and then lay uncovered on the sofa. In four to six hours he would have to make another bag exchange. Some routines, DeWalt, are more accommodating than others. He could smell the leftovers on the dining room table. He could smell the souring scent of wine.

The copper light of morning filled his eyes, a coppery taste upon his tongue. The sky looked like pounded metal. Sometimes this dichotomy of opposites, the beauty of a morning and the ugly feelings he had for himself and his life, sometimes they did not simply cancel each other out, sometimes they exacerbated one another. Now, as he drove home in the dawn light, still sleepy and chilled, the quiet beauty of the morning hurt him deeply.

Inside his small house he prepared to dialyze himself again. There had been only one spare bag in the trunk of his car, so he had had to come home for another one. He wanted to get back to Elizabeth's house before she

164

woke up. It would be bad enough when she awoke, but worse if she found him gone. He had this to do first and then he would return.

There was no morning inside his house. It was as warm and bright there as a fire that has gone out. Even with all the lights on there was no true brightness.

Sometimes he felt like disconnecting himself permanently. He was a prisoner to the tube and bag. He was chained to it. Every six hours he would reach the end of the chain's limit and be jerked back to the beginning. Sometimes he thought the inescapable repetition of it would suffocate him. When he tried to think into the future, to make plans or to entertain improbable ambitions, and he felt the chain dragging behind him, always shortening, growing heavier with each forward step, he actually became short of breath.

His body confined him and boxed him in. It had become what the Buddhists call an occasional Hell, had hardened around him like the lump of ore taken from a mine in Derby, England, a rock which when split open released a toad, barely but still alive.

Or like the split block of stone on display at the Smithsonian Institution from whose solid center a horned lizard was freed; unconfined, the lizard lived for two days.

Or like the fossilized form of the extinct newt found in a chalk quarry by a geologist from the University of Cambridge. When placed on a piece of paper in the sun, the newt began to move. When placed in a pond, it promptly swam away.

And maybe someday someone will free you from your occasional Hell, DeWalt. Maybe after the rock has formed around you so solidly that you cannot even wiggle a toe, maybe after you have survived in dormancy for half a million years, conscious of nothing but your pain and your past, maybe after you have had sufficient opportunity to reflect upon your mistakes, someone will serendipitously excavate you and expose you to the sun. You can take a startled breath then and stretch your atrophied muscles and then you will probably die. You will be released from this occasional Hell and if you are very lucky and good the one in your next life will not be so restricting.

Finished now with the bag exchange, finished for a while, DeWalt wound the thin plastic tubing twice around his waist and flattened the empty bag atop it. He reached for a clean shirt and pulled it on. His hands felt numb. There was no feeling in the skin, no awareness, sensitivity. Nothing felt right when he held it; not the tube, not the shirt buttons. It came and went, this numbness, here now for no apparent reason. He flexed his fingers—chalksticks; twigs. His hands, neck, knee joints, lower back, they were all turning against him, going their own way. He couldn't count on anything anymore. Not his body, not his mind. Not deduction nor reflex nor perspicacity nor hunch. Not the cautionary instincts of a tired, battered heart.

Chapter Twelve

Jan 6:	Notation on Alex's desk calendar, "Call D, ext. 236"
Jan 19:	Alex's note, "Call D, 236"
Feb 11:	" " " " "
Feb 18:	" " " " "
Mar 25:	" " " " "
Apr 3:	Report of Fort Erie discoveries, *New York Times*
Apr 7:	Alex withdraws $2500 State Teachers Retirement System
May 28:	Firebombing of Kinetics rehearsal garage
July 10:	Alex withdraws $4500 STRS
July 15–16:	Catanzaro family vacation in Niagara Falls
July 21:	Robbery of Fort Erie, *Toronto Times News*
Aug 16:	Alex Catanzaro murdered

Two entries on DeWalt's calendar of events kept drawing his attention. He was sitting in the Catanzaro kitchen in a chair pulled close to the telephone on the wall, waiting for the telephone to ring, prepared to snatch the receiver off its hook the very moment the ringer sounded. It was nearly ten AM but he did not want the telephone to wake Elizabeth. Before leaving his own home earlier that morning, DeWalt had made a call to Trooper Abbott, and he had given Abbott the Catanzaro number as the place he could be reached for the next few hours. At his feet was a plate smeared with honey and the crumbs of a blueberry muffin; the browning core of a Macintosh apple.

April 7, he read again. Why would Alex withdraw money from his retirement fund a month and a half prior to the firebombing of the Kinetics' garage? Had the time span between the two events been a matter of days, even a week, the connection would be tighter, more easily made. And why, just a few days before this withdrawal, had Alex ceased admonishing himself to call DeWalt? DeWalt could come up with only two reasons why Alex had been so insistent and yet so negligent to speak with him: He wanted to confer with DeWalt the writer; or, he wanted to confer with DeWalt the investigator.

The first explanation seemed the most plausible. "Hi, Ernest, Alex Catanzaro here, over in the History Department. Listen, the reason I'm calling is, I read your book and I really enjoyed it, and the thing is, I'm writing a book of my own. It's a historical novel, set in the early 19th century, but even so I felt I could benefit from the insights of a professional writer such as yourself. The truth is, I'm having a bitch of a time working certain things out. . . ."

That would have been a fairly simple call to make. Other people certainly had no qualms buttonholing DeWalt for free advice, a peek at their manuscripts, the name of a good agent. From the look of Alex's papers, though, he had barely yet begun to write the book. Maybe he was aware of his inability to get the book started, but he was embarrassed to admit it.

But Alex's repeated notations to call DeWalt seemed more than mere reminders. There was an escalating urgency to them. Was it mere coincidence that the firebombing had occurred *after* the final and most emphatic notation? DeWalt didn't think so.

Had Alex toyed with the idea of hiring DeWalt to somehow investigate Rodney Gillen? Perhaps even to harass, intimidate, or actually harm the boy? Of course it was possible: an erection will make a fool of any man. And it was not at all unusual, DeWalt knew, for people to assume that private investigators are well-versed in shady activities. *Suffer No Fools* had been riddled with violence and deceit. Had Alex made the all-too-common mistake of ascribing a book's personality to its writer?

This would explain, at least, why Alex, despite his own insistence, had been remiss in calling DeWalt. Alex, if he made the call, would be requesting an illegal service, or a service that would expose to another individual an adulterous affair that could wreck Alex's marriage.

Okay, DeWalt. Let's assume that Alex wanted you to do a job for him. A job on Rodney Gillen. A job he eventually took care of himself. What, then, was the *purpose* of the firebombing? Obviously, to frighten Gillen or one of the other band members. A message. And what might that message have been—please play "Hunka Hunka Burning Love"?

Probably not.

Okay, then: the other important date. July 21, the robbery of the Fort Erie museum. A week prior to this robbery, the Catanzaro family vacations in Niagara Falls, across the river from the museum. A week prior to this, Alex withdraws $4500 from his retirement fund. The money had been used either for a very expensive weekend vacation, or. . . . Could it be that Alex considered hiring DeWalt to rob the museum? DeWalt rechecked his calendar. No: announcement of the archeological discovery was not made until after Alex had apparently decided not to get in touch with DeWalt.

But Alex *had* hired somebody to rob the museum. DeWalt would stand by this suspicion unless and until Elizabeth could account for the entire $4500. Maybe Alex had tried to hire Rodney Gillen and/or the Kinetics, but they had refused. So he sent them a memo in the form of a Molotov cocktail: *No is an unacceptable response, boys. Perhaps you should reconsider.* And they, being young and impressionable, did reconsider. They, or Rodney, not only perpetrated the robbery on Alex's behalf, but they, or Rodney, went the extra measure and later introduced Alex at point blank range to the very weapon he had so coveted.

A neat and comprehensive explanation. DeWalt hoped it was not too neat. It all hinged upon information he needed from Abbott and Elizabeth. In the meantime he needed a sip of water, his mouth was dry, it tasted of smoke. He bent to pick up his breakfast plate and that was when he noticed her standing a few feet back from the threshold, watching him, hand to her throat and holding closed a very unflattering blue terrycloth robe, left arm locked across her waist.

She did not look good. That is, she looked ill. But even puffy-eyed and with hair uncombed, her small body concealed in the shapeless robe, feet bare, she stirred pleasant feelings in him.

"Good morning," he said, and tried a smile.

"Is it?" She walked over and took the plate from his hand, then carried it to the sink. "I'll get the coffee started in a minute. Do you want anything else?"

"How about if I make breakfast for you this morning?"

"I'm not hungry."

"Don't wash that plate, I'll do it."

"Don't bother. I'm used to cleaning up after a man."

"Nobody has to clean up after me," he said.

"I bet you like to think so, don't you?"

So, she was one of those people who could pass out from too much drink and the next morning remember everything that had transpired. He did not know if she was truly angry or if the anger was a cloak for embar-

170

rassment. He did not know what he would say in either case or how he might explain himself, but he stood to go to her because the first thing to do was to hold her. He had moved only two steps from his chair when the telephone rang.

"That's for me," he said. He turned his back to her and picked up the phone.

"The good news," Abbott told him, "is that yes, a musket was among the items stolen from the museum. A Pennsylvania long rifle in original flintlock condition. Made by one Joseph Honaker, Wythe County, Virginia, circa 1807. Valued at approximately $35,000."

"Bingo," said DeWalt. "But ... could such an item be made functional after 180 years in an interred condition?"

"She's standing there beside you, right?"

"More or less."

"When do you plan to tell her that her husband's a thief?"

"Could I refer you back to my previous question, please?"

"The item under discussion was not in an interred condition."

"How's that?"

"It wasn't one of the items that got dug up. It was donated by a private collector, on loan, actually, to round out the exhibit. But it was in mint condition, and could easily have been fired. Although to do so, and I quote the owner here, would be 'a crime of the utmost stupidity.' "

"Which implies the participation of an individual not particularly knowledgeable in these matters."

"You sound like a politician under indictment, you know that?"

"What else was taken?"

"Some buttons, brass insignia, powder bag, a handful

of musket balls—in total, the contents of one glass display case."

"What kind of security did they have?"

"Insufficient. One guard, who, when it suited his fancy, was also an unofficial tour guide. He wasn't even in the exhibit room at the time of the robbery. He was outside with some visitors, showing off his ramparts."

"This occurred during the daylight hours?"

"Between four-thirty and five in the afternoon, yep."

"Cameras and alarms?"

"Activated only at night."

"Can I assume that the security guard does not recall the presence of any suspicious-looking visitors at or about that time?"

"The ex-security guard. He's now a meter reader for the gas company. And no, he didn't see or hear a thing. Except for a certain pair of young women from Buffalo to whom he was extolling the superior design of his parapet."

"And that leaves us where?" asked DeWalt.

"We now know in all probability where the murder weapon originated. That's more than we knew yesterday. All we have to do now is to recover that weapon and match it to the ball we dug from the victim's brainpan. We also have reason to suspect that the robbery was perpetrated at the suggestion of, or under the direction of, the deceased. Did you talk to her yet?"

"I'll have to get back to you on that, give me an hour or so. How about the rock and roll connection?"

"The Kinetics arrived at the Theta Chi house at approximately 8 PM on the night of the robbery. All members present and accounted for. They started playing a half-hour later. Packed up and went home sometime after one."

"Could they have left the museum at, say, 4:35, and still arrive back here at eight?"

"Sure, if they were traveling by jet."

DeWalt heard his neat little premise collapse like a punctured balloon.

"Talk to your client, Ernie."

"I intend to. But I don't expect any revelations."

"At the very least he commissioned the job. You found proof of that yourself."

"I wouldn't exactly call it proof. Not yet."

"It's beginning to smell like proof though, isn't it? And as soon as you ask her to account for the money from the retirement fund, and I'll bet you a dollar to a doughnut she doesn't know a damn thing about it—"

"What's the chance of you getting access to the local bank records? Checking for deposits made in that approximate sum at that approximate time?"

"Approximately slim to none without a subpoena."

DeWalt could hear coffee gurgling through the coffee maker. Its aroma made his stomach feel hollow. He glanced over his shoulder at Elizabeth. She stood with both hands on the edge of the counter, leaning into it, staring blankly at the dripping coffee. But listening intently to every word he said; how could she not?

"Anyway," said DeWalt. "About an hour, okay? Will you still be there?"

"Just don't call with any more requests for information, all right? I don't like the impression that some people are getting around here. That I'm working for you."

"You're not working for me," said DeWalt. "I'm working for you." He realized then how this would sound to Elizabeth. "We're all working for the same thing, Larry."

"That's the plan anyway. But how about the next time, when you call, you give *me* the good news."

"The problem is, officer, we differ on the definition of good."

173

A few moments later he hung up the phone and turned to face her. "That was Trooper Abbott on the phone just now."

"And?" She stared at the coffee.

He pulled a chair away from the kitchen table and lowered himself into it. "Come sit down with me, all right?"

She faced him. "You think I can't take it standing up?"

"You just don't look comfortable there is all. You look tired."

"So what did the trooper have to say about me?"

"About you? Nothing. I thought maybe I had found a connection between Rodney Gillen and the murder weapon, but it didn't pan out the way I had hoped."

"Nothing ever does," she said. She crossed her arms and held herself tightly.

He waited, letting it build in her, letting her get herself ready.

The tendons in her neck tightened. "Did you think I wouldn't notice?" she asked then. "Did you think I was so drunk I wouldn't remember any of it? That's what you were hoping, wasn't it?"

"It wasn't meant to hurt you. Just the opposite, in fact."

"You couldn't bring yourself to make love to me . . . and I'm not supposed to be hurt by that?"

Quickly he thought of a half-dozen things to say, a half-dozen ready lies, off-roads, detours, switchbacks to lead her away from understanding. He dismissed them each in turn.

She said, "You weren't doing me any favors, you know. I might not be twenty-three years old but I'm not so desperate for attention that I have to go around asking men for favors."

"You're a beautiful woman," he said. "Age has nothing to do with it."

She softened just a bit. "Is it . . . are you gay, Ernie?"

He smiled. "Not since the carefree days of youth. And even then, not the way you mean."

Her eyes glistened. She was shivering. "Then why?" She was afraid of his answer but needed it. She steeled herself for it, told herself she was ready even though she knew she was not. "What happened last night was nice, it was very nice. But it wasn't what I needed, Ernie. I think you know that."

He looked down at his hand, fingers spread, foreign, unfamiliar. "Desire," he told her, "has never been so cruel to me," it sounded cold, phony, insincere, overpracticed, "as it was last night."

"Cruel? Why cruel? Because you couldn't *feel* any desire for me?"

"Because I felt so much. And still do."

Even though he wasn't looking at her, could not bring himself yet to meet her gaze, he felt her expression change. Anger and embarrassment melted into confusion. She sniffed back her tears. He heard the thickness in her throat as she swallowed. He felt the constriction.

It was this part of being human that he hated: one source of thoughts and feelings trying to convey its inarticulate truth to another source, which in turn must sieve this truth through the filter of its own thoughts and feelings, thereby warping, truncating, flensing the original. Two people live the same story under the exact same conditions and yet they end up with two different memories of it, two different understandings and two different stories to recount.

Yes, this is what it means to be human, DeWalt. To have a heart in conflict with itself and with every other heart. This is the original sin, to be made into a man or a woman, to be born into this occasional Hell, distanced, separated, evicted from heaven by your consciousness of self.

"I do want to talk about it with you," he told her. "I want to explain. But not now."

"Why not now?"

"Now's not the time."

Now she too smiled. "I'll understand," she said. "I can be a very understanding woman."

"You'll have to be." He looked down again. "Not now though."

The silence was not so heavy this time, not so dark. After a few moments she went to the cupboard, took out two cups, poured two cups of coffee. She set one close to his hand. "Are you sure I can't get you some breakfast?" she asked. "Or an early lunch?"

"I'm sure. But I would like to ask you a few questions, if that's all right."

She sat across from him.

"Your trip to Niagara Falls last July. What was the purpose of that?"

"Just a little getaway, I guess. A break in the routine."

"You, Alex, and the kids?"

"Yes. In fact, I guess the kids were the main reason we went. Alex thought it was high time they saw Niagara Falls."

"Had you been planning the trip for a long time?"

She shook her head. "Alex suggested it one night, and we left the next weekend."

"When did you leave? On a Saturday morning?"

"No, it was—" She stopped. Her eyes narrowed. "That son of a bitch. He said he had a couple hours of work to do in his office before we could go. So we didn't leave until after lunch."

"So when you got there—"

176

She interrupted. "He didn't want to miss a morning with her, that's what it was. That son of a bitch. That lying, duplicitous son of a bitch."

DeWalt said nothing. She deserved her anger. Anger is always superior to grief. Anger will often succumb to grief, or disintegrate into grief, but as long as it lasts anger should be coveted and protected. All those pinhead psychologists who claim that anger must be eschewed are in fact calling for the stagnation of human evolution. It is not love that makes the world go 'round, but anger.

He allowed her a minute to examine her anger, to find a place for it. Then he said, "So you arrived at Niagara Falls, what, around dinner time? And what did you do that night?"

"Checked into the hotel. Had dinner. Went out and looked at the Falls at night. That's about it."

"And was Alex with you and the kids all this time?"

She thought about it. "As far as I can remember, yes."

"And the next day?"

"Breakfast at the hotel. And then we did all the touristy stuff. Cave of the Winds, the observation deck, the trolley ride, Maid of the Mist ... everything, we did it all. It took four or five hours, I guess, altogether."

"Then lunch."

"Lunch, right. And then we took the ferry across the river to a museum Alex wanted to see."

"Fort Erie," said DeWalt.

She nodded. "It wasn't very interesting for the rest of us, but Alex was enthralled. The kids, in fact, were bored. In fact, as I recall, the kids and I spent most of our time outside. Skipping stones across the river, things like that. Waiting for Alex to come back out."

"How long was he inside?"

"I don't know, forty-five minutes maybe?"

"When you were inside with Alex, did you notice him speaking with anybody there? Or showing a particular interest in any one thing?"

"He was interested in everything. Remember, this was the War of 1812. The subject of his book. But no, I didn't see him talking to anybody. Who would he talk to? He took a lot of notes, of course, but he always did that. Took notes, made illustrations, things like that."

"And when he finished?"

"We got in the car and drove home. We stopped just south of Erie, I believe, at a fast food place. What's this all about, Ernie?"

"Less than a week after you visited the museum, it was robbed. One of the things stolen was a musket."

"You can't be serious."

"The newspaper clipping is among Alex's papers."

"No, I mean . . . you can't possibly believe that he had anything to do with it."

"What did he do with the money he withdrew from the retirement fund?" DeWalt asked.

He could tell by the look on her face that he had surprised her, Abbott was correct. From his shirt pocket he withdrew his calendar of events, unfolded it and flattened it on the tabletop.

"On April 7th he withdrew $2500," he said. "That was four days after the discovery of artifacts at Fort Erie. Then on July 10th, eleven days before the robbery of those artifacts and other items on display, he withdrew another $4500."

She took two slow breaths. "How do you know all this?"

"The withdrawal slips are in Alex's tax papers for this year. Do you know of any similar withdrawals he might have made last year? Or the year before?"

"He did the taxes himself. I have no idea."

DeWalt felt certain of what he would find when he examined those other papers. Alex had probably been making small withdrawals ever since his affair with Jeri Gillen began. How else to finance the affair without making Elizabeth suspicious? He had probably been a very generous man. His generosity was what had made him so attractive to Jeri and Rodney Gillen.

"What was the exact date of the robbery?" she asked.

"July 21st."

"What time?"

"Late afternoon. Between four-thirty and five."

She went quickly to the wall calendar beneath the telephone and flipped down the pages to July. In the block for the 21st was written, in her handwriting, *All-Stars, 6:00*.

She jabbed her finger against the calendar. "Here, you see? That was the day of the Little League All-Star game. Chris played left field. The game started at six, so we had dinner early, at about five. Then there was the game, then a weiner roast after. We were there all evening, Chris and Nikki and me and Alex. There's got to be at least a hundred people who can verify that."

"All right," said DeWalt. "Calm down." She could believe that her husband was an adulterer but not a thief. She could accept that he had been attracted to a lovely younger woman but to even suggest that he had ever done anything unwise or illegal was more than Elizabeth Catanzaro could tolerate.

DeWalt knew what would happen to her feelings for him, incipient and unevolved as they were, when, if, he proved her wrong. Still, there were things he needed to know.

"Anything on there for May 28th?" he asked.

She did not turn the pages. "That was our anniversary," she said.

"And you, what, went out for dinner?"

"And then a play at the community theater ... *The Gin Game*. It was the first time we'd actually celebrated an anniversary in, I don't know, five or six years. It was ... a lovely night." Now she looked at him. "Why, what happened that night? Was there a robbery in Texas or Florida or somewhere else you'd like to blame on him?"

"I'm working for you, Elizabeth, remember? I want what you want."

"It doesn't sound that way to me."

She was angry now and it made no sense to argue. He told her, "There was a disturbance near the college that night. It involved Rodney Gillen and his band. But never mind, I'm sure it's unrelated."

"I'm sure," she said.

So then, Alex had not been responsible for the firebombing. Not unless he had hired somebody to do that too. However, with no connection between the Kinetics and the Fort Erie robbery, Alex had no apparent motive for the firebombing. Still, it was interesting to DeWalt that Alex should have such unimpeachable alibis for both events. To a cynical man, it might even appear as something less than coincidence.

He returned the slip of paper to his pocket. He stood and smiled gently. "I'm going to have to leave now."

She only nodded. She did not inquire as to his possible return.

"I'll call you if anything should come up," he said.

"Fine."

"Do me a favor though. Think back, and try to remember what that $7000 might have been used for."

Her body tightened, went rigid as if in defense, as if she were about to turn and castigate him for his implication. But then it sagged; just enough to tell him that she had no idea where the money had gone. He left her staring at the wall.

Chapter Thirteen

Sometimes a man sinks so close to Hell that he can feel the devil's breath on the soles of his feet. And if the man has been cold for a long time, this sardonic warmth is inviting. A man who will allow himself to be seduced by this warmth is the kind of man who will stroll into a crowded shopping mall and, pirouetting slowly, not without some macabre turn of grace, will rain hot astonishment from an AK-47.

But you, DeWalt, you are not that kind of man, are you? You are beyond seduction. Immune.

I would try to be more discriminating perhaps. To get some good out of my time in Hell.

How so?

I would stroll not into a shopping mall but into a crack house or down a certain street corner or if I were back in Chicago into any one of a number of ethnic restaurants.

Of course one can not always be as discriminating as one desires. One has to accept that errors will be made. Errors, after all, are what have cast you in this drama.

Miscast, thought DeWalt. He started his car and, backing away from the Catanzaro house, glanced at himself in the rearview mirror. His eyes were no longer bright; not eager or alert; not even terribly interested. He did not recognize those eyes. I'm too young to be this old, he thought.

Even the car seemed sluggish, as if it too wanted to give up, quit, stop spinning its wheels for no reward. With his foot barely touching the accelerator he coasted down the driveway. He felt empty. Beyond recourse or reconciliation.

It was through the heart of this dark mood that a shadow of hope scurried past.

There are moments in life when out of the blue a connection is made. Unbidden and unexpected it is, a gift for no occasion, a surprise, many times undeserved. Henry James (or had it been James Joyce? Jesse James? Joyce Brothers?) called these moments epiphanies: a glimpse, a scent, a lost memory recaptured, a delicate kiss from the lips of truth. Writers are fond of epiphanies, of any device that will add strength to structure, shoring up a leaning tower, stabilizing edifice with artifice. That is why there are far more epiphanies in fiction than in life: a writer lives and dies by artifice. In life, we live and die unaided.

Still, DeWalt, life is not without surprises. Maybe it is because we sometimes let our guard down; give up; turn our attention elsewhere. We cease creating ourselves in the third person, or in any person at all. We fall resigned into the chair of forgetfulness. And that is when the thing ignored springs out: *Remember me?* But fuller, fleshier, in better light than we have ever seen it before.

This is how it happens: You are in your car, DeWalt, alone, driving lethargic and truculent down a long driveway, your foot hardly nudging the accelerator because you do not want to come too soon to the highway, where you will have to decide which way to go. Behind you is a farmhouse and a woman alone with a grief you cannot touch. It is morning, not yet noon, the sky as blue as a gas flame. Everything is August clear, everything except your thoughts, too cold and murky and weed-choked to plumb. So instead you wind down the window and drink a breath of summer. You hold it upon your tongue until it melts. You smell the hemlocks to your left, the needle-matted damp shade beneath them. The sun is high on your right, shining down broken through the oaks and chokecherries, shattered but as bright as a mirror. The air is hemlock sweet and country quiet and its beauty fills you with an unspeakable sadness.

You sit, DeWalt, at the end of the driveway. The day lies ahead, too long, it runs east and west, it waits, it requires your decision. You hold your foot on the brake. There is a song in your ear like the plucking of a single guitar string, a staccato metal sound, tight, repeating. You feel that your head is going to burst. The glare of the windshield stings your tired eyes.

Then up from the grass across the road flies a small bird, a yellow finch, a tiny burst of fluttering color. You nearly gasp out loud, DeWalt. The bird rises, dips, disappears again under cover of deep grass. It has nothing to do with anything; a moment in nature. It was not for you or about you; you are an anomaly to the moment, an accident.

But DeWalt, notice this: you have smelled the cat. More precisely, the remembered smell, a moldy, almost chemical odor—you place it precisely now—a cat's litter box. The odor you smelled in the Gillen's apartment and then again in Craig Fox's room. Why the other cat, the head in the kitchen sink, did not trigger this recognition, you do not know. Too many other concerns, perhaps. Revulsion. Compassion. You were trying too hard to know.

But all right. Here it is at last. Now you have something. You lift your foot from the brake. You pull out onto the highway, you wheel around hard to the left, you drive so fast that your tires squeal.

* * *

DeWalt had not been to his office on campus for several weeks now. The hallway seemed dim, most of the classrooms dark. A few students lingered near the water fountain; he nodded but turned quickly so as not to have to speak. In a few weeks this building would be so dense with highstrung bodies that he would find it difficult to walk to the faculty lounge for coffee without being drawn into a conversation of depressingly earnest young English majors, arguments he would be called upon to arbitrate: Post-modern neo-dadaism is, is it not, the only valid choice for a contemporary writer? Don't you agree that, pedagogically speaking, deconstructionalism is the hope and the way and the light of the world? By what ratio, do you think, should left-branching modifiers predominate right-branching modifiers in any piece of serious fiction?

Such confrontations were never easy for DeWalt. Fortunately he escaped unscathed today. He slipped into his office, turned on the light and locked the door. Seated at his desk, he dialed the extension for the registrar's office. A work study student answered.

"This is Professor DeWalt in the English Department," he said. "I need the class schedule for a student named Craig Fox, please."

"Greg Fox, okay sir. Do you want a copy of the schedule sent to your office?"

"It's Craig Fox, with a C. *Craig.* And no, just give it to me now. I'll wait while you punch it up. Just don't put me on hold."

Five minutes later he was climbing into his car again. Another seven minutes, 11:40 AM, and he was seated in a booth at the Colony Restaurant. A waitress he had never seen before, a sallow-faced brunette with a pit bull's underbite, poured his coffee, her eyes on his filling cup as if she were watching a toilet flush.

185

"Is Della working today?" he asked.

"This isn't her table though."

"If she's here could you tell her I'd like to speak with her, please?"

She walked away scowling. Half a minute later Della emerged from the kitchen. The scowler lingered nearby as Della approached his booth.

"Hi, Ernie! Ready to fly away with me on that lover's weekend to Hawaii?"

"I'm wearing my bikini trunks this very minute," he said.

She plopped down across from him, leaned close and whispered, "Look at her, she's not even pretending not to listen. What a weasel."

The other waitress blinked. When Della turned to look at her, she finally slithered away. Della flashed DeWalt a satisfied grin. "Now then, handsome. What can I do for you today?"

"Did Jeri have a cat?" he asked. "A kitten?"

"Yeah, she did. Why?"

"What color was it?"

"It was one of those, you know, what's it called when they're sort of reddish brown and white all mixed up?"

"Calico."

"There, you see, that's why you're a writer. So anyway, what about this cat?"

"I'm afraid I can't tell you anything else just yet."

"Ahh come on, that's not fair."

"Maybe next time I see you, okay?" He pulled a handful of coins from his pocket, sorted out three quarters and laid them on the table. Della, as he stood, scooped up one quarter and slipped it into his pocket. "Don't you dare tip her," she said, not at all softly. "We're trying to get her to quit."

Craig Fox's final class of the morning, the Laws of International Banking, ran from ten o'clock to twelve-

186

thirty. From an empty classroom on the second floor of Burney Hall, the Psychology building, DeWalt watched the main entrance of Collier Hall. Class ended a few minutes early, as it did most every class during summer session, and at 12:19 Craig Fox emerged.

Dressed in yellow seersucker walking shorts and a powder blue Polo shirt, Fox looked as slick as a full-page ad from the Spring issue of *GQ*. Strolling beside him was a very attractive young lady, bare legs and a flowered skirt, casual chic. They walked in no hurry up the sloping sidewalk, toward the cafeteria. Fox appeared to be doing all the talking.

Once Fox and the girl were well past, DeWalt came outside and followed them uphill. The cafeteria was crowded and noisy. Ten minutes passed before Fox and his companion reached the food counters. Then, still chattering to the girl, Fox set upon building a sandwich of cold cuts, meticulously layering slices of turkey breast between alternating layers of lettuce and tomato and cucumber.

DeWalt broke into line and stepped up behind him. Over Fox's right shoulder, he whispered, "Meeeow."

Fox turned, grinning, until he saw who was standing there. DeWalt's mouth held not a trace of smile. His eyes were hard and cold and they did not blink. Fox attempted to reform his own smile, but there was no confidence in it. "Good morning," he said. "I mean good afternoon, I guess."

"Not for cats it isn't."

Fox's smile fell apart. His head gave a little jerk, an involuntary twitch. He turned to face the counter again. DeWalt continued ahead of him down the line; he picked up an apple from the fruit tray, paid the cashier, and left the building.

On a street one block behind the Theta Chi lot, DeWalt parked his car. By watching between houses he

187

could keep an eye on all the cars in the lot. He knew that Fox would be moving cautiously now, trying to see in all directions at once, and he expected to wait much longer than he did. Not twenty minutes after DeWalt had left the cafeteria, Craig Fox emerged half-running out the back door of the fraternity house. He hopped into a shiny blue Nissan 4x4, that year's model, and sped away.

DeWalt remained several car lengths behind as he followed the student north out of town. It was unlikely that Fox knew what kind of automobile DeWalt owned, but DeWalt was taking no chances. He might be following him for a long time; Fox's family home was in Cleveland. DeWalt slipped a Rickie Lee Jones tape into the tape player. He unbuttoned his shirt, unwound the bag and tubing and tossed the bag onto the passenger side floor. So much for sterile fields. He was not due for another exchange quite yet but he might not have an opportunity later.

Rickie Lee's piccolo voice soon filled the automobile, impish and sexy, a sad little girl. DeWalt kept his eyes on the blue Nissan. The piano accompaniment tinkled like crystal, it played through the slender tube, it urged the dark weight of poison from his body. He had made the connection; he had broken through. He knew without knowing how he knew, without caring how he knew, that Craig Fox was leading him straight to Rodney Gillen. Maybe to Jeri Gillen too.

The feeling was returning to DeWalt's hands finally, hands warm with blood now, strong on the hard curve of the steering wheel. He would follow the Nissan all day and night if necessary; he had nowhere else to go.

By the time Rickie Lee began "My Funny Valentine," DeWalt had left the town far behind, was moving deep into green country now, into a quiet, uncultivated land. He hung the new bag of dialysate above the passenger window, where the sun could warm it as it emptied into him. He felt better now than he had felt in months. There were warm tears of gratitude in his eyes.

road, then followed the road for half a mile, but could
come further. Waves lapped at the end of the waves and
there your away world would fall.

Chapter
Fourteen

For nearly two hours DeWalt followed Craig
Fox north. The boxy blue profile of the 4x4 was easy to
track over the hillocks and gentle switchbacks of route
58. The two-lane highway cut through farmland and undeveloped countryside, past tiny hamlets built around
their churches—square stonewalled castles for the Cath-
olics, white clapboard cottages topped with groping
spires for the Methodists. DeWalt drove through state
game lands and a corner of the Allegheny National Forest, a part of the state he had always intended to explore
someday.

He was exploring it now, at nearly sixty miles an
hour. Fox was being careful: he drove as fast as possible but not fast enough to risk a patrolman's attention.
And he knew this road well, braking before blind turns,
accelerating through the curves.

Then DeWalt crested a long hill and saw laying before him a half-mile stretch of highway with no blue
4x4 in sight. He drove another eighth of a mile and
then noticed the entrance road to Honey Lake, the "private resort community" he had been reading about on
billboards for the past fifteen minutes, the 400-acre
manmade lake and shoreline community wherein "the
pleasures of boating, swimming, fishing, tennis and golf
on a picturesque 18-hole executive course await."

DeWalt made a left turn onto the macadam entrance

road, then followed the road for half a mile, but could go no further. Here the road was blocked by a gate similar to a cattle guard, a gate that Honey Lake residents could open by slipping a membership card into the scanner box. DeWalt had no membership card. He sat there and stared at the gate.

Craig Fox had either gone where the woodbine twineth—as DeWalt's Aunt Sara used to say—or he had driven beyond this gate. There was no other explanation for his disappearance. DeWalt felt confident that Rodney Gillen was in there too. Perhaps even Jeri Gillen; although this, for some reason, he doubted. In any case, he told himself, the smart thing would be to back up, DeWalt, drive to the nearest telephone and call in the state boys. But what if they arrived to find Fox sunning himself on an inflatable raft, all alone but for his ambitions? Things were already strained between Abbott and DeWalt; the trooper suspected DeWalt of misreading or ignoring certain facts, facts which clearly implicated Elizabeth Catanzaro. And hadn't DeWalt promised Abbott, almost three hours ago now, to telephone with an update of information gleaned from Elizabeth?

I've got to see him first, DeWalt thought. Then I can call up Abbott and tell him, "Larry, I saw Rodney Gillen, he's here and he's all yours, come and get him."

He backed away from the gate and parked his car along the side of the road. There was no fence blocking off the surrounding woods themselves, only numerous NO TRESPASSING signs, so DeWalt, on foot, set off through the trees on a path roughly parallel to the road. For ten minutes he ducked branches, brushed cobwebs from his face, and wended his way toward the lake.

When he came to the edge of the trees and could actually see the Honey Lake community, he was more than a little surprised. He had expected a few small cabins, a mobile home or two parked in the shade of a tree-sheltered lot: a semi-rustic setting, a kind of despoiled Walden Pond. But not this despoiled.

The lake was so crammed with small sailboats, row-boats, canoes, kayaks, inflatable rafts and inner tubes that an individual with a good sense of balance could hop from one craft to the other across the breadth of the lake, and never get his feet wet. On the far side was a tiny mall: a post office, laundromat, grocery and drug-store, a video arcade, a shop that rented boats and bicy-cles, a beauty salon, a community hall for bingo and dancing. Around the perimeter of the lake ran a smooth asphalt road, painted tennis court green. At the southern end of the lake, a picturesque arched footbridge tra-versed the exit stream. The lake road was not wide enough to accommodate automobile traffic except in the case of an emergency; travel here was restricted to transport by foot, bicycle, roller skates and, by all ap-pearances the most favored form of locomotion, by golf cart.

The "cottages" were all at least twice the size of DeWalt's house, each girdled by a sprawling wooden deck that seemed to overhang the entire lot. In front of the mall was a marina jammed with nonmotorized craft. Behind the mall, lots were terraced up the hillside. Hid-den somewhere amidst all this natural beauty were ten-nis courts and a golf course.

Jesus, thought DeWalt. What are you going to do now—go around knocking on doors? "Hi, sorry to dis-turb you, but are you harboring any criminals in there?"

He was trespassing. He had not registered for a tour and sales pitch and therefore would not be eligible for a free hibachi. And even if he could rent a bicycle or golf cart, it would take at least thirty minutes to walk around the lake to the mall and its rental shop, by which time he would have only enough strength left to collapse.

He was ready to say Fuck it. Go back to your car and call Abbott, don't be a fool. The hike through the woods had depleted his energies. His side ached, his chest ached, he was out of breath, sweaty and leg-weary. What was he trying to prove? He could feel the plastic bag sticking to his damp skin.

Then he thought of Elizabeth Catanzaro, of what she had endured, was enduring, stood yet to endure. She learns that her husband is having an affair—sucker punch, she falls to her knees. But she gets back up, decides to fight it out. Then her husband is murdered. She is implicated. She discovers the head of a kitten in her kitchen sink. She seduces the hired hand but isn't attractive enough, or so she believes, to give him an erection. He then suggests that her husband was not only an adulterer but a thief, a criminal. And still she remains standing, fists at the ready.

And here you are, DeWalt, feeling sorry for yourself because you're out of shape and short of breath. You make me sick.

He went out to the lake road, and with as much nonchalance as he could muster, he sauntered toward the mall. Every now and then he would take a quick glance over his shoulder, scanning the individual driveways for a glimpse of Fox's 4x4. Otherwise he kept his face to the lake.

During the first five minutes he was passed by a dozen or more golf carts, all occupied by couples or a solitary male. Finally one approached driven by a woman, the passenger seat empty. He turned and flagged her down.

"Out of gas?" she asked. She was in her sixties, a jowly pixie clad in a velvet jogging suit only slightly pinker than her hair, her face a crinkled chamois.

193

"In more ways than one," said DeWalt. "Listen, I'm new here, and I went out for a walk, and I seem to have lost my bearings. Could you point me in the direction of the Fox cottage, please?"

"I know a Wolfe but not any Foxes. What's the address?"

He grinned sheepishly. "I don't think I remember."

"Is it lakefront or wooded?"

He hoped his smile made him look charmingly stupid. "You'd think a person would remember something like that, wouldn't you?" In the cart's cup holder was a highball glass, empty but for a sliver of ice cube and a wedge of lime. "The truth is," he said, "there's not a lot about the last twenty-four hours that I do remember. Except that I'm staying at the Fox place, and that it's not wise to drink a quart of Chivas on an empty stomach."

She laughed brightly. "You just hop in here with me, honey. There's a directory over at the store. We'll get you home again, don't you worry."

By the time they reached the store she had driven off the edge of the road eight times, each time whipping the cart back on so forcefully that DeWalt's head jangled. During this tumultuous ride he learned that she was married to a radiologist, her third husband, that she had a handicap of fourteen, had recently acquired enough red points in bridge to qualify as a master, that her present mission was to secure a quart of Gilbey's, and that if she didn't get to a bathroom lickety-split she was going to raise Honey Lake another three inches.

She guessed that he was a doctor too. Probably a chiropractor. "Now how did you know that?" he asked.

"It's your hands. A man's hands don't lie."

He placed one on the back of her neck and squeezed the muscle. "I give good massage too," he said.

"Boy, could I ever use a good rubdown! Bucky, he's

my husband, he rubs me too but it's always the wrong way."

"If you use warm coconut oil, there is no wrong way." DeWalt squeezed her neck again, which sent the golf cart veering off the road.

"Whoops," she said. "You're going to be a lot of fun, I can tell that already."

"Fun is my middle name."

"And what's your first name?"

"Richard," he said. "But please, call me Dick."

"Ooooh," she said, and squirmed on the seat. "If I didn't have to pee so bad I'd take you into the woods with me right this minute."

"First things first," he said.

Without slowing she veered sharply into the covered parking lot adjacent to the store, narrowly missing a row of golf carts. She then slammed on the brake, bringing them squealing to a halt, but not before they struck the store's cement block wall with sufficient force to send the cart rebounding a yard back.

"Whoopsie doo!" she said.

DeWalt tried to smile as he rubbed his knee.

"That's the directory right there in front of you, Dickie. I'm gonna pee and pick up some goodies. Don't you run away, you hear?"

"I don't think I can run," he said. "I don't think I can walk."

She laughed and slapped his kneecap. "That part of the body isn't important anyway. Both of mine are stainless steel!"

According to the resort directory, which was mounted on the store wall not two feet from DeWalt's face, three Foxes owned property in Honey Lake. There was James Paul Fox, Ireta Fox, and William C. Fox.

C. for Craig, he thought, and hoped. William C. Fox, #2 Raspberry Lane.

195

Ten minutes later, his driver had not yet returned. He flirted with the idea of stealing her cart—she had left the key in the ignition. Instead he went inside the store. He found her standing before the soft drinks, a bottle of Schwepp's Tonic Water in one hand, a bottle of Canada Dry tonic in the other, a quart of gin tucked under her arm.

"Isn't it strange?" she asked. "I've forgotten which brand of tonic Buck prefers."

"Why not get both? Whatever's left over we can take a shower with."

"Oh, Dickie," she said, "you're going to get me into a world of trouble, I can tell. And I do love trouble!"

Along the way to the checkout counter he plucked a pair of aviator glasses off a rack, then a Honey Lake baseball cap. He chose a bright yellow one—suitable for a chiropractor, he thought.

Out in the golf cart he donned the glasses and cap. "How do I look?"

"Good enough to eat. Where should I take the first bite?"

"Tell you what. Drive me home so that I can get cleaned up a bit, and we'll meet for a drink later on. It's number two Raspberry Lane."

"Raspberry! I'm on #9 Plum! How about that?"

"How about that?"

"Plum is the road right in front of yours! We're only seven cottages apart."

"I'm a lucky man," he told her. "Always have been."

"I think I'm the one who's gonna get lucky." She backed out of the parking space so abruptly that his head snapped forward and the sunglasses popped into his lap. She laughed and shifted into forward. Speeding away she said, "I give a hell of a ride, don't I?"

He put the sunglasses on. "I'll ask Buck when I see him."

196

"You do that, Dickiepoo."

He braced himself and held on tight.

It never failed to amaze DeWalt how easily some people revealed themselves to strangers. Maybe in this case it was the gin and tonic, but he doubted it. He guessed she would be just as voluble sober. Some people use talk—and drink and sex—as a kind of lifeline to wrap themselves around other people, to rope them together, to create an illusion of unity. DeWalt had never been able to do that. For him, dialogue was a shield. Even in the days when he had been a fairly heavy drinker, alcohol had not allowed him to open up, to extend his grasp beyond that enclosing awareness of self.

He imagined it must be nice. A warm and comforting place. And addictive. Which was why so many people so gladly engaged in the loquacious kind of silliness this woman did. It was why they prattled on insensibly, lewdly, suggestively, harmlessly, intelligently, didactically, idly, desultorily, drunkenly, soberly, desperately—for the contact; the reassurance; the illusion.

"There's the gang!" she said. She shouted. "Beep! Beep!" and pretended to blow a nonexistent horn. The five people standing on the deck of #9 Plum returned her wave.

"Nuts," she said to DeWalt. "I was hoping we could slip past unnoticed. Then we could sneak over to your place for that rubdown you promised."

"Anyway," he said, and patted her leg, "we'll always have Paris."

She turned left at the next intersection. At the junction with Raspberry Lane he asked her to stop. "But that's only number seven, honey. We've got a ways to go yet."

He was out of the cart before it stopped moving. "I need to stretch my legs again. Poor circulation."

"Barbecue tonight at #7 Plum. BYOB. Five-ish. You play bridge?"

"Badly."

"How about Battleship?"

He could tell by the twinkle in her eye that she was setting him up. "That's a kid's game, isn't it?"

"Not the way I play it. In my version, you get into the hot tub, and I blow you out of the water."

"I'll bring my life preserver," he told her. "You're dangerous."

He sent her away laughing and that pleased him. He hadn't sent a woman away satisfied for quite some time. Flattery was so easy and so salubrious; he had learned its benefits from a black Georgian lady in Chicago, a thin almond-eyed gracious woman who flattered him, barely more than a boy, for a week and two days. Then, unable to stomach the city's rudeness any longer, she returned to Atlanta. But in that short time she taught him what balm kind words can be, what a salve to cool the friction burns of too much humanity scraping against each other.

There were not many kind words spoken these days, it seemed. Comedians made fortunes by slinging insults. Politicians blackened one another with dirty epithets. Newspapers thrived on the shit of slander. Court dockets bulged with libel suits. When, DeWalt wondered, had we become this country of denigrators?

Save that puzzle for tomorrow, he told himself then. You've got other business to attend to now. He pulled the bill of his cap low over his sunglasses, stuck his hands in his pockets, affected what he hoped was a casual chiropractic posture, and ambled down Raspberry Lane.

Very slowly he walked, counting the cottages that lay ahead. He saw it then, #2, the flat-roofed saltbox, the next-to-the last cottage on the road. On the roof deck were two figures: Fox at the forward railing, gazing across the lake, turning occasionally to speak over his shoulder. Behind him, seated on a lawn chair, hunched forward, elbows on his knees, was another man, an individual DeWalt had never seen before.

Gillen, he thought. Okay, you saw him. He's here. Now get your ass back to the store and call Abbott.

But he had not actually seen Gillen. Not close enough to match his face with the face in the photograph Abbott had shown him. What if DeWalt called in the cavalry? Would they come charging over the hill with sirens trumpeting and banners waving, only to have a hundred aging and inebriated vacationers mistake the police sirens for ambulance sirens, clutch their hearts and wonder which of them was checking out this time? No; the police would arrive without fanfare. First an unmarked car. Then a backup. Seal off all exits. Stroll in and make the arrest.

Still, what if all this transpired, and the second man on the terrace turned out to be Fox's brother? or father? or lover? or some other hapless innocent?

Get a closer look, DeWalt. What have you really seen? You've seen nothing. Forget about that tremor in your hands, those quivering knees. Forget about being unarmed and defenseless against two strong young men. Don't worry about getting shot in the gut again, there's nothing left in there to be hurt. So get along, little doggie, get along.

He crossed uphill between cottages #7 and #6, then followed along the edge of the woods parallel to Raspberry Lane. Both men now had their backs to him. He stayed in the woods until he was directly behind the Fox cottage. Now he could see that the second individual was slightly built, had a thin muscular body, long dark hair pulled into a ponytail. Not William C. Fox, in any case.

It's Gillen, he told himself. You know damn well it's Gillen. So go on, turn around, you're closer to your car now, go to it. Your safe little air-conditioned stereophonic womb. Come on, man, retreat. Retreat, you fucking coward. You gutshot chicken. You overweight snoop.

Briskly he walked down the grassy incline to the rear of the cottage, trying not to move too fast lest he lose his footing, fall and roll like a battered garbage can to bang into the wall. But he managed to get there standing up. At the rear corner he hunkered against the wall and tried to steady his breath. He waited, he listened. There had been no sudden movements above, nobody running to see who it was down there wheezing and gasping for air.

He could hear their voices as if from the clouds, the alternating hum of words as one man spoke and then the other, a sonorant drone of conversation distinguishable only by its tone of argument. An occasional obscenity, a vehement "No!" They were not discussing whether to barbecue steaks or chicken for dinner; of that, and little else, DeWalt was certain.

Gingerly he crept along the side wall, pausing every few seconds to glance up at the roof edge, to hold his breath, to listen. Then he continued on, one foot softly in front of the other. Steady, boy, steady as she goes.

"Who the fuck . . . ," DeWalt heard, and suddenly froze, his heart wild with adrenalin. In a glance he calculated that he could never outrace the boys to the woods, and so decided to head for the lake instead, the safety of conspicuity. He waited, poised, ready to run, hoping they would not attack from both sides at once.

But neither boy appeared. Above him, the staccato buzz of disagreement continued. DeWalt allowed his

200

heart another fifteen seconds to either fibrillate or slow, and then, finding himself still erect, still functional, he inched forward again, his shoulder to the wall.

The front screen door was closed, the wooden door standing open. Fortunately the front porch was a slab of concrete; no boards to creak beneath DeWalt's clumsy weight. He felt as graceful as a hippo as he moved to the door, as he gently squeezed the latch, eased the door open.

Inside, the floor was of bare polished hardwood, here and there an Oriental rug. Knotty pine paneling. Pine beams and textured plastered ceiling. A huge fieldstone fireplace. Stark Scandinavian furniture. A kitchen twice the size of DeWalt's.

There were two bedrooms on the ground floor. In the larger of the two, the one with a private bath, the bed was unmade, striped sheets twisted and hanging to the floor. The bathroom light was on, the window in the shower stall open, as was the shower door. Through this window he could hear the voices from above, amplified but still garbled as they echoed over the bathroom tiles.

On the nightstand beside the bed lay a .22 revolver. DeWalt stared at it a long time. He knew he should pick it up. Unload it. Pocket the shells. It was just a pipsqueak of a gun, but such an ugly thing. He knew it would be cold to the touch. He knew how it would smell; taste. Just looking at it caused a shiver to race up his spine.

The nightstand drawer was slightly open; he opened it the rest of the way. Inside was a bag of grass, matches and papers. Another bag, smaller, of coke. A razor blade and small silver tray. A packet of photos.

With the photographs in hand he returned to the bathroom. The light was better there and he thought that with an ear to the window he might be able to hear if Fox or Gillen came down off the roof deck. The photos

201

were from two different batches but mixed together, one group duplicates of the ones Elizabeth Catanzaro had shown him, the others shot with an Instamatic instead of with Alex's 35mm Olympia, shot indoors, either here in this cottage or in the Gillen's apartment. The subjects were Craig Fox and Jeri Gillen. The theme did not vary; only the postures changed. In three of the photos a small calico cat could be seen. The photographer, DeWalt guessed, had been Rodney Gillen.

Minutes later DeWalt realized that he had been paying too much attention to the photographs. He leaned into the shower, put his head close to the shower window, heard nothing. At that moment the screen door banged open. Gillen was already on his way into the bedroom. As he strode in briskly, angrily, DeWalt flattened himself in the bathroom's forward corner, the cold edge of the lavatory jutting into his side. He hoped the toes of his shoes did not extend beyond the doorframe. From his perspective, looking down, it seemed that they did. But his heels were tight to the wall, he dared not move.

Gillen sat heavily on the edge of the bed. DeWalt could not chance a peek around the doorframe and so had no idea which way the boy faced. In DeWalt's hand was the packet of photos. He tried to remember if he had reclosed the nightstand drawer. Was Gillen looking at it even now, wondering how it had come to be open? Had he glanced inside the drawer, noticed the photographs missing?

Now Fox entered through the front door. DeWalt paid particular attention to the footsteps; over carpet, bare hardwood, over kitchen tile. The refrigerator door popped open. From the kitchen Fox called out, "I'll get you some food to take. You hurry up and pack."

"I'm not leaving here on my own!" Gillen said.

"I said I'd drive you, didn't I? Just hurry up and decide where you want to go. I need to be back on campus by nine in the morning."

To this Gillen mumbled, "I'm running for my life and you're worried about missing a fucking class." DeWalt heard this and knew that Fox had not; that the words were not meant for Fox, they were meant for Gillen himself, an encouragement, incitement, a justification for what he would do next.

There was a creak of mattress springs as Gillen leaned slightly forward. The click of the revolver barrel against the top of the nightstand as the gun was picked up.

Be clumsy, DeWalt prayed, and drop the gun. Give me two seconds. Or change your mind and lay it down again. Or decide to take a piss first; give me one clean shot at your chin.

From Gillen came only silence, a terrible lack of sound.

Fox sat down somewhere in the living room. "The sooner we get started," he called, "the sooner it's over with."

Gillen laughed softly. "I guess that's right."

Silently, DeWalt groaned.

Again the mattress squeaked. Gillen took a few steps forward, toward the living room. DeWalt, with his nose to the doorframe, leaned forward half an inch. Gillen was standing just back from the living room threshold, the revolver in his right hand, pressed behind his thigh. In his right hand was a pillow from the bed.

DeWalt knew two things: first, that real people toting a gun are always more frightened and uncertain of their actions than are movie/TV/paper people toting guns; and secondly, that their own fear precludes the realization of how terrified and probably foolhardy is the person who confronts them.

DeWalt laid the photos in the lavatory and reached

for the most convenient weapon, which turned out to be a thick-handled six-inch black comb.

You're out of your mind, DeWalt. Risking your life for a yuppie? Do the world a favor and let Gillen finish him off first. *Then* you can stroll out and comb him into submission, or whatever it is you plan to do.

He might think it's a gun, it's been known to happen. I've got the element of surprise on my side.

The only thing you have on your side, DeWalt, is the lack of a next-of-kin.

"Freeze!" DeWalt barked. Was it his imagination, or did he sound more like Nervous Mary than Dirty Harry? He stepped around the doorjamb, armed with his comb. "Don't move. Don't even blink."

Unfortunately, he had misjudged Gillen's position. When substituting the photos for the comb he had heard Gillen move another step and had assumed it was a forward movement. But Gillen had backed up. So that now, when DeWalt stepped through the bathroom doorway, he was directly parallel to Gillen. Gillen had only to look out the corner of his eyes to see DeWalt coming toward him.

Another thing DeWalt knew was that you should never give a frightened man sufficient time to become ashamed of his fear, and so he strode toward Gillen briskly and authoritatively. He was two arm's lengths from him when he realized another thing: don't give a man, frightened or otherwise, sufficient time to recognize that a haircomb is not a gun.

Gillen pointed the revolver at DeWalt's chest. "Who the fuck are you supposed to be?"

DeWalt was about to say, "Vidal Sassoon," but before he could speak he smelled old blood pooling on a Turkish carpet, he tasted metal and stale smoke. Suddenly heavy with resignation, punch-weary, tired beyond utterance, he said nothing at all.

Chapter
Fifteen

Fox bound DeWalt's hands with a couple of silk ties from the closet. "Man oh man," Fox moaned as he cinched the knots tight, "there goes my career, there goes my future, there goes—"

"Shut up," said Gillen.

"Sure, what do you have to lose? I'm the one who—"

"I said shut up, fuckhead! Sit down there on the bed and put your hands behind your back."

"What are you talking about?"

"You're the one who led him here, idiot! He followed you!"

"Well what do you think, I did it on purpose?"

"Just shut up, man. Don't say another word."

"If you think—"

Gillen stuck the pistol in Fox's ear. "I said shut up and I mean it, fucker! Just shut up or I'll blow your asshole head off!"

He was a very agitated young man. Trying to be decisive but with not the faintest idea of what to do. He fumbled for a moment with a yellow silk tie, attempting with one hand to bind Fox's hands behind his back; finally he laid the gun aside and quickly completed the task. Had Fox himself not been scared witless he could have spun around during those ten seconds when Gillen was unarmed and wrestled him for the gun, could have

205

taken the chance, quite possibly the only one he would be given.

You would have taken that chance, wouldn't you, DeWalt? Which is exactly why you were not given the opportunity. Because Fate knows a fool when it sees one.

"What are you doing this to *me* for?" Fox whined. "Man, I thought we were partners in this."

Gillen bound Fox's feet and did not answer.

"In case it escaped your notice," DeWalt said, "he was on the way into the living room to shoot you when I stopped him."

"Yeah, right," said Fox.

Gillen said, "It's true, asshole, I was. And I might still do it if you don't shut the hell up for awhile."

He left both men sitting on the bed, DeWalt at the foot of the bed and Fox on the side, and went into the living room. DeWalt could hear him moving around out there, nervously pacing, muttering, locking doors, drawing curtains, occasionally banging his fist against the wall, occasionally kicking a chair. It was not long before he returned for the bag of cocaine in the nightstand.

"Rodney," Fox began.

"Shut up! Don't talk to me now!" He grabbed the bag and left the room.

Two minutes later DeWalt heard him snorting the powder, sniffing up his courage. A dangerous time, thought DeWalt. The sudden rush of invulnerability. It could all end right now.

DeWalt's next few minutes contained enough regret to last a lifetime. He went outside on the sound of somebody's lawnmower purring, he went home to smell the hay he and his uncle had cut that morning, slender stalks of stiffened sunlight. He looked through the window of his boyhood home and saw his mother there dressed in black, head down on the kitchen table. He saw his mother in a wheelchair, she was wearing the new flannel nightgown he had sent her two Christmases ago, she was an emaciated scarecrow, eyes empty of memory, void of recognition, she sat staring at a beige wall in an antiseptic hallway, there is nothing in her head now but the ghost of a child, I thought I had a son didn't I, will somebody hold my hand?

DeWalt had never been so cold in his life. He wondered how his blood kept running. When he came back inside on the sound of Fox's whimpers, on the movement of the bed as it vibrated to the boy's sobs, he realized that several minutes had passed. Gillen's rush would be fading into the sunset now. His sense of omnipotence dragging a shadow of doubt.

The living room was quiet, as still as concrete. An occasional voice, a trill of laughter, skipped across the lake.

Fox asked, whispering in a voice stiff and husky with fear, "What do you think he's going to do to us?"

DeWalt was glad to hear that the yuppie had stopped worrying about his career. First things first. Stay alive; then think about promotion.

The door to the living room stood open. DeWalt could not see Gillen out there but suspected that he sat facing the door, probably on the leather chair twelve feet from the threshold, revolver in his hand.

DeWalt did not whisper. "That depends on how smart he is."

"What do you mean?"

"He'd be crazy to shoot us here. No matter how careful he is, he'll incriminate himself. Besides the blood splatter, and there's always a little bit of blood, no matter what. But besides that, he's all over this cottage already. Hairs, clothing fibers—those DNA boys can nail somebody on a single flake of dead skin. Whether he

207

knows it or not, he's already written his name all over this place."

After the rush comes doubt. Susceptibility. Paranoia. A mind is a terrible thing to waste.

"The only thing he has going for him is that the cops don't know he's here. They have no reason to comb the place for evidence unless he gives them a reason. But if he shoots us and leaves the bodies here, that's an open invitation to being identified. They'd nail him as the murderer in two seconds flat."

"All that means is that he'll probably shoot us and then take our bodies out and dump them somewhere."

"Even if he manages to lug our bodies out of here without being seen, or leaving some kind of trail, all of which is highly unlikely, he won't get far."

"How do you know that?"

"A couple of hours ago, when I was following you, I lost sight of you for awhile. So I pulled over and called the police, gave them the make, model and license number of your 4x4. Ten minutes after that vehicle leaves Honey Lake, it's going to be surrounded by blue-and-whites."

"What if he takes your car instead?"

"That's why I lost you, it broke down about three miles from here. What's the name of that little town a couple of miles up the road?"

"Pigeonola?"

DeWalt nodded. "That's where I called the police from. Then I happened to go into this convenience store where I saw a stack of advertising brochures for Honey Lake. Seemed like the kind of place I might find a guy like you. So I hitched a ride. And here we are. Your folks use this place much?"

"So maybe you'd better tell him that, don't you think? I mean how's he going to know about my truck unless you tell him?"

"You think he'll believe anything I tell him? It'll sound like I made it up just to keep him from shooting us."

Fox's voice rose in pitch. "What choice do we have? Just let him go ahead and kill us?"

"If it's any consolation, Craig, I guarantee he won't get away with it. We can look down from Heaven and watch him sizzling in the chair. Or at least I'll look down from Heaven. You might have to apply for a travel visa."

"I don't *want* to look down from Heaven, man. I mean fuck that; if you don't tell him about my truck, I will!"

"Relax, he's not going to shoot us here. He'd be stupid to shoot us at all. Powder burns, the noise, it's a very messy business, believe me. At best, he'll be looking at thirty years in a six by ten room, where the only forms of entertainment are buttfucking and giving blowjobs to big sweaty men with tattoos on their lips."

Fox's eyes grew visibly wider. He shivered. DeWalt almost laughed out loud.

"So what's he going to do?" Fox asked.

"He's got three valid options here. The first one is to give himself up."

"Yeah, like he's really going to do that."

"I agree. It's the smartest choice, but I don't think he's smart enough to make it. His second choice is to leave us tied up and to try to get away on foot. Fill a bag with goodies from the cupboard, and take a hike. That's what I'd do if I were in his shoes."

"Not me, man. There's bears in these woods. Plus, if the cops are looking for my truck, they're going to be looking for him too, right? I mean they've already got an APB or whatever it's called out on him. How far's he going to get at three miles an hour?"

Thank you for your assistance, dimwit.

"His only other option is the lake."

"How's that?"

"Your folks keep a boat at the dock?"

"A sailboat, yeah. A twenty-six footer."

"What I would do, then, if I were in his place, is to do nothing until nightfall. Then I'd deck myself out in some nice respectable clothes there from the closet, and I'd march you and me down to the dock, and I'd make you sail that thing—you do know how to sail it, don't you?"

"Of course I do."

"So I'd make you and me sail him uplake to the opposite shore. Are there any towns up at that end?"

"Chelton."

"How big is it?"

"Not very. Eight or nine thousand, I guess."

"But big enough to have a car rental agency."

"I doubt it."

Help me out here, nimrod! "A bus station then. Every town's got a bus station."

"I don't know, I guess so."

"So we sail him up there, he takes all our money plus your identification, he gets on a bus, and he has breakfast in Toronto. Lots of coke, lots of music—it would be a good city for a guy like him to get lost in."

"So ... do you think he knows all that, though? I mean, do you think he's thought about that as a possibility?"

"I hope not."

"Why?"

"Because the cops couldn't touch him in Toronto. He walks across the border and he's free. No extradition." Don't contradict me now, kid, unless you're in the market for a headbutt. "It's the safest place in the world for him, and it's only a couple of hours away."

Fox was silent for a minute. So too was the living

210

room. DeWalt could almost see Gillen leaning forward to listen, considering it, finding hope, a rescue, salvation stolen from the enemy.

"But what's he going to do with *us*?" Fox asked. "I mean he can't just leave us there on shore, can he? So what's he going to do? He's going to fucking shoot us and dump us in the lake, that's what. So we sink into the mud for a couple of days, and by the time we swell up and bob to the surface, he's partying in Canada. Great, that sounds great, man. Well I'm not going to do it. I won't. I won't sail him anywhere. No way."

"Fine, don't. I know how to sail. Consider yourself expendable."

At that, Fox began to sob again. It continued for a long time and DeWalt was almost moved to comfort him. Then Gillen appeared on the threshold. He looked in at them, he smiled. The revolver was tucked into his belt now. He went into the bathroom, urinated, came back out zipping up his jeans, relieved. On his return to the living room he pulled shut the bedroom door.

DeWalt lay back on the bed and inched his way up to the pillow. He lay on his side, his back to Fox. There were lots of pleasant sounds outside he could listen to, to drown out Fox's sticky warble of grief. He tried to get some rest.

The afternoon is long but it is as timeless as a dream. Aromas of meat-laden barbecue grills filter into the room, the dinner hour, highballs and blackened steaks, the sweet numb optimism of leisurely intoxication. Over on #9 Plum, Bucky the radiologist and his perky wife and friends are probably moving into the pink nether regions of alcohol by now, the slur-heavy magnet of gin sweeping up the metal filings of their day.

DeWalt is heavy too but with another kind of poison. This is a natural poison, indigenous, endemic, and as it

211

filters into his bloodstream his lethargy will increase. He will become so heavy with surrender that no hope can escape, a human black hole, he will collapse into his own despair.

In actuality there is no great harm in missing a bag exchange or two, no real physical danger for a while. But he is connected psychologically as well as physically to the bag; he is bound to the routine, it is his solace as well as his torture, his asylum as well as his prison.

Gillen brings them both a sandwich. One at a time he unties their hands, sits across the room on a straightback chair, gun in hand, watches them eat. Fox eats first, he nibbles, no appetite, he mourns for a world that can be so easily circumvented by inferiors.

Good sandwich, DeWalt thinks. "You make a good sandwich, Rodney." Grainy brown pub mustard, lettuce, swiss cheese, a thick pile of chipped Virginia baked ham. Very generous executioner we have here.

But soon the sandwich is gone, a lingering taste of mustard. Gillen tells him to lie flat on the bed, face down, hands behind the back so that they can be retied.

"There's something I need to do in the bathroom, Rodney."

"You've got two minutes. Leave the door open."

"I can't do it in two minutes. It takes twenty."

Gillen laughs. "Yeah, right."

"I can do it here if you prefer. It doesn't matter."

"Do what? What are you talking about?"

"I'm going to lift my shirt to show you something. I'll use my left hand. Don't get nervous."

The clear plastic bag and the length of thin tubing. The pink scars. Gillen flinches, looks away. He looks again. "What the fuck is that, man?"

"My kidneys don't work, Rodney. This is how I get

212

rid of the waste fluids in my body. It drains into this bag. I have to do it four times a day."

"I don't want to watch something like that."

"That's why I suggested I go into the bathroom."

"What if I don't let you do it?"

"At first, nothing. I get very tired. Then weak. Sick. It's a relatively gradual process."

"How gradual?"

"I'd really rather not find out, Rodney."

"Maybe I ought to let you find out. Leave you here tied up while him and me go for a boat ride."

"Craig is a fine young man, Rodney, but do you really want to trust your life to him? He's been weeping now for what, three hours? Weepers, I'm afraid, aren't terribly reliable in a pinch."

At this, Fox puffs up indignantly. With a quivering voice, he says, "I'd be just as reliable as you."

"Of course you would, Craig. You've proven that already, haven't you? Anyway, Rodney, is that your plan then? You're going to escape by water?"

"None of your business. I'll tell you when you need to know."

"Any chance I could talk you into leaving both of us here, tied up of course, while you sail away?"

"He can't sail," Fox says. "He can't even swim!"

"Shut up, asshole! If I only need one of you, it's not going to be you."

"It's my boat! He doesn't even know which slip it's in!"

"Could we get back to the matter at hand, Rodney? I'd really like to dialysize myself now, if you don't mind."

Rodney has a glance at the bathroom window. Too small for a man to climb through. He cranks the louvres shut, closes the shower stall. "Leave the door open," he says.

DeWalt goes inside and sits on the toilet seat lid. He unwinds the tube and bag, lays the bag in the sink, makes it appear that something is happening. But nothing is happening, for Dewalt has no full bag of dialysate with which to complete the exchange. It is a charade, nothing more. A chance to think with hands untied; a chance, perhaps, to act. These are sad times for a tired old man, he thinks. These are sad, sad times.

There is a smell of marijuana smoke, sweet familiar gray. Get mellow, Rodney. Mellow out, man, we've got a ways to go yet, you and me. We've got some hours to kill yet in this sad sweet timeless time.

DeWalt sits there on the toilet lid, enjoying the smell of Rodney's high. The smoke scent helps him to put the stories together, the three voices, Fox's, Gillen's, Elizabeth Catanzaro's. The three stories become one. He knows what Abbott will say later, if there is a later, if DeWalt can make one: the dovetail joints are too neat, DeWalt, the seams too flush. Truth is never as smooth as a handpolished lie.

And yet, DeWalt is inclined to believe.

Fox's version had been garnered easily, all but volunteered by the blubbering boy as, hours earlier, he and DeWalt lay side by side on the bed. Then came Gillen's version, not conspicuously dissimilar but delivered with less alacrity, coaxed from him word by word not more than an hour ago after DeWalt had hopped comically into the living room and requested something to eat, and then in the kitchen, sandwiches being made, where he had assumed the role of hand-tied buddy, empathetic prisoner, victim-to-victim, and had found Gillen wonderfully voluble in the end, an eager confessor of sins, made garrulous by fear.

DeWalt had all three stories now, Elizabeth's too. Three glass balls to juggle in the air.

"What time was it when you called Craig, Rodney?

214

On that Saturday morning when Dr. Catanzaro was killed."

"I don't know exactly. I'd been sleeping, and the phone woke me up. I kept waiting for it to stop ringing, for, you know, for Jeri to pick it up. It seemed to ring forever. So I got up and answered it, and I talked to her, his wife, though it was more like listened really, for two minutes at the most."

"She did all the talking?"

"All I remember saying is hello."

"What exactly did you say, Elizabeth, when you called Rodney Gillen?"

"I said, 'I just thought you had the right to know what they've been up to. What they're up to right this very minute.' "

"She said, 'I think somebody should do something about them, don't you?' Something like that."

"What time was it when Rodney called you, Craig?"

"It was exactly twenty-three minutes till twelve. I've got a digital clock right beside my phone."

"And after Elizabeth called you, Rodney, after you had hung up, what then?"

"I guess I just sat there at the kitchen table awhile. Until I came up with the idea of calling Craig."

"Hey, Rodney, what's up? This is kind of early for you, isn't it?"

"I just got a weird phone call, man."

"Weird how? Was it another threat?"

"What kind of threat, Craig? What was said?"

"Around the first of the year Rodney started getting these phone calls whenever Jeri was at work. Told him he better quit dealing, or else."

"Did he know who was making the calls?"

"He assumed it was Dr. Catanzaro."

"Why would he assume that?"

"Because Jeri had made the dumb-ass mistake once

of trying to get the old fart to do some coke with her. And the guy threw a fit. Said he didn't want anything to do with her if she was going to fool around with that stuff."

"And?"

"And of course she swore she'd quit. You know, he was more important than getting high, blah blah blah, all that garbage. But I guess he didn't trust her because he went through her purse a couple of times, found her stuff. He'd explode, and she'd start crying and pleading with him, asking for his help, saying how hard it was to quit because the stuff was around all the time. . . ."

"Did she love him?"

"He loved her. Claimed to anyway. Treated her like gold. And she didn't get a lot of that from Rodney, needless to say."

"Did she get much of that from you, Craig?"

"She got what she wanted, I guess."

"Tell me something, Rodney. What kind of relationship did she have with Craig?"

"The only person Craig Fox loves is Craig Fox. He loved getting head and she loved giving it, that's all I know."

"And as for you, you didn't mind watching it?"

"Cheaper than a VCR."

"So did Jeri really quit using coke or not?"

"Not. In a way it was kind of pathetic. There she was fucking Dr. Catanzaro every Saturday morning, then later that same day she'd get high with Rodney and tell him all about it."

"She'd come home and tell me about it. I didn't care."

"You liked hearing it."

"So what if I did? Anyway, I don't know, she probably told him that I was forcing the coke on her, something like that. He seemed to think that if he could scare me . . . like there was only one place in town to get the stuff, you know? The asshole never even realized that he was buying the stuff for us."

"How's that?"

"All she had to do was to start crying the blues about never having any money. Cause I was blowing it all on coke or grass, stuff like that. Or that she needed a new coat, or new shoes, or new anything she wanted. Fuck, the guy was like a second income, you know? And all Jeri had to do was what she wanted to do anyway. What she was good at."

"Let's go back to the phone call a minute. When you called Craig, what exactly was said?"

"I told him I'd had a weird phone call and he asked if it was Alex calling to threaten me again. Ever since Alex firebombed our garage, Craig was paranoid that Alex was going to find out about him too."

"About how he was buying coke from you to sell on campus?"

"I don't sell coke, man. Never have. I wouldn't touch that stuff."

"It wasn't Alex who firebombed the garage, Rodney."

"Who was it then?"

"He was at a high school play that night. It couldn't have been him."

"Jesus, I just figured. . . . It wasn't always the same voice on the phone either, you know? But I just figured he was trying to disguise himself, you know?"

"What about your call to Craig?"

"So I say to Rodney, Weird how? And he says it wasn't Dr. Catanzaro this time, it was his wife. And I say, His wife? What the fuck did she call for?"

"Just to inform me that her husband and Jeri are parked down by the river fucking each other's eyes out."

217

"Holy shit. How'd she find out?"

"She knows where and everything, man. She knows the exact fucking location!"

"So what did you tell her?"

"I didn't say a damn word. What do you think I'd say—'Oh, yeah, I know all about it. Relax, it's cool'?"

"So what did you call me for?"

"Because she sounded pissed off enough to go and do something about it, that's why."

"What kind of something?"

"How do I know, man? What do women usually do when they catch their old man fucking somebody else?"

"Maybe all she needs is a good stiff one herself. You did offer, didn't you?"

"This is no joke, man. I mean what if she goes down there and *does* something? Who do you think she's going to go after, her fucking husband, or Jeri?"

"So what do you expect me to do about it?"

"Just go on down there before she does and scare them off. Jeri knows your truck. So just drive on in like you're going to go fishing or something, pull up close to the river like you don't even know they're there. If Jeri doesn't realize that something's up and gets them out of there, Alex'll see the college parking sticker on your bumper. Either way they're going to split, right?"

"So why don't you go?"

"Because he knows me, asshole. He hates my fucking guts."

"You afraid of him or what?"

"The guy threw a fucking gasoline bomb at me!"

"I don't know, Rodney. Did she just now find out about this? Did she say anything about—?"

"She was pissed, man. Fed up. I could hear it in her voice."

"The thing is, I've got a meeting with my advisor at one. . . ."

"So leave now and you'll be back in plenty of time."

"This doesn't have anything to do with me, Rodney."

"I got a bunch of pictures here with your bare ass in them that says it does."

"I still don't see—"

"If you want to keep getting what you get from Jeri, and you want to keep getting what you get from me, asshole, then you better do this for me. And I mean now."

"What did you find, Craig, when you got there?"

"I found that Dr. Catanzaro's wife had already come and gone. And that she was just as pissed as Rodney said she was."

"So you went back to Rodney and told him that Dr. Catanzaro had been murdered."

"So where the fuck is Jeri, man? Didn't you see her anywhere? Didn't you at least look for her or try to find her?"

"I never even got out of my truck, Rodney! The fucking professor's lying there with his head ripped open, you think I'm going to hang around?"

"Well we gotta go back right now! Jeri's probably still down there somewhere!"

"Jesus God, Rodney, use your head. She's gone, man. She's either dead too or maybe somehow she managed to get away. Either way, you'd better get lost and do it quick."

"Why should I get lost, I didn't do—"

"It's a setup, man! His wife calls you and tells you to go down there, right? Then she calls the police and tells them Hey, I just talked to Rodney Gillen and he threatened to kill my husband! It was just dumb luck the cops didn't show up while I was there."

"And what did Rodney do, how did he react, after you told him this?"

"He just stood there staring out the window. And

then he started crying. He was like, I don't know ... helpless. He said 'It's raining so hard now. She's going to be caught out there in the rain.' "

"So you hustled him away up here to the lake."

"He had to go somewhere."

"But why get yourself involved in it, Craig? Why not just let him fend for himself?"

"I guess I didn't think of it as getting myself involved."

"Did you think you were involved when you stuck the cat's head down Elizabeth Catanzaro's sink?"

"Cat's head? What cat's head?"

"How did Jeri get hold of his house key, Rodney?"

"He let her take the car one time to buy their lunch. He kept all of his keys on the same key-ring—car, house, whatever, a whole bunch of them. She had duplicates made of all of them."

"For what purpose?"

"Who knows? Maybe she was going to give them to him as a Christmas present."

"She and Rodney figured they'd rip him off royally someday. They knew he'd break up with her sooner or later."

"How'd you talk Craig into doing the thing with the cat's head, Rodney? You had a lot of leverage, of course. You had the photos of him and Jeri. You had a mutually beneficial business relationship. You had the threat of public exposure of all this. Which argument did you use to persuade him?"

"I appealed to him as a friend."

"You kept the kitten in your room at the fraternity house, didn't you, Craig? Just for a day or so, but long enough. I smelled the litter box. It was your idea what to do with it, wasn't it?"

"I finally convinced Rodney that Jeri wasn't going to be found alive. I mean, any woman who can blast her old man's brain away isn't going to be gentle with her old man's girlfriend, right? So, once he accepted that, we started thinking about some way to get the police off his ass. But it was Rodney who came up with this plan for a kind of campaign of terror. The first step was the cat's head."

"You thought that if you kept the pressure on Elizabeth Catanzaro, maybe made her believe her own life was in danger, that she'd finally confess to the murder?"

"Hey, it was worth a shot. Anyway, we had to do *something*."

"What if there isn't anything for Elizabeth Catanzaro to confess? What if she's not the murderer?"

"Yeah. Right."

"What if Elizabeth isn't the murderer, Rodney?"

"What if Elvis is alive and singing backup for Alvin and the Chipmunks?"

Chapter Sixteen

This could be your last impeachable night, DeWalt.

Your last opportunity to call the darkness to account. To resist. To impugn the integrity of surrender. To not go gentle.

There has never been a better time than tonight. The sky is clear and the stars each a brilliant tremulous white. Over the horizon to your right the moon hangs as if too swollen to rise, it awaits anxiously some disturbance in the earth's field of gravity, a loud cry, a splash, a gunshot, any rippling wave of abnegation on which it might ascend. You are moving with little awareness of movement over a body of water called Honey Lake, moving deeper into darkness, ever closer to the point of no return, and the irony is that you have been placed at the rudder, given charge of direction, charged with holding to the direction ordained. Your captain is less than half your age but he thinks he has a future and he grips that notion as urgently as he does the .22 revolver in his right hand and the bottle of beer in his left. He sits at the starboard rail, your other companion on the portside, watching the sail, believing his own improbabilities, correcting you occasionally as you veer off course. You hear the wind flapping the sail and the water splashing along the hull and you hear the buzz of all past misery fading, it is a buzz like that from an electrical transformer but you are moving away from it, it is somewhere back on shore, two hundred yards behind, three hundred, it is barely a hum now, no longer exacerbation but reduced to mere nostalgia, the incentive of indifference.

All right then. The past does not matter except that it gives you more or less reason to value the present. Whether you value the present more or less does not matter either.

You are sober and your blood is cool and your senses have never been more alert. You can smell the water and your own perspiration, you smell the beer in your captain's bottle, you smell the boy's fear. There is a vague scent too of wildflowers but it is not palpable enough to believe. You are leaving no one behind. You are expendable.

"I want you to know something, Rodney."

"Yeah? What's that?"

"I believe that you didn't shoot Alex and that you don't know where Jeri is."

"Sure you do."

"I do, Rodney. And if you would trust me, I could help you out of this mess."

"I'm helping myself out of it. I don't need nobody else's help."

"Once you step foot on shore, things will change."

"You better believe they will."

The beer has given him something, resolve or confidence; indifference. He has had three bottles of it, whatever it is. One as he led DeWalt and Fox to the dock at nightfall, the sixpack of beer concealing his gun. Three men out for an evening cruise. He had surprised DeWalt with his competency, his caution in maneuvering DeWalt and Fox to and onto the sailboat, always staying far enough from them that neither could disarm him with an unexpected move, but close enough that they could not anticipate escape either. Gillen had the edge because he was afraid and fear will always give a man the edge. Fox had gone beyond fear to abject terror, he could smell his red suspenders and yellow power tie and his cellular phones going up in smoke. DeWalt could have used a little fear but he had dropped too far below it. He did not know where he was exactly, this place was new to him, but there was no fear.

Where are your endorphins when you need them, DeWalt?

"Is that it?" Gillen asked. Lights on the eastern shore, approximately a quarter mile ahead. "What's the name of it?"

"Chelton," Fox answered.

"Is that it?"

"Yes." Fox was useless ballast now, and he sounded as if he knew it. His voice quavered when he spoke. He sat there whimpering, as he had whimpered all day. DeWalt wished he were sitting closer to the boy; he would cuff him alongside the head.

It would be so sweet just to brain the kid, to bash him a few times with anything handy. DeWalt could bash them both and leave them there to rot. He didn't have the stomach to shoot them but a full bottle of beer would make attractive dents in their foreheads. Two blows each would be sufficient. A week from now something would wash ashore and the smell would waft across Honey Lake. Fishermen would sniff their bait buckets. Sunbathers would wrinkle their freckled noses. God it would feel good to hurt these kids. It would feel so fucking sweet—a sweetness that might last him a lifetime.

"You're not aimed at the lights," Gillen said.

DeWalt told him, "I'm tacking."

"I don't care what the fuck you call it, I want you to head for those lights up there."

"Calm down, Rodney, this is the only way to do it. We don't have a motor, remember? We have to work with the wind, and the wind isn't precisely in our favor right now."

"It feels all right to me."

"It's tricky, Rodney, believe me. You're welcome to take over if you think you can do a better job."

"Just shut the fuck up and get us there as fast as you can, okay?"

"You're the captain."

DeWalt let a couple of minutes go by. He was beginning to feel very good. It was an unexpected and almost sexual feeling. He remembered being twenty years old and combing his hair in the dormitory mirror and smiling to himself because he knew that in a couple of hours he would be lifting a silky blouse off the shoulders of Katherine Lundeen, that her red hair would fall over her shoulders and he would kiss the warm flesh of her neck and back. There was no question that the night would progress in this fashion. Theirs was a temporary love but very real temporarily and the pleasure of thinking ahead to their time together and the certainty of it was almost more exquisite than the pleasure of their time together.

That was the feeling he had now. He couldn't help smiling. He smiled as he looked at the black-barreled pistol in Rodney Gillen's hand.

"I think Jeri's still alive," he said.

Abruptly Gillen turned toward him.

"It's just an opinion, of course. But it's what all the evidence points to."

"Like what evidence?" Gillen asked.

Yes, DeWalt, like what evidence? "If the murder was truly motivated by jealousy," he said, "why kill only one of the principals? Would a woman shoot her husband, let the only eye witness, her husband's girlfriend,

225

escape, and then go home and telephone the eye witness's husband? It's a ludicrous idea, Rodney. No, if Elizabeth Catanzaro were the murderer, she would have made damn sure that she got Jeri too. You don't leave somebody who can nail you wandering around freely. And if she does happen to get away from you, you certainly don't try to frame her husband as the murderer. Or you'll have Jeri popping up at the trial to point a finger at the real murderer."

Gillen thought about that for a moment. "So what you're saying," he said, "it still doesn't sound to me like a good reason to think she's alive."

"What I'm saying is, if Elizabeth Catanzaro were the murderer, Jeri wouldn't be alive. Her body would have been found right there beside Alex's. Or in any case, not far from it. But there wasn't a trace of Jeri anywhere. Not a single trace of evidence that she had been murdered. No blood, no tissue, no real sign of struggle."

"So. . . ."

"So, the only plausible explanation is that she got away." Will cocaine, marijuana, and beer render the specious plausible? DeWalt waited, smiling.

"But how? I mean she's naked, right? She didn't even have any shoes on."

"The way I figure it, Rodney, is that the moment Alex was shot, Jeri scrambled out of the car and into the woods. Whoever pulled the trigger would need at least a half-minute to reload, which would give her a sufficient headstart. So she's running through the woods, she's pretty fast because she's scared to death, and eventually the murderer has to give up and get his ass out of there. He can't spend all day chasing after her, right? Not unless he wants to take the chance of being caught."

"So where do you think she is?"

"Wait a minute, there's another scenario to consider

226

too. The only person to realistically suspect of having the kind of gun that Alex was shot with, is Alex himself. So there's also the possibility that Jeri shot Alex. Maybe by accident. Maybe not."

"I can't believe that," Gillen said.

"Actually, the question of who killed Alex isn't the important thing here. The important thing is, how did a naked barefoot girl escape without a trace?"

"That's exactly what I'd like to know."

"It's obvious. Somebody helped her."

"Somebody who?"

"Somebody she knew. Somebody she knew very well. Somebody she'd recognize on sight who just happened to come along at the right time. Somebody she trusted and was comfortable with. Maybe somebody she wanted to be with all the time instead of being with an old man who couldn't keep up with her, or with a husband who had, shall we say, certain sexual preferences that she didn't find particularly fulfilling. A husband she had already tried to leave on at least one occasion."

DeWalt cut a quick glance at Craig Fox, who was sitting stiffly upright now, eyes wide and disbelieving, head moving slowly back and forth. Then DeWalt looked at Gillen. Gillen sat leaning to his right, staring hard past the mast at a speechless Fox.

"It would have to be somebody smart enough to seize upon all the possibilities of the situation," DeWalt said. "Somebody who could afford to buy her a new set of clothes and then put her up in a motel somewhere until he could move her to a safer place. Somebody who, if he wanted her husband caught, and crucified, might actually lead an investigator to his hide-out."

There were more holes in DeWalt's story than there had been in Bonnie and Clyde's corpses but neither Gillen nor Fox was counting.

"That's crazy," Craig Fox muttered. Then louder,

more adamant, "You're crazy, you know that? You've gone fucking crazy, man."

DeWalt kept smiling. He had one hand on the rudder and one on the boom. It was such a clear and promising night, he felt twenty years old again.

Gillen, like Fox, was slowly shaking his head back and forth. To DeWalt they looked like a pair of novelty bookends. Then Gillen gradually rose to his feet. He lost his balance for a moment, set the beer bottle on the deck, and stood erect once more. He steadied himself by holding to the mast with his left hand. Still shaking his head, still negating some thought or misconception, he raised his right hand and the thing it held, he lifted a stiffly-extended arm until the revolver was leveled at Fox's chest.

Here it is, DeWalt. Now you either beg God to save you or you defy Him to destroy you. You demand a validation of existence through either compassion or cruelty, it does not matter which, either response is a declaration of being. It is now you force His hand.

DeWalt swung the boom hard to his right and at the same instant propelled himself backward, rolling over the low rail and filling his lungs and slapping harshly into the water. "Hey!" he heard, and grinned, it seemed such a funny thing to say.

For the first few moments his heart rebels. His chest hammers for oxygen, heart clattering, sensing death. The chill of the water goes straight to his blood and his blood turns as dark as the water, as thick as the darkness. Instinct orders him to fight for the surface, push up, break out and gulp the air, but he subdues this instinct somehow, this clawing animal. He turns not toward the stars but toward the center of the earth, pushes deeper into the chill and the darkness and whatever hope they conceal.

He is drifting down; falling, he imagines, like a large

228

heavy bird with wings outspread. Where is the gravity here? he wonders. Where the density and the grasping roots of fear? The water is cold and its darkness blinds him. He hears a humorous sound, *doink! doink!* That almost metallic report of bullets entering water. There is another muffled noise too but he can not isolate it, everything is everywhere and everything is nowhere, he thinks he might like to be a fish someday, he hopes the Hindus are right and he will someday get the chance.

He falls for maybe seven seconds and then feels the momentum change; the downward movement slows; stops. He does not want to start floating upward yet so he kicks his legs out straight and he scoops the water past him, pulls himself forward, swimming blind. He pictures himself plowing into a submerged tree. Conking his head on a sunken Buick, a fantailed American frigate. He swims as hard and as fast as he can through the chilling water and he has no idea in which direction he is headed.

And soon his lungs are burning, he must surface now. Noiselessly he rises, barely fluttering his hands, rising on the body's own buoyancy, its natural willingness to levitate. Rising in plenty of time so as not to have to gasp for air when he breaks the surface, the earth's hymen. Either he will take a bullet to the forehead or he will be all right. Life is very simple now. He wishes this moment could last forever. He isn't sure but he suspects that he has an erection.

The first thing he saw was the moon. He saw it from underwater as it floated above him, an undulating balloon of an egg. The moment his eyes broke the surface the egg retreated, solidified, gelled.

Get your bearings, DeWalt. Wake up or die.

He had no trouble staying afloat. Body fat saves the day, he thought. The air was cold on his eyes and forehead, his body warmer for a change. Water trickling from his hair blurred his vision but he could not risk wiping it away, making any anomalous splash no matter how small, and so he blinked in double time, scanning all that lay before him, a hundred and eighty degrees of darkness. On the left edge of his peripheral vision were several tiny lights—Chelton. To his right, nothing.

So he had emerged on the sailboat's starboard, he had his back to it. Would he turn just in time to see the grin on Gillen's face as he leaned over the rail, the pistol's fulminating red blink? DeWalt could take a breath and dive, swim for the shore, or push his luck no further and maybe accept this gesture from God as—

". . . just wait and fucking see."

That was Gillen's voice he heard. Over his right shoulder. The boat drifting closer, the boy muttering, pacing the deck. ". . . sonsabitches think I won't let you drown I will. I'll shoot you in the fucking water you assholes if you don't get back here right now this fucking minute!"

With a flutter of his left hand DeWalt did a quarter turn. Gillen had sounded not angry but terrified. The muffled splash DeWalt heard earlier had been the sound of Craig Fox abandoning ship. He was probably halfway to the western shore by now, sped by abject fear. So Gillen was alone on the boat, helpless. He knew nothing about sails and wind and in an instant his hopes had been deflated, became an empty canvas, a rudderless drift.

DeWalt watched the boat for a moment, its shadowed profile against a less-dark sky; he calculated its drift in relation to his. Gillen moved slowly around the deck, crabbing close to the rail, sliding against it, afraid to let go, the pistol scraping the chrome as he peered into the ink.

Again DeWalt filled his lungs. He pulled his palms up from hips to chest and sank below the surface and swam toward the boat. God could keep his petty gestures; a gesture wasn't enough. It would not be enough either to prove or to solve anything or to get yourself killed. But to force God's hand might come closer to enough. It might be as much of enough as is humanly allowed.

DeWalt did not really care which way it worked out. In the final end what would it matter? All that really mattered was the demonstration, the resistance; or maybe the belief in the illusion that it mattered.

He came to the surface but did not have time for a full breath because Gillen was moving aft along the port side, walking directly toward DeWalt who had emerged a few yards behind the boat. DeWalt pulled himself under again and swam forward. The movement of water dragged at the bag against his abdomen, tugged at the catheter where it entered his body.

His hand touched the slippery hull now. He felt along its curve until he found the ladder. He held to the bottom rung without pulling on it, lightly kicking, holding his breath, counting the steps he imagined Gillen taking as he came to the stern and moved past it.

When he could hold his breath no longer, he eased himself up, keeping the back of his head hard to the hull. Gillen stood directly above him, still muttering. His voice was clear for a moment but quickly changed in tone, became muted again as he turned and addressed the darkness on the starboard side.

DeWalt drew his legs up until he could get both feet on the edge of the short ladder's bottom rung. Reaching higher, he swung himself around as smoothly as he could. He felt the sailboat take his weight, felt the stern dip, and he knew that Gillen had felt it too, that Gillen in the next half-second would be turning to face him, pistol swinging toward him, and so he stood to his full height and leaning forward reached into the darkness to where he thought Gillen would be, where he hoped he would be, DeWalt's right arm stretching and swinging up quick, fingers as splayed and stiff as the prongs of a grappling hook.

Don't grab air, he prayed.

The moment his fingers met resistance they closed tight and pulled. DeWalt pushed his feet against the ladder, driving his torso backward. It seemed for an instant that he would lose his grip—he had grabbed Gillen's shirt just below the boy's left shoulder—but then the resistance broke and he went into the water on his back and he did not know if he had brought Gillen also or only Gillen's shirt until he felt the heavy splash and heard Gillen's startled cry filling with water.

Three hard strokes, and DeWalt had dragged himself back to the sailboat. He put a foot on the ladder and climbed up. Behind him, Gillen was fiercely battling the water, pummeling it with open hands. He would bob forward a foot or two, scream "Help!" and go under, only to bob up and scream again. His arms never stopped flailing. He was afraid to lower his face and therefore kept his body nearly vertical, doing far more hopping than swimming, and as a consequence was under water at least half the time.

DeWalt sat on the benchseat at the stern. His breath scraped in his throat, the air as abrasive as sandpaper. Gillen was making very slow progress but he seemed to be getting closer. DeWalt said, "You'll never make it to shore, kid."

Gillen's hands beat the water. "Throw me something!" he screamed, and went under.

When the boy's head bobbed into view again DeWalt told him, calmly, "Fuck you."

"I don't have . . . the gun man . . . help me!"

"You don't have a lot of things, Jack."

Gillen struggled forward, bobbing closer, gagging

232

and spitting with every inch of progress. When he finally pulled himself close enough to consider reaching for the ladder, DeWalt moved the boom, filling the sail. The ladder drew away from Gillen's fingertips.

"Ahh jesus, please!" Gillen cried.

"Aren't the stars lovely tonight, Rodney?"

"I'm going to drown here, man. For christ's sake!"

"Okay, enough's enough. Climb aboard." DeWalt luffed the sail.

Gillen clawed at the water until he dragged himself to the ladder again. Panting hard, wheezing, he began to pull himself up. DeWalt caught the tip of his chin with a crisp right jab.

A few moments later, when Gillen bobbed to the surface, DeWalt told him. "Involuntary twitch, man. Like sorry, you know?"

Gillen began to weep. Still slapping the water, kicking ineffectually, he sobbed convulsively, wave after wave of staccato wails.

"All right, knock it off," DeWalt said.

Gillen's misery echoed across the lake. DeWalt could hear it in the distant trees, a gathering of crows, a caucus of grief.

"Knock it off," he said, "and I'll let you come aboard."

Gillen sniffed and quieted, he paddled hard. The moment his shoulders came level with the aft rail, DeWalt punched him again.

This time when Gillen's head bobbed to the surface, DeWalt was standing on the ladder. Holding to the rail with his left hand, he leaned toward the water and grasped Gillen by an arm. "Are you ready to dry out now, Rodney?" he asked.

Gillen tried to nod but he was too weak to lift his head. His eyes rolled. Once again DeWalt struggled on board. He dragged Gillen along behind him, tugging

233

and sliding him over the rail, and then dropped him shivering, a gaffed fish, onto the moon-speckled deck.

DeWalt sat in the stern with one hand on the boom, one hand guiding the rudder. He sailed them toward the light. He tried not to shiver. He felt horribly alone.

The next afternoon was as gray as the late hours of loneliness, the sky a rough concrete floor. DeWalt looked up at the sky and thought, If that floor falls in, we're mush.

He and Trooper Abbott were standing in the grass just off the rear entrance to the courthouse. They had walked there together from the jail across the street, where earlier that day, Gillen and Fox had been lodged, escorted by the State Policemen who had taken Gillen off DeWalt's hands the night before. Abbott now lifted a panatella from his shirt pocket and, using a disposable plastic lighter, lit it up.

"I never saw you smoke before," said DeWalt. "I had you pegged as a man without a single nasty habit."

"I have maybe one of these a day. Usually at night." He laid his head back and blew out a long stream of smoke. "You know how I feel right now, Ernie? The first thing I'm going to do when I get home, and I do mean the first thing, is to throw my wife into bed. I feel like I could screw all night."

DeWalt smiled. Thunder stumbled across the sky. To DeWalt it sounded like a crippled caged animal pacing behind its bars, waiting for the keeper to come to feed him, to slip a hand too far inside the cage.

"You want one?" Abbott asked, meaning the cigar.

DeWalt shook his head. "It's been a strange summer, hasn't it?"

"How so?"

"Most days it's felt more like October than August."

"You think today feels like October? It must be eighty-five degrees right now."

"I don't mean the heat exactly. I mean the way the air feels. The way it smells."

Abbott laughed softly. "You writers," he said.

DeWalt could feel it coming now: something; some deep throaty growl of argument between them. Inevitable. Probably even necessary. With luck, cathartic.

"I already thanked those boys from the Chelton barracks for showing up so fast last night," DeWalt said. "But I'd appreciate it if you could pass the word along to the top. They didn't waste a second."

"The times are all logged in, it's part of the arrest report." Abbott puffed twice on the cigar. He held the smoke in his mouth as if it were a sip of wine, rolling it over his tongue, savoring it, particularizing its virtues and flaws. Slowly then he exhaled. "What did you think, we were going to make you babysit all night?"

DeWalt continued to gaze across the street at the jail's front door. The door stood open, two troopers and a local deputy just inside the dim lobby. They were laughing about something, a joke or anecdote. Grinning mouths, teeth, bobbing heads—a pantomime of humor.

"Where exactly did they pick up Fox?" he asked.

"About a half mile up the road from his folks' cottage. On his way back. The patrol car pulls up alongside him and he throws his arms into the air and yells, 'Don't shoot! Don't shoot! I surrender!' " Abbott shook his head and laughed. "What a MacGuphie."

"That's one I don't know," said DeWalt.

"I made it up. A MacGuphie's a machiavellian, greedy, parasitic, historically insignificant entity."

DeWalt smiled. "You cops," he said. He regretted it the moment it left his lips.

Abbott studied his cigar for a while. Finally he said, "That was one dumb-ass stunt you pulled, Ernie. Even just going into that cottage the way you did. I'd have thought you would know better."

"I'd have thought so too."

"You had no right to go in there, you know."

DeWalt kept quiet. It had to come out.

"No fucking right at all. Why the hell didn't you just go to a phone, Ernie? You think you're some kind of a Superman or what?"

"You're right," DeWalt said.

"You think you can stop bullets with your bare hand? Make them bounce off your chest? You think you can't get hurt?"

"All right," DeWalt said. "I agree with you, okay? I get the point."

Abbott looked down again, looked at the cigar burning in his hand. The coil of smoke drifted into DeWalt's eyes. He moved half a step away and turned to the side, but still the smoke found its way to him, it fouled the shaded grass-tree scent of the courtyard, it darkened the air and troubled the stillness. DeWalt was conscious of a nauseating chill deep in his stomach, in the hollowed-out pit of his solitude.

"Fucking amateurs," the trooper said.

DeWalt could have said something then and in fact considered it, he could have said that it took a fucking amateur to find them, didn't it, to find them right under your noses not three miles from the Chelton barracks. But there was no profit to such a statement. Truth can drop you into the red just as capriciously as it can lift you into the black.

"So what will they be charged with?" he asked instead.

Abbott played with the cigar, he twirled it between his lips. "What I've got," he finally said, "is I've got Fox on the thing with the cat, which he admits to. It's up to the DA to decide but we'll probably hit him with

236

unlawful entry and terroristic threats on that one. Maybe even cruelty to animals, just for the fun of it. We can also nail him with leaving the scene of the crime, failing to report it, aiding and abetting et cetera. Accessory to murder."

"Good luck on that last one."

"No luck needed. We stick Gillen in front of a jury, how do you think those folks will take to him? A small-time coke dealer with some fairly unusual sexual habits. Anyway people from around here will consider them unusual. Even though this might be everyday stuff where you come from, DeWalt."

DeWalt did not fail to notice the change of address. He said, "You really believe you have enough on Gillen to charge him with murder?"

"We've got circumstantial evidence by the bucketful. But who can guess the way a DA's mind will work? All I know is that neither Gillen nor Fox has an alibi. Opportunity they had, just like your client. It can also be shown that all three had motive."

"What's Fox's motive?"

"You working for him now?"

"I'm just wondering, Larry. Trying to put this all together, same as you."

"I don't have to be discussing this with you at all, you know. You're not her lawyer, I'm not required to do this."

"And I appreciate that. Because I value your friendship, and I wouldn't want to see it damaged by any of this."

Abbott looked away. He nodded stiffly. "The way I see it," he said a moment later, "is that Fox did pretty much what Gillen told him to do. After all, Gillen controlled his supply, and Fox didn't want shut off. Not from the cocaine and not from Gillen's wife. Motive."

"Okay," DeWalt said.

"As for the actual murder—or homicide, if you prefer—you heard them. Gillen claims Fox did it and then made off with his wife, and Fox claims Gillen did it and then sent Fox to the scene to get arrested. And when they're not pointing the finger at each other, they're pointing it at your client."

DeWalt nodded.

"And you already know how it looks for her. Here's a woman who's sick and tired of having her husband cheat on her every Saturday morning. She calls the husband of her husband's lover and suggests that something ought to be done about it. We don't know, by the way, that this is the only time she discussed this with Gillen. We'll pull the phone records, of course, but they probably won't tell us anything. She might have called from a pay phone, for example. Or maybe they met in person. In any case, we know they talked."

"Don't forget, though, Gillen knew about the affair. You might even say he encouraged it. So why would he murder Alex just because Elizabeth—and I am not conceding the point—just because Elizabeth might have suggested it?"

"Don't forget that somebody had already tried to turn Gillen into a crispy critter."

"It wasn't Alex, though. Two hundred people can verify that on the night of—"

"Gillen thought it was Alex, okay? Gillen's been getting threats. Then there's an actual attempt on his life. He's convinced that Alex Catanzaro is behind it. Enter the spurned wife, who just so happens to be in the market for a triggerman."

"Wait a minute."

"Hypothetically. For the purposes of argument, okay? So she gets in contact with Rodney Gillen, who, as luck will have it, would also like to see the guy dusted off, albeit for a different reason. And Gillen just happens to have a yuppie stooge who likes coke and blowjobs. Likes them so much that he's willing to decapitate a kitten for Gillen. Is it that much of a stretch to suggest he might be willing to do even more?"

DeWalt knew that the prosecution could make a case of such an argument, even though to DeWalt it smelled of smoke, it stung his eyes. "Anything turn up out at Honey Lake?" he asked. "Or in Fox's room at the frat house?"

"We didn't find the murder weapon, if that's what you mean. But I'll tell you where it is, it's at the bottom of Honey Lake. Either there or in the river."

"And Jeri Gillen?"

"Ditto. We'll drag the river again, and we'll drag the lake, and we'll find her."

"But why would Gillen off his own wife, Larry? Catanzaro, okay. But why Jeri?"

"Maybe she freaked out on him, who knows? Maybe she told him she didn't want anything more to do with him. Or maybe Gillen killed his wife by accident. Missed Catanzaro with the first shot and hit her instead."

"A musket is a single-shot weapon. Takes half a minute to reload."

"So maybe he had another weapon, ever think of that? The .22 pistol, for example. Maybe he shot her with that."

"No blood."

"Maybe he grabbed her first, took her somewhere else, and then shot her. Maybe he strangled her. Maybe he bashed her over the head."

"Maybe she's not even dead."

"Maybe not. Maybe the boys have her chained to a wall somewhere. Or strapped to a bed. A little S & M maybe? Tell me that's not a possibility."

239

"Spontaneous human combustion is a possibility too," DeWalt said.

"You think this is a joke?"

"I think maybe you're trying too hard to pin everything on Gillen."

"It's my job to try hard, all right? It's not your job, it's mine, let's get that straight. I don't know why I'm even fucking discussing this with you."

"Larry, wait." The air felt thick with smoke, and there seemed to DeWalt a kind of buzzing in the air, as if they were standing too near a high voltage fence. "I understand why you're pissed off, okay? And you have every right to be. I was out of line. The moment I found out Gillen's location, I should have called you."

"You got that right."

"And I apologize for that. I know you've probably been getting your ass chewed out all along because of me. I can imagine some of the heat you've been taking on my account."

"No you can't."

DeWalt chewed on the inside of his cheek for a moment. "Okay. I can't." If Abbott would not meet him halfway on this, what did concession avail? "Can we talk about the case, though? I need your help on this, Larry. On my side of it, I mean. I need your perspective."

Abbott continued to stand with his back to DeWalt. DeWalt imagined that to a passerby they must look like schoolboys refusing to shake hands after a playground tussle. Two women in this situation could throw their arms around one another and embrace and everything would be resolved in the warmth of physical contact, of touch, but such a solution did not exist in his or Abbott's repertoire of responses; they were too goddamn male.

"What do you need to know?" Abbott finally said.

He did not turn or look over his shoulder, he spoke to the horizon.

"It's the thing with the cat that bothers me. I just don't get it."

"What is there to get?"

"You've got two guys involved in a homicide, okay? Maybe even a double homicide. Why in the world would they risk discovery, risk everything, for that matter, just to frighten the wife of the man they'd murdered?"

"That seems fairly obvious to me."

"Only if you believe what you apparently do. That she hired them to kill her husband, and then reneged on the deal."

"Where else would two jerks like them, two fucking kids, Ernie, where else would they get their hands on a thirty-five thousand dollar Pennsylvania long rifle? She *supplied* it to them. Her husband's newest acquisition. Acquired illegally, by the way; which means she knew it couldn't be traced back to her. Hell, that rifle probably represented to her everything that was rotten about her marriage. What a joke, she must have thought, to kill him with the very thing he probably loved even more that he loved her *or* Jeri Gillen. She's got a terrific sense of irony, I'll grant her that."

DeWalt shook his head. "I just can't buy it, Larry. I've tried, I honestly have. But I just can't buy it."

"Maybe you could if you weren't sleeping with her." Abbott looked at his cigar, which had gone cold.

They had kept her house under surveillance, of course. There had been not only crows in the cornfield, but cops. What were you seeing, DeWalt, all those times you gazed into the trees and fields? Where were your eyes, man? Why didn't you smell them? Where was your nose?

The scent of cold cigar ash made DeWalt faintly nauseous. His mouth was dry. He tried to work up some saliva, and then to swallow, but it did him no good. His anger made him short of breath, so that he had to work hard to keep his voice low, his words evenly spaced and carefully chosen.

"I can't help thinking that we're missing something, Larry."

"Jesus H. Christ," the trooper said as he turned to face him. "This isn't a novel, this is real life, okay? Give your imagination a rest."

The look on Abbott's face then, the sudden blush of color, indicated how quickly he regretted his words. But they could not be reclaimed. He looked away for just a moment, then strode briskly toward the courthouse.

DeWalt remained where he stood. He stared at the opposite edge of lawn some thirty yards away, the cracked uneven sidewalk. There had been more to Abbott's statement than mere resentment that DeWalt had succeeded where the police had not. There was a deeper and more personal resentment, a suspicion confirmed, a mistrust.

It had to do with DeWalt's previous life as a writer. *This isn't a novel*, Abbott had said. *You writers. Give your imagination a rest.*

It had something to do with a common ambivalence toward writers, toward artists of any kind who labor in secrecy and in solitude, who do not publicly sweat except to preen and puff. There is something masturbatory about what they do. They are manic depressives, alcoholics and queers. They are intimate with madness. They know secrets.

The artist, even a mediocre one like DeWalt, even a pretender, is always watching, always listening. He keeps his own council. He communes with unseen forces, holds conferences with birds and grass and wind. He practices a strange alchemy, it cannot be quantified,

242

it is not predictable, it delights in nonconformity, in anarchy, it conspires for change.

DeWalt had not thought of himself as a writer for quite some time now. But he understood suddenly that other people continued to think of him as one, that because of one book he would be praised and condemned for a very long time. He understood too that he had been relying all this time on his writer's instincts. He was writing a story now even as he stood there, writing about himself thinking about himself, a story empty of epiphanies about a man staring at the juncture of sweet grass and dirty sidewalk, about an August that feels like autumn, a growl of closing thunder and a gathering of dusk, the scent of dead ash, and the chill thought that perhaps this man has been betrayed by his own heart, this man friendless and weary; this man is a fool.

Chapter Seventeen

The Catanzaro place is so quiet when DeWalt arrives, he feels as if he has driven up the long sheltered lane into a churchyard. A New England churchyard, survivor of three hundred years of progress. Anglican probably, venerated now for its age and remoteness, its indominatibility. Used only for weddings and Sunday services.

But today is not Sunday and there is no wedding to celebrate, no lovers joining lives. The sexton here, the caretaker of this solitude, is seated on the uppermost porch step, a dinner plate on her knees, a glass of iced tea by her hip. She is dressed in blue jeans and a long-sleeved blue cotton shirt, probably her husband's. Perhaps his scent still lingers on the shirt, and this is why she wears it. She is trying to fill those bottomless spaces of her solitude with something more tangible, more experiential than memory alone. Perhaps that is why she appears so small, so childlike: failure reduces all of us to our elemental virtues or flaws.

DeWalt did not consciously decide to park his car forty yards short of the house, he did not consciously reflect that he wanted, needed, to approach her slowly this time, needed to walk unhurried through the churchyard stillness with the sun dipping below the curtain of trees and the sky as gray as tomorrow's headlines.

She did not wave or call hello. The dogs were silent.

A killdeer screeched. Behind him, from somewhere near the tree house, a woodpecker rapped its jarring rhythm.

He smiled as he approached her, her brown eyes steadied now by a day of reflection; speculation. She held her plate with both hands. On the plate was a single ear of sweet corn, half-eaten, a shallow pool of melted butter, tiny black islands of pepper. Her lips were shiny with butter; her fingertips too. He wished this were a previous night so that he could kneel on the step below her and kiss the butter from her mouth, take her slippery hands in his, put her fingers to his lips. It would be a different night this time, an honest and more gentle night. He wished it were that other night now. Or a night five years in the past. Ten years. Or any other miraculous night wherein this now did not exist.

"Am I too late for dinner?" he asked.

She lifted the plate an inch off her knees. "This is all I made."

"It smells delicious." He watched her hands lower the plate again, watched them motionless, thumbs hooked over the rim. What did he want to say to her? And why can't you say it, DeWalt? He looked away, to the side of the house, as if there were something intriguing about the rain spout. Then into the sky.

"There'll be a good rain tonight," she said.

"A real thunderboomer."

She waited. Then she picked up her plate in one hand, her glass in the other, and stood. "Go on out to the garden and pick yourself some corn," she told him. "I'll get the water boiling."

"I was just kidding about dinner."

"Have you eaten yet?"

"No. But that doesn't—"

"You have to eat," she said. She turned and went in-

245

side, catching the screen door with her heel so it would not bang shut.

Not for thirty years had he walked through a cornfield and felt the long green leaves slapping his legs, the firm stalks bending against his hand, heavy tassles nodding as he passed. Back then it had been a hundred-acre stand of field corn and he had crept through it late one moonless night, he and three other boys filling a burlap bag with stolen ears ripped from the stalks. He had had to feel for the cornsilk in the dark, to search for its exquisite softness by sliding his fingers up the stalk, that womanly softness so fragrant and anomalous. He stumbled over a pumpkin once and fell flat on his face, the broken stalks gouging his stomach and chest and neck as he lay there laughing, the other boys whispering for him to be quiet, shut up, you want us to get caught? Until with the effort of suppressing laughter he had laughed himself breathless, and then remained against the cool dirt, safe in the fragrance of earth and corn and pumpkin vines, until his worried friends urged him away.

They had soaked that corn all night in a washtub filled with ice water, and late the next afternoon baked it on a bed of wood coals, the husks blackened and the golden silk seared away, the four boys and a dozen friends. Everybody laughed goodnaturedly when told how DeWalt had been felled by a pumpkin. The corn was tough but nobody complained because there were two quarter-kegs of cold beer and a clear starry night, and DeWalt had known since the party began that the long-legged girl sitting next to him would join him later on a blanket beside his mother's car. And when he tasted the butter on her lips that night and felt her warmth beneath him he had been grateful and pleased but the thought never crossed his mind that he might be engaging in an experience rare and finite, a soon past perfect joy. He had never suspected a day would come when he would hunger without hope for the taste and touch of a woman and the moment shared, or that a handful of cornsilk could bring it all back to him now, so new and fragrant and impossible to sustain in a hand nearly fifty years old.

"I'm ready when you are," Elizabeth called from the back door.

He looked up at her.

"Water's boiling!" she said.

He laughed at himself then, stiff old scarecrow, pumpkin-stumbling romantic. Quickly he plucked three ears of corn from the stalks and shucked them bare, green husks trembling heavily to the ground. He stroked away the tufts of cornsilk, and let them fall, and shook the last golden strands from his fingers. The air smelled of rain.

In the kitchen Elizabeth rinsed the corn under the tap and then slipped the three ears into a pot of boiling water, its steam rising into her face. She remained facing the stove then, her back to him. DeWalt knew she did not want to turn because she sensed somehow the coming of bad news, had seen it on his face perhaps, his reserve, the sadness of his eyes.

But it's bad news *and* good news, he thought, and then dismissed the phrase as something he would never say. A cliche, supposed to be medicinal, but astringent, wounding. The bad news always outweighs the good, he thought. Nullifies it.

Which do you want first, the good news or the bad?

Better give me the good news first, doc.

The good news is, if you take care of yourself you can expect to live a reasonably long and productive life.

Hey, great. And what's the bad news?

You can't drink, fuck, hope, trust, feel young, be in-

247

nocent, wear a swimsuit in public, or sleep soundly ever again.

Can't you give us a prescription, doctor? Can't you do something?

Certainly. Repeat after me, son: *Now I lay me down to sleep.* . . .

Elizabeth said, without turning, feeling his eyes on her, "I'll bring it out to the porch when it's ready."

So he walked past her then, toward the living room and the front door. In doing so he trailed his fingertips over the nape of her neck. She reacted with a shiver, and moved closer to the stove.

Later he sat alone on the porch step, the plate in his lap, three golden ears of corn, kernels bursting with sweetness. No butter for DeWalt, no salt or pepper. He wanted the taste of the corn itself, the taste of yesterday pure and undiluted. She had also made him a salad: slices of ripe tomato, Vidalia onions and provolone cheese, a few drops of olive oil, three broken leaves of sweet basil. He ate hungrily, gnawing off an entire row of kernels before pausing to wipe his mouth or to take a bite of salad. She had brought a glass of tea too but he could not drink it all. He poured it out off the side of the porch.

He was glad she did not stay to watch him eat. Eating corn on the cob is not a thing to invite spectatorship. As a boy at family reunions he used to cringe when the platter of corn was passed down the long picnic table, uncles and aunts and cousins and strangers crowded elbow to elbow. What an assault of the senses would ensue! His uncle, the farmer, did not raise pigs but DeWalt had no doubt he knew exactly how they would sound, a dozen snouts pushed deep in the slop. And they would talk, those good country people, with mouths full; they would laugh and grin with mouths dripping butter and split kernels. Since then, DeWalt had never been able to

248

fully enjoy the pleasures of corn on the cob except when alone.

The same held true for onion and avocado sandwiches. It was good to have nobody around for his breath to offend. Sleeping late when he didn't have to teach—could he do that if not alone? Not shaving on weekends. Being able to pass a mirror without feeling compelled to look in it. Being responsible to no one but himself. Being needed by no one. Neither valued nor desired.

When he finished the dinner he carried the plates into the kitchen. Elizabeth was seated at the table, a glass of white wine in her hand. The glass was full. Either she had not drunk any of it yet or she had recently refilled it.

"That was the most delicious dinner I have ever had," he told her.

"You're easy to please." There was an edge to her voice, an extra facet.

He dumped the cobs into the trash, then went to the sink and began to wash the plates. "I'll do that," she told him. "Leave them."

He said nothing. He washed the dishes quickly, dried them, put them away. When he faced her again he saw that the wine glass was still full. "Would you rather talk here or out on the porch?" he asked.

She took half a minute to answer. "Outside, I guess."

They sat together on the porch glider and did not turn on the overhead light, though the night was dark enough now to illuminate fireflies winking against the far bushes, dark enough to hide if not her face from his at least the deeper emotion of her eyes. It was she who set the glider in motion, establishing with the pressure of her feet a rhythm for him to follow, a slow scrape backward, a glide forward, the repetitious drag, he thought, of a jazz drummer's brushes, beat keeper for the blues.

Oh I went down to the St. James Infirmary, I saw my baby lying there, stretched out on a long white table, so cool so sweet so fair. . . .

"We brought Gillen in today," he told her. "He was caught late last night. He's in custody now."

"Oh my god," she said. He felt her quivering exhalation of relief. At least he hoped it was relief. He did not think he could be wrong about her. But there was always the possibility of error.

"He was staying in a cottage at Honey Lake," he said. "A boy from the college had set it up for him. It seems they were involved in a kind of business relationship. Selling cocaine on campus."

"You're kidding," she said.

"I wish I were."

"Was . . . the girl with them? At the cottage, I mean."

"No," he said.

"Well, did he . . . say where she is? Or confess to anything?"

"The boy from the cottage admitted to the thing with the cat. Apparently Jeri had had duplicates made of Alex's keys. Without his knowledge, of course."

"But why would she do something like that? If she cared about him, why would she steal his keys?"

Because she wanted what you have, he thought. What you had for a while and what she imagined you continued to have in spite of her. DeWalt recognized in himself then a certain sympathy for Jeri Gillen, a response he did not quite understand. He was beginning to feel a sympathy for everybody, and he did not particularly appreciate that emotion, it blurred the lines, it weakened him. He hoped he had not used up all of his anger. He had a long way to go yet and he had counted on the anger to take him there.

"Their story," said DeWalt, "Rodney's and the other boy's, Craig Fox, is that you set Gillen up. You called

250

and asked him to go down to the river, knowing he'd find Alex dead. And that while looking for Jeri, he'd leave fingerprints or some other evidence, or better yet, the cops would arrive and find him there."

"And is that what you believe too?" she asked.

"The police think they're lying."

"Then I'm not a suspect anymore?"

He watched the fireflies for a moment, their dance of lights in the trees at the far end of the yard. There was something sad in their aspirations, that almost desperate blinking for attention. Meager lights of ardor calling *Here I am, here I am,* so transient and unsustainable. They seemed so close to one another out there, yet unable to find each other in the dark.

"The police believe that one of the boys did the actual shooting," he said. "But at your suggestion. That you hired them to kill Alex, that you supplied the murder weapon, and that you then refused payment or lowered the price, which is why they then sent you the cat as a warning to reconsider."

She nodded, understanding all this, having presumed and feared as much for several days now. Her breathing was shallow and rapid. It was DeWalt who kept the glider going; he thought it important somehow that the motion, the illusion of movement, did not stop.

"Am I going to be arrested?" she asked.

"There's no hard evidence against you," he said. "No powder burns, no prints, nothing but that one phone call to implicate you. But that doesn't mean they can't lock you up for forty-eight hours if they want to. If you are taken in, and I'm not saying you will be, in fact I don't think you will be, but even so, it's high time you talked to a lawyer."

"I can't believe this is happening," she said.

"You might never even need a lawyer, I don't know. But it's foolish not to be prepared."

251

"I thought it would get better. I thought it had to."

"It will get better, believe me. It's not as bad as I'm making it sound. You'll probably be questioned again, but you can handle that. They'll want to search the house again, and Alex's study and his office at school. You might even feel that you're being harassed or intimidated. And that's why you need a lawyer, Elizabeth. You need somebody who can protect you in ways that I can't."

"I was hoping to bring the kids back home," she said.

"I don't think that's wise yet."

"I miss them so damn much."

She tried not to cry but the tears came anyway. He laid his hand atop hers. She turned her hand then so that their palms touched, and she squeezed his hand tightly for a while. Finally her grip relaxed. She withdrew her hand from his and with a fingertip pulled the tears from her eyes.

"Tell me the rest," she said.

He searched his mind for a beginning, the right place to start.

"Tell me why Jeri Gillen would make duplicates of Alex's keys."

"Bear in mind," he told her, "that much of this information comes from Rodney Gillen and his friend Craig Fox. By that I mean, be wary of accepting it as the absolute truth."

That's the way, DeWalt; give her hope where none exists. Throw her a book of matches as she stands stranded on the ice flow.

She nodded. "Go on."

"Apparently," he said, "Rodney knew all about Jeri's affair. You might even say he . . ." *participated?* Wrong word, DeWalt. Watch your step.

"Alex wouldn't have been aware of any of this, of course, but Rodney had a set of photographs; copies, in

252

fact, of the set you showed me. Indications are ... he enjoyed looking at them. He liked the idea of Jeri being with another man."

"Oh god," she said. "Oh jesus god."

She was breathing very rapidly, hands pressed flat to her stomach, feet flat on the floor as she leaned over her knees. "I feel like I want to throw up," she said.

DeWalt stopped himself from touching her. That was no way to go at it now, no way to get this thing done. He crossed his arms, then uncrossed them. Clasped his hands in his lap. Pulled them apart. Nothing felt right. "Tell me when you're ready," he said.

A minute later she nodded. "I'll be all right, I promise. Just go ahead with it."

He stared at the fireflies. "It seems that Alex was very generous with Jeri."

"Nearly half of his retirement fund is gone," she said.

"You checked the records."

"He's been making withdrawals ever since he started seeing her."

"How much altogether?"

"Over eleven thousand dollars."

"Whew," he said.

"I hope like hell she was worth it."

Good, he thought; let's see some more of that. That's the thing that will get you through this.

"So you can imagine what a windfall that was for her and Rodney," he said. "Alex bought Jeri clothes, gifts, gave her money whenever she asked for it. The money, most likely, financed their cocaine habit. Jeri swore to Alex that she had quit, but of course she hadn't. My guess is that hardly anything she told him about herself was the truth. One of the other things Alex didn't know was that Jeri was also involved sexually with Craig Fox. And again, with Rodney's approval."

Again she leaned slowly forward, this time until she

253

was completely doubled up, head to her knees, a tight bundle of grief. DeWalt could see through her shirt the hard curve of spine and he wanted to cover and protect it for her, to shield her with his own body as if mere flesh could turn the pain away. He wanted to hold her and somehow ease the rise and fall of labored breath, somehow quiet his own chill by quieting hers.

"Alex didn't know any of this?" she asked, voice muffled, back taut.

"You knew him better than I did. Was he the kind of man who would have tolerated such things?"

She sat up and took a deep breath, but continued to hold tight to herself. "Of course not," she said.

"In my opinion, I think he truly cared about Jeri. And I think he believed she cared about him in the same way."

"I don't know if that makes it any better or not."

Nothing makes it better, DeWalt. "Anyway. She was smart enough to know that Alex would catch on to her sooner or later, or that he'd just get tired of her, something like that. And that's why she made duplicates of his keys. Whether for kicks, or revenge, or just for the money, who knows? She and Rodney must have figured it would be an easy job. Watch the house until everybody goes out for a movie or whatever, then walk in and take what they want."

"She didn't love him at all," she said.

"Cocaine has a way of rendering love insignificant."

"I hope she is dead," she said. "I hope whoever killed her did a damn good job of it. I do. I'm sorry, Ernie, but I do."

He liked the sound of that, the sincerity. It told him what he most needed to know. It gave him back some confidence.

"There are a couple of other things," he told her.

254

She looked at him now. She thought she had heard the worst of it.

"There was an incident last spring. A garage in town was firebombed. Rodney Gillen was the probable target."

"No," she said. "Alex would never try to hurt anybody. Never."

"You've already established that he didn't do it. It was your anniversary. You went to a play."

"Then what . . . ?"

"Alex didn't do the actual firebombing, no. But it does seem likely he was behind it somehow. That he probably hired somebody to do it for him."

"That's impossible. It's ridiculous."

"I think it's why he wrote down my phone number so often, why he wanted to get in touch with me. You yourself said he read my book, which, let's be honest, is a violent book. Maybe it was the book that gave him the idea. I don't know."

"That's right, you don't know," she said. "You don't know Alex, or you could never even suggest such a thing."

"Somebody made several threatening calls to Rodney Gillen. The police pulled the phone company's records, and all of the calls originated from the same pay phone. The booth outside the suite of carrels on the second floor of the library."

"Anybody in the world could walk in and use that phone."

"It was somebody who knew Jeri's schedule, knew she wouldn't be home at the time of the call. Somebody who wanted Rodney to quit supplying his wife with cocaine."

Whatever she was thinking, she kept it to herself. DeWalt now realized that he had given her the information in the wrong order. He had told her first about

255

Jeri's deception and exploitation of Alex, which in Elizabeth's mind turned her husband into a pitiable figure, a man betrayed by the foolish but understandable error of obeying his heart. Elizabeth was listening to her own heart. It was a heart with a history, a history that would not succumb to any revisionist's speculations. So he could merely tell her what he knew, what he believed to be the truth. It was what he had been hired to do.

"The murder weapon was probably among the items stolen from the Fort Erie museum last month. During the robbery that took place one week after Alex's visit to the museum."

"And you know very well, don't you, where Alex was the night of the robbery. I already told you that, didn't I? Or have you chosen to forget that too?"

Anyway, he had told her. He had told her everything she and her lawyer would need to know. Everything the police knew or thought they knew. He saw that it was raining now and he wondered when it had begun, a fine quiet rain that stirred the sweet smell of grass. Even as he watched the rain came down harder, all but invisible except for the first layer of the curtain just off the edge of the porch, raindrops glinting like glass beads as they caught the dim light from inside the house. The porch glider no longer moved so there was no "St. James Infirmary" to accompany the rain now. But the rain had a song of its own. This was a Miles Davis tattoo being laid down. "Bitch's Brew," shadowy with cloud-scent. Black rain swatting shingles and porch steps and soggy black earth. It was a long song too; it was going to play all night.

"I don't think I'll be requiring your services anymore," she told him.

DeWalt nodded. He put his hands on his knees, pressed hard, pushed himself up. He went to the edge of the porch and looked across the yard. His car was out there somewhere, out there in all that darkness and rain. There were no fireflies now to guide him, no hopeful blinking lights.

"Tell your lawyer to call me at home," he said. "So that I can fill her in on what I know."

"What makes you think you know anything?"

He stepped out into the rain. It was cold on his neck and even colder running down his back. It was cold on his face and his hands and wherever it soaked through his clothing. By the time he reached his car he was shivering. He climbed inside and closed the door, started the engine and shivered. This is August, he thought. Isn't this supposed to be August?

He turned on the heater but it would take a minute or two to warm up. The wipers swatted urgently back and forth, clacking loud at each turn. With the headlights on he could see Elizabeth still seated on the glider, she had set herself in motion again, was vehemently rocking, eyes staring straight into the long beams of light.

DeWalt could not stop his teeth from chattering. This must be what Hell is like, he thought. He gripped the steering wheel hard as if trying to strangle some warmth from it. Hell is cold. There is no fire in Hell, DeWalt. That's just a myth, a come-on, there is not a single warming spark. But ice burns too, you know; as does an icy rain. And that is what Hell is: ice, the great preservative. Hell is the place where not even Death is allowed the final blessing of rot.

Elizabeth stood then and went inside. She went inside behind her new locks. She went inside to the lights of her living room, the warmth of her anger and wine. DeWalt drove home shivering, windows fogged. There was nothing but static on the radio.

"I can't help but think that we're missing something," was what DeWalt had said to Trooper Abbott and what he now said to himself as he lay on his bed and listened to the rain. He lay flat on his back with several blankets pulled to his neck. He was dry now but not much warmer than when he had left the Catanzaro house. Even so he kept the window behind his head open a crack. The rain was better company than the television. The rain not only spoke but had a scent and a presence and what it said was more often worth listening to.

"I can't help but think we're missing something," said the rain. Again and again it reiterated. Yes, DeWalt answered. And I know precisely what it is. We are missing a body and a murder weapon. We are missing a murderer too. We are missing everything we need.

He believed that Abbott held the tail of the elephant and that he, DeWalt, held the trunk, but there was a lot of gray space between the two appendages. Abbott seemed willing to settle for what he had, to imagine the head and ears and the great gray bulk. He assumed that to hold the tail was to hold the entire animal. Sooner or later he might even convince the DA of that fallacy. More than one case had been built and won on the evidence of the tail alone.

A basso tremble of thunder asked him then what is all this to you, DeWalt? You have been relieved of your duties, remember? You are not in the elephant chasing business anymore.

Why could he not let go? Was it mere meniscus that held him? surface tension? that human quality of adhesion which sticks abraded hearts together?

In two and a half weeks he would be back in the classroom. Baggy corduroy jacket with worn leather elbow patches. Sophistry and sex in the air. There you will be, DeWalt, wading through the thick of it, perpetuating the myth. Good writing matters, you will say, it really matters. And your students will compose stories about killer Coke machines and cynical overweight cats because they read the bestseller charts and ask, Whoever this William Gass guy is, when was the last time he was on television?

Yes, you are a recidivist old fart, DeWalt, but it is the only profession you have the guts for. So go to sleep, DeWalt. Shut it off now. Close your eyes and listen to the rain. Breathe the darkness. Search for the scent of wild mustard. . . .

After a while he admitted to himself that he would need the television or something like it to silence the noise in his head. He did not want to abandon his bed for the night-chilled room, so he concentrated on trying to remember the *Twenty-third Psalm*. He found it in his memory in bits and pieces and it was good work to put it together again. In his voice the joints did not dovetail as neatly as they had when he was a boy, and he worried that he was leaving something out when he could not find any more pieces of it anywhere.

I'm not praying, he told himself as he began it again in full. This isn't praying. It's for the rhythm and the poetry and nothing else. It's for myself alone.

Inside his head then he repeated it time after time. It was on a loop of memory and would run continuously now until sleep shut it off. And not even then would it leave him completely, for he dozed off once and then awoke suddenly in mid-verse, *a table before me in the presence of mine enemies, thou annointest my head with oil my cup runneth over,* and he was finally asleep again.

A while later it was not the prayer that pulled him up from sleep but the scream of the firehouse siren at the end of town. It blared unwavering for two solid minutes, calling volunteers from their beds and barstools, a common enough plaint in the nights of a countryside summer, but always startling, an almost predatory shriek. This time it was probably a lightning fire, a rended tree, a split power line whipping and snapping at the highway. Good entertainment for a dull rainsoaked night.

Three minutes after the siren fell silent, the firetruck roared through town, its own siren warbling. DeWalt listened to the shrill noise fade, heard it echo in his memory. Afterward he had to struggle to bring his attention to the rain again. He had had enough of the *Twenty-third Psalm* for one night. It was not a good habit to get into, he thought, this over-reliance on intangibles.

As always when he had slept a few minutes and awakened he had a hard time coaxing a return to sleep. It seemed to him there was something flawed to the structure of a human being. The mind should be able to turn itself off anytime it told itself to. But the mind would not obey itself, even when it knew it should. Nor would the body obey the mind. Who the hell are you listening to? DeWalt asked his own thoughts. Who's giving the orders here?

He disobeyed himself a while longer. He lay there and wanted sleep but the desire did nothing to hasten it. You can desire until your head falls off, DeWalt, and it will not do you any good.

He said, "Gimme a break," and rolled onto his side. He had no choice but to lie there and wait.

Chapter
Eighteen

In the morning DeWalt did not feel like cooking for himself and then having to clean up and he did not feel like going to the Colony either, where Della would want to talk about all the things he no longer wanted to think about. So he drove to a market on the way to campus, he bought two oranges and a newspaper, and he went to Tower Hill.

It was called Tower Hill because of the mushroom-shaped water tank on its summit, a pale blue hundred-foot morel encircled at the base by a high cyclone fence, discouragement to unauthorized climbers. DeWalt and other professors sometimes held their classes on the gentle slope of Tower Hill, even though trying to teach a class there was an exercise in futility, the female students gathered around him in a half-circle as if he were a guru about to reveal the secret path to literary satori, the males lower on the hill so as to better gaze up the girls' skirts, inspiration for yet another science fiction story. DeWalt himself could be distracted by clouds scraping across the sky, the suggestive scents of autumn, the breath-rhythm of a coed's distended decolletage; too distracted to be of any use except to urge his students to awaken their senses, to not only see the grass and sunshine but to smell and feel and hear it as well. He would toss them a handful of Hemingway's old chestnuts, and since few of the students had ever read Hemingway they believed that DeWalt was being riotously original. Sometimes he even thought of himself as a character in a Hemingway novel, one of the lesser characters, a parody, a Harry Morgan, an El Sordo dying on the hill.

It was what DeWalt would soon enough be doing again, instructing and having his instruction ignored, fighting against the allure of mediocrity. You have to get below the easy surface of impressions, he would tell them. Get below the grass is green and the sun is bright. You have to plumb deeper, he would tell them, and they would titter, sex first and foremost in their minds, and he would recognize again his uselessness to them.

He did not like to think now of September coming, another school year. There was not much of anything he liked to think about anymore. To stop himself from thinking he began his own exercise, the one he would have his students try when they gathered on the hill.

Buzz of cicada was the first thing he heard, building to a susurrous crescendo, fading out. The low whoosh of distant traffic, a delivery truck grinding down a narrow campus avenue. Somebody's lawn mower purring several blocks away. A catbird squawking. The vague bass thump from an open dormitory window. A clicking noise—what was that? A honeybee batting against the blue shell of the water tank, trying to penetrate the world's largest flower. DeWalt could smell the water inside the tank, fluoridated, chemically pure. He could smell sunshine baking the blue paint, the hard stretch of metal, silent pressure of the underbelly. He could feel gravity pulling hard on those thousands of gallons of elevated water, the water wanting to go home again, deep into the cool earth, hating the cool sling of metal that held it aloft, not understanding this resistance, imprisonment, curtailment of an innate need to flow, move, redefine. . . .

He felt the cool grass and the warm ground beneath his legs, he felt his legs, feet, toes itchy in heavy socks. Food aromas wafting from the cafeteria. The scent of orange peel oils on his hands, sticky fingers, orange memory in his mouth. The pungent scent of grass clippings smoldering in somebody's yard. . . .

This last scent reminded him of something and he stopped the exercise. He sat very still for a moment, pulling the memory together. Then he snapped open the newspaper and spread it open on the ground. He scanned the pages. He was curious, he told himself; nothing more. Expecting nothing, really. A confirmation of no suspicions.

But even as he searched the newspaper he was gathering the bits of memory together, isolated images that had floated into his consciousness last night as he lay in shallow sleep, near-sleep, that gray room between wakefulness and dream. Each image had washed briefly ashore like something from a shipwreck, each piece of flotsam hinting at the ship's identity but then pulled to sea again, dragged under, pushed into the mud. Now the scent of burning grass clippings had reminded him. And now, finally, he found it in the newspaper, a one-column paragraph near the bottom of page eleven:

At approximately two thirty this morning local firemen responded to an alarm in a wooded area of Claridge R.D. 3, Adams Township, seven miles north of town. Because of the rain and the firemen's quick response, the blaze was confined to less than three acres of woodland. Fire chief Bob Landers cited lightning as the probable cause of the blaze. This was the fifth brush fire in the heavily wooded river area in the past twelve months.

Even after he finished reading the paragraph, DeWalt did not move or look up. What he felt and what brought

263

a kind of tight-lipped smile to his face was not so much surprise as ... as what? Vindication? No, not that; not just yet anyway. But maybe. ... Maybe he had caught a whiff of the elephant.

The question now was how to properly track the elephant.

First of all, he told himself, kill the metaphor.

He refolded the newspaper, rolled it up and shoved it into his hip pocket. On his way to the car he dumped the paper and the orange peels into a trash can. Then he drove to the station house. He was familiar enough with volunteer fire companies to know who would be at the station house at this time of day: an unpaid EMT or two hanging around to answer the phone and activate the alarm—a housewife, a college student, or an unmarried man, somebody hoping to escape the daily dullness of his or her life.

But he did not know what his story would be until he saw who the EMTs were. He entered through the building's side entrance, directly into the kitchen. Seated at opposite ends of the long table, watching a game show on the color TV on the counter, was the young man who worked evenings at Lonnie's Sub Shop on Third Avenue, and his partner, more than twice his age, a decade older than DeWalt, Amy Weesner, indefatigable public librarian.

When DeWalt first moved to town, Amy Weesner had placed *Suffer No Fools* in the library display case, and had kept it there so long that the jacket grew sunfaded. At least six times she had asked him to autograph copies of the book, gifts for friends, she told him. She was a widow whose husband, a lumberyard baron, had left her with a great deal of money. Shortly after DeWalt arrived in town she announced that she would donate to the library $10,000 worth of new books, and then asked DeWalt to recommend specific authors or titles.

When he returned from his survey of the shelves, he had asked, "Do you think $10,000 will be enough?" And she laughed. "You see why I had to take matters into my own hands?"

With his help then, which she certainly had no need for, they compiled a list. They played a kind of alphabet game, taking turns naming authors: Atwood, Annunnzio, Bellow, Boll, Beckett, Borges, Barth, Camus, Crane, Conrad . . . "Maybe I'll have a special Southern Writers Collection," she mused. "Percy, Styron, Conroy, Robert Penn Warren, Eudora Welty. I have a special fondness for the southern writers," she had said. "They, at least, know how to act decorously even when they don't mean it. Are you a southerner, by any chance, Mr. DeWalt? I sense in you a great respect for civility."

She purchased four additional copies of DeWalt's book, two for the shelves and two for "the archives."

"It is absolutely thrilling," she told him once, "to have a real live writer as a patron in my library."

"Even a writer who writes commercial trash?" he asked.

"Nonsense. You have a gift for characterization which very nearly rivals Mr. Faulkner's."

"I'll try to write a *Sanctuary* someday," he told her.

"Isn't that book a hoot? I just laugh and laugh everytime I read it. And all those wonderful Snopeses of his. I just can't get enough of those people. They remind me of my Board of Directors."

By virtue of his one-shot profession, then, he had acquired a champion. Now, seeing her there at the station house table, a copy of *Library Journal* open before her, he knew suddenly how to get all the information he required.

265

"I should have known you'd be involved here," he told her. "You just don't know how to rest, do you?"

"There is no rest for the wicked, Mr. DeWalt. I must admit, though, that I'm surprised to see you here—you're feeling all right, I hope?"

He realized then that he had his hand on his chest. He had been short of breath ever since reading about the brushfire.

"I'm fine," he told her. "The reason I'm here is," and he smiled conspiratorially, "I'm thinking about starting a new book."

Amy Weesner's face lit up like that of a Jehovah Witness told that Jesus is waiting outside for her in his private limo. "I have been waiting so very long to hear you say that, Mr. DeWalt."

He felt a flush of shame, but continued. "The main character is a volunteer fireman. And I was wondering, you see I'll need to know something about the daily life of a firehouse. How many calls you receive, and of what types, that kind of thing. So what I was wondering is, would it be possible for me to have a look at your logbook? I'll need to go back at least a year. Preferably more. For verisimilitude, you know."

The young man, nodding vigorously, was on his feet even before DeWalt had finished speaking. "I'll get the logs," he said.

Amy Weesner showed DeWalt to a meeting room—a long folding table and twelve hard folding chairs—where he could examine the logs in privacy. He borrowed a pen and paper from her. She tiptoed away and closed the door quietly, reverentially, which made him feel all the more guilty for the deceit.

The guilt all but evaporated, however, after he had spent an hour with the logbooks—the boy had brought four of them, each covering six months of activity. From these records DeWalt learned that of the five brush fires in the wooded area on the western side of the river north of town, lightning was listed as the probable cause of three, and the two others, occurring as they had in drier weather, were "of unknown origin. Arson suspected." The firemen had also responded to four separate sightings of smoke in the same general area, only to arrive to find the ground charred, trees scorched, but the fire extinguished.

Altogether, over the past two years, thirteen brushfires had been reported within a few miles of the inlet where Alex Catanzaro had been killed. In other words, within a few miles of the Jewett home. DeWalt considered again, as he had fleetingly considered last night during those moments of troubled gray sleep, the scorched back door of the Jewett house, the burned-away steps, the blackened ground several yards from the house.

Somebody likes to play with matches, he thought.

DeWalt tried to reconstruct what little he knew of the psychological profile of an arsonist. Somebody who feels weak and ineffectual, dominated by circumstance. Somebody, perhaps, with a repressed or aberrant sexuality. Repressed hostility and self-contempt.

Somebody like me, DeWalt thought, and smiled at the irony of it, the bitter taste.

Or somebody like Draper Jewett.

Somebody who, if hired to intimidate or injure a third party, might choose as his weapon a Molotov cocktail?

Excited then, almost breathless with excitement, DeWalt returned the logbooks to Amy Weesner. He thanked her and the young man for their help and hastily said his goodbyes. Outside again, hurrying toward his car, he inhaled deeply, he filled his lungs with the August sweetness. He felt certain finally that his prey was near, that he had stepped in a pile of fresh, steaming elephant shit. It smelled wonderful.

Passion is a child born of unknown parents, a child of
surprising gifts sometimes; sometimes disturbing; a
willful child, enlivening and unpredictable; uncontain-
able. Even here at this inlet, this place of death sudden
and violent, this violated place marked by memory with
the stain and scent of blood and the quivering echo of
a stifled scream, even here DeWalt felt something akin
to passion.

Which isn't so strange after all, DeWalt. You needn't
be ashamed of it. There is blood too in every cathedral
nave, is there not? And yet passion stirs souls there, else
every nave would stand empty. There is passion in the
streets of Soweto, the alleys of Beirut, the Serengeti
plain and the Amazon jungle, in Central Park and Wall
Street and in the Hollywood Hills: all places irrevocably
stained, violence upon passionate violence.

And so maybe we know the child's parents after all,
he thought. He wanted to understand this passion, to de-
fine and use it. You were brought forth from sorrow,
child, in violence and in pain. Sorrow is your mother.
Your father is the quiet side of darkness, the pale morning light, breathless, hopeful and fearing, a silence that
trembles.

DeWalt studied the cattails standing tall on pencil-
thick stalks at the edge of the water, the brown water itself and the earth and the enclosing trees. We ascribe
our passion to you, he thought. As if it comes from you,
reaches out from you to touch and move us here outside, separate. We ascribe to you what in fact is gestated
within each of us. It is only in every man and woman
alone, not in trees or rivers or sun or sky, it is in man
and woman alone that both parents of passion are sanc-
tioned to conjoin.

And so this is what passion is: no bastard after all.
No orphan. It is a child at home, a child abundant in

feeling but with nowhere to project those feelings but outward, out through the windows and onto the world, because there are no mirrors in the soul, the mind can not see itself, and even if this were possible there exists no soothing image to reflect, the face in the mirror is flat.

A bass rose to the surface then and struck at a small green dragonfly, in an instant seized and pulled it under, a ripple of brown rings, a shadow moving toward the mud. DeWalt watched the concentric rings until they had shivered away, the river calm. He turned then, and, sensing the passion, the quickening of blood, he regarded the weeds and the tangled growth of brush around the area where Catanzaro had so often parked his car.

He would find no evidence here, nor did he expect to. The police had examined the area numerous times, and they were better trained to see the invisible than was he. Then why are you here, DeWalt? For courage? Resolve?

No, not even that.

For the passion, then. The smell of blood.

Maybe so, DeWalt. Maybe so.

Not far away was the narrow path that led uphill to the Jewett property. DeWalt considered the hike to the top, a mere half-mile. But he knew how he would feel at the end of that hike, lungs and calf muscles burning, heart hammering against his chest.

Remember when you could have sprinted up this hill and not even be out of breath, DeWalt? That's a way you'll never be again. A way you were for too short a time and never paused to appreciate.

What you should do now, old man, is to climb back into your air-conditioned car, drive into town, find Abbott. Have a talk, be nice. Inquire as tactfully as you can if the Jewett house or truck has ever been searched.

Were the Jewetts checked for powder burns, scratches, fibers or hair or blood? Can they provide alibis for the night of the firebombing, the day of the Fort Erie robbery? And will their alibis, like the ones for the day of Catanzaro's murder, be confirmed by no one but themselves?

Unfortunately, DeWalt could hear that conversation already, he knew how it would go.

"What about the Jewetts, Larry?"

"What about them?"

"You don't think it's peculiar that in a year and a half they never saw or heard Jeri and Alex down at the inlet? That they didn't hear the gunshot?"

"You have to understand who you're dealing with there, Ernie."

"I'm trying to."

"We've got families like them all over the county. All over the state, for that matter. Reclusive, suspicious, backward—if you didn't go looking for them, you'd never even know they exist."

"I'm not unfamiliar with the type."

"All I'm saying, Ernie, is yes, I do think they would have at least heard something. But do I expect them to admit it? No. Do I see anything incriminating to their reticence? No again."

"What about the high incidence of fires in that vicinity?"

"Arson isn't murder. Not in this case anyway."

"It might be attempted murder, though. The Kinetics might very well have gone up in flames."

"There's only one Kinetic we're concerned about now, and he's in custody. And as far as I'm concerned, Ernie, his premise sounds a lot more believable than yours."

"The Jewetts are involved in this, Larry, I know they are. They're involved up to their eyeballs."

"Show me the proof."

And that, of course, was the very thing DeWalt lacked. So he could not go to Abbott yet, it would be a waste of time. Just as standing here at the inlet was a waste of time. No bottle was going to wash ashore with his proof inside it. No blackbird could whisper the truth in his ear.

If there was any truth to be found or heard, it was where it had always been, where no one had ever yet looked. He climbed back into his car and drove to the Jewett's house.

He approached the house cautiously, driving slowly until he saw that the blue pickup truck was gone. Aleta, probably, would be the only one home. At most, Aleta and Draper. DeWalt could say he had come to inform them that the suspected murderer was now in custody. He could watch their eyes, observe the emptiness within. Maybe remark casually about last night's fire. The high incidence of brushfires hereabouts. Ask about the back door and steps, how had they come to be burned? Ask once again about the possibility of having heard a gunshot on the day of the murder, about hearing Jeri's screams.

Ask Draper if he was absolutely certain he did not know Alex Catanzaro; if, upon reflection, he was still sure he and his brother had never met the man who every Saturday morning used Draper's favorite fishing hole, posted NO TRESPASSING, for his own private lover's lane; sure he and Clifford had never spoken to Catanzaro, never worked for him, never spied upon him and his naked girlfriend.

That's all he would do, he would watch their eyes. Aleta's eyes, he knew, would reveal nothing. But Draper's, perhaps, those yellow poisoned eyes might have a thing or two to say. They would tell DeWalt nothing he could take to court, nothing that might mend a friendship or insure abiding love or reverse the damage of time, but it might be something to hang a hunch upon. It might be something finally to vindicate an unrequited passion, a passion more dormant than moribund but re-awakened now, rewanted, the only heat now left to him, that unavailing, impractical, untenable passion for truth.

Chapter Nineteen

The Jewett house stood as silent as ice, all doors locked. The sound made by DeWalt's knuckles rapping on the front door seemed swallowed by the wood itself, wood dry and chipped and warped, thirsty for attention. There was no echo to the knocking, no answer from a barking dog. He let the screen door close quietly, not wanting it to bang shut, not knowing why. He made his footsteps light too as he descended the wooden porch and went to the side door, as light as the leaves of the oak trees scratching the breeze, high dry branches creaking.

Because the steps to the side door were all but burned away—there remained only a skeletal black frame that would support no weight—he had to stand close to the house and reach above his head to put a hand through what was left of the screen door—it too little more than a blackened frame, the rectangle of wire mesh melted from its bottom upward to the corners like an intricate cobweb touched by a cigarette. He tried the knob of the charred wooden door. This door too was locked. The outside veneer of the hollow door had been burned through; it would be no trouble, not even for DeWalt, to put a fist through the flame-weakened panel that remained.

Easy enough, he told himself, but he did not do it. He looked at the smudge of soot on his hands, smelled the smoky stench of the door. What you need to do now, DeWalt, is to walk away from here. Walk back to your car. Drive into town. Find Abbott.

So there've been a lot of fires in that area, Abbott will say. So what? What does that prove?

Nothing, DeWalt answered. Zero.

The lock was an inexpensive Weiser, the type that could be opened with a coat hanger or screwdriver, the type that protected with the illusion of protection a hundred thousand homes across the country. DeWalt had a very nice set of screwdrivers but they were in the basement of his home, too far away. Everything he needed, would ever need, was, it seemed, too far away.

He walked to the rear of the house. Here he found a half acre of detritus stored, a lifetime of junk. A strip of fiberglass panels, braced five feet off the ground on a framework of two-by-fours nailed against the house, provided an awning for, gathered in no discernible order, birch and oak logs, an assortment of lumber, bricks and building stones, old truck tires and naked rusting rims, plastic and metal buckets, a washtub filled with dirt and, DeWalt guessed, fishing worms. There was a bicycle frame, wheelless and without a seat; at least two coffee tins filled with oxidized nails; half a pair of sewing scissors; tools including a trowel, handrake, spade, hoe, pickaxe and maul, all with blades either rusted or caked with dried mud; a wooden crate containing over three dozen railroad flares wrapped in clear plastic sheeting; two sets of antlers, a five-point and a nine-point; a piece of animal hide thrown over a stump, the hide so weathered that DeWalt had no idea what species of hapless creature had been stripped of it; and, sticking out of a rotted black work boot, a plastic-handled steak knife and a forked sassafras twig, the twig scraped clean of bark, incipient handle for a slingshot.

DeWalt picked up the steak knife and holding it flat

against his leg returned to the side door. He glanced toward the driveway. He should not be doing this. He didn't yet know whether he would do it or not. Why *should* you do it, DeWalt? What's any of this to you? Go home and watch television, DeWalt. Go home and piss through a tube.

He stood facing the side door, steak knife in his right hand. Another glance down the driveway. Surely if the Jewetts returned while he was inside he would hear the truck pulling up out front, he could slip out the side door and into the woods. That was how it would work in an ideal world.

No, not quite. In an ideal world you wouldn't be doing something like this. He pushed the tip of the knifeblade into the keyhole, twisted the knife side to side, probing, and heard the lock click. Worthless, he thought. What good is a lock that any six-year-old can pick? He returned to the woodpile then, wiping the knife clean on his trousers before he dropped it into the leather boot.

He held open the screen door and knocked again on the charred wood, louder this time. He took a long look down the driveway. Then, pushing the heel of his palm against the doorknob, he turned it, he swung the door open. Careful then not to lean on the catheter tube or the plastic bag folded against his abdomen, he pulled himself up over the threshold and into the kitchen. Quickly he stood; looked out; quickly and quietly reclosed the doors.

He was here now and did not know why. Do you really think you'll find anything now, DeWalt, so long after the murder? After all that has happened, how can you remain such a romantic?

A cancelled check would be nice, he thought. A check signed by Alex Catanzaro, with note attached: *Thanks for a good firebombing and robbery, boys.* It

275

would be nice to stumble across the murder weapon too. With several nice sets of usable Jewett prints all over it. And nearby, Jeri Gillen's body. No, make that Jeri Gillen, alive and well.

And then DeWalt thought, *alive and well,* that's an oxymoron.

But hey, as long as you're fantasizing, DeWalt, why not find a couple of kidneys and a healthy liver too. Maybe they're over there in the sink. Soaking in ice water.

He made himself stop it then. "Concentrate," he said aloud. He would find nothing in here, though: this was Aleta Jewett's domain, her enclave and escape. This kitchen was as clean as her memory, as sterile as her crystal gray eyes.

The kitchen opened onto the living room, and, to his right, the dining room. He only glanced into the dining room, which housed no table, but a sideboard, an armoire full of knickknacks and plaster figurines and a few china plates, a bent hickory rocking chair beside which, on one side, was a basket stuffed with skeins of yarn, and, on the other side, Tippy's wicker red-cushioned bed. This, too, Aleta's room.

It was just as easy to see who owned the living room: two recliner chairs, separated by a small table on which set an ashtray filled with cigarette butts. The chairs faced a color TV. A 26–inch color TV, new, DeWalt told himself. Eight, maybe nine hundred dollars. Maybe he had found that cancelled check after all.

The house was warm and smelled vaguely of damp shade. It was silent but for a constant hissing sound, so low in volume that DeWalt could not determine where it was coming from, could not in fact ascertain if it originated inside or outside his own head. Maybe I've sprung a leak, he thought.

He looked again at the living room. A brown worn

sofa. White plastic end-table holding a telephone. Nothing else here, no Pennsylvania long rifle mounted on the wall, no naked girl chained to the wainscoting.

He went to the front door and glanced outside. An empty driveway. He turned and, walking on his toes, crept up the stairs.

The first thing he noticed was that the hissing noise grew louder as he mounted the steps. From the second floor landing he could peer down the narrow hallway to the far end of the house. On his immediate right were two bedrooms, both doors open. On his left was the bathroom, then a linen closet, then a room with its door closed. It was the closed door that drew him. Doors are kept closed for one of two reasons: to keep something in, or to keep someone out.

Even before his hand touched the doorknob, DeWalt had identified the hissing noise. He knew it was coming from inside the room and he knew what the noise signified, what that pale blue odor of natural gas signified, a yellow towel stuffed against the inside bottom of the door, protruding through the crack like sunlight too thick to escape. His initial thought was that the door would be locked and he would have to kick it open, but the door had no lock. He turned the knob, pushed steadily but firmly, and a wave of natural gas washed out through the opening, shimmering, a heat mirage of soporific poison.

At first glance the room seemed unnaturally bright, already filled with flame. But it was only the afternoon sunlight pouring through curtainless windows. It was all DeWalt could see for a moment, the quivering golden light. Dizzy from the initial blast of scented air, he did not move, he remained on the threshold, squinting, holding his breath, until finally he located the source of the hissing noise, a gas jet low on the right-hand wall. Attached to the gas jet was a small space heater, flameless, the dirty ceramic burners cold. The hiss echoed inside the white enameled heater before venting into the room, a room effectively closed off, sealed, until DeWalt had opened the door.

DeWalt went first to the gas jet, but the knob on the release valve had been removed; he would need a pair of pliers to shut off the hissing gas, and there was no such tool in sight. He glanced across the room at the bed pushed into the corner. Draper Jewett lay fully clothed atop the bed covers, clothed but for his shoes as he lay in the center of a neatly made bed. His skin was yellow and bloodless, his limbs even thinner than DeWalt remembered. His eyes seemed huge—dots of empty black on swollen yellow balls. They were watching DeWalt. DeWalt looked at him for just an instant before turning to the window. With the heels of both hands he pounded on the upper sill. But the window would not budge, would not slide up. DeWalt's lungs felt about to burst but he did not think he should chance a breath yet, not until the room had cleared a bit more. He hammered at the window.

"Get away from there," Draper said. His words were slow and flat and thin, a moan, a breathless dream-speech.

"Don't be stupid," DeWalt told him, tasting the gas. It tasted of cold metal, impossibly dry, a hard blue clot of poison.

He gave up on the window then and went to Draper's bed. Leaning over Draper, he slipped one hand beneath the fleshless knees, another beneath the brittle wings of his shoulder blades. But before DeWalt could begin to lift, Draper's left hand rose lazily, dreamlike, from between the bed and the wall, bringing into view the pistol it held, the longnosed .38's gleaming silver barrel turning heavily toward DeWalt, sleepily, finding him then, the round little killing mouth pushing into his gut.

It is not difficult to snatch a gun from a man's hand if you do not hesitate. You must react without thinking. DeWalt had been that quick and sure for a time in his life. This time he was neither. Whether it was gas or pistol or memory that caused it, he felt suddenly awash with nausea, submerged in it. Only by driving his knuckles into the bed, his hands still beneath Draper Jewett, could he keep himself from falling atop the man. Haltingly he backed away, gagging, his stomach in spasms.

DeWalt, bent nearly double, nodded as he backed into the hallway. Just as he cleared the threshold he saw Draper begin to rise up, turn, try to find him again. ". . . that door," Draper seemed to say.

But DeWalt was in the hallway now, breathing, sucking cool shade into his lungs. Christ, he thought, trembling, because for an instant he had actually believed it was going to happen again, had to happen, over and over without change. But he was moving down the stairway now, heavy-footed, moving as if through a narrow tunnel with the bannister rail smooth and cool beneath his hand. His feet were finding the steps, hard and sharp. He kept expecting to hear a gunshot, and then, as anticlimax almost, a heavy wallop breaking his spine. He kept expecting his legs to give out. Jesus fucking Christ, he thought. There was no air in the tunnel, he could not satisfy his lungs. He felt his heart slamming hard against his throat.

When he was halfway through the living room he stopped. He turned to face the stairway, but Draper was not behind him, no silver-rimmed black eye staring, no wink of light, the stairway was empty.

Slowly the tunnel expanded and his breath came back to him. He was getting hold of the nausea now, squeezing it into something smaller, containable, a lead ball in his belly. The house seemed to be roaring, but it was the blood in his head, the crashing wave after wave of his pulse. In the midst of this thunder came a dull thud—it took him a few seconds to realize that Draper had closed the bedroom door again, was probably stuffing the yellow towel into the crack.

So be it, DeWalt thought.

He sat on the swaybellied sofa, elbows on knees. He would not wait out the suicide, Draper had too far to go yet. But DeWalt had his own long walk ahead of him, outside and to his car. He needed to steady his legs first, quiet his head. Clifford could come home and find his brother dead. Or Aleta could find him. Anybody but me, thought DeWalt. I'm through with this.

Maybe Clifford and Aleta already knew what they would find when they came home. Surely they knew. This day or another, sooner or later, they knew. Draper had been dying for a long time now. Since birth, DeWalt thought; just like the rest of us. He almost felt sorry for him. For everybody.

Christ, cut it out, DeWalt. Thoughts like that will ruin you for sure.

The world is fucked, remember that. It's fucked for always now, for an always as long as will matter to any living man and his children. And probably for the bigger always as well, the one that will end the always always and forever.

So what does a man do in the meantime, DeWalt? A man with such knowledge. He can quit doing anything at all and learn to live with his uselessness. Lots of people do. Is that what you want to do, DeWalt? Is that why you are here now, in this house, in this life, with a plastic tube in your side?

A man can do what he does best, he thought. For no

other reason than that he *can* do it, and that doing it well pleases him and maybe a few others.

That and cowardice, he told himself, is all you need to keep yourself going. Cowardice and hope. Hope and Crosby. No, Crosby is gone. We still have his records, though. We still have our memories. And maybe that, not cowardice or hope, is what keeps the world alive: the way we remember it. The way we remember the way we thought it would be.

He slid to the edge of the sofa then and reached for the telephone, a squat black rotary model. Not many of these left, he thought as he dialed the numbers, 9–1–1. He would summon an ambulance, then go outside and toss a rock through Draper's window. No easy death this time, buddy. There are still a few things to be answered for.

He gave the dispatcher the address and asked her to notify Trooper Larry Abbott of the Pennsylvania State Police, Menona Barracks. The patient was armed, dizzy but dangerous.

As the dispatcher repeated the address DeWalt's eyes focused on what he had been staring at for several moments now, staring without recognition, a small colored glass in Aleta's armoire, a juice glass among the figurines and china plates. He was too far away to read the lettering but he could make out the blue waterfall and the rainbow mist it made. He hung up the phone, stood, and on still-shaky legs, stepped up to the armoire. NIAGARA FALLS, NY, the glass read.

He swept an antimacassar off the small table beside Aleta's rocking chair and used it to open the armoire. He could see the juice glass clearly enough, but even so he felt compelled to look at it with no obstacle between them, this beautiful evidence, this connection. He would not touch it, though. He would leave it here for Abbott. Could Abbott refuse then to check the hotel registries in

Niagara Falls, to find a clerk, a waitress, anybody who would remember seeing Draper or Clifford Jewett in the area on or about the time of the Fort Erie robbery? Could Abbott refuse then to turn this house upside down, to search the grounds, subpoena the Jewetts' bank records, ask them to explain how a family living on welfare could afford a new 26–inch Sony?

Damn it, he thought, I knew they heard the gunshot.

He heard it himself then, startling, too near. And an instant later he knew that it was not a remembered gunshot but a real one. Simultaneous with this realization, the sound of Draper's .38 blossomed and exploded again, an explosion to dwarf the gun's bark, a sonic boom that blew out the front wall of Draper's bedroom and seemed to lift the entire house off its foundation.

DeWalt found himself sitting on his ass on the bare floor. He could hear window glass raining over the porch roof, wood creaking and snapping, a crackling of fire. A china plate rolled out of the armoire, rolled almost delicately, fell lethargically, and burst at his feet. His eyes seemed to want to peer in different directions, he could hold nothing steady in his gaze.

His head was still ringing when, ten seconds later, he smelled the smoke and understood it, understood the plaster cracking above him, popping off in small chunks. He turned onto his hands and knees, steadied himself, pushed himself up. He wobbled closer to the armoire. Lying on its side in the corner of the armoire, unbroken, was the souvenir juice glass. Using the antimacassar—he was surprised to find it still clutched in his hand—he picked the glass up. He stumbled to the front door and, moving dreamily, smiling at the small glass, turned the lock. Feeling simultaneously floating and submerged, weak but desperate, a water-filled balloon pushing through dirty sunshafted water, he ran awkwardly away from the house, far out into the shaded yard before he stopped, nearly falling, and looked back.

The top portion of the house was a solid box of flame. Even the oak tree that had pressed against Draper's window was burning, the tip of a limb slowly taking fire. There was very little smoke just yet but that would come too. DeWalt could feel the heat on his face, tightening his skin, pulling his mouth into a hard frown. Even the glass in his hand felt warm. He looked at it, his evidence. Illegally obtained. What good would it do him now? He slipped the souvenir into his pocket and waited for the authorities to arrive.

In Abbott's car, parked along the edge of the Jewetts' driveway, fifty yards back of the fire company's trucks, the two men sat, car windows sealed to keep out the smoke that still billowed from the shell of the house. Both men's faces were shiny with perspiration, hands damp, shirts sticking to their backs. Even with the windows closed DeWalt could hear the old boards crackling, furniture sizzling and spitting beneath the continuing arc of water. The ambulance crew, with nothing to do now, stood by their vehicle, as curious as any of the machinations of death; maybe a bit more curious.

On the middle of the dashboard, midway between the two men who did not look at each other now, who had looked at each other maybe twice, uneasily, since Abbott's arrival thirty minutes earlier, was the souvenir drinking glass. Occasionally Abbott's gaze was drawn from the fire to the glass, from the liquid orange to the frozen rainbow of blue and red. Reflected on the side of the glass were the flames and the running shadows of smoke and steam; they made the glass come alive, made the static blue waterfall flow. Abbott had not yet touched the glass. The antimacassar lay just above

283

DeWalt's left knee, an old lady's doily flattened beneath his hand, a spinster's diversion. His finger picked absently at the cobweb design.

"So he either shot himself," said Abbott, still working it out, not yet satisfied with the logistics, the turn of cause and effect, "and that's what touched off the explosion. Or else he fired into the space heater . . . could that do it, though? Ignite the gas?"

"Either way, it was suicide."

"If the room was full of gas, though, I guess the spark would do it. No matter which direction he shot."

"He told me once, more or less, that he was going to do this. Said he'd rather shoot himself than go on dialysis."

Abbott shook his head. "Goofy bastard. Probably didn't have any idea what could be done for him these days."

DeWalt said nothing.

"I have a cousin on dialysis. He's run a greenhouse now for almost twenty years. Kidneys failed, they figure, because of all the chemicals he's used on the plants over the years. So now he takes dialysis a couple times a week. But hell. It's hardly changed his life at all."

Again, DeWalt kept quiet.

"Damn lucky for Clifford and Aleta that they weren't home today."

"And Tippy the dog," said DeWalt. "Lucky, yeah. Lucky and convenient."

"Second Monday of the month," Abbott said.

"What does that mean?"

"If you ever went shopping for groceries on the second Monday of the month, you'd know. It's the day the welfare checks come out."

"That's where you think they are now, at the supermarket?"

"Aleta, anyway. Clifford's probably not far away. Just across the street at Scipio's Bar and Grill. Anyway, don't worry, they're in town somewhere. I'll find them."

He drew a hand across his forehead then, looked at the sheen of dirty perspiration on his fingers. "I can't stand this heat," he said. He started the engine and turned on the air conditioner. A few minutes later, DeWalt was shivering. His own perspiration, the dampness beneath his arms, on his chest and down his spine, had turned to ice water.

They sat in silence then, watching the fire and the heavily-jacketed men superimposed upon it. Then a gunshot sounded from inside the house. Quickly the firemen backed away, crouching, dragging the hose, moving toward their trucks.

Then came a second shot, a flat toneless bark, but unmistakable. "Jesus fuck," said Abbott as he and DeWalt ducked forward, putting their heads below the level of the dashboard. More reports followed, in quick series of two or three, until what had probably been several boxes of shotgun, pistol and deer rifle shells were exploded—several minutes of DeWalt breathing the air between his knees, the catheter tube pinching his skin.

Finally there was nothing but the sound of flames. Then firemen shouting at one another, going back to work. DeWalt and Abbott sat erect at nearly the same time.

DeWalt, sitting up, glanced briefly at the trooper. Abbott's face looked strained, mouth rigid. DeWalt knew it would start now, the questioning, the getting down to brass tacks. The sound of gunshots can do that to a man, the possibility of being shot—time is short, they seem to remind us. Quit pussyfooting around.

Abbott put both hands on the steering wheel. "All

right," he said, watching the fire. "How about telling me just what you think you were doing in there."

"There have been thirteen brushfires in this general area in the past two years," DeWalt said. "Several of them of a suspicious nature. There was also evidence, although it's gone now, that somebody had once set fire to the house itself. There was evidence of another fire not far from the house. All in all, it seemed to add up to the presence of a firebug. Somebody, it seemed to me, who might know something about a firebombing apparently aimed at the husband of the lover of the man who was killed not a half mile from here."

"Use names," Abbott said. He sounded tired; a man who wants to sleep but is not allowed to close his eyes.

"Draper, in my opinion, fits the psychological profile. Which isn't to suggest, however, that Clifford wasn't involved in the firebombing. You can't honestly tell me, Larry, that you've never once wondered how realistic it is that the Jewetts could be totally ignorant, as they claim, of a man who parked on their private property for several hours every Saturday."

"That doesn't prove they had a deal going."

"It doesn't prove it, no."

"It doesn't prove much of anything, does it?"

"All I have is theory, okay. Theory and no proof. Do you want to hear my theory or not?"

"What good is theory without something to back it up?"

"It's a starting point, Larry. That's all I'm suggesting."

Abbott watched the juice glass vibrating slightly, the thrum of the engine blurring the rainbow lines, shaking the waterfall. Half a minute later he said, "I'm listening."

"Okay, let's suppose this. Suppose that maybe the first or second time Alex takes Jeri to the inlet, one of the Jewetts shows up and tries to chase them off. But Alex says Hey, listen, you know how it is, a man's got needs, right? So he offers Jewett, what—ten, twenty bucks? It's cheaper and safer than a motel, am I right? And everybody comes away happy."

"Tell me when you get to something significant."

"You'll know," DeWalt said. Then, "So okay, this goes on for a while. In the meantime Alex is trying to get Jeri off cocaine. Being one of those over-educated naive types, he imagines he can accomplish this by convincing her husband to quit supplying her with it. But how does he go about such nasty business? He can't soil his own hands, of course; he doesn't have the temperament for it. So, whose help can he enlist? Certainly none of his colleagues or friends; he can't afford to expose his affair. So who? For a while he toys with the idea of hiring me—"

"You? He contacted you about this?"

"He never contacted me, no. But I think he intended to. My phone number appears several times on his desk calendar. The last time, less than a month before the firebombing."

"Why wasn't this made known to us?"

"It's just my phone number, and he never did call. It's all theory and no proof."

DeWalt was looking at the antimacassar on his leg but he could feel Abbott's eyes on him. DeWalt looked up and smiled. Abbott was chewing on the inside of his cheek.

"I wouldn't keep anything important from you, Larry. Have I yet? Haven't I, in fact, been trying all along to *give* you information?"

"Not information," Abbott said. "Guesswork, maybe."

"And a little information here and there."

Abbott nodded slightly and looked away. A concession.

"Okay, so where was I? Alex toys with the idea of hiring me to do his dirty work, because after all, I obviously know all the tricks, they're in my book. But he doesn't call me. It's too risky. What if I say no? I'm establishment now, I'm a perfessor, for christ's sake. So. He remembers how easy it was to rent his parking space at the inlet. How quick the Jewetts were to take his money. Maybe he asks around, inquires of their history, criminally speaking. Which is what, by the way?"

Abbott thought about it. "Barfights, drunk and disorderly, the usual kind of things when they were younger. Draper was arrested once, I don't know, maybe ten years ago, for pissing on main street. And a long time ago, Clifford couldn't have been more than ... he had just turned twenty-one, as I recall. He did a year or so on a vehicular manslaughter charge."

"In other words, they've got a history."

"Not an uncommon history, but a history. Just off the top of my head, though, I could name a dozen upright citizens who've each done more jail time than Draper and Clifford Jewett put together."

"Sure, but Alex doesn't know them, he doesn't rent a parking space from them. The Jewetts he knows."

"Granted."

"So he goes to them and he says, Fellas, I've got a problem. Are you interested in a little work? The hours are short and the pay is high. Here's what I want done, he says. How you do it is up to you. And, since at least one of the Jewett boys has a fondness for incendiaries, voila, it's Molotov cocktail time."

Abbott laughed softly and shook his head.

DeWalt continued. "That deal works out fairly well. After all, Jeri swears she's off the stuff, and that's exactly what Alex had hoped for. Some time passes, everything's going along just swell. And then Alex reads about the archeological discovery at Fort Erie. Then about the display of 1812 relics. He checks it out, takes his family along as a cover. And what does he see on display? An authentic Pennsylvania long rifle valued at upwards of $35,000. It's setting there in a glass case, practically his for the taking. And he deserves it, right? He's worked so fucking hard his entire life, a man of his intelligence, his potential, he deserves that rifle, right? So then, back to the Jewetts. How would you boys like a vacation to Niagara Falls? he asks. You can take Tippy and Aleta along too. My treat. There's a little something I'd like you to pick up for me while you're there, but hey, it will only take you a couple of minutes."

He tapped his fingers to the dashboard. "And one of them, Aleta probably, brings herself home a little souvenir."

"A souvenir which does us not one damn bit of good."

"Not in court, no. But look at it, Larry; you can't deny its presence. You can't deny what it suggests."

"That's right, I can't deny that I've seen it. So are you telling me that Draper came downstairs and invited you in and then gave you that glass as a present?"

DeWalt smiled, looking at his hands.

"Because unless you're willing to swear that that's what happened—which would then give rise to some other questions—Clifford and Aleta could have you arrested for burglary, you know that?"

"I know that."

"Did you know it when you took the glass?"

"I had to show you the connection, Larry. It won't be admissable evidence. I understand that. But I had to show it to you. Now all you have to do is to place the

Jewetts in the Falls or Fort Erie area on the date of the robbery."

"Don't tell me what I have to do."

"I didn't mean it that way."

Abbott stared straight ahead, his mouth a thin unsmiling line. He was motionless for half a minute. He put his hand to the gearshift then and yanked it into DRIVE. The juice glass fell off the dashboard and onto the seat as the car bucked forward, turning across the driveway. DeWalt looked at the glass but did not touch it.

"I better go find the Jewetts," Abbott said. He drove the hundred yards to the mouth of the driveway, where DeWalt's car had been reparked. Stopping alongside DeWalt's car, staring into the windshield's glare of sunlight, he held his foot on the brake, he waited.

DeWalt sat for a moment with his hand on the door release. Then he said, "You'll probably want me to come in and make a statement for the records."

"I know where to find you," Abbott said.

DeWalt climbed out then, closed the door and started toward his own car. He had his hand on the door latch when he heard Abbott's door open. Abbott walked to the passenger side, DeWalt's car between them, and stood there for a moment, looking past DeWalt at the trees behind him, the silent apse of trees.

DeWalt watched him for a few seconds. Then he said, softly, "You're holding the wrong guys, Larry."

Only after a half minute of silence did Abbott respond. He drew back his right hand, cocked it, and hurled something high over the deep stand of trees. DeWalt watched the juice glass go sailing from Abbott's hand and into the sunlight, glinting as it turned over and over, moving in a rainbow arc only to drop unnoticed but for the delicate splash of leaves.

"There's no evidence of that," Abbott said. He returned to his car then, climbed in and drove away. DeWalt stood there a while longer, looking to the ground at the intricate white design half-flattened by a treadmark, the antimacassar that had slipped off his knee when he got out of Abbott's car, a muddied cobweb, a lonely granny's distraction.

Chapter Twenty

DeWalt sat alone in his small backyard in a collapsible chaise lounge of aluminum and plastic. He sat in the pre-midnight darkness without comfort of drink or companion, legs crossed at the ankle, fingers laced atop his chest, head only slightly more elevated than his feet as he considered the cool pastille of moon.

All day long he had been thinking too many things, none clearly enough, and the thoughts had made him slow-moving and indecisive. He thought of Elizabeth Catanzaro and how he wished he had had a chance to meet her children. Children are important, he thought. Everybody should have some children in his life. He felt a terrible void in his existence because of the absence of children, his own or nephews or nieces or even neighborhood children who knew and liked him well enough to stop by unannounced for a glass of lemonade, a game of catch. The teenagers at the college did not fill this need, in fact they exacerbated it. All but rarely their innocence was already and ineluctably gone.

He was getting old too soon, he knew that. There was nothing to slow the years for him, to help pull back the reins. There was no joy, all melancholy and regret. All was hope betrayed.

I'm too easily worn down these days, he thought. No reserves of strength or faith. Every small effort defeats me. But doing nothing defeats me sooner.

As a boy you were strong as a bear, DeWalt. Remember? You could work, roughhouse, play, make love, drink and carouse for a full day at a time. Then you would rest for an hour and start it all again. But now the time ratios have been reversed. And now all but one of your favorite activities has been struck from the list.

Yes, but a new activity has been added. It seems to be your favorite now. You have gotten very adept at wallowing, haven't you, DeWalt? You've become a virtuoso in the music of self-pity.

He turned his attention to the moon again, the most convenient thing to look at so that he would not have to look at himself, not have to acknowledge the faint taste of metal in his mouth. It was a full moon but thin, as pale white as a Japanese lantern. The moon's face had been worn so thin in that smalltown sky that the black tunnels of space could be seen behind it. The moon was as thin as rice paper, paper naturally thin worn thinner with age, neglect, indifference. In the cities the moon could no longer be seen at all. In the cities no one ever looked up at the sky unless he was lying in the streets dying, and by then it was too late for either him or the moon.

Maybe it is too late here too, thought DeWalt. The moon is so thin that I could put my hand right through it. Put my hand through and grab . . . what?

Whatever was up there behind the moon, he wished he could grab it, wished he could wrench it into the open, confront it, challenge it face to face once and for all. He was angry but it gave him no comfort, a bastard anger born of helplessness. He had come out here into the yard to try to relax, but he was still stiff with anger, his body as twisted as a braid of chain, all that torque with nowhere to go.

Two hours earlier Abbott had telephoned. I found Aleta and Clifford Jewett, he had said.

And?

They weren't surprised. Pretty upset about the house, but they weren't surprised about Draper.

Did you ask Aleta about the glass?

I don't know anything about a glass.

We can't pretend I wasn't there, Larry. I called for an ambulance from their phone, I gave the dispatcher my name.

There was a pause then. DeWalt could hear in it the trooper's weariness, his desire for an end. He pictured the trooper lying in bed beside his sleeping wife. They had made love but it wasn't very good. Then Abbott couldn't sleep. He called DeWalt and spoke softly, too tired for bitterness.

Here's what I remember you telling me, Abbott said. You went there to ask a few questions, knocked on the door, nobody answered. You turned around to leave, but then you caught a whiff of gas. The house was full of gas, you couldn't help but smell it. You picked the lock on the back door, went inside, went upstairs and found Draper. You tried to carry him out but he pulled a gun on you. You went downstairs and called the ambulance. Bam, the house exploded. You were lucky you weren't killed.

Is that what you told the Jewetts?

That's what you told me, isn't it?

DeWalt had wondered then if it might yet be possible to save this friendship, if something salvageable remained at a deeper level, something that could not be insulted or demeaned.

Did you ask if they've ever been to Niagara Falls? said DeWalt.

Clifford said that if he wanted to see a lot of water splashing, he'd climb a tree and take a piss.

He's fairly witty for an atavist, isn't he?

He's not as dumb as he looks.

How about the house? Did your boys find anything?

Ashes. We found a whole lot of ashes.

Any lumps of melted lead that might once have been musket balls? Or a bullet mold? Or, I don't know, a brass nameplate signed and dated by Joseph Honaker?

It doesn't take much to make you happy, does it?

So you didn't find anything.

We're still going through it, okay? You don't mind if we wait until the ashes cool, do you?

Sorry, Larry. I don't mean to push.

Anyway. So I had an interesting talk with Craig Fox earlier tonight.

Yeah?

He's starting to remember how strangely Gillen was acting the morning Gillen sent him down to the inlet. Like maybe Gillen already knew what Fox would find there. Like maybe Gillen and his partner, if he had one, wanted Fox to be there when the police arrived.

That's just paranoia talking, Larry. The kid's scared.

I would be too in his position.

Elizabeth Catanzaro had absolutely nothing to do with her husband's murder.

I hear you're not on her payroll anymore.

I'm not on anybody's payroll.

Then what am I talking to you for?

You called me, Larry.

Thanks for reminding me. You've been cut loose now, so . . . try to think about something else from now on, all right? Go write another book, why don't you?

Yes, it was a very thin moon and it was wearing thinner all the time. It was wearing out because nobody ever looked at it anymore to marvel and to wonder. Nobody except DeWalt and maybe teenagers exhausted from making love on a blanket in a wheatfield and maybe children resting from chasing fireflies and maybe dogs penned up in a kennel and with nowhere to run.

DeWalt remembered how he and his father had used to study the moon. His father had loved being out of doors at any time of day or night. He would have his first cup of coffee each morning on the front porch, no matter what the season, the coffee steaming into his face even as the dawn's ghosts of fog were rising. Look out there, DeWalt's father had said once, the boy, still heavy with sleep, having climbed shivering into his father's lap. See the ghosts getting up out of bed, Ernie? Look at the way they stretch. They're going back to heaven now. Back up with the angels. At night they come down here to sleep with people they used to know, but in the morning they go back up to heaven. I think that one out there is your grandmother, Ernie. You remember her, son? Hi, mom, I sure do miss you, sweetheart. Tell all the angels Ernie and me said hi.

DeWalt wondered now if his father had somehow known that he was destined to die early. Maybe he knew he had a bad heart and that his luck could not last very long. These days a man could live quite a while with a bum heart, but not in Ernie's father's time. In those days you took what God dished out and you did not hope to tinker with it.

Maybe that was why Dad liked sitting on the porch during thunderstorms, DeWalt thought.

Bradley, get in this house here before you get struck with lightning!

If God wants me, Rose, he'll find me no matter where I hide. So I'm not hiding.

Then send Ernie in, for pete's sake. He's going to catch a cold.

He's not hiding either, are you, son?

DeWalt's father had loved thunderstorms and big winds and the river ice breaking up and tearing free in

296

the spring. Calm nights, dark woods, waterfalls and blizzards. The fiery turn of leaves in autumn. The stark black bones of a tree in the dead of winter. Stars. The northern lights. The red dot of Venus. And every pale or bright configuration of the moon.

And so now, without comfort of drink or companion, DeWalt considered the moon. Without comfort of a blanket or pillow he lay through the tremulous night and studied the moon until his eyes refused to consider it. He closed his eyes then and thought that if the early morning chill did not chase him inside, it might be nice to awaken out here, here with the thin ghosts of morning. It might be nice to consider those rising wisps as they stretched, to scrutinize them for familiar shapes, to watch them into Heaven as he had not done now for a very long time.

This was his intention but he was not able to do it. He awakened well after midnight to a suffocating scent, gagging even as he sat up. It was a charnal reek he breathed, an odor of putrefaction, a stench that faded quickly, leaving only the foul taste of it sticking in his mouth.

Whether the scent was real, carried past him on a breeze of night air, or whether it had blown over him in a dream, he did not know or care. What mattered was the knowledge the scent carried. He sat there shivering, clutching his rigid stomach, on the verge of being sick. He knew where to find Jeri Gillen.

The river was white in the morning, buried beneath a thick bed of sleeping ghosts, a narrow but dense fog-bank which clung to the cool water even after the land ghosts had fled. Less than half a red sun had yet cleared the high horizon but enough light shone into the fog-bank to make it an unearthly white, the white of transcendentalist painters, the white of a soaring imagination made weightless by too little sleep.

DeWalt had tried to be a painter once but his hand refused to reproduce the pictures inside his head. He was just a boy then, not even old enough to vote. He had tried writing songs on a guitar too, had in fact composed a basketful of songs, but no one ever thought them as wonderful as he had expected them to be.

For a while in his life he had dreamed of becoming a creator of things beautiful but had learned to his great disappointment that he had no talent for beauty. And so I became a man who expresses life's ugliness, he thought. Until I lost my talent for that as well. And now I am a man with no talents at all but I can admire the white of a fogbank at dawn and appreciate the cool brown music that flows beneath it.

He could appreciate too the growl of the backhoe half a mile away. He could appreciate that muffled roar of finality, the mechanized sound of satisfaction, of end. It was what warmed him despite the chill of morning. In a minute or two he would hear the machine stop, and a few minutes later they would find Jeri Gillen's body and they would find the murder weapon too.

The certainty of this should have made DeWalt happy as he stood there at the inlet, listening, staring into the fog, his right foot on a stone in the ring of stones encircling the long-cold firepit. But there was a sadness to the morning, a sadness which had nothing to do with DeWalt himself. A sadness external to him, originating in the day itself, the air, the deep damp green of the leaves and weeds, the creaminess of sky. There was no good reason for him to feel sad and so he knew that what he felt was because of what he breathed, what was absorbed into his skin.

Maybe it was the trees who resonated sadness and he was empathetic to them. He had always had a fondness for trees. The scarlet-berried sumac and the white-barked birch. Black oak and tulip maple. Sassafras, hemlock, the bloody leaves of dogwood. Maybe the trees knew how soon the winter would come and what would happen to them then. There was a sadness inherent to nakedness, as they would soon be. A sadness of vulnerability. A shame.

You could not tell just by looking at them that the trees were sad, but if you were sensitive to their dilemma you could smell their musty sadness every time you breathed.

Maybe all emotions are external, DeWalt thought then. What we think we feel is mere reflection. We are not the generators of emotion, but receptors. Nature broadcasts her laughter and tears in undulating waveforms which we then pick up and reflect in our faces and movements and words. Some people are sensitive to trees, and some to water, to clouds, to rocks or flowers or sand or fields of golden weed. Some people pick up only the high modulation; some the low. Some unlucky people are susceptible to the entire range of frequencies.

And some people think too much, DeWalt. If you are going to stand here thinking nonsense as an excuse for waiting for the backhoe to stop digging, waiting for yourself to be proven a sage or a fool, at least try to think of a happier nonsense. Think of the look on Larry Abbott's face when he comes walking down the hill to tell you you were right.

No, DeWalt. Don't think of that.

He wondered if Abbott had recognized, three hours earlier, after DeWalt's telephone call awakened him, the reluctant tone of deception in DeWalt's voice. DeWalt himself had certainly been aware of it. He was not in the habit of lying to a friend.

"It was Draper *and* Clifford," DeWalt said a moment

after the trooper's mumbled hello. "They were both involved, and I can give you the proof."

"Jesus fucking Christ," Abbott had muttered, not yet sufficiently awake to be angry.

"In a couple of days, Larry, I swear to God I *know* this, in a couple of days your men are going to place the Jewetts at Niagara Falls. I think you know that too. That will put the murder weapon in their hands, but you'll need more. And I can give it to you, Larry. I can tell you where to find Jeri Gillen's body and the rifle used to kill Alex Catanzaro."

Abbott was silent for a moment, suddenly awake. "This better not be a dream I'm having," he said.

"It's the end of your nightmare is what it is."

"I'm listening."

"First of all, my guess is that Draper Jewett, and maybe Clifford too, routinely spied on Alex and Jeri. I mean think about it. They know what's going on down there in that car every Saturday morning. In and outside the car. You don't think they'd take a peek every once in a while?"

"I've thought of that," Abbott conceded. "It's a possibility."

"For Draper, certainly."

"Why? What's special about Draper?"

"I'll get to that in a minute. First of all, in a couple of days, as I said, you'll be able to link the Jewetts with the museum robbery. They've got the murder weapon. They know exactly when and how to deliver it to the man who commissioned the robbery. They go down to the inlet to give it to him—"

"Loaded? A valuable weapon like that?"

"I don't know why it was loaded, Larry. I haven't figured that out yet. Maybe the Jewetts didn't know the rifle's value. Didn't know they'd be endangering it by actually firing it. Maybe they thought they'd do Alex a

300

favor by showing him that it was still fireable. I mean who knows what went through their heads?"

"You're presuming that you know."

"Not on motive. On motive I'm guessing. And what I'm guessing is this. Draper and/or Clifford carried the rifle to the inlet to hand it over to Alex. But when they got there, things were hot and heavy inside the car. Whoever was holding the rifle got a little too stirred up by it all. Got carried away. And Alex got killed."

"An act of passion."

"Just as we always surmised. Except that we had the wrong cast of actors."

"Somebody got a hard-on for Jeri, killed her old man and then took Jeri, where, back to the house?"

"Eventually, yes."

"And you think it was Draper."

"Not necessarily."

"Fuck, DeWalt, get to the point, would you? It's after three o'clock in the fucking morning."

"I'm not saying it wasn't Draper who pulled the trigger. In fact I'd guess it probably was. But I'll tell you this. There is no way in hell that Draper Jewett could have carried Jeri Gillen a half mile through the woods. The man was dying even then. He was little more than a ghost."

"Maybe he didn't have to carry her that far. Maybe ten, twenty yards. Just far enough to put her in his truck."

"I don't care if it was three feet, he couldn't have done it. Because first he would have had to subdue her. And the evidence points to the fact that she ran down the lane in an attempt to escape. Remember the spilled purse? He never could have caught her."

"He threatened her with the rifle."

"It's a single-shot weapon. By the time he reloaded, she'd be out of range."

"Maybe she didn't know that. She was panicky, hysterical. Maybe he had another gun with him."

"Maybe," said DeWalt. "But I'll tell you something else. A guy's kidneys shut down the way Draper's did, a guy is that far gone, and his pecker shuts down too. In all likelihood, Draper Jewett was impotent."

Abbott was silent for a moment. Then, "That sounds to me, Ernie, like it weakens your argument more than it supports it."

"I'm not saying the desire isn't still there. In fact, it's probably stronger than ever. Precisely because it can't be satisfied."

"So then . . . he could still *want* to screw her?"

"He wants her so badly it's driving him crazy. And maybe that's why he shoots Alex. Frustration. Jealousy. Who knows? In any case, Alex is dead. Jeri takes off running. Is Clifford there to catch her? He has to be. Either that, or Jeri goes running up the hill to the Jewetts' house. Unaware, of course, that it's the Jewetts' house. She's sitting there naked and shivering, telling her story. And pretty soon, who comes dragging in but Draper himself."

Again Abbott said nothing for half a minute. Then, tiredly, his voice evincing a lack of expectation. "The first thing you said when you called was that you know where the body is. Do you or don't you?"

He thought he knew, yes. But now was no time for speculation, for guesswork. He needed certainty now; a convincing lie.

"The first time I went to the Jewetts' place, Clifford and Draper were excavating the septic tank. Just as I got there, they were pulling the cover back onto the tank. But later Clifford told me that the honeydipper would be showing up within the hour. So why would they be recovering the tank if it hadn't been cleaned out yet?"

302

"Maybe they wanted to take a last look at their shit," Abbott said.

"Or maybe they were putting something *into* the septic tank. And maybe if you contact all the honeydippers in town—there can't be more than one or two, right?—maybe their records will show that they did *not* do any work for the Jewetts that day."

"It's a lot of maybes," Abbott said.

"Two phone calls at most. That's all it will take to find out."

"Two phone calls and a court order."

"Or wait a week and give Clifford a chance to dispose of the evidence."

This time the silence was a long one. Finally Abbott said, "I'll think about it," and hung up.

Nearly four hours later, DeWalt's telephone rang. "We'll be out at the Jewetts' place by seven-thirty," Abbott had said.

And DeWalt answered, "I'll be waiting at the inlet."

And now, waiting for the backhoe to fall silent, he stared into a fogbank. He tried to identify individual wisps streaming off from the main configuration to twist and dissipate in the sky. He saw a movement on the right edge of his peripheral vision and turned to face it. But it was only a leaf, a small brown heartshaped leaf, already dead, suspended it seemed in midair between two cattails, fluttering but not falling, a miracle of levitation.

He stepped closer and saw the silvery filament stretched between the cattails, the spider's thread upon which the stem of the leaf was caught, a single sticky tightrope. DeWalt felt an inclination to pluck the leaf free—he felt its sadness, perhaps—to let it fall to the ground where it belonged, to the wet and warmth of a natural decay. But he stopped himself; at the last instant he drew back his hand. The leaf vibrated on its tether, a harp string almost plucked.

Who was DeWalt, after all, to intervene? Things get caught, tangled up; that was how it went. True for a falling leaf, for a fish on a hook. True for a man in his lover's arms. Things get trapped. Forever stopped. Interruption previous to an expected end becomes the end itself. It is how life goes.

Still looking at the leaf then, the dew-jeweled thread, DeWalt realized that he could hear nothing but the river. The backhoe had stopped digging. How long ago? he wondered.

They will be sliding the cover off the septic tank now, he thought, and he gave them time to do so, the heavy lid stuck at first, grinding and scraping, Abbott standing back to watch the two young troopers who had accompanied him, Abbott still not convinced, reluctant to believe but with the grudgingly obtained court order in his pocket, the backhoe operator remaining in his machine, hands on silent levers.

First would come the awful stench, the charnal reek of it. Quickly they would move to the upwind side of the septic tank. DeWalt saw it happening inside his head, he watched the work proceeding. One of the young troopers pushes a long hooked pole into the muck, pushes it almost delicately, almost tenderly probing. In a minute or two, the hooked tip finds something. The trooper looks up at Abbott. Abbott moves closer, although his inclination is to do the opposite. The young trooper swivels and jostles the gaff until the hook catches hold. He struggles with the weight as he pulls against the muck's thick gravity. The other young man helps. Maybe there is a police photographer there too, snapping pictures. The flash of his camera seems as bright as lightning in the dimness of the trees. Some object breaks the brown surface and is pulled onto tram-

304

pled earth. It is unidentifiable except by shape, but shape is sufficient; it is more than enough.

The men look away. DeWalt looks out across the river. Nobody wants to see the body like this. It will have to be moved, touched, identified. But all of that can wait.

"See if there's anything else in there," Abbott says, meaning the rifle, the murder weapon. He knows now that there is. It will take the men longer to find this object but they are glad to turn back to the sludge tank now, glad to be so engaged.

DeWalt turned away too to another scene, to the evanescing white of the fogbank. It was smaller now by half; it would soon be gone. He wondered if Elizabeth Catanzaro was awake yet; if the crows had awakened her. Her children could come home now. Home to the too-large house. He wondered if she would stay or move, knowing now what she knew about her husband, what she would sooner or later have to believe, what her neighbors, the town, would be so quick to believe.

Move, he answered.

He then had a terrible thought. He understood it all, the desperate passion of it. He understood Alex's need, a man too aware of his mortality, his limitations. He understood Draper's choices. How many mornings had Draper crouched behind a tree, watching, hearing the wild lovetalk of a beautiful young woman, a girl more beautiful than any he had ever touched or could ever hope to hold? He listened until the words and liquid sounds took over for his own heartbeat and instructed him to do their will. Or maybe it was Clifford there behind the tree. Maybe he had lived with her inside his head until his head felt it would explode if he did not find relief, and so he came to the inlet that morning with but one intention, and accomplished it.

It was even possible, he supposed, that Jewett had

kept her alive for a few days. Desire is seldom sated with an isolated taste. He kept her at the house, did not hide his activities from Aleta. Maybe it was Aleta who had finally killed her. Maybe that was what had put the gray in Aleta's eyes.

The complications were too myriad to consider now. The coroner would take over from here, and he would toss it into the lawyers' venue. Let some younger hound take up the scent now, some young nose fresh to the fragrant splash of blood.

As for DeWalt, he stood there by the river and inhaled its morning scent. He felt something opening up inside him. He felt his self-pity, so long hoarded and relied upon, so long tended in darkness, he felt it blossoming in new light. He felt the anger-curled petals begin to unfold. And from this wild bloom arose a fragile scent, the scent of all the world. Tears wanted to come to his eyes but he held against them, he allowed a warm blurring of his vision but would permit no grief evident to an observer, even though there was no one watching, no eyes but his own.

If there is a God—this DeWalt suddenly knew without knowing the source of his knowledge, his certainty—if there is a God I've been wrong about Him. He isn't to blame.

He had caught the scent of God's fear, perhaps. The fragrance of regret, of apology. God, he knew, is little more than human. All too human but on a grander scale. Everything DeWalt had ever heard about God was a lie. Omniscience, omnipotence, infallibility. It was all a lie, a palliative for a frightened mob. A perfect God would create a perfect world. But an imperfect God, a lonely God, a curious God would do the best he could with what little he had. Only to realize too late that he had overextended himself. That he had tossed too many glass balls into the air, had started too many plates spinning. And now what was he to do, he was not tireless, he could not be everywhere at once. He had not counted on such gravity, this human compulsion to fall.

It was a terrible thought DeWalt had, and yet it comforted him. God was not responsible for humanity. It worked the other way around. It was an extra burden, a seemingly unbearable weight. And yet, strangely, somehow, it gave DeWalt hope.

Soon September, he thought, another academic year, another crop of minds to cultivate, hopes to till. Soon the pumpkins will be ripe; fat orange suns to be tugged from withering vines. Hay will stand baled into monolithic wheels, millstones with no inclination to roll. Apple butter bubbles will pop in churchyard kettles. Cider presses will creak, juice splatter, sticky arms and faces, voices joined in praise to God's bounty, lord hear our prayer, amen.

Screens to take down and storm windows to put up. Festivals of trees blown bare. The air will be sad with leavesmoke. A tremulous air, quivering between lucidity and a sodden gray. Between afternoon sun and morning frost. Promises made and promises broken. The river will swell with October and thicken with mud. Questions will be asked, answers found, answers lost.

A woman will find strength in her children, in the consuming routine of helping them to grow, to adapt to a lacerating world. She will need no interference from DeWalt but perhaps she will allow it anyway, perhaps he has something valuable yet to give, the emollient of his own need, his balm for hers. . . .

And suddenly Abbott's voice interrupted the calm. "Ernie, hey."

DeWalt turned to see Abbott stepping past the line of trees and onto the lane. Then the trooper paused for a moment, brushed something from his face, a cobweb, a damp strand of dew.

DeWalt walked toward him, back toward the center of life, away from the shore. He tried to remember something Melville had written to Hawthorne, one weary whale-chaser to another. *As long as we have anything more to do, we have done nothing.* Somehow DeWalt liked the idea that he had done nothing yet, he was now at the start, another chance to begin.

Another winter was coming, it would not last. The seasons are too wise and old to vary; the seasons understand what man can not. Let winter have its turn; without the chill there is no comfort in dreams of days of warmth. Yes, though the wind will sting and numb and blow the reek of death, it must have its season, it must claim its due; no hope and no fear can intervene. When the river is thick and slow with silt is the time to cross to higher banks; when life's moments are fast with flood, we must think like water. Surely man with all his theories understands himself the very least: and he must seek to justify his pride forever.